PENGUIN BOOKS
Daughter of Chaos

A.S. Webb is the *Sunday Times* bestselling author of *Daughter of Chaos* and *Daughter of Fate*, the first two instalments of The Dark Pantheon trilogy. She holds a BA in English Literature and Theatre Studies from the University of Leeds and is inspired by stories rooted in history and mythology. She lives in London with her family.

Daughter of Chaos

A S WEBB

PENGUIN BOOKS

PENGUIN BOOKS

UK | USA | Canada | Ireland | Australia
India | New Zealand | South Africa

Penguin Books is part of the Penguin Random House group of companies whose addresses can be found at global.penguinrandomhouse.com

Penguin Random House UK,
One Embassy Gardens, 8 Viaduct Gardens, London SW11 7BW

penguin.co.uk

First published by Penguin Michael Joseph 2025
Published in Penguin Books 2026

001

Copyright © A S Webb, 2025

The moral right of the author has been asserted

Penguin Random House values and supports copyright. Copyright fuels creativity, encourages diverse voices, promotes freedom of expression and supports a vibrant culture. Thank you for purchasing an authorized edition of this book and for respecting intellectual property laws by not reproducing, scanning or distributing any part of it by any means without permission. You are supporting authors and enabling Penguin Random House to continue to publish books for everyone. No part of this book may be used or reproduced in any manner for the purpose of training artificial intelligence technologies or systems. In accordance with Article 4(3) of the DSM Directive 2019/790, Penguin Random House expressly reserves this work from the text and data mining exception

Printed and bound in Great Britain by Clays Ltd, Elcograf S.p.A.

The authorized representative in the EEA is Penguin Random House Ireland, Morrison Chambers, 32 Nassau Street, Dublin D02 YH68

A CIP catalogue record for this book is available from the British Library

ISBN: 978–1–405–96208–7

Penguin Random House is committed to a sustainable future for our business, our readers and our planet. This book is made from Forest Stewardship Council® certified paper.

Author's Note

This book contains themes of a sensitive nature – please refer to the author's website, webbandpen.com, for specifics.

For Sam, always

*Before the earth and the sea and the all-encompassing
heaven came into being, the whole of nature displayed
but a single face, which men have called Chaos.*

Ovid, *Metamorphoses* (translated by David Raeburn)

The Cave

Danae's breath danced like little ghosts in the gloom. She rolled away from the dark belly of the cave and looked out onto desolate whiteness. She was in a crevice halfway up an indomitable mountain at the end of the world, shrouded in a freezing fog of never-ending clouds. No one had ventured this far for centuries. No mortal, anyway.

Squeezing her eyes shut, she fought to recapture the warmth of her dream. But no matter how hard she tried, she could not go back. The cold of the mountain was in her bones.

Surrendering to reality, she untangled herself from her bag and turned her attention to her throbbing hands. Biting down on the tips of her goat-hide gloves, she tugged her fingers free. Blood oozed from the cuts she'd sustained during the climb. Sucking in a sharp breath, she placed a hand on the wall and pushed herself up, leaving a smear of red. On her knees, she shuffled deeper into the cave, away from the biting flares of wind. Her mouth tasted of salt. She lifted a bloody hand to her cheek and realized she'd been crying.

She'd dreamt of a beach. Plumes of white sand streamed behind her brothers as they raced down to the rock pools at the edge of the sea. She'd been sprinting to catch up, desperate to be the first to capture a crab. Her sister watched them from the bank, Alea's chuckle skipping across the breeze.

Danae barely recognized her younger self running along the shore. Her childhood felt like it belonged to someone else, as though she were harbouring the memories of a stranger.

She looked down at her battered hands and thought of what they'd done, what she had done, to get here.

She'd been eighteen when she left Naxos. She must be almost twenty now. It felt like she'd been gone for days and decades, all at once. She thought of her parents, her brothers and her little nephews. Through everything they were her anchor. She'd clung to the hope of returning to them, but now when she tried to conjure their faces, they slipped through her memory like smoke.

She adjusted the lion hide draped over her shoulders. The beast's jaw yawned over her head, its fangs rested on her temples and its shaggy mane flowed down the length of her back. It was said to be impenetrable to any blade, torn from the body of the infamous Nemean lion by the greatest hero who'd ever lived.

Her stomach twisted at the thought of Heracles discovering it stolen. Her need was greater than his, but she couldn't stop imagining the expression on the hero's face the moment he realized she'd betrayed him.

'Enough,' she muttered to the empty cave.

She reached for her bag and tugged out an ink-black dress, then set about slicing off strips of fabric with her blade. Once her fingers were bandaged, she inspected her arsenal. She had a knife, a waterskin, the shard of omphalos stone, her pipe, a near empty pouch of herbs, a purse of drachmas, her midnight cloak and one and a half stale biscuits.

Her stomach groaned. After a breath of deliberation, she ate the half-biscuit then tilted the waterskin to her lips.

She swore.

The water was frozen. Pulling it under her furs, she gasped as the icy vessel stung her skin. Hopefully the heat of her body would melt it, or she would die of thirst before she reached the summit.

Her eyes wandered to the last biscuit, then she noticed a mark beside it on the cave floor. A groove scored into the rock. She moved the biscuit to reveal a set of claw scratches. Scouring the ground, she found more. Her brow creased. What bird would make a nest in such treacherous conditions?

She crawled deeper into the cave, hope flickering in her chest. If there was a nest, there might be eggs. The light dwindled the deeper she moved, but the cave was deceptively large at the back. The ceiling expanded upwards into a kind of antechamber, high enough for her to stand in.

Her foot crunched on something hard. She bent down and picked up a shard of bone. It must be a large bird. Big enough to catch prey the size of a goat, given the length of the bone. She flattened herself against the wall, allowing as much light as possible to flow into the back of the cave.

The floor was littered with objects. Twigs, coins, rocks, broken pottery, shreds of fabric and fragments of what might have once been armour. Her pulse quickened. No birds hoarded like this, not even magpies.

A piercing screech cut through the wail of the storm. Danae threw herself to the front of the cave, fumbling for her knife. A moment later a mass of feathers hurtled in, claws scrabbling across the rock.

At first, she thought it was an eagle. Its feathered head loomed towards her, yellow eyes wild and curved beak tipped with frost. It filled the cave, tawny wings blocking out the light as they bashed into the sloping walls. Then she saw the rest of its body.

From the wings down the creature had the torso, hind legs and tail of a lion. Its front legs were a grotesque hybrid of the two animals, powerful and muscular like a giant cat's but scaled like a bird's, ending in long arched talons.

It was a griffin. A creature she'd only heard of in legend.

In another life she'd have been petrified, but this beast was a mere drop in the ocean of horrors she'd faced.

Half blinded by the dark, she dived to avoid the griffin's talons. Not fast enough: she cried out as claws raked her forearm, catching her skin below the cover of the lion hide. She thrust up with her knife, but only managed to nick the edge of a wing. The griffin made a guttural sound, somewhere between a shriek and a growl, and its attack became more frenzied.

She was so weary. She wouldn't be able to keep this up for long.

There was always another way.

She gasped, her elbow slamming into the cave wall as she threw herself against the rock to avoid another strike. No, she was too weak to use her powers. Her lower arms were already torn to bloody shreds, and she barely had enough strength to keep dodging the griffin's talons.

What would Heracles do? He'd fought a dozen creatures more terrible than this and lived. Although, he had the advantage of supernatural strength. Without using her powers, all she had was a knife and an impenetrable lion hide that could be ripped from her back as easily as tearing the wings from a butterfly.

The *lion hide*.

The griffin lunged at her again. If this went wrong, she was dead. The creature had almost driven her to the back of the cave. Soon she would be pinned against a solid wall of rock, then the beast would rip her apart anyway.

She lowered her head, so the lion's face was pointed directly at the griffin, and roared with all her might.

Just for a moment, the creature hesitated.

Clutching her knife in both hands, she threw the full force of her weight behind it and stabbed upwards. The blade sank through feathers into flesh. The griffin's scream curdled in its throat as the weapon pierced its windpipe. Blood gushed over Danae's hands. She held on while the beast struggled, only letting go once it slumped to the floor.

She wanted to collapse too, but she had to act fast. In a few moments the power of the griffin's life force would be lost. She placed a hand over the wound, feeling for the rhythm of its waning pulse.

Her vision doubled. Overlaying the physical world were the glowing threads of energy that animated all living things. She could see them beneath her own skin, coursing through her veins, ever moving in a cyclical tapestry of power. And there were the griffin's life-threads, seeping out between her fingers and disappearing into the darkness as the creature lay dying. She focused her mind and willed each fleeing strand towards her hand. The life-threads changed course and began to flow into her palm, snaking up her arm to join the web of light that spread through her entire body.

The griffin's eyes dulled as the last tendril wound up Danae's fingers. The pain in her limbs melted away, and her wounds knitted together as the creature's life force rushed through her veins. She sat back and breathed in the euphoria of containing so much life.

So much power.

PART ONE

1. Three Years Before the Cave

'Today of all days!' Danae's mother fussed over the gathering of her sister's tunic. 'We're going to be late!'

Danae was engrossed in a large fishing net, splayed across the wooden table that dominated the centre of their small hut. She and her father were huddled over it, their fingers working together to untangle the netting. Her face was taut with concentration, her mother's words nothing but background chatter.

Alea slipped from their mother's intrusive fingers and crossed the room to place a hand on Danae's arm.

'Come on, we won't hear the end of it if we don't leave now.'

'If you've marked that dress . . .' Her mother stood by the doorway, hands on hips.

'Just this one . . . last . . .' Danae grasped a stubborn piece of flax between her nails and twisted.

She was rewarded by a satisfied sigh from her father as the netting unfurled into its intended pattern.

'Thank you, daughter. You have such clever hands. Now go on.'

She smiled and was about to follow her sister, when she caught a shadow darting across her father's weathered face.

'Are you all right, Pa?'

He swatted the question away. 'I will be if you're not late. Go.' With a gentle nudge, he steered her towards the door.

Her mother ushered the girls into the yard, then paused in the doorway to squeeze her husband's hand.

'Odell, they won't be chosen,' she whispered. 'I know the

crops haven't been plentiful this year, but that doesn't mean Demeter will demand . . .' She drew a breath. 'Even if she does, Alea is betrothed and Danae . . . well,' she glanced at her youngest daughter, 'it's usually the quieter girls.'

Her father kissed her mother's fingers. He looked like himself again, a man whose cares had slipped from his shoulders like water from oiled wood.

Mopsus and Pilops trotted out from under the lean-to at the side of the hut to investigate the commotion. Danae tore her gaze from her parents and lifted a palm to stroke Mopsus' muzzle, as the goat stuck her head through the fence of their little enclosure.

Quickly, she delved into her tunic pocket and drew out a squashed honey cake.

'Don't tell,' she whispered as the goat gobbled it then licked the crumbs from her palm.

'Come on, Danae!' Her mother strode past, herding Alea out of the gate and down the dusty track.

Danae gave the goat's ear a final scratch before running after them.

'Be good for your mother,' her father called, his wiry frame silhouetted in the doorway. 'Bring blessings on our village!'

Danae knew this was directed at her. She turned and winked at him, then hurried towards the crowd of women flowing along the coastal road.

To the west, the dying sun spilt gold over the turquoise waves. Despite the heat that still clung to the land, Danae shivered with anticipation. She looked ahead at her mother and sister. They were so similar; both tall and delicate, crowned with the same auburn curls, their olive skin painted with matching freckles. Danae had always been told she looked like her father. She was proud to have his strong features, but no one had ever called her a beauty.

The crowd swelled as more women joined the procession, the air bustling with the click of cicadas and nervous chatter. This was the only occasion on which the women of Naxos were allowed out without their men. On this night every year, women from all over the island made the pilgrimage inland to the temple of Demeter for the Thesmophoria.

It was vital to honour the Goddess of the Harvest on this sacred night. If Demeter was displeased with their offerings, the following year's crops would fail and children would be born lifeless.

And this year, both the wheat and barley crops had been crippled by blight.

Evidently, last year's offerings had not been enough, and if the goddess was not placated by their gifts tonight, only one thing would quench her rage.

Danae had witnessed four human sacrifices in her lifetime, and each year the harvest was poor, the threat of it circled over the heads of the unmarried girls like vultures over carrion. But she was not afraid. As her mother had said, the priestesses always chose the blood of the meekest unmarried girls to appease the goddess. Never anyone who irritated their mother as much as she did.

She looked around at the women in their swathes of coloured fabrics. The wives of the island were draped in their finest dresses, while their virgin daughters looked like lambs, bobbling behind them in tunics of white. Some hid their fear well, others couldn't stop their lips from trembling.

Heads tilted as she passed. Some were subtle, some stared openly as her family walked by. She tugged at the darned hem of her greying tunic, suddenly self-conscious. Glancing up, she almost caught someone's eye, but the woman's gaze slid past her to settle on Alea. No one was looking at her.

The band her mother had fastened around her tightly coiled hair itched, and she prised her fingers under the stubborn fabric to scratch.

Her hand was slapped away.

'Leave it alone.' Her mother sighed. 'It already looks like a bird's nest.'

Danae glanced at her sister and rolled her eyes.

Alea giggled, then whispered, 'I think your hair looks beautiful.'

She knew it wasn't true, but she loved her sister for trying. There wasn't a curl out of place on Alea's head. She wore a striking green headband woven with yellow ears of corn. It was the band their mother had worn the day she married their father. No wonder people were staring; Alea looked more beautiful than the harvest goddess herself. Not that Danae would ever say that out loud. The gods were always listening.

'Eleni!'

Melia the blacksmith's wife waved at them across the crowd. Her daughters, both clad in white, were trailing along behind her. The two families navigated through the stream of bodies, until they were walking side by side.

Both Eleni and Melia opened their mouths to say the sacred greeting at the same time, but the blacksmith's wife was faster.

'The Twelve see you and know you,' Melia said swiftly, her lips spreading into a satisfied smile.

Of course Melia would make sure she was the first to say the words that welcomed the gods into every crevice of their lives. Her mother smiled graciously and touched her middle finger to her forehead, showing that she returned the sentiment.

Melia's eyes swept over Alea. 'Oh, doesn't she look stunning?' She moved closer but didn't lower her voice. 'You must tell me when we can expect the wedding. It's going to be the event of the season! That is, if Odell can afford it.' She patted Eleni's arm. 'Well, you won't have to worry about that for much longer. A merchant's son no less, I still can't believe it.'

Danae bit the inside of her cheeks. She hated having to be polite to odious village gossips. She glanced at Alea and her jaw tightened at the deep flush that had spread over her sister's face.

Alea's betrothal was an unusual one and not everyone was pleased. There were mutterings around the village that Alea's intended was lowering himself by marrying the daughter of a fisherman. There were even whispers that he'd compromised her and been forced into the marriage by their father. They could all go to Tartarus in Danae's opinion.

'I'm sure it will be easier to find a match for Danae once Alea is wed. Are there really no fishermen's sons that will have her?'

Alea reached for her hand, but it was too late.

'Are either of your daughters promised, Melia?'

The blacksmith's wife blinked as though she'd forgotten Danae was there. She opened her mouth then paused before her lips formed the word 'no'.

'Well then, perhaps you should keep your advice to yourself.'

'I'm sorry,' Eleni muttered as Melia turned a sunset shade of crimson. 'We should, ah, we'll see you at the festival!' Without giving the other woman time to reply, she took hold of her daughters and dragged them into the crowd.

'Danae,' her mother said wearily.

'I'm sorry, but she always talks like she's got one of her husband's pokers shoved up her arse.'

Alea snorted.

Her mother sighed. 'You can't speak your mind whenever you feel like it.'

Danae glanced at her sister, who smiled encouragingly. Alea was betrothed to a wealthy man whose company she could tolerate; as a woman you couldn't wish for more. She should be happy for her sister. Yet a familiar weight dragged at her chest as she thought of Alea's impending marriage. It was selfish, but she was dreading it. She would be the last child left at home. Her brothers, Calix and Santos, had long ago moved to huts of their own to make space for their growing broods. She missed them, but with Alea, it felt as though she would be losing half of herself.

At sixteen, she was only a year younger than her sister and knew that she too was expected to start a family of her own. She'd been aware of it ever since men's eyes began to linger as she passed. Their hunger made her skin crawl. But that wasn't why she'd given every farmhand and fisherman that dared approach her the sharp side of her tongue. Once a woman married, she was shackled to her husband's hearth, and lenient men like her father were a rare breed.

The desire to marry well seemed to dominate the minds of the other village girls, but even a rich husband couldn't buy you freedom.

As the procession wound its way inland, the anticipation simmering in Danae's stomach ignited. She could see Demeter's temple. Flanked by protective hills, the white stone pillars stood stark against the gritty golds and greens of the surrounding land. It always made her think of the bones of a great leviathan, picked clean and gleaming after being washed ashore centuries before.

The crowd was funnelled down a road lined by tall cypress

trees. Then the sun dipped below the hills, and a cavalcade of shadows stretched out behind the women. By the time they reached the floral path leading up to the temple, darkness had fallen. The braziers were lit, their smoke muddling with the sweet scent of the blooms to form a heady concoction.

The temple garden was an oasis of flora and foliage that would never survive without the dutiful care of the temple hands and the water they walked miles every day to fetch. Opulent fuchsia flowers nestled in bushes of waxy emerald leaves, and beds of yellow and orange blooms were surrounded by clusters of tiny ocean-blue petals. Even in the brazier light the colours were luminous.

'Eleni, Danae, Alea! Over here!' Kafi, Danae's sister-in-law, shouted across the garden, waving vigorously. She'd saved their usual spot. Next to her was Calix's wife, Carissa. A pretty woman, whose appearance was rather spoiled by her mortification at the disapproving glances garnered by Kafi's booming voice.

They fought their way through the crowd towards the two women. Kafi grinned at Danae with her big, gap-toothed smile and drew her into a tight hug. Danae liked her. She was loud, unapologetic and had chosen to marry Danae's brother, Santos, because the first time they'd met he had – in Kafi's words – made her laugh so hard she was almost sick.

Kafi released her, and Danae turned her attention to the temple. A temporary altar had been erected in front of the sacred building. It was piled high with bowls of ripe figs, crisp apples, pomegranates and stacks of vegetable-laden baskets. Sacks of grain, barrels of fish, amphorae filled with olive oil and bronze dishes of wine mixed with water were nestled around its base. The men of each household had delivered the produce earlier that morning in addition to the monthly temple tithe. Every family gave more than they could spare.

Danae's stomach growled. They'd fasted since dawn in memory of Demeter's own refusal to eat when her daughter, Persephone, had been held hostage by Hades, God of the Underworld.

As she stared at the offerings, she noticed a quiver of movement to the side of the altar. The air oscillated like something was distorting it. For an unsettling moment, she thought she saw a pair of disembodied red eyes. Then she blinked and they vanished. It must be hunger and the intoxicating aroma of the garden playing tricks on her.

Then the pounding of drums cut through the chatter of the crowd.

'This is it,' Alea whispered.

Danae took her sister's hand.

Three women emerged from the temple. They walked slowly, with purpose. The first priestess was dressed in green, a band of gold across her brow and ivy wound around her arms. She was Demeter. The second wore a deep crimson robe, her face obscured by a fearful mask with twisted horns. Hades. The third wore white, her thin dress fluttering in the evening breeze. She was Demeter's daughter, Persephone. Four temple hands kept pace behind them, beating wide drums fastened with leather straps around their necks.

As the procession reached the altar, the priestesses came to stand side by side in front of the offerings. All three raised their arms. Painted on each of their palms was the all-seeing eye, the symbol of the Olympian gods' omnipotence. Demeter was the patron deity of Naxos, but all twelve gods shared dominion over mortal lives.

The priestesses lowered their hands to face the crowd, pointing the eye of the gods at the women of Naxos.

The congregation grew still as a windless sky.

Danae's mouth was dry. This was the moment of judgement, when the Twelve would enter their souls and lay bare what was inside. They would know if anyone had held back something which should have been offered.

There was no hiding from the gods.

'May the Twelve see you and know you,' the priestesses intoned.

In response, all the women raised a finger to their foreheads.

The Demeter-priestess sang out a long piercing note. Her sisters joined her, their three voices melding into one. Then the Hades-priestess backed away into the shadows and Demeter and Persephone took each other's arms and began to dance.

Danae grinned. The play was her favourite part of the ceremony.

The priestesses twirled and skipped, the drumbeat chasing their feet. Danae's heart raced with their ever-increasing speed.

Suddenly Hades lunged out of the dark and grabbed Persephone's arm, spinning her away from the altar. Danae gasped, despite having seen the performance many times before. The drums slowed, and Demeter made a show of searching the crowd. Unable to find her daughter, she collapsed to the ground, her head in her arms. Then Hades and Persephone re-emerged to stand in front of the altar. Hades plucked a pomegranate from a bronze dish and gouged it with her fingers. Wine-dark liquid trickled down her arms as she proffered half the fruit to Persephone.

The crowd screamed for her not to take it. Everyone knew that by eating the fruit of the Underworld, Persephone would be condemning herself to remain with Hades for all eternity. The cries reached a crescendo as Persephone took the pomegranate and lifted it to her lips. Juice poured down the priestess's chin, staining her white dress.

The women gasped again. A standard had emerged behind the drummers. They parted, bowing as deeply as their instruments would allow. On top of a long pole, carried by a sweating temple hand, was a golden eagle. The symbol of Zeus, King of the Gods. A hush descended over the crowd. Demeter prostrated herself before the great bird, then rose, her face wet with tears – that part always impressed Danae – and moved to stand beside her daughter.

'Persephone ate six pomegranate seeds,' said the Demeter-priestess. 'Therefore, the Father of Mankind, in his infinite wisdom, decreed she would remain on Olympus with her mother for six months of the year. During this joyous time Demeter blesses the earth with life and abundance. But for the remaining six months, Persephone must live in the Underworld, with Hades. During these terrible months the earth grows cold and withers with Demeter's grief.'

The crowd bowed their heads in recognition of the Harvest Goddess's suffering.

'Tonight, women of Naxos, we give praise to she who blesses this fertile land. Praise to she who guards our crops from pestilence. Praise to she who provides for us, so we may bloom and our children may flourish. Demeter, we pray you continue to watch over us all here tonight, our families at home and those who have joined the Missing. We pray, one day, they will return to us.'

The Missing were the people who disappeared. It had been happening ever since anyone could remember. Every so often someone would just vanish. The average on Naxos was around five people a year. On the mainland it was far more. Even the priestesses couldn't explain it. Despite beseeching Demeter every year to bring back the Missing, so far no one had ever returned.

'Demeter watch over us,' the crowd murmured.

Two temple hands walked forward, guiding a large pig towards the altar. This was the part Danae liked the least. The drums returned, slow and steady.

The priestesses smoothed the beast's back, cooing as they held it still in front of the altar. Another temple hand ran forward and dropped to one knee, a long silver blade balanced on his upturned palms. The Demeter-priestess curled her fingers around the knife and raised it high above her head.

A reflected sliver of moonlight slashed through the air. The drumming reached a crescendo as the animal squealed. Blood splattered the priestess. She sliced open the animal's belly and reached into the incision. Tugging out the intestines, she held them up to the moonlight. The organs glistened as she ran them through her fingers, inspecting every single segment.

The crowd was so quiet, not a breath could be heard.

The priestess dropped the offal into a bronze bowl beneath the altar and turned to face the women of Naxos.

'The omens have spoken. Demeter sees all, hears all, knows all. She has looked into your hearts, and she has found you wanting.'

There were gasps. Someone cried out, 'But we've given everything we have!'

'Your offerings are not enough,' the priestess continued. 'Someone amongst you has kept back what should have been given to Demeter. Someone thought they could lie to the goddess.'

A few of the younger girls began to cry. Danae's fingers tightened around her sister's hand. Her mother wrapped her arms around them both so firmly her nails dug into Danae's skin.

The priestess lifted one painted palm to travel over the crowd, while with the other hand drew a smear of blood down her forehead. Danae's ribs tightened around her lungs as that hand drew closer. Then stopped.

The priestess made her choice and pointed.

'No!'

Melia clung to her daughters as the priestess's gaze settled on her youngest girl.

The temple hands barged through the crowd. The blacksmith's wife sobbed, refusing to relinquish her daughter as they tried to pull her away.

A shriek ruptured the air. Startled, Danae looked around, but all she could see was her own confusion mirrored in the faces around her.

They appeared from nowhere, clambering out of bushes and leaping from behind trees, their hair tangled with twigs and bracken. At least twenty women, all completely naked.

They were the Maenads, the followers of Dionysus, God of Wine and Pleasure. Women who'd forsaken their families to live wild in the forests. They were said to give their minds over entirely to their god, drinking so deeply of his wine they fell into an ecstatic trance and performed frenzied dances to please his salacious will. It was even rumoured that during one of their rituals, they tore a baby limb from limb with their bare hands.

Like wolves amongst a flock of goats the Maenads scattered the crowd, their laughter echoing through the garden. Statues were overturned, flower beds trampled, and two Maenads even clambered onto the altar and stuffed offerings into their mouths. They only managed to devour a few fistfuls before the temple hands dragged them away, but the damage was done. Demeter would be furious.

Eleni grabbed hold of Danae and Alea's hands.

'Don't let go of me, girls.'

She bundled them towards the floral pathway, but panic had infected the crowd and they were battered by frightened women, tripping over each other in their attempts to flee.

Melia hurtled past with her daughters, having freed the youngest from the temple hands, and barged into Danae with such force she was thrown to the ground. A stampede of legs trampled her. She needed to get back to her mother and sister, but the onslaught of bodies kept her pinned down. She raised her arms over her head and curled up to protect herself. Then someone grabbed hold of her and dragged her out of the crushing mob. She was helped to her feet and found herself looking into the face of one of the Maenads.

Her skin tightened, the breath imprisoned in her chest, as she waited for the woman to strike.

The Maenad's eyes rounded with concern. 'Are you hurt?'

Danae opened her mouth but was too stunned to speak. She shook her head.

'Good.' The woman grinned, slapped her shoulder, then darted off into the bushes.

'Danae!' Her mother came battling through the crowd. 'Thank the gods, I thought I'd lost you.' She pulled her daughter into a tight embrace. 'Where's your sister?'

'I thought she was with you?'

Her mother paled. She clenched a vice-like hand around Danae's wrist then turned back to the crowd.

'Alea!'

Danae's heart raced at a sickening pace. She too called for her sister, scouring every face that rushed past, but there was no sign of Alea.

They searched the garden until their throats were raw and everyone had disappeared, save the temple hands who were left to clear up the wreckage.

'Have you seen my daughter? White dress, green headband, looks like me,' Eleni croaked for the hundredth time.

The man shook his head and returned to sweeping a heap of broken pottery.

Danae turned to her mother. 'What do we do now?'

Eleni, who always had an answer, said, 'I don't know.'

2. Two Daughters

When Danae and her mother returned home and told her father that Alea had disappeared, Odell immediately ran to gather her brothers and search the island.

News of what had happened at the Thesmophoria spread swiftly through the villages. Doors were barricaded and the all-seeing eye of the Twelve was daubed across the lintels. There was little the islanders could do to exact punishment on the Maenads. In the past, attempts had been made to discover their encampment, but the men who hunted them always returned bloody and battered, muttering that Dionysus protected his flock. The people of Naxos would have to leave their punishment to the gods.

By noon the following day, the news of Alea vanishing had reached her betrothed.

Philemon was a thin man of twenty with milky skin, sandy hair and forlorn eyes. He reminded Danae of an ear of wheat. She and her mother were fixing the awning of the goats' lean-to when he and his father came striding up the path. Thaddeus couldn't have been more different to his son. He was thick-set and bullish, dressed in a maroon tunic which did nothing for his ruddy cheeks. He shoved open the yard gate, Philemon scurrying behind him.

'Odell!' he bellowed, wiping beads of sweat from his brow with a meaty hand.

Her mother hurried over to greet them.

'Thaddeus,' Eleni inclined her head, muttering the sacred greeting.

He responded then barged past her to stick his head through the hut door.

'Is it true? Has my son's intended run off with the Maenads?'

'How dare –' Danae began, but her mother interrupted.

'My daughter was terrified when those women attacked the festival. She would never run with them. Alea was lost in the mayhem, but Odell's taking care of it. There's no need to worry, she will be home soon.'

Thaddeus did not look convinced. 'Well, if she hasn't gone with those whores, she must have joined the Missing.' He turned to his son and shook his head. 'She was your choice.'

Philemon looked down at his feet.

Danae dug her nails into her palms. 'Alea hasn't joined the Maenads or the Missing. Pa and my brothers are out there searching now. They'll find her.'

Thaddeus turned to Eleni as though she had been the one to speak.

'If by some miracle they do find her . . .' He paused. 'She'd better be intact.'

Danae felt like he'd punched her. The shame of it. She imagined taking her father's fishing spear and ramming it into Thaddeus' ham-like face.

'Of course she will be.' Her mother did well to keep the anger out of her voice. But Danae could tell from the pulsing vein in Eleni's temple that she, too, was furious.

'Father,' Philemon took half a step forward, his eyes still firmly downcast. 'I want to help search.'

'It's a waste of time.'

Philemon mustered a glance at his father. 'Please.'

Thaddeus sighed and rubbed his face. 'Where have they looked?'

'They've searched the fields around the temple and our village. They moved on to Sangri this morning.'

Thaddeus nodded. 'We'll take my ship around to the other side of the island. See if anyone there knows anything.'

'Thank you.' Eleni's hands twitched.

Thaddeus responded with a gruff 'huh' that jarred Danae to the back of her teeth. If they didn't leave soon, she was afraid she'd say something she'd regret.

'We'll find her,' Eleni said to Philemon. 'And the two of you will be married before you know it.' Her mother presented a brave mask, but Danae sensed the reassurance was really for herself.

The boy shot Eleni a weak smile.

'Come, son. We've got work to do.' Thaddeus placed a hand on Philemon's shoulder and steered him out of the yard.

Danae watched them walk away along the path.

'What a bastard.'

'Thank the gods the son is nothing like the father,' Eleni muttered. 'I pity his poor mother.'

Danae looked at her palms and the rows of crescent moons imprinted by her nails.

'Ma, what if Thaddeus is right?' She hesitated. 'Do you think Alea has joined the Missing?'

'Listen to me,' her mother said with the heat of a newly forged blade. 'Your father will find her. We just have to be patient.'

Danae nodded under her mother's fierce gaze. All they could do was wait.

It was the blue hour. That quiet time between night and day, when the moon fades before the sun has risen, and the sky belongs to no one.

Danae ran down to the beach, an empty pail swinging in

her hand. Normally, she'd never be sent out of the hut alone, but she couldn't sleep, and her mother had grown tired of her relentless pacing, so had sent her to 'do something useful'. In this case, collect brine for the cheese they made from Mopsus' milk. She was glad. If she spent any more time waiting in the hut, she would lose her mind.

She slowed as the dirt track gave way to white sand. The itch of the grains between her toes was a familiar comfort. This was the beach she had grown up on. It was in these waves she'd learnt how to swim and caught her first fish. This was her true home.

She broke into a sprint, the pail bumping her side. She didn't have long and would have to make every moment of freedom from her mother's supervision count. As soon as she reached the rocks she began to climb. Pail slung over her shoulder, she clambered the well-worn route, over rock pools she'd plundered as a child, up onto the shallow cliff. Once at the top, she padded across the craggy surface until she could see the concealed cove below.

She dropped the pail with a clatter, pulled her tunic over her head and slipped off her sandals. A shiver of anticipation sang through her body as she dived. Sleek as an arrow, she sliced into the sea, the cool water drawing the tension from her sun-bronzed limbs. She needed this. As much as she wanted to be at home when news of her sister came, the sea was a salve to her racing thoughts. Besides, she wouldn't stay long.

She surfaced, took a big gulp of air, then dived under again.

The cove held a secret. She liked to think it was one that belonged only to her.

She opened her eyes. The salt water burned but she was used to it. Then the ruins came into focus. She swam down, past swathes of mottled seaweed to the long-forgotten stones.

It must have been a special place. Many of the slabs were worn smooth by the grind of the tide, but some still had markings on them. She swam, following the circular layout, to her favourite stone. It was almost as tall as she was and stuck out of the seabed like a lone tooth. Carved upon it was a tree, its branches bowed with fruit mostly erased by the ocean. She stretched out a hand and traced the groove of its trunk.

There was something about the image that fascinated her. Perhaps the stones had once been part of a temple. Probably constructed to honour Poseidon, God of the Sea.

She flattened her hand against the carving.

Please watch over my sister, Lord Poseidon. Help my father and brothers bring her home.

Her lungs started to ache. Reluctantly, she left the ruins and kicked up towards the surface. She broke the water and gasped in a deep breath of cool, salty air. Lying on her back, she stared at the brightening sky through beaded lashes.

Her father used to call her his little Nereid, his sea nymph. Even as a babe she had loved the water. As a young child she would splash after lightning-quick shoals of red tunny, desperately wishing she had fins to match theirs.

Things were simpler in the water. The ocean could be a dangerous beast, but it had always held her and never let her fall.

Danae ran back along the beach, the pail sloshing in one hand, her sandals clacking together in the other. The blush of dawn had already fled the sky. She'd stayed too long.

As she ran up the track to her hut, she almost collided with Carissa hurrying in the opposite direction.

Her pulse quickened. 'Any news?'

Carissa shook her head, pursing her lips at Danae's sodden

hair and sand-splattered legs. She carried on her way without a word.

Her body heavy as stone, Danae dragged her feet through the yard gate.

Her mother looked up from where she sat in the goat pen, a bucket of milk beneath Mopsus' belly.

'Was Carissa here about Alea?'

Eleni shook her head. Her cheeks were pale. 'It's Melia's daughters. The temple hands dragged them from the blacksmith's hut and sacrificed them before dawn.'

Danae almost dropped the water. After the commotion of the Maenads' invasion and Alea's disappearance she had forgotten that Demeter had demanded blood at the Thesmophoria.

'Both of them?'

Her mother's hands shook as she smoothed the flyaway hairs that had escaped the cloth tied around her head.

'Demeter, in her wisdom, desired an additional life to amend for the desecration of her festival.'

Her legs suddenly weak, Danae set down the pail and leant against the goat fence.

'The goddess chose two daughters from the same family?'

Her mother held up a hand. 'It's not for us to question the will of the gods.'

'No, of course,' Danae said quietly.

Eleni let out a shuddering breath. 'Gods, I am not fond of Melia, but I would never wish this on anyone . . .' she trailed off and wiped her face. 'They'll be reunited in the Asphodel Meadows. As will we all one day.'

There were three realms of the Underworld, all presided over by the god Hades. The Asphodel Meadows were the plain where all the souls who'd lived a devout and honest life passed to after their death. Danae's grandparents and her uncle Taron were already there. It was a blissful land of sunlit fields and undulating hills, carpeted with eternally blooming flowers. A place of endless peace and joy, always spring and never winter.

The paradise of Elysium, where souls were sent to be anointed with immortality, then raised up to the heavens in the sky, was reserved for great warriors and heroes who died in battle. Danae always thought it sad that those brave people didn't get to spend eternity with their loved ones. No matter how splendid it was, heaven would feel empty without her family.

Last of the three realms was Tartarus, a place of torment and everlasting pain for those souls deemed to have led an unworthy life. Imprisoned in this deepest, darkest level of the Underworld were the Titans. An evil race of giants who had sought to destroy the world before the Twelve defeated them in a great battle known as the Titanomachy. Danae owed the ground beneath her feet to the courageous Olympians. All mortals did.

Eleni's hands fidgeted in her lap. A drop of blood dripped onto the skirt of her tunic from where she'd absentmindedly torn the nail bed. She didn't seem to notice.

'Ma?' said Danae.

Her mother blinked. 'Come on,' she said gruffly, hefting the milk towards the hut. 'The cheese won't make itself.'

Danae watched her for a moment, then followed her inside.

Her mother tipped the milk she'd collected into an iron cooking pot, set on the blazing hearth. 'She's not producing as much these days. Poor girl's getting old.'

Steam billowed into Danae's face as she added a splash of brine, then reached for a small clay jug beside the hearth, pouring a dash of vinegar into the milk.

Eleni had just dipped a wooden spoon into the mixture when Danae heard the creak of the gate. She dived through the doorway and skidded into the yard.

Her father was running up the path; he looked like he hadn't slept in days. Behind him were her brothers. Alea was draped over their arms, her auburn curls cascading towards the dusty earth.

Her father caught Danae as she hurtled towards her siblings. 'Is she alive?'

'She is.' Her father held her back. 'But we need to get her inside.'

'Alea!' Eleni rushed towards her brothers as they entered the yard and ushered them into the hut, cradling her sister's lolling head. The boys gently laid Alea on the pallet where the sisters slept. She was pale as marble.

Her mother raised Alea's eyelids. She did not respond.

'Where was she?' asked Eleni.

Her father sank into a chair. 'One of the priestesses found her this morning at the feet of Demeter's statue.'

Her mother drew in a sharp breath. She knelt down by the pallet and took Alea's hand in hers. 'The goddess has returned her to us. She was pleased with the sacrifice and gave us our Alea back.'

Danae didn't know how to feel. 'When will she wake?'

Her father shook his head. 'I don't know, Danie.'

She caught her brothers sharing a look. Unease prickled her stomach, and she stared at Santos until his eyes met hers. She twitched her head and stepped out into the yard. A moment later he followed her.

'What are they not saying?'

He shifted his large feet in the dirt.

'Santos.'

'Pa told us not to say anything to you.'

Danae punched his arm. 'Tell me. I'm her sister, I have a right to know.'

'*All right*.' Santos rubbed his bicep and glanced towards the hut. 'Alea's been drugged.'

Her frown deepened. 'Why would . . .' The words turned to ash on her tongue at the sight of Santos' eyes, awash with grief and fury.

Odell emerged from the hut looking as though he had aged a decade in the last three days, Calix following behind him. 'Your mother needs some time alone with your sister.'

Before he could grab her, Danae darted around him.

She entered the hut to find her mother peering between her sister's legs. Eleni looked up, her face stricken, and a stony weight settled in Danae's chest.

There was an unspoken need to keep busy the next day. Calix and Santos had gone back to their families, her father had risen before dawn to fish and so Danae and her mother were left alone in the hut with the still sleeping Alea.

Eleni kept vigil by her sister's side, endlessly mopping Alea's brow with a damp cloth, Danae loitering behind her.

Her mother loosed a sharp sigh. 'Make yourself useful – go to the riverbank and collect a bushel of sideritis. The herb might help revive her – remember it's the one with the little yellow flowers.'

Eager to help, Danae grabbed a hessian bag from its peg by the door, but before she'd stepped into the yard, her mother cried out. She turned to see Eleni bent over the pallet, arms wrapped around her sister.

Alea was awake.

Danae rushed forward and threw herself in a heap on top of them. They stayed entangled until Alea rasped, 'I can't breathe.'

'Fetch her some water, Danae,' her mother shouted.

She rushed over to the hydria that lived next to the fireplace, poured water from the large vase into a bowl, then hurried back to Alea. Her mother took the vessel and lifted it to her sister's lips. Alea spluttered before she pushed herself up and took the bowl in her own hands, drinking deeply. As she wiped her mouth, a furrow formed between her brows.

'How do you feel?' Eleni took the bowl from Alea.

'Like a herd of cattle have trampled through my head.' Her frown deepened as she looked down at her crumpled tunic. 'Weren't we just at the festival?'

'Alea, you've been gone for days,' said Danae.

Confusion creased her sister's face.

'But . . . we were just at the Thesmophoria. We watched the play and the pig being sacrificed and then . . .' Her breathing quickened.

'What's the last thing you remember?' her mother interrupted. 'Did you see a man?'

Alea shook her head. She looked on the verge of tears.

Her mother smoothed her sister's hair. 'All right, enough for now.' She turned to Danae. 'Go to the village and get a chicken from Myron, to celebrate.' She was already on her feet, whirling about the hut. 'Calix and Santos must come for dinner too. The whole family. Here,' she pushed Danae towards the door while scooping up the bag she'd dropped and pressed it into her hand, then a coin into the other.

'But –'

'Go on! Or he won't have any left.'

With a last look at Alea, Danae stepped out of the hut.

She ran down the coastal track that led into the heart of the village, her sandals slapping the sun-dappled path, the cerulean sea her constant companion.

At the edge of the village, she sprinted past the little shrine dedicated to Dionysus, only slowing when she reached the ramshackle collection of canopied stalls that lined the village square. She took a moment to catch her breath, then headed straight for the butcher's awning.

Her determination to return to Alea as quickly as possible was jeopardized by the arrival of a fisherman's wife from the next bay. Ceto, a thin woman with sallow skin and sharp eyes, stepped squarely into Danae's path. She quickly mumbled the sacred greeting before asking, 'Is it true? Has your sister been found?'

'Yes. She's home.'

'Bless the mercy of the gods.' Ceto clutched her hands to her chest. 'Has she said what happened?'

'I really must get on . . .'

But Ceto wouldn't let her pass. Biting her lip in frustration, Danae dodged right and broke into a run towards the butcher's stall.

'We're all so glad she's home,' Ceto called after her. 'But only time will tell if it's a blessing or a curse!'

Her words unsettled Danae so much that she ducked under Myron's faded awning with a scowl. The butcher, a man with the stature and complexion of an oak tree, was hacking slabs of meat from the carcass of a goat. She was used to the smell of fish, but she always found the metallic sharpness of Myron's hut unpleasant. He glanced up, wiping a bloodstained hand across his brow.

'The Twelve see you and know you,' she said breathily.

He touched a bloody finger to his forehead. 'You shouldn't go around with a frown like that. Wind might change and you'll end up looking like me.'

'I just ran into Ceto,' said Danae.

'Ah. Say no more.'

'I'm after a chicken if you've got any?'

Myron nodded and thudded his cleaver down into the stained wooden block. He shuffled through his hut, then out to the yard at the back. After a few moments, Danae heard a squawk and the fluttering of feathers. Then a crack.

Myron re-emerged, the chicken dangling from his fist. Danae opened her hessian bag for him to place the bird inside and held out a small copper coin.

He looked at her with a twinge of discomfort.

'The price has, ah . . . it's two obols now.'

Danae looked at the coin in her hand, and her heart sank.

'I've got another little one on the way and what with the temple tithes going up . . .' The butcher scratched his bald head. 'I hate to do it, but I've got no choice.'

'That's all Ma gave me.' Danae held her head high. 'But I'll go home and get another. Here.' She held out the coin and her bag containing the chicken.

The pity in his eyes brought heat to her cheeks.

He took the coin and pushed back the chicken. 'Just this once.'

Danae hoisted the bag onto her shoulder.

'I'm glad your sister's home.'

'Thank you,' she said quietly.

The butcher cleared his throat and took up his cleaver. Relieved the interaction was over, she darted out of the shop.

3. Ripe Fruit

Six weeks later, on her way out to feed the goats, Danae discovered Philemon dithering on the doorstep. He wore a new red tunic, trimmed with gold stitching. It didn't suit him.

They exchanged the sacred greeting.

'I've come to see Alea.' Proudly, he held up a small, cloth-wrapped parcel.

Danae sighed inwardly. Philemon had visited every week since Alea's return. She couldn't bear the thought of another afternoon spent listening to his dull stories and was about to tell him her sister was resting and he should come back tomorrow, when her mother appeared behind her.

'Philemon,' Eleni beamed. 'Just one moment. Danae, entertain our guest while I ready Alea.'

The door shut behind her, and Danae was left standing nose to nose with her sister's intended. He backed away and picked at the wrappings of his present at a safe distance.

They stood in silence for a while. Danae crossed her arms and scoured her mind for something polite to say. She settled on gesturing to the package in his hand.

'What's that then?'

Philemon's face stretched into a satisfied grin as he tapped the side of his nose. 'Ah, *ah*. I don't want you ruining the surprise.'

She raised an eyebrow.

'What I can tell you,' he conceded, 'is that this is a very special gift, all the way from –'

'Athens?'

Philemon's father owned a large olive grove and traded his produce in the city. From what she'd overheard of his conversations with Alea, Philemon endlessly went on about the latest fashion, the food and the superior culture. Apparently, even the air was sweeter in Athens.

A slight frown appeared between his brows. 'Yes, actually.' He drew himself up. 'I was there only yesterday on very important business with my father. I wish I could take Alea to see the new Temple of Athena. It really is the most stunning building. Did you know it took ten years to complete? The friezes alone were . . .'

His words became a drone in her ears. What really irritated her wasn't that he was boring, monopolized Alea's time or turned into a gibbering jellyfish whenever his father was around, but that he got to go to the mainland. When Danae was younger, she loved going out on her father's boat and helping him sell his catch at Naxos port. But her mother put a stop to all that. Young women on Naxos didn't leave their huts, except to do washing in the river and run errands in the village. And they definitely didn't get to go to Athens.

They were saved further interaction by her mother opening the door and ushering Philemon inside. Danae went to follow him, but Eleni stretched out an arm and blocked her way.

'Give them some privacy.' From behind her back she produced a broken wicker basket. 'Make yourself useful and mend this.'

Danae took the basket and glowered at her. 'You're staying inside then?'

'Of course. I'm her mother.'

'Fine.'

She sat down next to the goats and began weaving the broken pieces of straw back into the lattice of the bowl. She finished long before Philemon re-emerged, wearing a deeply irritating grin. As soon as he'd left the yard, she sprung to her feet and ran indoors.

Alea was sat next to the hearth, her cheeks flushed, their mother busy pinning something to her tunic. As Danae moved closer, she saw it glint. It was a brooch. An owl moulded in bronze with feathers carved into the metal and two little green gems for eyes.

Her sister gazed down at it, her face radiant.

'Danae, isn't it beautiful? Have you ever seen such a lovely thing?'

'No,' she said honestly.

'Ma, don't you agree?'

Danae glanced at her mother, expecting her to share Alea's joy, but she looked distant.

'Ma?'

Eleni returned to the room and beamed at her eldest. 'It's stunning, my love, a mark of the strength of his affection.'

As much as Danae disliked Philemon, she couldn't help smiling.

Suddenly, Alea lurched off her chair and staggered towards the door. Danae ran after her to find her retching in the yard behind the goat pen.

She held Alea's curls and rubbed her back.

'Should we send for the healer?' She glanced up at her mother, who had followed them out.

Eleni looked around, as though worried someone might see them.

'No,' she said through tight lips. 'I know what's wrong. Come back inside, quickly.'

Alea sat on the pallet, gazing at her lap, her eyes unfocused. Danae reached for her sister's hand, but Alea twitched her fingers away.

Danae looked at her mother. 'Are you sure?' she asked solemnly.

'I think so. I had the same sickness with all four of you children.' Eleni knelt beside her sister. 'And, Alea, your monthly blood still hasn't come.'

Whoever had done this to her sister deserved to have their genitals mutilated, and their limbs ripped from their body while they still breathed. Danae's rage boiled over into tears. She turned away and quickly wiped her eyes. Alea wasn't crying. If her sister could be strong, so could she.

'Alea, listen to me.' Her mother tucked a curl behind her sister's ear. 'This changes nothing. You will still marry Philemon.'

'How?' Alea's voice was barely audible.

'We'll go to Thaddeus and ask him to bring the wedding forward. I'll think of something to convince him. Babies arrive early all the time, no one will know it isn't Philemon's.' Her mother straightened up and crossed the room to the wicker chest at the foot of the girls' pallet. She began pulling out dresses. 'Which one is his favourite again?'

'Will Thaddeus agree to it?' asked Danae.

'He'll have to,' said her mother, inspecting a sky-blue tunic.

'I don't want to lie to him.'

Her mother lowered the dress.

Alea lifted her head, crystal clarity in her hazel eyes. 'I don't want to deceive Philemon. I want to tell him the truth and if he won't have me any more . . .' her voice wavered, 'then I'll stay here.'

Danae felt a surge of love for her sister. Beautiful, noble Alea. She moved to stand next to her and placed a hand on her shoulder.

'I'll help Alea look after the baby. We could do it together.'

She imagined the two of them running across the beach, a chubby infant swinging between their arms. They could be their own little family, and neither of them would have to get married. They could get by on selling cheese, and she could fish like her father.

Eleni's eyes blazed. She dropped the dress and paced across the small room to grab Alea's chin.

'Look at me. You *must* marry that boy.'

'Ma –' Danae began, but her mother rounded on her.

'Gods help me, Danae, you're a woman now. You should know better. Your father and I can't support you forever. How do you think you would live? We would be shunned, all of us.'

Danae pressed her lips together and bit down on the inside to stop them trembling.

Her mother smoothed her apron and sighed. 'We're going to get through this. But you must trust me, both of you.'

It was agreed that Danae, Alea and their mother would visit Thaddeus the following morning. Her father should have been with them. But that night, when Odell returned home and her mother told him of Alea's condition, he didn't say a word. Instead, he took himself off into the yard with a jug of wine he didn't bother to mix with water.

The girls lay on their pallet and tried to ignore the clashing of their parents' voices outside.

Alea faced the wall, her back to Danae.

'Are you afraid?'

There was a pause.

'No.'

'Good, because I'm going to be with you. For everything.'

'I know.'

Danae wondered how to articulate the thought that had

gnawed at her since Alea's return. It felt so large and tangled she didn't know how to begin.

Eventually she said, 'I know you don't remember, and you don't have to talk about it if anything does come back . . . but you can if you want to . . . I just . . . I want you to know that.'

More silence. Her bones felt heavy as she rolled over.

She closed her eyes, but even after her parents grew quiet and retreated inside, sleep ran from her like a shadow chased by the sun.

Danae stared at the large wooden door as her mother rapped the iron knocker. She squeezed her sister's hand, hoping to reassure her. In the end, her mother had chosen the blue tunic for Alea. She looked perfect, if a little pale. Her hair was elaborately coiled, the owl brooch proudly pinned to her chest. There hadn't been much time for Danae after preparing her sister, so her mother had just wound a strip of fabric around her unruly mane and put her in one of Alea's old green tunics.

Even dressed as they were, people were staring. Philemon and his family lived at the other end of the village, where the big houses were. They had separate rooms and proper wooden shutters. Danae was excited to see inside. She'd never been to a merchant's house before.

The door opened. Philemon's mother stood in the doorway. She was blonde and willowy like her son. Her face was unnaturally pale, painted with white lead. It was a trend that had floated across the water from Athens. Fashionable or not, she looked half dead.

Philemon's mother smiled dreamily and intoned the sacred greeting. 'You'd better come in.' She stood back and wafted an arm towards the interior of the house.

Danae suppressed a gasp as she stepped inside. The house

was built around a small garden. A large olive tree grew from a central patch of perfectly manicured grass, stretching up to the sky between an open square of terracotta tiles. Stone pillars held up the roof and rooms sprouted from each side of the garden.

'You have a lovely home,' said Eleni.

Philemon's mother breathed a soft 'hmm' and beckoned them into the garden. They sat on benches beneath the olive tree, specks of sunlight sprinkled on their laps.

Philemon's mother clapped her hands, and a boy in a loincloth scampered out from one of the rooms. Danae glanced at Alea. It was rare for a merchant to be able to afford a slave. Thaddeus' business must be doing very well indeed.

'Bring wine.'

'Oh, just water for us. Thank you,' Danae's mother said quickly before the boy could leave.

Philemon's mother sighed, 'Bring both.' She threw them another languid smile that didn't quite reach her eyes. 'We weren't expecting you.'

'Yes, sorry to surprise you like this. I was hoping to speak to your husband.'

'He's out. He and Philemon might be home soon . . . or not. You never can tell with Thaddeus.'

The boy returned, and Philemon's mother took a cup of wine from the tray, immediately raising it to her lips.

Danae looked up at the olives. Their green skins were so shiny they looked like they might burst. Her hands worried the edge of her tunic. No one was saying anything.

'How do you make olive oil?' she blurted into the silence.

'Danae,' her mother hissed as she passed a cup of water to Alea.

'What? I'm just making conversation.'

She was spared further reprimand by the front door

opening. Thaddeus and Philemon entered the garden. Philemon's face shone when he saw Alea, his eyes never leaving his intended. Danae's heart twinged. He really did seem to care for her sister. Gods, she hoped their mother could persuade Thaddeus to bring the marriage forward.

Danae's mother rose to her feet. 'Sorry to impose on you unannounced, but –'

'Where is Odell?' Thaddeus interrupted.

'He's fishing. It's a very busy time for him. He wishes he could be here.'

Thaddeus sat heavily next to his wife while Philemon pulled up a stool next to Alea.

'Go on then. What is it?'

Danae's mother smoothed the skirt of her dress. 'After everything that's happened, we feel that these two young people shouldn't be made to wait any longer. Demeter herself returned Alea to us, and we want to honour that by bringing the wedding forward to the month of ploughing.'

Philemon looked excitedly at his father. There was a tense pause before Thaddeus laughed.

'You do remember who's paying for this damned wedding?'

Eleni's lips tightened. 'Odell is contributing what he can.'

'A pittance,' Thaddeus spat. His wife flinched. 'We agreed, the month of the goddess. All the arrangements have been made. Do you have any idea how much it will cost to bring the preparations forward?'

'We're happy to scale back the celebrations if it means –'

'Scale back? My only son is not getting married in some peasant ceremony. That might be what you're used to, but by the gods my family is not.' Thaddeus' gaze slid to Alea. 'Why the sudden rush?'

Alea looked like she was melting under his scrutiny. Danae's pulse quickened. She could see the perspiration beading on her sister's brow.

'Like I said,' her mother dived in, 'we believe we would be honouring Demeter by marrying the pair as soon as possible. The goddess, in her mercy, returned Alea to us so that she and Philemon could be together and –'

Silently, as though kissed with sleep by a mischievous god, Alea crumpled.

Philemon lunged, catching her as she slumped forward and Danae fell to her knees beside her sister, the luscious grass staining her skirt. Alea was pale as stone.

'Boy!' Thaddeus shouted. 'Send for the healer.'

'No.' Eleni jumped to her feet. 'She just fainted, she'll be fine in a moment.'

'Give her some wine,' said Philemon's mother.

Thaddeus ignored them as the boy entered the garden. 'Fetch Iatromea, now.'

'Really, Thaddeus, please don't go to any bother; you know what women are like, she's just overcome with excitement about the marriage.'

There was panic in Eleni's voice. As the village healer, Iatromea had delivered countless children, including Danae and her sister. They couldn't let her near Alea in her condition, especially not in the home of her intended.

Thaddeus turned to her mother with a glint in his eye. 'She's my future daughter-in-law. I'm not leaving anything to chance.'

'Wider.' Iatromea prodded Alea's tongue with a gnarled finger.

Alea stretched her mouth so the healer could peer inside. Danae glanced at her mother. Eleni was staring at the back of Iatromea's head as though she might be able to see the woman's thoughts if she just looked hard enough.

Philemon sat next to Alea on the bench. He hadn't let go of her hand. It would have been a touching scene, if it weren't for the secret growing in Alea's stomach.

'Well?' Thaddeus said impatiently. 'What's wrong with her?'

Iatromea grumbled something incomprehensible, then proceeded to prod and poke Alea in various places. Once satisfied with her examination, she straightened up.

'Heat exhaustion.'

'There,' her mother's voice was light with relief. 'Didn't I say? Nothing to worry about.'

'Women,' grumbled Thaddeus.

'Father.' Philemon rose to his feet. He was trembling. Danae noticed his knuckles had turned white as he clung to Alea's hand. 'I too wish for the wedding to be brought forward. It was the worst time of my life when Alea was gone . . .' he glanced down at his intended and swallowed, 'and I don't want to waste another moment.' He raised his head and looked his father dead in the eye.

Danae thought this might be the bravest thing Philemon had ever done.

Thaddeus stared at him as though he couldn't quite believe what he'd just heard. Philemon stood firm, like a hardy blade of grass against the withering heat of the sun.

'I . . . I am a man now, and it is my right to marry when I wish.'

There was silence as Thaddeus considered his son. Danae held her breath.

Then Thaddeus let out a booming laugh. 'It is good for a man to speak his mind. And yes, you are a man now. To get anywhere in life you must go after what you want and not give up until it's between your teeth.' He slapped Philemon on the shoulder. 'All right then, you shall have your wedding in the month of ploughing.'

Philemon looked so shocked that Danae wondered if he too was going to faint.

'Oh, Thaddeus, thank you –' Eleni began, but he interrupted her.

'There, you got what you wanted. Now,' he gestured towards the door, 'I'm a very busy man.'

'Yes, of course.' Eleni took both her daughters' hands and backed away. 'We won't take up any more of your time.'

Iatromea coughed.

Thaddeus grunted and shouted for the boy to fetch his purse.

'No, we'll pay, I insist.'

Danae looked at her mother, brow furrowed. Thaddeus was infinitely wealthier than they were. He probably wouldn't even notice the missing coin, whereas paying the healer would mean no bread for her family for a week.

Philemon showed them out, still flushed from standing up to his father. He waved them off into the heat of the day and shut the door.

Danae slipped an arm around Alea's waist as their mother turned to the old healer.

'How much do I owe you?'

An unpleasant smile hooked the corners of Iatromea's mouth. 'Five obols.'

Eleni baulked. The healer's eyes slid past her to rest on Alea's stomach.

Danae's blood ran cold. She knew. She'd known all along.

Her mother's lips turned white as she pressed them together and rooted around in her purse. She drew out two obols.

'It's all I have on me. But you will receive the rest tomorrow.'

Iatromea snatched the coins. 'By sundown.' She threw a

contemptuous glance at Alea, then shuffled off down the dusty road.

'Ma?' Alea said in a trembling voice.

'It's all right,' Eleni said quickly as she ushered the girls away from the house. 'I'll take care of it.'

They began to walk back through the village.

'I'm sorry,' Alea said so softly it was barely audible.

'It's not your fault. These things can happen early in a pregnancy. I should have gone on my own.'

Danae watched Alea with an iron weight in her stomach. Intuiting her sister's mind used to come as naturally as breathing. Now she felt like a stranger. She was slipping away, and Danae didn't know why.

Her gaze trailed over the large, sun-bleached houses to her left and lingered on one with blue-painted shutters. She comforted herself with the knowledge that their mother's plan had worked. Perhaps her sister would end up living in a house like one of these, with her own courtyard garden and an apple tree in the centre. Apples were Alea's favourite. Danae smiled. She'd sneak out to Timon's orchard when they got home and bring her sister back a skirtful.

She stopped walking. In the shadowy gap between two of the houses was a pair of red eyes, the same crimson orbs she'd seen at the Thesmophoria. The air around them seemed to ripple, as though the eyes were attached to a body that was somehow there and not there at the same time.

'Danae.' Her mother touched her arm and she blinked. The eyes were gone. 'What are you staring at?'

'Nothing,' she said as her mother pulled her away.

A couple of weeks after their visit to Thaddeus, Danae and Alea were lugging their family's hydria along the dirt track to the village. With each step the vase grew heavier. Danae readjusted her grip as the handle slipped between her moist fingers. The midday sun was relentless. Normally, they would make the journey in the cool of morning, but Alea's sickness had delayed them.

Before Alea's disappearance, the sisters would chatter all the way to the well. But the gulf between them was widening, gorging itself each day on their silence. Danae could not shake the sense that there was something Alea was not telling her.

Sticky and irritable, they finally reached the square. After hefting the hydria across the last stretch of dirt and setting it down against the bricks of the well, together they heaved the heavy iron handle and hoisted the pail up from its watery depths.

A crash of broken pottery echoed from the far side of the square. Philemon and his father were standing outside the blacksmith's hut, shattered fragments of an amphora scattered around Philemon's feet. He didn't seem to notice. His eyes were fixed on Alea.

Behind them, Melia emerged from her husband's hut. She'd halved in size since the death of her daughters, a grief-ravaged skeleton of the woman she'd once been. She staggered past Philemon and Thaddeus, her face twisted with hatred.

'You don't deserve to be alive,' she shouted. 'My beautiful daughters are gone but *you* are still here. Disgusting, depraved . . .' She collapsed to her knees, sobbing. Her husband ran forward and half dragged, half carried her back inside.

Danae couldn't breathe. Melia knew.

Thaddeus seized Philemon by the scruff of his tunic and barked something in his ear before shoving his son in the direction of the sisters. By now, a crowd had gathered, waiting in rapt silence for the drama to unfold.

Watching Philemon walk across the square was agonizing. When he finally reached them, he looked like he was going to be sick. For the longest moment nobody moved. Then a peal of laughter rippled around the square. Anger flushed his cheeks.

'Philemon, I –' Alea began.

With as much violence as if he'd hit her, Philemon spat in Alea's face.

4. The Followers of Dionysus

The tension ruptured. All around, the villagers shouted, given permission by Philemon's act of condemnation.

'Filthy animal!'

'Whore!'

'You aren't welcome here!'

Through the commotion, Danae spotted Iatromea in the crowd. She wore a look of satisfaction, reserved for those who believe themselves the agents of justice.

'How could you?' Danae shouted, wrapping her arms around her sister. 'You promised! You took our coin!'

Iatromea raised her wrinkled chin. 'My soul sickened with your secret, so I went to the priestesses. They told me I must bring it into the light, for all our sakes.' She glanced at Philemon. 'He had a right to know. We *all* had a right to know there was a Maenad hiding among us!'

'I knew she'd run off with them that night,' said Ceto. She pointed at Alea's stomach. 'She danced with those wicked women then spread her legs for the first man she saw!'

One boy, Karan, whom Danae had cared for when his mother was sick, picked up a stone and threw it. He aimed for Alea's head. Danae threw herself in front of her sister, pain spiking across her skin as the stone caught her arm. The child immediately bent down, scrabbling for more ammunition. Others followed his lead, throwing anything they had to hand: sticks, clumps of dirt, stale bread and fruit that had turned rotten in the heat.

The sisters backed away from the well, but the crowd closed in on them. Danae tried to shield Alea, but the onslaught came thick and fast. These people had known the sisters all their lives; the village was like one extended family. But in a single breath, hatred had poisoned them. Danae feared if they didn't get away, they might be stoned to death.

A shadow passed overhead. The crowd looked up as a large bird soared above them, momentarily blocking the glare of the sun.

'An eagle!' someone cried.

'The sacred bird of Zeus!'

A few people backed away, their makeshift weapons discarded.

'Come on!' Seizing the opportunity, Danae grabbed her sister's hand and dived through a gap in the crowd.

They sprinted down the sun-baked path, stopping only when they were well beyond the outskirts of the village. Panting, Danae fell to her knees, then looked back to make sure they weren't being followed. The dust was already settling on the empty road.

She wiped the sweat from her eyes and turned to Alea. 'Are you all right?'

Her sister's tunic was filthy, her hair plastered with pulp, and there was a glistening cut on her forehead. Danae took her sister in her arms and hugged her tight. Alea's body spasmed. As her sister's tears soaked into her shoulder, she pictured herself back in the square. Instead of fleeing, she launched herself into the crowd, punching and kicking. She clawed her nails down Iatromea's hateful face and smashed Philemon's head into the well over and over again until it cracked.

She forced herself to take deep steady breaths.

'It's all right, it's going to be all right,' she muttered, even though she had no idea how it could ever be all right again.

She desperately wanted to take her sister's pain, suck it out like it was poison from a bee sting. But there was nothing that could save Alea now.

News of Alea's condition tore through the village like a hurricane. Overnight Danae's family became outcasts; at market, her father found his catch was worth half of what it had been the day before, many of the shopkeepers refused to sell to them, and they were no longer welcome to scrub their clothes with everyone else at the river behind the village. So, Danae and her mother were forced to take the long path into the hills on washing day. Alea didn't accompany them. After the attack at the well, her mother had forbidden her sister to leave the safety of their yard.

They paused for breath halfway up the rocky track, wicker baskets piled with dirty tunics balanced on their hips. Danae looked back. The village lay beneath her at the edge of the sea. The houses looked tiny from her vantage point, clinging to the land like the barnacles on the underside of her father's boat. From here the villagers didn't look like people at all, just a cluster of ants. She bent down and picked up a stone. Closing one eye, she held it out above the dwellings. She wondered what it would feel like to have the strength of a god and crush anyone who hurt the ones she loved.

'Danae, stop dawdling.'

She dropped her hand and let the stone tumble back onto the path.

They trudged up through sparse, yellowing grass, which gave way to a woodland track, until eventually they emerged onto the broad rocks of the riverbank.

They set down their loads and dipped and scrubbed the soiled clothing in the water. It was quiet, save for the rush of the current, the clicking of cicadas and the occasional call of a kestrel. Danae breathed in the verdant air, thankful to be away from the oppressive atmosphere of their hut. She wrung out a sodden tunic and splayed it flat on the rock to dry. As she delved into the basket to retrieve another, she heard a tinkle of laughter. Her head snapped up. Had they been followed? Then she spotted someone further down on the opposite bank.

The woman slid into the river, gasping as the crisp water lapped over her mahogany skin. She submerged herself, then broke the surface and threw back a slick of hair. Another woman emerged from the trees and launched herself bodily into the river, showering the first in spray.

Danae glanced at her mother. 'Maenads?' she whispered.

Eleni nodded, a wary frown creasing her brow. She raised a finger to her lips.

Transfixed, Danae watched the women giggle and splash each other. She had never seen two people so free from inhibition. She knew she should look away, but she'd never really seen a naked body before, apart from accidentally catching a glimpse of her sister's when she was dressing. The Maenads' breasts bobbed in the water, the tufts of hair under their armpits wicked into curls. Their skin folded, rolled and stretched as they moved. They were mesmerizing.

She was so captivated by their bodies, she barely noticed their faces. When her eyes did finally travel upwards, recognition jolted through her.

The first woman was the Maenad who'd saved her from the stampede at the Thesmophoria. Before she knew what she was doing, she was on her feet. Her mother was hissing at her to sit down, but like a hound with the scent of a rabbit, she could not let go.

'Maenads! I want to talk to you!'

The women froze. When they caught sight of Danae, they immediately swam for the bank.

'Danae!' Her mother tried to grab hold of her, but she slipped through Eleni's fingers and dived into the water.

Her mother's cries were drowned out as the river enveloped her. The current threatened to bear her downstream but she struck out, her limbs strong from years of battling sea tides. She knew her mother couldn't follow her. Eleni had never learnt to swim.

By the time she reached the far side, the Maenads had vanished into the trees. She grasped fistfuls of grass and heaved herself out of the water. Catching sight of a trail of wet footprints in the earth, she ran after them.

As she tracked them through the woodland, it occurred to her how dangerous this was. The Maenads were wild, capable of anything. She ground the fear between her teeth. These women must have taken her sister from the Thesmophoria, it was the only explanation. They probably dragged Alea through the woods, then left her to be preyed upon by the first man that found her. Danae didn't care how dangerous they were; she would kill them, all of them, with her bare hands.

Then she thought of the woman who'd helped her at the festival, recalled the genuine concern in her eyes. The flame of her rage sputtered out. She shivered in the shade of the trees as her wet tunic clung to her body and suddenly realized that she had no idea where she was.

Then something hit her in the back.

She twisted to see an apple roll across the ground behind her. Then another smacked her in the shoulder. She spun around.

Laughter pinged between the trees. She couldn't tell which direction it was coming from.

'Come out, you cowards.'

'Come out, you cowards.'

This was a game to them. Her anger flared again. 'I know you took my sister the night of the Thesmophoria. I know it was you.'

The laughter stopped.

The Maenad who'd saved her stepped out from behind the trees. Danae was disarmed by her nakedness, the dark tuft between her legs, the way her wet hair slicked over her full breasts and the round curve of her stomach. She dragged her gaze upwards and clenched her jaw.

The woman's eyes were deep and serious. From the lines around them, Danae realized the Maenad was older than she'd first thought.

'We do not kidnap women.'

Danae took a step back and stumbled on one of the apples. 'I don't believe you. I know what you Maenads do. I saw you at the festival.'

'You saw us dancing. We disrupted your ritual, but we did not harm anyone. I helped you, remember?'

'But . . .' Danae couldn't argue. Then she recalled what had happened to Melia's daughters. 'An extra girl was sacrificed because of you.' She couldn't hide the tremor in her voice. 'You brought the wrath of Demeter down on us.'

The woman's eyes swelled with sadness. 'I am sorry to hear that. It is a terrible demand for a god to make.'

Danae stared at her. How could she utter such blasphemy?

The other Maenad emerged from the trees. She was younger than the first, her curly hair dripping onto her sun-rouged shoulders.

'We didn't take her, but there is one who might know what happened to your sister.'

Danae's heart lurched. 'Who?'

The Maenads glanced at each other.

'Come with us.' The first woman stretched out a hand.

Danae hesitated. Her mother would be frantic on the other side of the river. She should go back, tell her she was safe, but she doubted the women would wait for her to return.

Swallowing her guilt, she took the Maenad's hand.

The Maenads' encampment was chaos.

A grove of wild fruit trees was scattered over the hillside and the air was sweet with the scent of apples, figs and pomegranates. The trees were all mixed together as if someone had muddled their seeds and thrown handfuls in the air, leaving their fate to the wind. Vines too were tangled around the branches of the mature fruit trees, kissing their boughs with indigo clusters of grapes.

There were Maenads everywhere. Women old and young, all naked, some balancing baskets on their hips as they harvested the fruit. Animals and children ran about their feet, chickens squawked and goats nibbled on low-hanging fruit.

Beyond the grove was a ramshackle structure. It looked as though it had once been a large house that over the years had spawned additional extremities and was now a rambling collection of dwellings all joined together.

The two Maenads led Danae through the grove to an older woman who sat with a brood of infants on the steps of the house.

'Ariadne,' called the first Maenad. 'This is . . .' She looked at Danae.

'Danae.'

Ariadne stood slowly and gently shooed the children away. Her skin was the colour of fresh cream, her grey hair so long it fell past the silver stretch marks on her abdomen. She walked forward and drew Danae into a tight embrace.

Danae stiffened at the proximity of this stranger's naked body to her own. Drawing away, she said, 'My sister was taken from the Thesmophoria. Your . . .' She looked at the younger Maenad.

'Oenone,' prompted Ariadne.

'Oenone said you might know what happened to her.'

Ariadne's pale eyes darted to Oenone then back to Danae. 'I cannot say for sure. I can only tell you the warning I was given by my husband.'

'You're married?'

The stories she'd heard told that the Maenads were an all-female community who didn't interact with anyone outside their sect. Looking around, Danae could see no men anywhere in the grove.

Ariadne smiled. 'I am the wife of our lord, Dionysus.'

'You're married to one of the *Twelve*?'

Ariadne's lips twitched at the incredulity in her tone.

'The gods of Olympus have taken mortal lovers since the dawn of mankind. Is it so strange that our two souls wish to live in union for the time I have upon this earth?'

Danae didn't know what to say. She rubbed her face and tried to focus. 'What was the warning? Tell me.'

Ariadne took Danae's hands in hers. Her skin was soft and wrinkled like an overripe peach.

'My husband warned us that a creature would come to our island. An unseen beast with scarlet eyes that hunts mortals. He called it a shade, and its victims, I believe, you call the Missing.'

Danae felt the cold breath of fear on her neck. She'd seen it. Twice.

'But the Missing never come back. The shade can't have taken my sister because she was returned to us. It must have been a man because . . . she's pregnant . . .' Her words dissolved at the pained expression on Ariadne's face.

Her lips parted, but she couldn't ask the question, could not voice the horror that had just taken root in her mind.

Ariadne put her arms around Danae, and she crumpled, sobbing as though crying out all the pain would undo what had happened to Alea.

Eventually her heaving shoulders stilled. She pushed Ariadne away, raw and embarrassed.

'I am sorry,' Ariadne said softly. 'We do not know for sure that it was the shade who took her, but even so, what happened to your sister is an evil crime. I am glad at least that she has you. I wish, in my time of need, I'd had my sister.'

There was an ache in Ariadne's words, a river of understanding that Danae had unknowingly touched. She wiped her face. 'What happened?'

Ariadne loosed a small sigh. 'I was a foolish girl who betrayed her family for a prince and an empty promise of marriage. He took what he wanted and left me here to die. He is King of Athens now, I believe.' Her face softened. 'But it has been decades since my Dionysus found me, and look.' She gazed at the grove. 'Time is kind. It may bring pains to the body, but it heals those of the heart.'

A headache was beginning to pulse behind Danae's eyes.

'What happens to the Missing? Did your husband tell you?'

Ariadne shook her head. 'He only said that once someone has been taken by a shade, they are as good as dead. He would speak no more on the matter.'

'Why didn't you make him tell you?'

Ariadne laughed. 'My husband is a god, child. A benevolent one, but a god nonetheless. He cannot be made to do anything.'

Danae's frown deepened. 'But Alea came back. I don't

understand; why would the shade return Alea to the temple, and why would it . . .' she couldn't bring herself to say the word, 'do that to her?'

Ariadne tilted her head. The pity in the Maenad's eyes shuddered through her like a stone striking metal.

'I do not know. There are creatures in this world that delight in the pain and suffering of others. Be thankful your sister is alive.'

'Will it come back?' Danae whispered.

Ariadne did not answer immediately. 'I would be wary. There is a reason your sister did not join the Missing. The shade may have unfinished business with her.'

The child. A wave of nausea washed through her.

Ariadne placed a hand on her arm and said gently, 'You should go home, your family will be worried.'

Danae nodded, and let the Maenad guide her towards the grove.

'You and your sister are always welcome here. We do not judge any woman on the hardships life has weighed upon her. Do not give up hope.' Ariadne pulled her into one last embrace. 'Take care of yourself, Danae.'

She took a step towards the forest, then turned back. 'Is it true . . . do the Maenads really kill babies?'

Ariadne shook her head sadly. 'We are liberated women, not monsters.'

Danae swallowed. 'Thank you for telling me about the shade.'

As she turned once more towards the trees, Ariadne called out, 'Remember, my Lord Dionysus protects his flock. It would be unwise for you to speak of where you found us.'

She glanced back, then set off at a run through the

grove. The last thing she wanted was to incur the wrath of a god.

Danae sprinted all the way home, but the sun had already melted into the sea by the time she reached the yard. She'd been gone for most of the day.

She crashed through the gate, doubled over to catch her breath, then pushed through the hut door. She barely had time to take in the room before her mother crossed the space and grabbed her by the shoulders.

'Where have you been!? Are you hurt? What did they do to you?'

'I'm fine.'

Eleni stared at her for a heartbeat, then slapped her. Stunned from the pain, Danae stayed rooted to the ground.

Her sister let out a small sob. 'Oh, Danae, we were so worried.'

'How could you?' Her mother was trembling.

'I'm sorry, I –'

'Your father is out there now, searching for you.'

In addition to the throbbing in her skull, a sickening weight settled in Danae's stomach.

'I cannot believe, after everything we've been through with your sister, you would run off with those *women*.' Her mother spoke quietly. It pierced Danae deeper than if Eleni had shouted.

'I'm sorry, I truly am, but I learnt something important.' She turned to her sister. 'The Maenads are nothing like we've been told; they were kind, and they told me there's an unseen creature with red eyes who's been taking the Missing – they called it a shade – and . . .' she gulped in a breath, 'that's what took you from the festival, and Ariadne said it might have unfinished business,' she looked at her sister's stomach, 'so we need to be careful —'

'Enough of this nonsense!' Her mother grabbed Danae's arm. 'You want to keep the company of animals? Then you can sleep outside with the goats.'

'Ma, please,' Alea protested, but Eleni ignored her.

She picked up her husband's old fishing rope and tied it in a knot around Danae's wrists, then pushed her out into the goat enclosure and secured the other end to the fence.

Danae was too stunned to fight back. Rage had distilled into diamond-hard resolve in her mother's eyes. Eleni disappeared back into the hut, then emerged with a blanket, which she threw at Danae's feet. Without another word, she bustled Alea back inside and slammed the door.

Danae slumped down against the wall of the hut, underneath the goats' awning. She nudged the blanket over her legs. Pilops came trotting over and nuzzled her. She pressed her face into the goat's musty fur and groaned.

In the silence, the terror she had repressed since the Maenads' camp stirred.

If it was a shade that took her sister, what was the thing now growing inside Alea?

Danae woke to the creak of the yard gate. Her body ached from a fitful night tossing and turning on the hard earth. She had barely slept, her mind a roaring torrent, each thought more terrible than the next. Yawning, she cricked her neck and looked over to see her father staring at her. His eyes were rimmed with shadows. The blanket slid to the ground as she scrambled to her feet.

'Pa, I'm sorry . . .' she began, but her father turned away without a word and disappeared into the hut.

She sank back down and pulled the blanket back over her legs. A moment later, she sat up again as her father re-emerged with fishing nets slung over his shoulder. Hope fluttered in her chest, then sank. He didn't look at her as he crossed the yard and took the path down to the sea. She cradled her head in her bound hands, guilt gnawing at her insides.

Hearing the door again, she glanced up. Alea walked towards the goat pen carrying a cup of water. Her sister let herself into the enclosure and sat down beside her. Danae took the cup and drained it in a few gulps.

'Thanks.' She wiped her mouth, and her eyes drifted to Alea's stomach. Her throat tightened.

'You might be sleeping out here for a few more nights.' Alea took the cup, then began to pick at the knotted rope around Danae's wrists. 'Ma's still furious.'

Danae forced herself to smile. 'That's all right, I sleep better out here anyway. The goats don't snore.'

Her sister rolled her eyes, as the rope fell loose in her hands.

Danae rubbed her wrists. 'Alea, if it was this shade creature that took you . . .' she glanced again at her sister's stomach, 'I don't want to frighten you, but . . . the baby might not be human.'

Alea held her gaze and said calmly, 'You're right.'

Danae saw Alea's secret rise, until it floated just below the surface. She didn't dare speak, afraid to send it scampering back to the depths.

'I should have told you before. But I was afraid you wouldn't understand . . .' Alea hesitated. 'I know who my child's father is.'

Danae's mouth went dry.

'At one point, I woke . . . and I saw his face.'

She felt sick. Alea had known all this time.

'Is it the shade?' she asked flatly.

A prickle of unease crept up her spine at the smile spreading across her sister's face.

'It's Zeus.'

5. Blood and Bark

Everyone had heard the tales of mortals being impregnated by the gods, and the heroes their demi-god children went on to become. But that was something that happened to people far away, not on their island. Not to the daughters of fishermen.

'Danae?'

The world came back into focus. Alea was watching her, waiting.

'That's . . . it's . . .'

'Wonderful.' Her sister placed her hand over her stomach. At the expression on Danae's face she said, 'I know, I was scared at first too. I couldn't remember anything and I thought I had lost my mind. Then one night it came back to me. An eagle flew through my dreams, and when I woke, I could recall Zeus' face. I can feel it, Danae, the divine spark growing inside me. Do you see now, all the hardship, all the pain will be worth it.' She beamed. 'Can you believe it? The King of Heaven chose me.'

Pity choked Danae's heart. 'Alea, I don't blame you for wanting to turn what happened into something –'

Her sister reached forward and gripped Danae's hands. 'This is why I didn't tell you, I knew you would find it hard to believe, but you must trust me.' She placed Danae's hands on her stomach. 'I can feel the seed of Zeus inside me. And remember the day the villagers attacked us? An eagle came to save us. Don't you see? The King of Heaven was protecting his child.' A thread of silver leaked from her gleaming eyes.

Danae pulled back, her stomach hollowing. She had thought the chasm between them would close once she learned her sister's secret. But as she looked at Alea, the gulf grew wider than ever. To be admired by a god was a high honour, but even if it was true, Danae could find no joy in her heart for what had been done to her sister. And if Alea really was carrying Zeus' child then she was in grave danger. As infamous as her husband's fondness for mortal beauty was his wife, Hera's, vengeance upon those who inflamed his lust.

And there was always the chance that Alea had imagined it all, to protect herself from the terrible truth, that she had been abducted and raped by a shade.

'Let's keep it between us for now,' Danae said quickly. 'You were right not to speak of it; other people might not understand. Even Ma and Pa.'

For a moment she was worried her sister would disagree, but Alea's face softened and she nodded.

'Our secret.'

The following night, Odell returned home with a bruised jaw and a swollen nose.

'What in Tartarus?' Eleni was immediately upon him, cloth in hand, dabbing at the blood crusted on his lip. 'Who did this?'

He did not reply as he gently pushed her away and reached for the amphora of wine beside the hearth.

Danae shared a glance with Alea as her mother grasped his arm.

'Odell. Who struck you?'

Her father loosed a weary sigh and without meeting his wife's eye muttered, 'Calix.'

Danae stiffened.

'What?' Eleni breathed, her grip tightening on her husband's arm.

'It was a disagreement about fishing territory, it's nothing.' Odell made another feeble attempt to reach the wine.

'It is not nothing.' Eleni blocked his way, her cheeks flushed. 'Our son struck you.'

Calix had not set foot in their hut since the news broke of Alea's pregnancy. Santos at least had visited a handful of times, but Calix had severed all ties.

Danae glanced at Alea, and her stomach twisted at the tears blooming in her sister's eyes.

Before the thought had fully taken form, she was on her feet, sprinting from the hut. The sound of her name being called was soon drowned out by the rasp of her breath as she ran along the path that led to the north of the village.

Dusk had spread its indigo wings over the sky by the time she arrived outside Calix's hut. She hammered on the door.

Her brother opened it, his handsome face falling slack at the sight of Danae, dusty and sweating on his step.

'You shouldn't be here –'

'How could you?' she spat. 'Your own father.'

Hastily he stepped outside and shut the door behind him.

'You have no idea what it's been like,' he hissed. 'I've had to work damned hard to rid myself of Alea's taint just to keep food on the table, and Carissa's pregnant again.'

'*Taint?*'

He drew himself up. 'Carissa has helped me see the truth. This is our parents' fault. Both of you should have been married off years ago, not left to roam the island like a pair of Maenads. And Pa taking you fishing, teaching you to spar – it is unnatural, Danae. Unnatural and wrong. It's a wonder something like this didn't happen sooner.'

She couldn't prevent the tears from blurting down her cheeks.

'You abandoned us, your own family.'

'The people inside this hut are my family.' Calix wrinkled his nose. 'Go home.'

She tasted metal. She'd bitten down so hard on her lip she'd drawn blood.

Calix turned to step back inside.

The storm within her erupted. She kicked out at the back of his knee and brought him crashing to the ground. Calix snarled and scrambled to his feet as she struck out again, this time with her fist, catching him in the stomach. He staggered backwards into his door, the breath wheezing from his lungs.

'Unnatural am I?' Danae aimed a blow at his jaw.

Gathering himself just in time, Calix dodged and tackled her around the waist, hurling them both to the ground.

The hut door swung open. Carissa shrieked at the sight of her husband scrabbling in the dirt with Danae.

'I'm your sister, I'm your fucking sister,' she sobbed as she sank fist after fist into Calix's ribs.

A hand grabbed her shoulder, and without looking she hurled her next blow upwards. Carissa flew back, clutching her nose as blood dripped onto her dress.

Danae's limbs sagged, horror spreading through her as Calix staggered to his pregnant wife.

'I'm sorry, I didn't mean to . . . is she all right?'

Carissa moaned, and Calix turned to her with hatred in his gaze.

'You are not my sister.'

Eyes burning, Danae turned and ran.

When Danae was a child, she was sometimes gripped by fits of anger so violent she would fall to the ground and beat the earth until her rage seeped away like rainwater.

One day her father had taken her to a rocky outcrop above the village. An old tree stood amongst the jagged stones, its long dead branches twisting into the azure sky.

'Don't tell your mother. This is where I taught the boys to fight.'

Danae scowled, her little fingers tracing the grooves in the peeling grey bark. Her father took her hands and bound them in strips of cloth.

'Now, hold your fists like this, see?' He curled her fingers into her palm. 'Make sure your thumb's on top; if you tuck it in you'll break it.'

She looked up at him, at the creases that ran down his cheeks into his beard.

'Who will I fight?'

He smiled at her, his eyes warmer than the sun. 'No one, Danie. I'm teaching you this so you don't end up fighting yourself.'

'Don't be silly.' She turned to the tree. 'I would only fight bad men.' She chewed her lip, picturing them. 'Pirates and bandits and thieves and enemy soldiers and . . .'

Her father laughed. He smacked the tree with his palm. 'Let's start with old Greybeard here. We can pretend he's a pirate if you like.'

Danae nodded enthusiastically and narrowed her eyes, her imagination morphing the tree into a fearsome pirate.

'Now,' her father came to stand behind her, 'hold your hands up like this. Keep your gait loose, shoulders relaxed. Aim for where you want to hit and land the blow with the flat of your fingers.'

After that, her father brought her to the tree every day. Soon she was training with her brothers, until they grew too tall and strong to spar with.

Since that first day, she never had another episode. Her

mother thought it a miracle and was so relieved she'd never asked Odell where he took their daughter for an hour each day.

Now, Danae stood before the tree once more. Her chest heaved and her hands ached from fighting with Calix. Her eyes were raw with salt, but her tears had dried. She looked at the rivets their little fists had left in the dead wood, like they had been potters moulding clay.

Her father hadn't had much skill to pass on, save how to throw a punch and not break her hand. But sparring with her brothers had been the only time she felt truly in control. They were a team, their own little army.

Now it was just her.

She flinched at the cry of a bird soaring overhead. For a moment she thought it was an eagle silhouetted against the sun-bleached clouds. Her pulse quickened, but as she shielded her eyes against the glare, she realized it was just a falcon.

She dropped her hand and as it swung by her side she sucked in a breath. In one smooth motion she drew back her right fist and drove it into the silver bark. She hit the trunk with such force a tiny crack appeared in the wood grain. As she pulled away, blood trickled down the peeling bark. Against the wine-dark fluid it looked like bone.

'Goodbye, Greybeard,' Danae whispered and turned away, dripping blood onto the soil as she walked.

6. Son of Thunder

Six months later, the hut reeked of bitter herbs, sweat and blood. Danae massaged her sister's back while Alea knelt on all fours, blankets spread underneath her swollen belly.

'Danae,' Alea groaned.

She leant close so their mother wouldn't hear.

'I don't want her watching.' Alea's eyes darted to the wooden figurine of Hera their mother had set on the table.

Zeus' wife was the patron deity of childbirth. The statue had been present for the births of all Eleni's children and was something of a good luck charm to their mother, who knew nothing of what it would mean to her daughter.

Danae nodded and scrambled to her feet.

'Get more cloths,' Eleni barked.

Danae glanced back. Her mother was kneeling between her sister's legs, far too preoccupied to notice her turn the figurine away from Alea.

During the long months since Alea had confided in Danae, she had become increasingly anxious about Hera taking revenge on her child. To comfort her, Danae told her stories of Heracles, the mortal son of Zeus, and the greatest hero who'd ever lived. She recounted the tale of Hera sending a pair of venomous snakes into Heracles' crib. The hero had grasped them in his little fists and shaken them so hard he addled their brains. It was said that the following morning he'd been found asleep, cuddling the dead reptiles like a pair of dolls. Alea loved that story, but Danae came to regret telling her, as, from then on, her sister's new obsession became pondering what special demi-god powers her child would inherit.

She had considered sharing the burden of Alea's secret with her parents. But she barely saw her father any more; he rose before dawn and returned after dark, working twice as hard to bring in half the coin. Her mother's edges had sharpened under the strain of holding the family together. Eleni's temper had become so volatile, Danae hadn't dared bring up Zeus, the shade or the Maenads again.

Alea's labour had started in the early hours. Danae had woken in the dark to discover their pallet soaked. Her father had already left for the day's fishing. She and her mother had busied themselves with preparing boiling water, tearing up old tunics and burning sacred herbs.

She imagined it would be like delivering a baby goat, intense and visceral, with the ordeal being over swiftly. But Alea had been struggling all day. She could see the strength draining from her sister with each spasm. As time crawled on, her vague feeling of worry had become a writhing knot in her stomach.

Alea rocked back and forth, lowing like a wounded heifer.

What if the child wouldn't come? What if the baby was a kakodaimon, an evil spirit, that would kill her sister by tearing its way out?

Her mother wiped the sweat from her brow and pressed the sides of her sister's stomach. She looked up, face tight with fear.

'The baby's turned the wrong way.'

Alea bellowed as another contraction racked her body.

'Danae.' Her mother beckoned.

She moved to Eleni's side.

'I need you to help me,' her mother whispered. 'I've got to turn the baby the right way round or it will suffocate. As soon as I say push, I need you to make her do it, understand?'

Danae nodded, swallowing the saliva pooling in her mouth. She moved back to face her sister and wriggled her fingers between Alea's clenched fists.

'Hold onto my hands.'

As her mother turned the baby, Alea screamed. The air rushed from Danae's lungs as her sister gripped her fingers so hard, she thought they would break. Then Alea's head sagged onto their tangled fists, only for her body to clench a breath later, as another contraction broke through her.

'Now, push now!' Eleni called, her arms slick with Alea's blood.

'I can't,' Alea sobbed. 'I can't do it.'

Danae pressed her forehead against her sister's. 'You can, we'll do it together. I'm with you.'

A sob lodged in the back of Alea's throat. She nodded.

Danae tensed with her sister as the next contraction came, the air expelling from both their lungs in unison. Again and again they strained, riding the tide of the birth together, until with one last heave, the baby slid free of Alea.

Heart in her throat, Danae peered around her sister and glimpsed a very human-looking foot. Relief washed through her.

'Danae,' panted her mother. 'Get the knife, and make sure you sterilize it.'

She rose to her feet and staggered to the table. Fumbling the blade into her hand, she held it over the fire, then returned to her mother. She stared in amazement at the tiny person in Eleni's arms. It was a boy. Underneath all the slime he was perfect, down to each tiny toe and the little hands resting on her mother's arm.

'Cut the cord.'

Hands shaking, she sliced through the sinuous rope and

her mother whisked the child into the air, patting his back. The baby did not cry.

'What's happening?' her sister murmured weakly.

No one answered. Danae sank to her knees, staring at the tiny blood-soaked body, while her mother continued to try and activate his lungs.

Finally, a cry pierced the air.

Her mother let out a long sigh and lay the wailing child against her shoulder, bobbing him gently up and down.

Suddenly her sister sank back on her knees, gripping her stomach. She groaned.

'What's wrong with her?' Danae rubbed her sister's back, powerless but to watch Alea endure yet more pain.

'The afterbirth.' Her mother's attention was still on the child. 'Get her on her back and press down on her stomach.'

For a moment, Danae thought her legs were going to give way, but she forced her limbs into action and eased her sister onto her back, laying her shaking hands on Alea's stomach.

'That's it.' Her mother hovered over her with the baby. 'Help it out.'

She pressed down on her sister's abdomen. Alea gasped and the last of the birth slid from between her legs. Danae stared at the bloody sac. It was strangely beautiful. Rootlike veins unfurled from the trunk of the umbilical cord and wound around the membrane, like a tree taking nourishment from its own little pouch of earth.

Then the door swung open, and her father entered the room. His eyes roved across the carnage of blood and bodies to settle on his grandchild.

'All is well.' Her mother smiled. 'A boy.'

Dropping his nets and ropes, he hurried over to Alea and gently patted her shoulder. 'Well done, my girl.'

'Ma,' Alea breathed through waxy lips.

Their mother wiped him then lowered the squalling baby onto Alea's chest. Danae watched the little body rise and fall with her sister's breath. As his mother held him, the child quietened.

She edged closer. There were downy hairs on his face. He changed from moment to moment. One minute he had the wrinkled brow of an old man, the next his little pink tongue protruded like a budding flower. Warmth swelled inside her. She hadn't expected this. Even the red patches on his face were perfect.

The baby squirmed, and his small, swollen eyelids opened for the first time. She held her breath. His eyes were deep pools of blue that looked much older than the brand-new creature they inhabited.

Alea looked up at her, eyes shining through her tears.

'Arius.'

'Hello, Arius,' Danae whispered.

She reached out, and he gripped her finger in his fist. She marvelled at the strength in his tiny hands, each nail a pearly fragment of seashell.

In that moment, the entire world was contained in their hut. Then Danae looked up and saw something that sent a jolt of fear down her spine.

A pair of crimson eyes was watching them through the window.

7. Offerings

They set out at dawn. A cool breeze brushed their cheeks, and the ripe scent of fish wafted from the basket rocking between them. Danae stole a glance at her mother. Eleni looked as terrible as she felt, her eyes bloodshot, ringed by puckered purple skin. It had been three weeks since Arius' arrival, and none of them had slept for more than a couple of hours at a time. Despite being such a small creature, his lungs were like a pair of hunting horns. Alea had lost so much blood during the birth, she barely had the strength to nurse him, her milk drying by the day. It took all Danae's resolve not to break at the sight of her sister, withering with each turn of the sun.

'What do you think he'll give us?'

Her mother glanced down at the basket of scaly bodies. 'I don't know,' she said tersely. 'As long as we get enough for Alea, that's all that matters.'

'She needs meat,' Eleni had said before they left the hut. They'd already been forced to sell the goats to a family from a village on the far side of the island, but they still barely had enough coin for grain. So, her mother had taken a portion of Odell's morning catch and was hoping Myron, the butcher, would be willing to trade.

They did not speak again until they reached the village. The square was quiet. Only a couple of awnings were out, unfurled by early-rising shopkeepers. Her mother quickened her pace towards the butcher's hut, and Danae had to stride to keep up. Eleni had insisted they visit the butcher before his stall opened, as their family had been banned from doing business in the village, and Myron was unlikely to trade with them under the hateful eyes of his other customers.

Her mother raised a fist and rapped quickly on the butcher's door. A few moments later, the door creaked open, and Myron peered out, his face still crumpled with sleep. Before he could speak, Eleni grabbed the basket of fish from Danae and proffered it to him.

'We have no coin, but we need meat. Goat, chicken, whatever you can trade us.'

The butcher's gaze slid from their faces to the square beyond.

'You shouldn't be here,' he muttered.

'Myron,' Eleni's voice trembled, 'my daughter is near death, and her child will starve if she does not recover. If you have a bone of compassion in your body, please . . . help us.'

Danae felt as though there was a fist around her throat as Myron twisted his hands, his eyes darting everywhere except their faces.

Finally, his shoulders sagged. 'All right.' He took the fish. 'Wait here.'

As he disappeared back inside his hut, there was a burst of laughter behind them. Danae turned. Three farmhands, likely on their way to the inland fields, were crossing the square. One of them shouted, 'Give your whore sister a kiss from me!'

In a heartbeat she was pacing towards them.

'My sister is not a whore.'

'That's not what Davos says,' the boy sneered. 'He said he had her for a stale lump of bread.' He laughed again. 'She couldn't wait to open her legs.'

'Liar!' Flames of fury licked over Danae's skin. Her mother was calling her name, but she paid no heed as she planted both hands on his chest and shoved. The lad stumbled back, then a nasty grin spread over his face.

'Want some too, do you?'

He lunged for her. But Danae was quicker and dodged out of his way. The farmhand might have the physical advantage, but she had years of brawling with her tall, strong brothers in her arsenal. And she had rage. She pivoted, throwing all her weight behind her fist, and punched him square in the face. His nose cracked, spraying them both in a shower of ruby droplets. She roared and hit him again, thumping his flesh with her fists, elbows, knees. It took both the other two farmhands to drag her off him and throw her bodily to the ground. The boy lay on his back, whimpering through broken teeth.

'Get away from her!' Eleni's voice rolled like a tidal wave across the square.

The boys rounding on Danae backed away as her mother advanced, holding a leg of cloth-wrapped goatmeat like a club.

'Animal,' one of them spat at Danae as they helped their battered friend to his feet.

Eleni grabbed Danae by the scruff of her tunic and yanked her up. It was only then she noticed how many people had come out of their huts. Some were holding sticks. A couple had knives. She stumbled as her mother pulled her into a run. She did not look back.

As they sprinted along the coastal path, she was suddenly aware of the intense throbbing in her hand. She glanced down and saw the skin had split across her knuckles.

Her mother would not slow until they reached the path leading up to their hut. Danae finally braved a glance at her. The anger she'd felt in the square paled in comparison to the rage radiating from her mother.

'Ma –'

'No.' Eleni's voice was an iron blade. 'You do not get to speak.'

She knew she would pay dearly for what she'd done, and it was unlikely Myron would help them again. But even as her hands trembled and her body ached, she did not regret it. After everything that had happened to her family, it had been worth it – even just for a moment – to feel powerful.

The earth bloomed. Petals fell to make way for ripening fruit, and the sun began its descent in the sky, arcing lower with each passing day. As the glaring brightness of summer melted into the deep reds, yellows and browns of autumn, Alea regained her strength. Slowly, colour returned to her cheeks, and the hollow caverns of her body filled and softened. Danae could not say which day it was, only that one morning she looked at her sister and realized the fear that woke her each dawn was gone. Alea would not leave them for the Underworld, not yet.

'You promised me, as soon as he was old enough, you would take him to the temple.' Arius gurgled happily and grasped a fistful of Alea's hair. She winced and attempted to free the captured strands. 'It's been six months!'

'Exactly, *only* six months.' Danae pummelled a lump of dough with her fists. Her promise had been made in a moment of sleep-deprived weakness and she had hoped Alea would forget about it.

'Why don't you want to take him?'

Danae reached into a pot of flour and dusted the table. 'I've told you before, after what the Maenad Ariadne told me, I think we should stay away from the temple.' She glanced into the yard, where her mother was sweeping out the old goat pen. She could have done with Eleni's support.

'You're not still worried about the shade? Danae, that was months ago, surely it will have gone away by now.'

Scarlet eyes peering through the hut window were seared across her memory. She opened her mouth to speak, but fear stilled her tongue.

'The timing is perfect,' continued Alea. 'You can take our offerings for the Thesmophoria and bring Arius to receive Demeter's blessing.'

She sighed. 'Alea, please –'

'Don't you love your nephew? Don't you want to protect him from Hera's wrath?'

'Shh,' Danae hissed.

Alea set her jaw. 'His father will surely come to visit him soon, which will reveal everything. If he is under Demeter's protection, *she*,' Alea glanced skywards, 'is less likely to harm him.'

'He's safe here, at home. Gods know what might happen to him out there.' Danae flung flour across the room as she gestured. 'You've not been out of this hut. You don't know what it's been like for me and Ma –'

'At least I'm not starting fights!'

'I was defending you!'

'Enough!' Their mother stepped through the doorway. 'I am sick to the back teeth of this endless bickering.' She turned to Alea. 'You must calm yourself, it's not good for you.'

Danae poured her frustration into the dough and hurled it onto the table with a vigorous slap.

Her mother took Arius from her sister. 'You should rest.'

'I'm fine.'

They all knew that was a lie. As she looked at her sister, Danae felt a stab of guilt. Though stronger than she was in the first weeks, Alea hadn't been the same since the birth.

She tired easily and barely had any strength. Arguing like they were would cost her.

Danae sighed. 'I'll take him tomorrow with the offerings and intreat Demeter to bless him.'

She half expected her mother to tell her that she would do no such thing, but Eleni nodded sagely.

'It is only right. Demeter returned Alea to us after all.'

Her sister's pale face lit up. She smiled at her mother then looked to Danae.

'Thank you.'

Alea's fears might be placated. But taking Arius away from the safety of the hut meant facing her own.

The sky was a deep hyacinth blush, but the chill of night still lingered in the air. Danae was glad. The summer heat had remained longer this year, and when the sun crested the horizon, it wouldn't be long before the earth was baking.

She pushed open the yard gate. Arius was strapped to her chest, a full bag of cheeses and a loaf of bread slung over her shoulder. There was at least a week's worth of food in her pack; far less than her family had offered at the previous year's Thesmophoria, but still more than they could spare. She ground the resentment between her teeth.

By the time they reached the tree-lined path that led through the valley, a hazy heat had settled over the land. Danae tugged the cloth of Arius' swaddling over his head, shading him from the sun's glare. They would most likely have to shelter in the temple for the hottest part of the day before returning home. She sighed at the thought of spending hours trapped under the scrutiny of the priestesses.

She tugged the waterskin from her bag, took a large gulp, then stowed it away again. Arius' lip trembled. She placed her little finger in his mouth, stretched her face wide, then puckered it tight. He laughed, and his effervescent chuckle banished her irritable mood. But at the removal of her hand, his little face contorted, and a wail erupted from his mouth.

'Shh, now.' She bobbed him up and down, but nothing would calm him, not even the return of her finger.

She carried on walking, Arius' wails serenading them until they reached the tree-swathed path leading towards the temple valley. Having worn himself out, Arius fell asleep, his tear-stained face resting on her chest. She breathed in the quiet.

Then something darted across her vision. She looked towards the shrubbery. The leaves were still, and there was no sound except the clicking of cicadas. She took a breath to quell the fear that rose like bile in her throat. Then she set off, striding along the path with renewed speed.

Soon her pace grew lethargic with the heat, and she took another deep draught from the waterskin. Mercifully, the trees on either side of the road were becoming denser, dappling the ground with patches of shade.

She stopped. Ahead of them, a cloud of dust was settling on the path, as though someone had just run across it. But there were no other travellers in sight.

'Hello?'

No one answered.

Then a faint crack, barely audible over the cicadas, drew her eyes to the bushes on the left. She wrapped one arm around the sleeping Arius and bent down, fingers curling around a stone. The hairs on her arms were raised despite the heat. Part of her mind was screaming for her to run, another was trying desperately to work out what she found so uncanny.

It was the leaves. There were a clump in the centre that

were the exact colour and shape of the others around them, but they looked flat, like those painted on a fresco.

Then the bush unfolded. She stumbled back, the leaves and branches twisting in front of her, unfurling and blurring into a mottled, green-brown mass. Briefly, she saw the silhouette of a man, before his outline melted away into the foliage. She stood transfixed, wondering if the heat had warped her mind.

Then, where the shape of a head had been only moments before, opened a pair of piercing red eyes. They were even more terrible up close. Ink-black pupils, surrounded by irises that bled scarlet into where the whites should have been.

The stone tumbled from her hand and, almost tripping in her haste, she pelted back along the path. Arius, woken by the movement, howled. She clutched him tighter but kept running, the sound of her own ragged breath blasting in her ears.

She should never have let Alea talk her into taking him to the temple.

Just as she had feared, the shade had come for Arius.

She only slowed once the glade was far behind them and they'd reached the road that wound past the village towards their hut. She sank to her knees, wheezing. Her head was throbbing like it had been pummelled. Arius' cries had subsided to a whimper.

'It's all right,' she whispered between gasps of air. 'I won't let it take you.'

Once Arius had been born, she was sure he could not have been fathered by the shade, he looked so human. She smoothed the downy hairs on his little head and wondered if he was just a mortal boy, why was the shade haunting him?

Could Alea be right? Could he really be the son of Zeus?

She glanced back at the path behind them. The air shimmered with the heat of the midday sun, but no dust danced above the track. She kept thinking she could see those red eyes staring at her, but when she blinked, they vanished.

She staggered to her feet. There was a little shrine dedicated to Dionysus only a stone's throw ahead along the path. After a moment's hesitation, she paced towards it. Delving into her bag, she retrieved the Thesmophoria offerings and laid them beside the dish of water that sat in front of the stone, flowers floating on its mirror surface. The visage of the god carved into the shrine looked welcoming. Vines crowned his head and grapes dangled from the curls of his beard. There was a softness to his face and a playfulness to the tilt of his eyes. He looked after Ariadne and the Maenads, perhaps he would answer her prayer. This way, at least she'd kept part of her promise and entreated a god to keep her nephew safe.

She bowed her head and touched her finger between her brows. 'Please accept these offerings, Lord Dionysus, and in return watch over Arius and see no harm comes to him.'

Her prayer released into the world, she ran for home.

'That was quick.'

Her mother was sitting on the hut step, darning a pile of faded tunics.

Danae shut the gate and glanced back over her shoulder. 'We didn't make it to the temple.'

Eleni set down her needle. 'What happened?'

'There was . . . on the road, there was something waiting in the bushes.'

'Was it someone from the village?' Eleni put down her sewing and walked over to them. She untied Arius' swaddling and took him in her arms.

Danae drew a breath. 'It was a shade.'

Her mother's eyes flashed.

'I know you don't want to hear this, but it's been watching us ever since –'

Eleni let out a sharp sigh. 'Oh gods, Danae, please not this again –'

'Listen to me!' Her body still sang with fear. 'I saw it at the Thesmophoria, it was looking in through the window the night Arius was born, and it was waiting on the path today. I should never have taken him.' She punched her last sentence into the air with more violence than she intended.

Arius began to cry, but Eleni did not seem to notice. She looked so weary. She was thinner, they all were, and the skin on her face was beginning to sag. Danae used to believe there was no problem her mother couldn't surmount. But she was no longer a child and could see Eleni was as lost as she was.

'Do you believe me?'

Her mother looked at her as though she were the source of all her worry. 'I don't know what to believe any more.'

She took Arius inside and left Danae standing alone in the yard.

8. Dance of the Deep

Since the unsuccessful visit to Demeter's temple, there had been no sign of the shade. Now, there were even days where Danae barely thought about it. Perhaps Dionysus had answered her prayer after all. Or perhaps the creature was biding its time.

'I think I should tell Ma and Pa today,' said Alea.

Her sister stood by the table they'd carried into the yard, Arius balanced on her hip.

'Hmm?' The heat of the outdoor oven blasted Danae's cheeks as she peered in, watching the honey cakes she'd just slid into its fiery belly.

'It's Arius' first birthday, what better time to tell them who his father is?'

Danae's head snapped round. 'Alea, I don't think that's a good idea.'

Given their mother's reaction to Danae trying to convince Eleni about the shade, she could only imagine the reception Alea claiming Arius was Zeus' son would have.

'But what if he comes to see his son today? He will come eventually, Danae, he must. And Ma would never forgive me for not warning her.'

Danae's chest tightened at the hopeful expression on her sister's face. Every time Alea brought up Arius' father, she was forced to face the kernel of doubt buried deep inside her. The little voice that whispered that Alea had created this fantasy of Arius being a demi-god to protect her from the truth of what had happened to her.

Danae could not explain why the shade had taken her

sister, or why it had continued to watch her nephew, but try as she might, she could not convince herself that of all the women in Greece, the King of Heaven had looked down from Olympus and chosen her sister. Heracles' mother was a princess, as was Perseus'. Alea was beautiful, but she was cut from the same humble cloth as the rest of their family.

No, the terrible truth was that, however strange the events surrounding the Thesmophoria, Alea must have been raped by a mortal man. And if it was brought to light, their parents' scrutiny might tear down the walls her sister had built around her pain. If that happened ... she didn't want to dwell on what Alea might do.

'Don't let those cakes burn, Danae!' Eleni shouted as she emerged with a jug of water, which she set on the table. 'The honey alone cost ...' she trailed off, watching Arius gurgle with happiness as he played with Alea's hair. A contented smile spread across her lips, and she bustled back into the hut.

The yard gate creaked.

Alea gasped, and Danae spun around to see Santos stepping into the yard. His young sons, Egan and Minos, scampered out from behind his legs.

'Danie! Danie!'

Cakes abandoned, she rushed over to them. The boys flung their arms around her, and she hugged them tight.

'Look how big you've got, little bears!'

Minos puffed out his chest. 'I'm not a bear, I'm Heracles!'

Egan shoved him. 'No, it's my turn to be Heracles! You're the hydra!'

They began to chase each other around the yard. Their mother, Kafi, came striding from behind her husband. She made straight for Alea and Arius.

'He looks so like you. He'll grow to be a strong, handsome man, I can tell.'

Alea smiled. 'Would you like to hold him?'

Kafi's face broke into a toothy grin, and she took her nephew in her arms.

'Danae, the cakes!' With a clatter, her mother set down the bowls and cups she'd carried from the hut and rushed towards the smoking oven. 'You had one job!'

She had been so absorbed in watching the exchange between Kafi and Alea, she'd forgotten the honey cakes. She winced as the tray emerged, the cakes blackened at the edges.

'Don't worry, Ma, I like them charred.' Santos strode across to their mother and pulled her into an embrace. As he drew away, he looked at his feet. 'I'm sorry we've not come as often as we should.'

Danae threw an arm around her brother. 'You're here now.'

He smiled and walked over to Alea. 'I was inspired by my own sons when making Arius' birthday gift.' From his tunic pocket he drew out a wooden figurine of Heracles.

Alea took the doll and ran her fingers over the carving. It was lovingly detailed, even down to the famous lion hide the hero was known to wear.

'Oh, Santos, it's perfect. Now he will know what his brother looks like.'

Danae's heart tripped a beat. Santos looked quizzically at his sister.

Not now, not like this. Please let us have this day.

She felt a tug on her tunic. Egan was beside her.

'Play with us!'

She seized the opportunity to create a distraction. 'You are *both* the mighty Heracles, and I am the terrible many-headed hydra!' She launched after the boys, gnashing her teeth and jabbing her hands like pincers, as her nephews squealed and scurried away.

Santos laughed and ran after them, holding his fingers to

protrude from his jaw like tusks. 'And *I* am the fearsome Erymanthian boar!'

'Honestly, you two, we're about to eat!' The scold in Eleni's voice was tempered by the smile she could not prevent from curling her careworn mouth.

Alea laughed and took Arius back from Kafi, her world narrowing to the rosy glow of her son's face.

As Danae sprinted across the yard, the knot in her stomach loosened. Alea's secret was safe once more. At least for now.

Danae woke drenched in sweat. The mat she'd slept on since Arius' birth was sodden. She rolled over to stare at the pallet her sister now shared with her nephew. As the darkness solidified into shades of grey, the clarity of their sleeping bodies came into focus, and her fear abated.

She'd been woken by the same dream for weeks.

In a starless sky, the moon and sun loomed together over the beach, both burnt to blood-red craters. Danae stood paralysed in the shallows, feet rooted to the seabed by some invisible bond. Then threads of golden light cracked through the darkness. They cleaved the air, growing brighter and brighter, until the night shattered. She threw her arms over her head, expecting to be flattened by a falling shard of moon or sun, but the blow did not come. She lowered her arms. The celestial bodies were gone; so too was the spider's web of glowing threads. The heavens were empty, and her limbs were coated in a fine film of black dust.

Her mother told her once, dreams come through two gates, one of horn and one of ivory. The dreams fashioned from horn reveal the truth of what is to come, but those cast from ivory are woven with tricks.

Her gaze drifted to the wooden figurine of Heracles

lying forgotten on the floor. Towards the end of the day, Alea had shut herself away in the hut. Her mother had accepted the excuse that her sister was weary and needed rest, but Danae knew the real reason. Zeus had not come, and Alea was bitterly disappointed. Despite the lie tasting acrid on her tongue, Danae had tried to convince her sister that a mortal celebration was too lowly a place for the King of Heaven, and he would surely honour his son in his own way. But Alea had still cried herself to sleep. Danae didn't know how much longer she could keep doing this.

She blinked. Perhaps some remnants of sleep still lingered, or the night was casting illusions, but she could have sworn the miniature Heracles just moved.

A ripple seemed to pass through the air, drifting beside her sister's pallet. Danae rubbed her eyes. It was as though she was looking at the bed through an undulating pool.

Then the breath solidified in her chest.

Arius was floating. One minute he was asleep in Alea's arms, the next he was levitating in the air.

She must be dreaming. She pushed herself up and dug her nails into her palms. Pain spiked across her skin. She was definitely awake. At the sound of her movement, the air around the baby blurred and dread seeped into her limbs.

Then a pair of crimson eyes twisted towards her.

She screamed.

In a heartbeat, the creature bolted for the door, Arius in its clutches. Danae staggered to her feet and raced after it. Half blind in the dark, she ran through the yard, following her nephew's cries through the swinging gate. She barely heard her sister's screams as she tore down to the beach. Stones cut her bare feet, but she didn't slow. As her toes sank into sand, the moon emerged from behind a cloud, illuminating the earth in silver light. She scoured the sand, searching for the shade's footprints. But there were none.

Frantically she ran back and forth, calling Arius' name into the night. For a wild moment, she thought she heard the beating of wings. But both sky and land were empty.

Arius was gone.

When her family caught up with Danae on the beach and she told them what had happened, Alea collapsed onto the sand. The cry that tore from her sister cut her to the bone. After that, Alea would not move. Eventually, her parents had to carry her between them. Danae walked behind, like a spectre, watching their bodies shake and strain in the moonlight.

Alea wept for days. The sound of her sobs accompanied the silence of their exhaustion. It was a painfully familiar sight, watching her father leave at first light to hunt for Arius. Odell searched the beach, the village and the surrounding land. This time, only Santos accompanied him. No one else was interested in wasting precious time on the bastard of a whore who danced with the Maenads.

Eventually, Alea stopped crying. Somehow that was worse.

Arius' absence was like dust. Its particles drifted through the air, catching in the throat and scratching the eyes. There was not one corner of the hut, one crumb of bread, one breath of wind it did not smother.

Danae felt as though she were trapped in time, watching the grains of her life trickle past, one by one. At night, the walls edged towards her, and each morning she woke to find the hut smaller. Sometimes, she would lie awake in the darkness, watching the mud bricks out of the corner of her eye, but she could never catch them moving. Sometimes, she thought she could hear them whispering. Even the walls blamed her.

After three days of searching, her father came home.

'I'm sorry, Alea.' Her sister wouldn't look at him. 'We've done all we can.'

He picked up a jug of wine and took it into the yard. Danae could see his shoulders shaking with silent sobs through the doorway.

'You were right about the shade.' Her mother sat hunched over the table, staring at the wood grain. 'I should have listened.'

Danae had longed to hear those words, but now she wished for all the world that the creature had been a figment of her imagination.

They waited for weeks, hoping in vain for a temple hand to come running to their door, panting that a baby had been left at the feet of Demeter's statue, just like Alea had been. But as time trudged on, their hope stretched thinner and thinner until it vanished.

No one spoke of what Arius' disappearance meant. They didn't need to. Arius had joined the Missing and, unlike his mother, he would not come back.

She walked with purpose, guided by the ever-constant stars. The moonlight threaded silver through her hair, and the sea whispered; it was time to come home. Her feet carried her over dirt, over rocks and over pebbles, until finally, her toes melted into sand. She met the tide like an old friend and fell willingly into its embrace. Her dress billowed around her as she waded deeper and deeper, until the last glinting curl disappeared, and the surface was unbroken once more. The nymphs of the sea rose to greet her and teach her the dance of the deep. She twirled and spun as the ocean washed her clean of pain, until there was nothing left.

The dream lingered, like the smell of charred meat. Danae rolled over to find herself alone on the pallet. She propped herself onto her elbows and looked around the hut. Her sister wasn't there. She rubbed her face and shrugged off the shiver that scuttled over her skin.

Padding quietly across the floor, she slipped on her sandals and stole outside. After an unfruitful sweep of the yard, she eased open the gate.

There were a few places Alea might go, but she knew where to look first.

She felt oddly calm as she jogged down to the beach. Dawn was creeping over the horizon, and the sea rippled like shards of broken glass in the cold light.

It didn't take her long to spot the footprints meandering towards the shore. It was unlike Alea to go for an early-morning swim. She followed her sister's tread. Then her eyes fell on a dark mass floating in the shallows.

Time slowed as she realized it was a body.

She pushed forward, the tide tugging at her legs. The body lay face down, gently rocked by the waves, a crown of seaweed tangled in its drifting curls. Blood thundering in her ears, she grasped it under the arms and dragged it onto the shore. Clear of the sea, she reached forward with shaking hands, earthquakes of panic rumbling through her as she pulled back the salt-soaked strands.

Her world imploded as she stared at the mottled skin and misted eyes of Alea.

She vomited onto the sand. She wanted to turn away, run forever and never stop. But she forced herself to look.

Her beautiful sister. Her best friend. Alea's spirit had gone to the Underworld and left behind a sea-bloated corpse.

She screamed and fell onto her sister's body, a tempest of rage and grief flaying her from the inside out. Then she felt a tugging sensation down her arms. She lifted her head and saw glowing threads of light seeping between her fingers. She jerked her hands away, but the shining ribbons continued to fan across Alea's skin, until they lined the length of her ribs.

There was a crunch and a crack. She shuffled back as Alea's tunic ripped, the skin beneath splitting as her sister's chest opened like the wings of a butterfly.

A green shoot sprung from Alea's still heart. It twisted up, past the splayed fingers of bone, towards the sky. Horrified, Danae lunged forward and desperately tried to smother it, but the tendril would not be stopped. It forced its way between her fingers and grew into a sapling, continuing upwards and thickening until its trunk was wider than Alea's body. Its twisted branches sprouted leaves, and in the space of a few moments, a tree loomed over her. Danae slumped back on her heels, her eyes wide as moons. Then buds opened into blossom and fruit grew, branches bowing with radiant, golden apples. They were brighter than the sun, so luminous they even eclipsed her pain.

Everything physical melted away. It felt as though she was suspended in a vat of liquid light and all that existed was her and the tree.

Entranced, she reached up and, as though offering her its fruit, the tree lowered a branch to meet her fingers.

She plucked one, perfect, golden apple and took a bite.

9. The Heart of a Tree

Danae woke in agony. It felt as though her body had been crushed under a quarry of rocks.

She was in the yard, and the midday sun loomed high above the hut. She tried to move her arms and couldn't. It took her a moment to realize that they were tied around a post in the goat pen. There was a smell in the air that did not belong. Something sweet she recognized but could not place.

She had no idea how she'd got there. She could recall flashes of a strange dream, a tree with golden fruit. Her mouth tasted bitter. She had the distinct feeling she was forgetting something. She could feel the imprint of it in her bones. Why could she not remember?

She cast around and saw a bowl of water beside her. She lunged for it, suddenly gripped by a raging thirst. She cursed as she bashed the bowl with her forehead and water slopped onto the ground.

'Ma,' she rasped. But her mother did not come. 'Ma?'

Still no answer.

She leaned over and dragged the bowl towards herself with her teeth. Then she dunked her face into it, lapping like a dog. Her skull felt like a trampled egg. Why in Tartarus was she tied up?

Water dripping down her chin, she shouted, 'Ma!'

This time, the hut door creaked open. Her mother lingered in the doorway, one hand on the frame, the other clutching the handle of a carving knife.

'Ma?'

Her mother took a step into the yard. The sweet smell intensified. Eleni wouldn't meet Danae's gaze. As she approached, she touched her forehead, tracing the all-seeing eye of the Twelve onto her skin. The knife trembled in her other hand.

'You're scaring me.'

Her mother took a deep breath and lifted her gaze.

The look in her eyes chilled Danae to her core. Eleni was terrified. She was looking at Danae as though she wasn't her daughter, but something monstrous.

'Don't move.' Her mother's hand tightened on the handle of the blade.

'I don't understand . . .' Danae tugged at her bindings.

Tears tumbled down Eleni's cheeks, and she turned away as though it caused her physical pain to look at her daughter.

Danae scoured the yard, and her eyes fell on the table, visible through the hut door. She suddenly realized what the smell was. Embalming oils.

A pair of mottled feet lay on the wood, protruding from a white winding cloth.

With earth-shattering clarity, everything came back to her.

'Alea,' she whimpered.

'Don't say her name, kakodaimon,' her mother hissed.

Danae tore her gaze from her sister's body. 'What?'

'I don't know what I did to deserve this.' Eleni's mouth stretched into a soundless howl, snot-muddled tears dripping from her chin.

Danae's pain-addled mind tried to fit the pieces together. It was as though she'd somehow stepped into a nightmare world that looked just like her own. Perhaps she'd died and gone to Tartarus, and this was her own personal torment.

'Ma . . . it's me.' She could barely get the words out.

'I saw what you did to her.' Eleni's eyes were wild, her voice strangled with grief. 'I found her heart in your hands.'

Danae stared at her mother, her head pounding with every word.

'I didn't . . . I would never hurt Alea. Ma, please –'

'No!' Eleni raised the knife between them as Danae struggled against the rope. 'You will not use your evil magic on me.'

'Evil magic? Ma, I'm Danae. I'm your daughter . . . I didn't kill her!'

The knife shook in her mother's hand. 'You may have taken her skin, but you are not my Danae.' She twisted her face away. 'I can't look at you . . . you're so like her.' She drew a deep breath. 'They will be here soon, then it will all be over.' She turned and ran back into the hut.

'What do you mean? Who's coming? Ma!'

Her mother shut the door.

'Don't leave me!'

Danae screamed herself raw, but her mother did not come out again.

Maybe she *was* possessed. Her thoughts kept returning to the tree, the deep pull she'd felt, the warmth bleeding out from her hands across Alea's skin and those strange threads of light. The sight of her sister's body had unleashed a tide of memory. In her trancelike state, the twisted branches and golden apples had seemed so real; the sand, sea and Alea were like a dream.

It was impossible; a tree could not sprout from a dead human heart and grow to maturity in a matter of moments. Only the gods had that kind of power. She searched every corner of her mind, but the last thing she could remember was taking a bite out of one of the golden apples. Then nothing.

A sob lodged in the back of her throat. This was all wrong.

She should be inside helping her mother prepare her sister's body for the burial rites. Alea would be on her way to the Asphodel Meadows now. Death had finally done what Danae could not and taken away her sister's pain.

She stiffened. There was movement in the distance. Someone was coming up the path. Fear came flooding back. Squirming, she tried desperately to prise her hands free.

As the figure drew closer, she stopped struggling.

With the habit of one who'd spent a lifetime rising early and creeping out of the hut, her father silently eased open the yard gate.

Danae opened her mouth, but he raised a finger to his lips.

Swiftly, he ran to her, and with fisherman-nimble hands, undid her bindings. His sweat reeked of stale wine, and his eyes were sunken and bloodshot, but he looked at her like he always did, like she was his little Danie.

Her legs were stiff from sitting, and he had to help her to her feet. She caught sight of her hands and faltered. They were crusted with dried blood.

'It's all right,' he whispered and took her stained fingers in his calloused ones.

As they crossed the yard, she stared at the hut door, convinced at any moment it would burst open and her mother would fly at her with the knife. But they ran through the gate without discovery.

'Pa,' she gasped as they sprinted down the pebble-strewn path. 'I didn't do it.'

'I know.'

She faltered when they reached the sand. The beach stretched out before them, turquoise waves lapping at the shore. The only place she'd ever felt truly at home, the place that had taken the one she loved the most.

The tree wasn't there.

'Come on.' Her father tugged her arm. 'We need to get to the boat.'

'Why?'

'I'll explain when we're at sea.'

Dragging her eyes from the spot where she'd found Alea's body, she let him pull her across the beach to the little cove where Odell kept his fishing vessel, clinging tightly to his large warm hands.

They waded into the water, and her father untied the mooring rope while she clambered aboard. It was a small tub, just a pair of oars and one sail, and it always stank of fish, even when it was empty. She stared at the stained planks, shimmering with loose scales. Her father wound the rope around his arm and heaved himself into the boat, easing down between the oars with a grunt.

'Pa, what's happening?'

Hurriedly, her father began to row. 'Your mother called the temple hands.'

Danae's stomach dropped through the bottom of the boat. If the temple hands believed she was possessed by an evil spirit, they would kill her.

'I won't let them take you, Danie. I'm not losing another daughter.'

At the sound of her childhood name, she began to cry. Amidst all the chaos, her father and his boat were a lifeline to everything that had been ripped away.

Once they were hidden behind the crag of the next bay, he heaved in the oars. Then he put his arms around her and wiped her tearstained cheeks.

She felt sick. She couldn't banish the image of Alea's ribs peeling away from her body.

She extracted herself from her father's arms. 'I think the gods have cursed me.' Terrified as she was of him looking at her the way her mother had, she told him everything that had happened, from finding Alea's body in the sea to the strange golden apple tree.

Odell looked at her long and hard. 'Oh, Danie, I'm sorry. I don't understand this any more than you do. Sometimes, I think the fates just roll a die.'

She looked up at the yellow-legged gulls soaring above, cawing to each other as they searched for nesting spots on the cliffs.

'I've got to leave Naxos, haven't I?'

Her father nodded, an ocean of sadness in his eyes. 'It's the only way you'll be safe. The temple hands will hunt you to the ends of the island.'

She knew he was right. It didn't make it any easier.

Her father delved into the pocket of his tunic and brought out the owl brooch Philemon had given Alea. He pressed it into her hands. She traced the little green gems with her fingers. It felt like a lifetime had passed since she'd first seen it pinned to her sister's breast.

'Go to the oracle at Delphi. This will pay your entrance. The oracle knows everything. Whatever's happening to you, if you *are* cursed, the Pythia will tell you how to fix it. Then you can come home.'

Delphi. The mainland. She'd never even been to Athens, let alone the land beyond.

'I've never been anywhere but Naxos . . . how will I find my way?'

Her father took her by the shoulders. 'Take this boat and sail north-west past the islands until you reach the mainland shore. Then follow the coast west for two days until you reach Mount Parnassus. There you'll find Delphi.'

'But if I take your boat, how will you fish?'

Odell's eyes were heavy. 'I'll find a way.'

'You and Santos rely on it; I can't take it, you'll all starve!'

'You have to,' his voice wavered. 'You have to get off the island.'

Danae chewed her lip. 'What if I took another ship?'

Odell's lined brow furrowed.

'Merchants sail from Naxos to Athens every day. I could stow away on one of their vessels.' She reached for her father's hand. 'I can do it.'

He broke down then and held her, their tears muddling with the scales at the bottom of the boat.

An hour later, the mouth of Naxos Port yawned before them, ships of all shapes and sizes protruding from the jetty like jagged teeth.

'Get down,' her father whispered as they approached.

Danae curled herself into the bottom of the boat. It wasn't long before she felt the gentle jolt of their vessel knocking against the jetty. Odell gathered up the tether and attached it to a wooden mooring pillar.

The air hummed with the steady chatter and clatter of merchants and their wares, punctuated by the wet crack of octopuses hitting stone as fishermen slapped their catches onto the rocks to dry. She breathed in the scent she knew so well. Fish, sweat, spice and oiled wood. She wanted to remember every note. She had no idea when she would smell them again.

Her father made a show of bending down to check the rope. 'See the ship directly behind me?' he whispered.

She peered discreetly over the lip of the boat and saw a small merchant vessel half full of wheels of cheese.

'I know that man, he trades in Athens. You could hide in between those cheeses.'

She stole another peek over his shoulder. The merchant

was standing next to his ship, drumming his fingers irritably on the prow. He was portly with a lavish beard, overseeing a boy, Danae presumed to be his son, unloading more cheeses from a mule-led cart.

'How am I going to get aboard without them seeing?'

'I have an idea, trust me.' He squeezed her hand. 'And remember, Danie, all seas are the same beast. When we're riding her, no matter how far apart, we're riding together.'

He opened his palm to reveal a pebble. 'Are you ready?'

She nodded. He threw the stone.

It whistled through the air and caught the mule square on the behind. The creature reared then bolted down the jetty, cart in tow, scattering traders in its wake.

'My cheese!' bellowed the merchant.

His son tore off after the mule, and while the merchant's back was turned, Odell hissed, 'Go!'

A piece of her soul was wrenched away as she leapt from her father's boat. She sprinted across the jetty, vaulted the prow of the merchant ship, and landed in a sprawl amongst the cheeses. Hastily, she folded her limbs between the stacked wheels and nudged the wax tarpaulin over herself. Clamping a hand over her mouth, she fought the urge to retch as the sour stench of cheese clogged her throat.

Eventually, a dejected clip-clop signalled the mule's return.

'Bloody useless animal,' she heard the merchant say. 'Get on with it.'

The ship rocked as the boy continued to load the rest of the stock. With each sway she tensed, waiting for the tarpaulin to be pulled back and her position revealed, but the moment did not come. Then the vessel dipped as the merchant and his son climbed aboard.

'Just a moment.' A different voice. 'May the Twelve see you and know you.'

There was a pause as the merchant presumably returned the sacred gesture.

'What is it? I'm due in Athens in three hours.'

'We won't keep you long. Do you have a licence for these . . .'

'Cheeses,' finished the merchant curtly. 'Yes, of course.'

'Is that all you're carrying?'

There was a rustle of parchment, then the edge of the tarpaulin twitched. Danae's heart thumped so loudly she was sure they would hear it. There was nowhere to run. If they searched the boat, it would be over.

A crack of sky appeared, light pouring over the mottled cheese rinds as the cover was drawn back. Danae's entire body tightened as she readied herself to fight her way out.

Then someone shouted from across the jetty, 'Telchis, look at this!'

The cover stopped moving just before her leg was revealed. The man stepped away, muttering to the merchant, 'Everything seems to be in order.'

Relief coursed through her at the sound of footsteps walking away down the jetty and the hiss of the tarpaulin being pulled back over the cheeses. She squirmed a hand between her legs, found the owl brooch she'd pinned to the inside of her tunic and traced the rivets in the bronze.

Whatever was happening to her, the oracle would have the answer.

10. Ledgers and Liars

The blast of horns vibrated through Danae's teeth. They must be nearing Athens. Thank the gods. After several cramped hours, she longed to stretch her legs and be free of her cage of stinking cheeses.

The ship shuddered as it jarred against something hard. Then the vessel dipped as someone climbed ashore. She heard the merchant instructing his son to unload the stock. Her pulse quickened. Any moment now.

The tarpaulin shivered. Then it was peeled away, and she rushed to push upwards, her elbows sinking into cheese as she pulled herself onto the side of the ship. The merchant's boy stared at her like she was a creature from the deep. Her legs screamed in protest, but she seized the moment and sprang. The boy lurched out of her way and toppled into the sea as she leapt from the boat, onto the jetty. For a heart-stopping moment she thought her legs would give way, then she stumbled forward, sprinting as fast as her tingling body would allow.

'Stop!' The merchant wheeled around. 'Stowaway! Stop her!'

The harbour was vast, at least five times the size of Naxos Port. She barely had time to take it in as ships blurred past her. The vessels on either side of the wide jetty were so tall, it felt as though she were running down an avenue of giant, leafless trees. The great painted hulls were punctuated with three layers of oar holes, like hundreds of eyes, watching as she whipped past.

She dodged around merchants unloading their wares, skirting crates of silks and barrels of olives, amphorae of scented oils and packs of smoked meats. The ships and their merchants all brought with them the scent of their homes, and the air was so overladen with different aromas she could barely smell the sea.

People, so many people, talking, shouting, more people than she'd ever seen in her life.

A dash of blue caught her eye. She glanced to the left and saw a fleet of warships gliding into the harbour. They were magnificent – enough to momentarily arrest the fear pumping through her limbs. They moved as one, their prows curved like swan necks, and their uniform cerulean sails were emblazoned with the royal crest of Athens, the twelve-pointed sun. Thanks to those visits from Philemon she knew a great deal about the city she'd never seen.

She tore her eyes from the ships a moment too late, and crashed headlong into someone standing at the entrance to the jetty.

'Watch it,' the man growled and wrinkled his nose at the lingering smell of cheese.

'Guard, stop her!'

Danae glanced back and saw the puce-faced merchant pursuing her down the gangway. She tried to lunge past the guard, but he was quicker and grabbed her by the arm. The harder she struggled, the tighter his grip became.

The merchant finally caught up to them and slumped against a pile of crates, wiping the sweat from his brow.

'That girl,' he panted, 'is a stowaway. And she's ruined half my stock!'

The guard looked down at Danae as though she were a mosquito that had just bitten him.

'I see. You'd best follow me.'

The merchant drew himself up. 'I hope this won't take long. I should be in Athens already.'

'Aren't we in Athens now?' asked Danae.

Both men laughed.

'She's soft, this one.' The guard continued slowly, 'This is Port Phalerum. Athens is six leagues that way.' He pointed east. 'Not that you'll be going anywhere near it.'

She twisted, trying to squirm out of his grip, but the guard was as strong as a bull. He yanked her arm up behind her back, and pain spiked through her shoulder.

'Where are you taking me?' she gasped.

The guard pulled her away without an answer.

In front of the jetty was a bustling road. Carts and riders on horseback hurtled past in both directions. The guard dragged Danae with him, holding up a large hand to halt the traffic as they crossed the road. She looked around wildly, searching for someone, anyone who might help her. But the passers-by averted their eyes, as though it were a common sight to see a young woman being hauled through the street.

Once they reached the other side, she was marched up the steps of a long stone building topped by terracotta tiles. Sun-bleached pillars ran along its open front in an orderly crescent, and long tables littered with scrolls and ledgers nestled behind the columns.

The guard pushed past a queue that stretched up the steps. Ignoring the disgruntled mutterings, he shoved Danae in front of a clerk, who peered at her over a precarious stack of licences. The man was thin and almost completely bald. He reminded her of a walnut.

'Graeculus, we've got a stowaway.'

The clerk shifted ever so slightly to glance at the growing line behind them. 'I see.' His voice was as dry as his skin.

The merchant stepped forward, said the sacred greeting, then declared, 'I am Memnos, a purveyor of fine cheeses from Naxos. This girl stole aboard my ship and ruined my stock. I seek reparation.'

Graeculus sighed, returned the greeting and surveyed Danae wearily.

'It seems you owe this man for passage aboard his vessel and the cost of the stock you damaged. How will you pay?'

She gaped. 'I can't, I have no coin.'

The only item of value she had was the brooch, and she needed that to gain entrance to the oracle.

'Hmmm.' Graeculus' fingers itched towards a scroll. 'If you can't pay then I will have to send you back to the authorities at – Naxos, was it?'

She couldn't let them send her home, she had to get to Delphi. 'I can work off the debt, I'll do anything, please just don't send me back.'

Graeculus' hand paused. He met her pleading gaze, then his eyes slid down, crawling over her body. She stiffened. The clerk looked at the guard. Something unspoken passed between them.

With the scraping of wood on stone, he unfolded himself from under the desk. The merchant followed him through a doorway behind, and the guard pushed Danae after them.

The room was cool and musty. It smelt of dust and parchment, and the walls were lined floor to ceiling with stacked scrolls.

'Off the record,' Graeculus said in a low voice, addressing the merchant. 'You're not going to recoup your losses. The girl evidently has nothing, and port officials bear no responsibility for stowaways.'

The merchant's expression darkened.

'However,' Graeculus lowered his voice further. 'There is a way you can make a profit from this unfortunate situation.'

Memnos' lip curled. 'Go on.'

Fear pulsed through Danae. She was very aware of how large the guard was, his hulking frame towering behind her.

'My colleague here, Elias, and I have an arrangement. Not strictly by the book, but I'm sure a man of your business acumen will appreciate that sometimes steps need to be taken outside of what is strictly legal.'

Memnos made an open gesture with his hands.

The clerk smiled. 'A healthy young woman like this would fetch an excellent price at the flesh market.'

Danae stared at Graeculus. 'You can't do that!'

Elias clamped a hand over her mouth.

'We would take our cut of course, but I'd wager she's worth at least ten drachmas.'

Memnos folded his arms. 'What exactly would that cut be?'

Blood thumped in Danae's ears. She writhed against Elias' grip and bit down on his palm. The guard swore but didn't let go. He tightened his hold, his fingers digging into her cheeks.

Through the panic, she remembered something her mother told her when she and her sister were blossoming into womanhood. 'Be wary of men, always go about your tasks with your sister, never alone, and if anyone lays a hand on you, kick him between the legs and run.'

Her struggles appeared to grow weaker as she feigned exhaustion. Elias loosened his grip, ever so slightly. She glanced down to gauge the position of his feet, then kicked back with all her strength. Her heel connected with something soft, and the guard let go, groaning like a wounded bear.

Quick as a minnow, she darted towards the door, pulling a flurry of scrolls off the shelves as she ran. Pulse racing, she pelted out into the sunlight. White pillars flickered past, and merchants dived out of her way as she sprinted down the row of customs desks.

Finally, she reached the end of the building and dodged around the side. She bent over, hands clutching her knees for support, sucking breath into her aching lungs. Glancing back, she was relieved to see she was alone.

She straightened up, then a fist collided with the side of her head.

11. Chains and Tales

Danae noticed the smell first. The air was stifling with the scent of overripe produce and rotting spice. And something else, something bitter and human. Then came the pain, blossoming from her left temple and pulsing its way across her skull.

Slowly, she opened her eyes. It was dark. The only source of light shone weakly through one slit of a window. Filthy straw lined the floor. She became aware of something hard and cold on her skin. She looked down and saw an iron cuff secured around both wrists. It was chained to a metal loop screwed into the wall. She twisted her hands, searching for any weakness in the chain. But the harder she tugged, the deeper the metal bit into her skin.

A clink at the other end of the room startled her. She squinted through the gloom and saw that she was not alone. There were others, attached to the same long chain, bolted at intervals around the walls.

'The new girl's awake.'

A man sat against the wall to her right. He was shrouded in shadow except for a sliver of light across his tanned, bearded face.

'Where am I?' Her voice was hoarse, her mouth parched.

'Port holding cell.'

'How long have I . . . ?'

'A few hours, give or take.'

She ran her hands under the hem of her tunic and was relieved to feel the bronze owl. She mumbled a silent 'thank you' to the gods for giving her the foresight to conceal the brooch before arriving in Phalerum.

She glanced back at the bearded man. He was watching her. She twitched her hands away from her clothing.

'What happens now?'

The bearded man shrugged. 'We wait until someone takes us to market and if we're lucky we might get a bit of food in the meantime.'

The word 'market' sent a shiver down her spine.

'The flesh market?'

The bearded man tilted his head. 'A word of advice: keep quiet and don't anger the guards.'

She swallowed. It was a bit late for that.

She was acutely aware of the others listening to their conversation. As her eyes grew accustomed to the dim light, she tried to make them out. To her left was an elderly woman with wispy white hair. Opposite was a boy who looked a few years younger than her. His legs were folded into his chest, his face half hidden behind his knees. Next to him was a man with the shaved head and red kilt of a Spartan soldier. His skin was a patchwork of scars.

Footsteps echoed from somewhere outside the room, accompanied by the jangle of keys. Danae shuffled into the shadows as far as her chain would allow.

The heavy wooden door creaked open, and a thick-set guard stepped into the room, carrying a pail of water. Some of the prisoners stretched towards it. The vice of panic around Danae's chest eased slightly.

'Get back!' he snarled and aimed a kick at the old woman. She shrank away from the guard, but her eyes never left the bucket. At the sound of the sloshing water, Danae's mouth ached.

The guard moved around the room, pouring water from a

roughly hewn cup straight into the waiting mouths. He took little care, often spilling the liquid over their faces.

When he finally reached Danae, the guard paused, the cup poised tantalizingly over the pail. She waited, longing for the sweet taste of the water. The guard continued to stare at her. Then, to her relief, his hand dipped into the bucket and a full cup was drawn out. She opened her mouth. Before it reached her, the guard flicked his wrist and the water splashed onto the floor. Without pausing to think, she lunged forward, licking the dirt between the straw, desperate to catch the liquid before it was absorbed.

The guard laughed and kicked her in the gut. Spittle and grime flew from her mouth as the breath was punched from her.

'Filthy bitch.' He spat on her and walked away, the pound and jangle of his footsteps echoing in her ears long after the door slammed behind him.

She stayed where she'd fallen, each breath a sharp spasm of pain.

'You're lucky.'

It took Danae a moment to realize the bearded man was speaking to her.

'Another guard came when you were out cold.'

She felt sick. It had nothing to do with the pain in her stomach.

'Terribly angry he was. Going on about wanting to settle the score and so on . . .' He paused. 'Would have done it too, if the fat one hadn't stopped him.'

Danae raised her head to look at the man. He was twirling a piece of straw between his dirty fingers.

'Not allowed to damage the goods, you see. A few bruises are to be expected, but no one wants to buy a sullied slave.'

She curled her legs into her chest, tugging the hem of her

tunic down as far as it would stretch, and turned away from the bearded man. She didn't want him to see her cry.

From the smatterings of conversation, Danae gathered most of the others had been in the cell for at least a few days. The boy had arrived just before her.

'What's your name, lad?' asked the bearded man.

The boy sniffed. 'Lycon.'

'Where are you from, Lycon?'

The boy's pink tear-stained face appeared from behind his knees. 'Crete.'

'Are you now? I've heard it's a beautiful island. Some say the finest in all of Greece.'

Lycon nodded, a hint of a smile tugging his mouth. The bearded man's tone was friendly, but he reminded Danae of a mountain lion playing with its food.

'Are you old enough to remember the Minotaur?'

The boy shook his head. Despite her foreboding, Danae was intrigued.

'The old King of Athens used to send fourteen children, just like you, from Athens to Knossos every year. Their parents would dress them up in their finest clothes like it was a feast day – well in a way I suppose it was.' He chuckled. 'Then they would be sent over the sea to Crete and be paraded through the city to the palace. Do you know what happened next?'

Lycon shook his head.

'Autolycus, leave the boy alone,' said the old woman.

The bearded man ignored her. 'They were fed to the creature that lived in the labyrinth below the palace. A terrible beast, with the body of a man and the head of a bull, always thirsty for human blood. The children would scream and scream but no one –'

'Oh, be quiet!' The old woman shook her head.

Autolycus looked hurt. 'I'm only trying to cheer the boy up by reminiscing about his home. Such a lovely island. I, for one, have fond memories of the yearly sacrifice.' He sighed. 'Until our most noble and righteous king slaughtered the monster and put a stop to it. Shame really, it would have been much more fun if the Minotaur had killed Theseus.'

Lycon started to cry again.

'You'll get us all put to death with that kind of talk,' muttered the old woman.

Autolycus laughed. 'We're as good as dead already.'

Danae hoped he was joking.

Suddenly, the Spartan soldier jerked into motion. He grasped the chain either side of him and whipped it against the floor with an echoing clang.

'Enough.' His voice was rusty from disuse.

They all fell silent.

Danae had heard tales of the Spartan army. Wild stories from farmhands and fishermen's sons. It was said they took boys from their families aged seven to start training. At ten, to weed out any weakness in their ranks, they were paired against each other and forced to fight to the death.

There was no more talk that night. She was glad at least that Autolycus left her alone. She was in no mood to be toyed with.

As the hours stretched on, she couldn't tell if the gnawing in her stomach was from bruising or hunger. She thought of home, of her father. Silently, she begged the gods to spare him punishment for her escape.

She pushed the memory of Arius being taken, the image of her sister's drowned body and the terrible look in her mother's eyes into a deep hole and imagined piling boulders on top. She couldn't let herself dwell on those thoughts. If she did, she would shatter, and she didn't think she'd be able to piece herself back together again.

I will make it to Delphi. I will find a way.

She chanted the words over and over in her mind, until eventually she fell asleep.

'Psst.'

Danae curled her arms around her head.

'Pssssssst.'

Groaning, she rolled over. 'What?'

Autolycus grinned. In the morning light, she noticed he was missing several teeth.

'I want to know your name.'

She eyed him warily, but supposed it couldn't do much harm, and if she told him he might leave her alone.

'Danae.'

'Ah, *Danae*.' He rolled her name around his mouth like it was a fine wine. 'There was another by that name once. She was beautiful, they say. A princess so radiant, her father locked her in a bronze chamber deep beneath the earth, safe from the gaze of men. It was prophesied his grandson would kill him, you see, so he did everything in his power to prevent her conceiving a child. But Zeus had already spied her with his eagle eye. And no walls of bronze or stone can keep a god from what he desires.'

He stared at her. She blinked.

'But you look nothing like her, so I doubt you'll have that problem.'

She huffed a sigh through her nose. 'What do you want?'

The playful glint vanished from Autolycus' eyes. 'Eternal life.'

They were interrupted by the rattle of keys.

The cell door creaked open. Straw crunched underfoot,

and two new men accompanied the plump guard into the room. One was slight with small, darting eyes and a scraggly beard. He was dressed in a navy travelling cloak and carried a whip strapped to his waist. His companion was large and muscular. Scars decorated his meaty forearms. He shadowed the smaller man, right hand never leaving the handle of his sword.

'What do you think, Kakos?' said the guard.

The slight man's gaze slid from one captive to another, all the while fingering his whip. The hairs on Danae's neck prickled as his gaze lingered on her.

'I'll take them all.'

Kakos passed a pouch of coins to the guard. He weighed it in his hand before swiftly pocketing it.

Kakos' lips stretched back to reveal yellowing teeth. 'Time to go to market.' He snapped his fingers. 'Bring them.'

The guard moved around the cell, detaching the chain from the iron rings. Once his task was complete, he clapped his hands.

'You heard him. Outside!'

Danae hesitantly pushed herself to her feet, taking comfort from the weight of Alea's brooch against her thigh. She wondered if she could use the pin to pick the lock of her cuff once they were outside.

The line jerked, and she stumbled forward. Not fast enough.

The large man grabbed her arm. She winced as his thick fingers crushed yesterday's bruises.

'Move,' he snarled, yanking her out into the corridor.

As they shuffled along, she could see more of the building they'd been held in. It had low ceilings with doors at intervals along the right of the passage. At the far end, the stone wall was replaced by iron bars encasing the final room.

Confiscated wares were stacked floor to ceiling. There

were crates of fruit and vegetables in a rainbow of colours, including an orange fruit covered in spines Danae had never seen before. Disordered amphorae of oils and wines lay on the floor with sacks of grain slopping over them. A pair of ruby earrings glinted between a stack of ceramic plates, and backed into the far corner was a human-sized statue of the goddess Aphrodite. A sword dangled from a scabbard slung over her outstretched arm, and a jumble of bright silks was wound around her neck. It was jarring to see the statue of a goddess treated in such a careless way.

A small black pot at Aphrodite's feet caught her eye. It was cracked down one side, but the emblem was still visible: a painted tree, its twisted branches bowed low with fruit. Danae stared at the pieces of gold leaf pressed onto each tiny apple. Her skin tingled. Then the chain pulled taut, and she was forced to move on.

The large man herded them into the belly of a wagon and bolted the door behind them. Danae scrambled onto her knees and held onto the iron bars of the window, pressing her face against the cold metal. She shuddered as the wagon moved, and the world outside leapt with each stone under wheel.

'Where are they taking us?'

'Didn't you hear the man?' said Autolycus. 'Flesh market.'

'I know, but where?'

Autolycus laughed. 'Athens, of course.'

Danae peeled her face away from the bars. She was going to Athens. She felt a ripple of hope. Athens was one of the largest cities in Greece; there must be people travelling to and from Delphi every day. If she could somehow escape at the other end, she could still reach the holy city.

12. The Flesh Market

As they left the wrought iron gates of Phalerum behind, the wagon swung round to enter a vast stretch of road. At either side of this giant highway were towering walls that looked designed to keep everything and everyone out. Or in. The ground had been worn smooth by thousands of hooves and wheels, and even at this early hour, the road was teeming with travellers. Wagons, riders and carts of all sizes bundled past.

Eventually, they approached another pair of vast iron gates, bearing the Athenian twelve-pointed sun. The wagon left the main road and the huge walls peeled away, to be replaced by buildings of the same bleached stone as the customs office in Port Phalerum. Danae caught glimpses of tall, pillared houses and men in richly dyed tunics sauntering along the street.

They came to a sudden stop, and a few moments later, the door opened. The flesh merchant's enforcer stood, silhouetted, against the sunlight. He held a waterskin and a loaf of bread in his large hands.

'Kakos don't want anyone fainting.' He smirked. 'Share nicely.' Then tossed the victuals into the wagon, and slammed the door.

For a heartbeat, nobody moved. Then they all lunged forward. Heads butted together, chains stretched, and Danae's nails scratched painfully against someone's cuff as she clawed for the waterskin. When the tangle of limbs unfurled, it was revealed the Spartan soldier held the loaf, and Autolycus clutched the waterskin.

Three sets of eyes darted between the men.

'Well now, look at this.' Autolycus grinned at the Spartan. 'I'll trade you half.'

The Spartan stared at him impassively. Then he ripped the loaf in two.

Danae's heart sank. She was so thirsty, her mouth was like dust. Autolycus took a long swig from the waterskin, then licked his lips, eyeing the half-loaf expectantly. He frowned as the soldier proceeded to tear the halves into quarters.

'I can chew it myself, I don't need you to –'

He stopped speaking as the Spartan tossed the first piece into Lycon's lap. The boy stared at the bread, then the Spartan, then shoved the entire hunk into his mouth before anyone could take it from him. The Spartan tossed the remaining pieces to each of the prisoners in turn. He left none for himself.

'Share,' the Spartan nodded at the waterskin.

'Will you look at that, it knows more than one word.' Autolycus held his piece of bread in one hand, the waterskin in the other.

The Spartan fixed him with a piercing stare. 'If you do not share, you will die.'

There was a pause. Autolycus laughed, but he didn't sound as confident as before. 'You can take the soldier out of Sparta . . .'

He snuck a last swig before re-stoppering the skin and begrudgingly tossing it to the soldier. Again, the Spartan didn't drink himself but passed it to the old woman. She hurriedly took a glug, then quickly handed it to the boy, muttering, 'Thank you.'

Watching the skin being passed around was agonizing. When it finally reached Danae, she was relieved to find there was some water left and gulped it down. It wasn't much, but thirsty as she was, it tasted like liquid life.

'What I want to know,' said Autolycus, 'is what a man of your abilities is doing chained up with a ragged bunch of misfits. Surely you could have escaped by now?'

The Spartan was silent for a moment. Then he said, 'There is no honour after being captured. Without honour, life is meaningless.'

Autolycus raised his eyebrows. 'Sorry I asked.'

After what felt like hours, the wagon stopped for the second time. Then the large man turfed them out onto a gravelled road.

To their right, sloping away from the wagon, was a dense forest. Far in the distance Danae could see the outline of the city walls. They funnelled the wide road that linked Phalerum and Athens, then broke apart to expand around the whole city, which included its own woodland. To her left was a large theatre, a semi-circle of curved wooden benches staggering up from a raised platform.

Philemon had said the theatre of Athens was where the citizens gathered to cry over tragic plays, laugh at comedies and take umbrage with the latest thinker's enlightened philosophy.

He'd failed to mention it was also used to sell slaves.

Danae looked up. The theatre was built onto the side of a hill, smatterings of trees peppering the land around it. At the top, guarded by more walls – like a small city in itself – was the acropolis. The royal palace and surrounding buildings presided over the rest of Athens from its height, and at the very peak was the new Temple of Athena.

Danae could see why Philemon had waxed lyrical about this building. It was magnificent. A temple six times the size of Demeter's back on Naxos, its polished pillars, thick as ancient oaks, stood proud against the blue sky. It was said to be the most expensive temple ever constructed and it was dedicated to Athena, the Goddess of Wisdom and Warfare.

The rest of the city was hidden on the other side of the acropolis hill, though Danae could hear it. The air was thick with the cries of street peddlers, children, smiths, fishmongers, butchers, the rumble of carts, people eating and drinking outside numerous kapeleia and so many more sounds she couldn't decipher.

There was something different about the air here too. Something was missing from the mix of hot stone, horses and the sweet scent of the forest.

It was the sea.

That fresh, salty tang that had been constant her whole life was gone.

'Follow him,' the large man barked and pointed after Kakos as he strode up onto the stage.

Danae breathed in sharply as they trudged after the flesh dealer onto the wooden platform. There was barely a seat unfilled on the benches fanning out above her. Hundreds of people sat upon them, pointing down at the stage and talking amongst themselves. She spotted Memnos, the cheese merchant, in the front row. No doubt waiting to collect his coins after her sale.

She and her group were not the only slaves being auctioned that day. A couple of other people stood further downstage, also in chains, escorted by a man she presumed was another flesh merchant.

She noticed two guards at either side of the stage, identical in their bronze armour and blue cloaks, embroidered with the twelve-pointed sun. There were more dotted throughout the seating. She glanced behind her and saw that another two guards had appeared behind the stage.

Her hope of escape shrank to barely a flicker.

A tall youth was being unchained at the front of the stage. His flesh dealer pushed him forward.

'Do I have five drachmas for this strong fellow?' The man slapped a hand on the lad's shoulder.

Several men stood, raising their hands and calling their bids.

'Six, seven, eight, nine . . . ten. Ten to the man in the green tunic, last chance –'

'Eleven.'

The crowd murmured. But no more bids were made.

'Eleven drachmas! Going once, going twice . . . Sold!'

One of the guards stepped forward and pulled the youth towards a small stone building at the side of the stage. An elderly man in a white tunic began to make his way down the seating to collect his purchase.

Next, a young girl was brought forward. She was trembling. As the bidding began, Danae noticed a pool of wet around her bare feet. It was barbaric. She was only a child.

Her gaze slid beyond the girl into the crowd and settled on a figure in a hooded charcoal cloak. The men on either side sat slightly apart, as though they found the person's presence unsettling. The figure's hood was pulled low, the face beneath hidden in its depths and the hands encased in black leather gloves. For a wild moment Danae wondered if there was a person under there at all.

'Sold to the man in brown.'

She'd been so distracted by the cloaked stranger she'd missed the bidding.

A guard moved forward to take the girl away, but she stayed rooted, shaking like a sapling in a gale. After a moment he threw her over his shoulder and carried her off the stage.

Kakos pointed his whip towards Danae. 'She can go first.'

The large man unlocked her cuff, and Kakos dragged her forward. This was the moment. She was finally free of her chain, but there was nowhere to run. The heat of hundreds of eyes bore into her. The air smelt of fear and piss. She blinked away budding tears and imagined she was made of iron. Cold, immovable iron. She would not let them see her cry.

Kakos circled, squeezing her shoulders.

'A young woman of childbearing age,' he called to the crowd. 'In the peak of physical health. You'll get many years out of this one and you can work her hard – do I have five drachmas?'

A squat, balding man raised his hand.

'Excellent! Do I have six?'

A tall man with a pinched face bid. Then another and another. Her eyes flitted from one bidder to the next, trying to work out what type of master they might be from the tilt of their head or the set of their chin.

She was drawn back to the cloaked figure. The voices of the bidders faded away as she looked into the depths of that hood.

She thought she'd been afraid before, but that was only a shadow of the terror she felt now.

From the darkness under the hood stared a pair of crimson eyes.

Suddenly, the crowd was on its feet, shouting and pointing behind her. She twisted around to see the Spartan soldier had somehow got hold of a sword. Lycon, Autolycus and the old woman fell to the ground as he swung the weapon, yanking their shared chain, to decapitate Kakos' enforcer with a single blow. The large man's severed head sprayed an arc of blood through the air before rolling across the wooden platform.

The guards surged onto the stage in a flurry of blue. Despite his cuffed hands and being attached to three other people, it took five guards to slow the Spartan's attack. He fought like a wild beast and killed three before he was finally disarmed.

Blood leaking from a myriad of stab wounds, he roared, 'Sparta!' and went down smothered by a sea of blue cloaks.

Danae glanced back at the seating. Many of the buyers had fled. But the grey cloaked stranger remained, staring at her with his terrible red eyes.

She didn't hesitate a moment longer and while the guards and Kakos were distracted, bolted across the stage and leapt down onto the path.

She could hear Autolycus shouting behind her, 'That's it, girl. Run, Danae, run!'

Expecting to feel the clamp of a guard's hand on her shoulder at any moment, she sprinted as fast as she could across the gravel and plunged into the forest.

13. City of the Sun

Leaves whipped Danae's face, and twigs clawed at her limbs, but she did not slow. Then a root caught her foot and sent her tumbling to the ground. Scrambling onto her back, she stared at the trees behind her, expecting to see Kakos, the guards, or the hooded stranger burst through the foliage.

But no one came.

She stayed on the forest floor while her breathing calmed. Perhaps, in the chaos, they'd given up on her.

The air was close, sickly with the sap of trees and damp earth. Sunlight glinted through the leaves, but its warmth didn't reach the ground. She shivered. It was like being underwater, watching the light dance on the surface above, as though it belonged to another world. But she knew the sea, its tides and the creatures that dwelt within it. This forest was a different beast altogether.

She looked down at the welts on her arms and the tears in her tunic. Now her pulse was no longer deafening, the rustle of leaves and chitters of unseen animals pressed in. She flinched as an owl hooted in the canopy above. Then her hands flew to the hem of her tunic. She sighed. Alea's brooch was still there.

She thought of the Spartan soldier. He was the only person who'd been kind to her since leaving Naxos. She knelt and said a prayer to Hades, God of the Underworld.

'Please look mercifully on the Spartan who died at the Athenian flesh market today. Please command the ferryman to carry him across the River Styx, even if he has no coin to pay.'

She doubted Kakos would perform the burial rites and place obols on the Spartan's eyes. But she hoped his soul wouldn't be left to wander the bank of the Styx until the end of time.

She rubbed her face and sat back on her heels. She was alive. She was free. She was in Athens. The terror of the flesh market still vibrated through her body, but she had to get to the city. It was the only way she was going to find the road to Delphi.

Doggedly, she pushed herself to her feet and began to pick her way back through the broken vegetation.

Hours passed, and the light above faded. Her head was throbbing by the time she found a stream trickling through the undergrowth. Throwing herself into the shallow water, she drank until her belly ached. Then she pushed herself up and kept walking, only stopping when she could barely see the trees in front of her.

Night was upon her, she was exhausted, and she was completely and utterly lost.

She sank against a large tree, determination seeping out through her sandals. Her stomach growled. The meagre ration of bread consumed in the wagon seemed a very long time ago. The last thing she wanted was to spend a night in the forest, but she needed rest, and it would be impossible to find her way in the dark.

She heard a rustling nearby. Her pulse quickened. She looked around, straining against the gathering gloom for somewhere safe to sleep, somewhere she wouldn't be discovered.

Her eyes travelled upwards.

She grasped the lowest branches of the tree and pulled herself up. She climbed, clenching her teeth as the bark raked her palms. Unlike the rocks she was used to scaling back home, the tree seemed displeased with its invader and bent under her weight. One branch dipped so violently it almost sent her tumbling back to earth.

Finally, she reached a sturdy branch that was thick enough to safely bear her load and high enough to be hidden from the ground. She wedged herself into the crook between the trunk and the branch, and in this space between sky and earth, waited for sleep.

A giant wolf with a charcoal coat prowled the base of the tree. Danae clung to its branches, her trembling body shaking the leaves. The animal reared up and planted two large paws on the trunk. The tree shuddered under its weight, but she told herself it couldn't reach her, she was safe.

Then the beast began to climb.

She stared in horror as its tawny eyes ignited into red. Its limbs twisted, claws elongating into black gloved fingers and its hide unfurled into a sweeping cloak, the hood shrouding a face dissolved in darkness, except for those terrible crimson eyes.

She tried to kick it away and found her leg was not a leg at all but a branch. Threads of light coursed through the bark that was her skin. The creature tumbled from her twisted branches, and she knew it would not climb her again. She could feel life surging through her trunk, through her leaves and down into her roots buried deep in the earth.

She was the tree but at the same time she was so much more. She was everything the tree was connected to. She was the soil and all the beings it contained. She was every ocean and all the creatures that swam in their depths. She was the whole world. She was the infinite tapestry of life itself.

The blast of a horn jolted Danae awake. Rosy-fingered dawn blushed the sky. She winced as a twig dug into her back. Carefully manoeuvring herself onto her belly, she clung to the branch beneath her and peered through the leaves.

The wolf was nowhere to be seen. It was just a dream.

But what was the horn?

For a breath she was still, her body frozen with indecision. Then she eased herself off the branch and began to clamber down the trunk. She couldn't waste time waiting in her bower; she had to reach the city, find food and directions to Delphi.

Dropping from a lower branch, she landed sprawled on the forest floor. Her legs were stiff, her muscles aching from overuse and undernourishment. As she got to her feet, she heard the rumble of hooves. The horn sounded again, much louder than before. Whoever they were, they were close. Perhaps the guards were still searching for her after all.

With no time to climb back into its branches, she ducked behind the tree. A heartbeat later, a man burst through the bushes and hurtled past. He was young, with olive skin and dark hair, dressed in a ruby-red tunic. His eyes bulged with fear, and his spittle-flecked lips were drawn back as he gasped for breath.

A pack of hounds tore after him, followed by a group of men on horseback. In the lead was a thick-set man in a royal-blue tunic, a gold band nestled on his greying curls.

King Theseus.

Danae flattened herself against the trunk and stayed very still until she was sure the hunt had passed, then peered around the tree. The little clearing was calm once more. She took off carefully along the path the horses had trampled. Now, at least, she had a route to follow out of the forest.

A few moments later, she froze as screams ruptured the air, accompanied by the snarling of hounds who'd found their prey. She pressed her hands over her ears, but she couldn't block out the man's agonizing cries and the last pitiful sounds of him begging for his life.

She broke into a run and sprinted along the hunt's trail as fast as her aching legs would let her.

When she eventually emerged from the forest, she found herself not far from where she'd entered it the day before. Her heart sank, but thankfully, there were no wagons parked outside the theatre.

She lingered in the last row of trees, scanning the area for guards. The gravelled road seemed to be deserted. She chewed the insides of her cheeks, then decided to risk it and sprinted across the path to the smattering of trees on the other side.

A crow soared overhead. She watched it beat its wings against the sun, then turn sharply and dive towards the theatre.

Curiosity snaring her, she left the little clutch of trees and scuttled towards the wooden seating. The bird had landed in the centre of the top row of benches, and was pecking the spike-mounted head of the Spartan. His grey flesh was already sagging in the heat and trickles of dried blood stained the wood beneath his severed neck.

A wave of nausea cramped her stomach.

She recognized the landmarks of Athens from Philemon's stories, but this was not the city she'd imagined. He'd described it as the height of civility, culture and sophistication. All she'd seen so far was cruelty and violence. The sooner she could leave this place for Delphi the better.

She looked up towards the acropolis at the peak of the hill, the Temple of Athena its crowning jewel. If anyone knew the way to Delphi, it would be a priestess of Athena. It was said the Athenian treasure house was the largest in the sacred city, and it was always fully stocked. The trade-off being, whenever Athenian royalty or nobility wanted to visit the oracle, they got to jump the queue. Apparently, there was even a statue of Athena at the entrance to the city, despite Apollo being the patron deity.

She turned and ran up the ground to the left of the theatre, darting behind the sporadic clutches of trees. As she reached the ground level with the crest of the seating, two guards stepped out in front of her. She skidded to a halt. They stared down at her, helmeted heads obstructing the sun. Had they been at the flesh market? She couldn't tell.

'What were you doing down there?' said the first guard. 'The theatre's closed today.'

Thank the gods, they hadn't recognized her. Thinking quickly as she returned the sacred gesture they had given her, she rounded her shoulders and bit her lip, hoping she looked young and helpless.

'I'm sorry, I just went into the forest to look for food. We haven't had much since Pa died and now Ma's sick . . .' she trailed off, staring dejectedly at the ground for added effect.

She willed herself to keep calm as the guards scrutinized her.

Then the first said, 'You're lucky the king's hounds didn't find you. He's hunting today.'

She wondered who the man he'd been pursuing was, but she didn't dare ask.

'Get out of here. Don't let us catch you again,' said the second guard.

Fighting the urge to bolt, she forced herself to walk calmly around them towards the city, then, as soon as they were out of sight, broke into a run towards the acropolis steps.

The only way into the Temple of Athena was through the acropolis compound, up winding stone steps, flanked by more guards. Even at this early hour, a queue of people was already making the ascent. Many of the women's faces were painted with white lead, contrasting starkly with their brightly dyed dresses. They looked like ghosts, dragging their finery to the gates of the Underworld.

Danae waited a moment, then hopped over the low wall and slipped into the current of bodies. As the crowd surged upwards, she looked down at the city. Athens fanned out beneath her, a sprawling mass of formal pillared buildings, houses, squares, market awnings, ramshackle stalls and stables, spreading over so much land she could barely make out the city wall in the distance. The only thing she could compare it to was if someone had taken all the villages on Naxos and squeezed them into the valley where Demeter's temple stood.

She bobbed behind a pair of gossiping noblewomen as a guard looked her way. Despite the crush of people around her, she felt exposed. Her tunic was tattered and dirty, and she still stank of cheese. She wasn't exactly blending in with the well-groomed Athenians around her. But she managed to ascend unhindered until finally the entrance building loomed ahead. It was so grand, if she didn't know better, she would have thought it was the Temple of Athena itself. Tall fluted pillars supported the pediment, carved with the likeness of the goddess. She floated above the worshippers, clad in full battle armour, her watchful eye on her devoted subjects as they passed beneath.

Once clear of the entrance, Danae flowed with the crowd into an open courtyard. The palace lay behind gilded gates to her left, and in front of her stood the Temple of Athena. Her body tingled with anticipation. She was almost there.

As she mounted the last set of steps up to the temple, her heart sank to see that the open mahogany doors were flanked by yet more guards, their bronze spears crossed over the entrance. She concealed herself behind a group of men in long white robes, peering between them to look into the sacred building.

The inside of the temple was vast. Tall, uniform columns held up the open roof, and set into the centre of the floor was a rectangular pool, its water still as glass, mirroring the sky above. And at the back of the temple was a likeness of Athena that captured divinity itself. It was over forty feet tall, sculpted entirely from bronze and ivory. The goddess was crowned with a five-pronged helm, her spear and shield rested at her side, and she was draped in a flowing dress that looked like it had been fashioned from liquid sunlight. Athena's skin seemed to radiate its own pearly light and her sapphire eyes, each one larger than Danae's head, were so piercing she was convinced the goddess could see straight into her soul.

She held her breath as the guards' spears parted for the men in front of her, and once through the doors, darted round them.

She was immediately yanked back by the neck of her tunic and the guard threw her down the steps. Her hip and elbow jarred against the stone as she smacked into the ground.

'No begging in the temple.'

'I'm not –' she began but the guard lowered his spear and advanced towards her.

'Get back to the streets, scum.'

She scrambled back from the tip of his spear. Athenians cringed away from her as she half ran, half stumbled across the courtyard. Fear clutched at her chest as she suddenly became aware of how visible she was. She had to get away from the crowd.

She weaved her way back down the acropolis steps, like a rock sinking against the current of a river.

Her first attempt might have failed, but she would find someone who could direct her to Delphi. She had to.

*

When Danae reached the bottom of the acropolis steps, she found herself surrounded by makeshift stalls piled with miniature likenesses of the city's patron goddess. The sellers shouted over each other, fighting to be the loudest to advertise their wares.

She paused in front of one of the stalls. A tray of brooches was balanced on top of a barrel. They were all the same. A bronze owl with eyes of green stone.

'Three obols – it's a good deal – cheapest on the stretch. Aren't they pretty? Sacred bird of Athena. Why don't you try one on?'

She backed away. 'No . . . I don't want –'

'Two obols. I'm robbing myself here.'

She turned and fought her way through the sea of haggling traders. Ducking into a side street, she leant against the wall, fighting back tears. She thought of Alea's glowing face when their mother had pinned Philemon's owl brooch to her chest. It had looked so special surrounded by the shabby interior of their hut. But it was just one of many. And next to the real wealth of the acropolis, she saw it for what it was, a cheap copy.

Shame stung her throat. Philemon was wrong, Alea would have hated it here. She rubbed her eyes and breathed out slowly through her nose. She couldn't let herself be distracted. There had to be someone in this infernal city who knew the way to Delphi.

She carried on down the street and found all the doors and windows bolted shut, so she pressed on and emerged into a large market square. The shops were shaded on all sides by colourful canopies. She was overwhelmed at first. There were so many people. Who to ask? She lingered by a stall of apples, deciding the shopkeeper looked friendly.

'Excuse me?'

The man had his back to her.

She cleared her throat and was about to speak again when he turned around. Eyes bulging, he grasped a broom from behind the doorway of his shop and jabbed it into her stomach.

'Fuck off. You're not getting any food.'

She staggered back. Athenians knocked into her as she was buffeted through the square. She tried to ask the people she passed but was met with much the same reaction. Some shooed her away, some simply ignored her. It was like a dream she'd had once, where she was a ghost and everyone she approached to help her find her body walked straight through her.

After a while, her stomach began to ache. Wearily, she eyed the produce of the nearby stalls. There were plates of ripe figs and barrels of olives, trays of sweet pastries and bowls overflowing with nuts. There was so much food it was obscene.

She spotted a thin man stacking a pyramid of oranges. She watched as one teetered on top of the pile, then tumbled to the ground, rolling away from the stall. The merchant sighed and turned to retrieve it. But she had the urgency of hunger on her side. Her fingers closed around the fruit, then she was off.

'Stop!' the merchant yelled.

But she was already darting down an alley. She ran through street after street until she was certain she'd lost him. After what she'd seen of the city, she didn't want to find out what the penalty was for thieving.

She must have come to a district where the nobility lived. On either side were pristine villas with white walls and terracotta roofs. People looked at her with disdain, but no one threatened her or chased her away. She was grateful for that at least.

She dug her nails into the orange's skin. The tang of zest filled her nostrils as she peeled back the rind. Juice spilled over her fingers and she licked them greedily, not caring about the dirt on her hands. The fruit was deliciously sweet and succulent. She was so engrossed in eating that she almost walked headlong into a man emerging from a doorway. He tossed the contents of a bucket in front of him, and piss slopped over her sandals, before trickling away down one of the gullies that ran along either side of the road.

She swore and backed away.

The man glowered. 'Watch where you're going!'

'Wait!' she called as the man ducked back inside. He paused in the doorway. 'Do you know the way to Delphi?'

The man's eyes narrowed. 'How much is it worth?'

She glanced down at the half-eaten orange, ripped off a piece and offered him the dripping segment.

The man wrinkled his nose and slammed the door in her face.

She sighed, continuing along the road while finishing the last of her fruit, its flavoursome flesh a small distraction from her aching feet.

'. . . from the holy city.'

Her ears pricked. Two men were walking ahead; one wore the bronze armour and blue cloak of an Athenian soldier, high-ranking by the look of his plumed helm. His companion was draped in the white robes of a scholar.

'Perhaps I should consult the oracle again?' asked the officer.

'I do not think it wise, Aristides. Prophecy is not a friend you can question until you receive the answer you desire.'

They emerged onto a bustling, shop-lined street, and a group of women stepped in front of Danae. She weaved around them, but by the time she'd navigated past, she could no longer see the two men. Clenching her teeth in frustration, she darted down the street, peering through the various doorways and windows.

But her search proved futile. She'd lost them.

Danae asked the way to Delphi so many times the words turned to gibberish on her tongue. She must have spoken to more people in one day than she had in her entire life.

She wandered for hours and found herself in a less affluent part of the city. The buildings here were made of wood. They were lower and closer together, washing hung off lines that stretched between the roofs, and barefoot children ran through the streets, not seeming to care that they were splashing through human waste. The gutters here were evidently not maintained like they were in the wealthier districts.

At least the people didn't look at her like she was vermin.

A few streets along, she noticed a change in the air. Something was drawing people from their homes. They flitted like fruit flies from doorways to windows, conferring in hushed voices.

Something had happened.

Most people were now walking in the opposite direction, back towards the heart of the city and the acropolis. She turned around and let the flow carry her back the way she'd come.

She passed a bathhouse and overheard a group of men talking animatedly as they stepped onto the street.

'I don't see how Theseus can recover from this.'

'That's what you get for marrying a woman from Crete.'

Their laughter faded into the throng of passers-by as they were absorbed by the crowd. She darted after them, snippets of conversation flitting around her.

'I heard one of the servants caught them.'

'Lying with her own stepson! It's an abomination.'

The streets nearer the acropolis were packed. Danae weaved through the throng, straining to catch more information.

As the great stone steps up to the acropolis swung into view, a commotion broke out behind her. The crowd was peeling back from the road. Pushed towards the buildings on the left, she fought to see what was happening over the heads of the people in front.

A procession was making its way down the road.

Danae stretched onto her tiptoes. At the head of the procession was King Theseus, his shoulders draped in a cobalt-blue cloak that pooled over the rear of his chestnut steed. The band he'd worn on the hunt had been replaced with a golden crown, and his grey eyes were cold as a winter sky.

She weaved forward, squeezing her way through the first line of onlookers just in time to see the rope stretching from the back of the king's saddle. Her stomach lurched when she saw that it dragged the body of the man she'd seen pursued through the forest. He was so battered, she almost didn't recognize him. He was naked, and his lithe frame was torn and punctured with bite marks, his skin crusted with dried blood.

He is King of Athens now.

She remembered what the Maenad Ariadne had said about Theseus. This was the man who had lain with her then abandoned her on an unknown shore. He had always been cruel, even before his heart was poisoned with vengeance. To be cuckolded by his own son was a grievous wound indeed, but to hunt his child like an animal then defile his body was beyond brutality.

Behind the body of Theseus' son walked a woman. She wore no jewels, and her long silk gown trailed around her bare feet. Danae gaped. The resemblance was uncanny. She was younger than Ariadne, her long silver hair still streaked with blonde, but the tilt of her mouth and shape of her jaw were the Maenad's replica. This must be the sister Ariadne spoke of. Danae wondered if this woman knew what had happened between the Maenad and her husband.

The Queen of Athens stared down at her stepson's broken body, as though the crowd were not there and the two of them were all that existed. She didn't cry, but her pale-green eyes were caverns of grief. A step behind her were six guards, two abreast. They wore full Athenian battle armour, their blue-plumed helms masking their faces, hands resting on the pommels of their swords. Danae had the feeling they were there to guard the queen rather than protect her.

Bringing up the rear was a woman with a severe brow and light-brown skin, mounted on a grey dappled mare. Her dark hair was cropped short, like all her kind, and she was swathed in a black robe. Despite the horror of the procession, the sight of her made Danae's skin tingle. She must be the royal seer.

Danae had only seen one other seer, a long time ago in Naxos Port. Men and women who became seers were chosen from a young age to study under a master and learn the secret arts of divining the omens. They then chose which king or military commander they would serve. A female seer was an anomaly, a woman outside of the confines of societal restraints. Even a queen was ruled by her husband's whims, but a seer could travel anywhere with anyone and command respect. A woman who decided her own fate.

King Theseus dismounted at the base of the acropolis steps and began to climb. His seer followed him, and the guards detached the body, dragging it up to the middle of the stairs. The queen, still flanked by the guards, was positioned next to it. It was a chilling sight, the king surveying his citizens, his wife and the mangled body of his son below him.

Theseus raised his hand, and silence descended.

'Athenians, may the Twelve see you and know you all.' He spoke in the manner of a prince who'd never had to fight to be heard. 'Your king stands here today, before his people, to address the rumours that I'm sure by now you've all heard.' He paused. The city was so quiet. Even the memorabilia sellers were silent. 'Adultery has been committed. Let none of us forget, for a woman to betray her husband is a sin against the gods. It is a sickness that must be driven out and cauterized. No one is above judgement, not even royalty.' The tension in his voice betrayed how difficult this was, but Danae couldn't see the pain of heartbreak on his face, just the fury of wounded pride.

The seer nodded slowly as he spoke. Danae wondered if Theseus had been forced to make the admission. Kings may rule their people, but priestesses ruled their kings.

'My son, Hippolytus, was mine to deal with.' Theseus glanced at his seer. 'But I leave the fate of Queen Phaedra to Athena.'

The crowd muttered amongst themselves, then fell silent again as the seer lifted her arms to the sky. Her eyes rolled into the back of her head, then she opened her mouth and a language Danae didn't understand poured out, the guttural tones raising the hair on her arms. This woman was communing with the gods.

The crowd waited, spellbound.

After a while, the seer lowered her arms and looked around as though waking from a trance.

'Athena has spoken. The queen's life will be spared.'

Many gasped. It wasn't like the gods to be merciful. Theseus' mouth twitched; he almost looked disappointed.

'But,' continued the seer, 'she must be cleansed and atone for her sins. Athena wishes Queen Phaedra to travel to Delphi immediately to be purified by the oracle. If she does not, a terrible plague will befall this city.' The seer turned to Theseus. 'The fates have aligned, my king. The chosen novices are due to travel to the holy city tomorrow to be presented as candidates for the new Pythia. The queen must accompany them.'

Phaedra blinked and said nothing. She didn't seem to care that her life had just been spared. There was a pause while the king looked intensely at his seer. Then he turned back to the crowd.

'Let Athena's will be done.'

Danae didn't pay attention to what happened next. While the people around her drifted back to their lives, she remained still.

And began to form the outline of a plan.

14. Burning Gold

'Please let this work,' Danae whispered as she cradled a stone in a strip of material she'd torn from the hem of her tunic.

She bit her lip and took aim.

The first stone fell short, pinging off the steps of Athena's temple. The second hit one of the guards on his bronze breastplate. He didn't so much as flinch.

She swore under her breath.

Flattening herself to the pillar she was hiding behind, she glanced back at the palace, then gazed down at her torn clothing. She had discarded her initial idea of how to distract the guards as too risky, but she looked so terrible it might just work.

Muttering a swift prayer to Hermes, the patron god of tricksters, she ran across the courtyard.

'Help! Someone help!'

The guards' heads swivelled towards her, and she let the horror of what she'd been through in the last few days pour rivers down her cheeks.

'A man in the palace. He killed a guard then attacked me; he was looking for the queen.' She fell to her knees, sobbing.

Between her fingers, she saw both guards bolt towards the palace. A moment later she was on her feet, pacing up the temple steps.

Stage one was complete. The next would require stealth and patience.

She waited, concealing herself behind one of the broad stone pillars, until the last worshipper left the temple and the doors were bolted shut. Athena's painted eyes stared down at her as she crept from her hiding place. The stillness of the vast hall sent a shiver down her spine. The mirrored pool was so calm it seemed to capture the moon, emitting its own ghostly light. She desperately needed to wash, but bathing in the holy water would be an unspeakable act of sacrilege.

Each step she took felt clumsy, each breath louder than the last. She didn't belong in this sacred place, in the presence of a goddess. Even one made of bronze.

Averting her eyes from Athena's ivory face, she sank down behind the statue's plinth, and pressed her back into the cold marble. Her body desperately needed sleep, but she was afraid of what dreams would come if she closed her eyes.

Instead, she focused on what would happen next. If the priestesses of Athena were anything like the sisters of Demeter, they would start each day with morning prayers and blessings.

That was when she would strike.

Danae bolted from the temple like a horse stung by a gadfly.

She ran faster than she'd ever done in her life, a pale-blue cloak clutched in her fist. People dived out of her way, but she didn't stop, not even to glance behind her. If Phalerum had taught her anything, it was to make damned sure she'd given her pursuers the slip before slowing down.

While the priestesses were occupied with the morning ceremony, she had crept from her hiding place and skulked through the shadows as the novices derobed. It was all going so well until one of the novices spotted her, and she'd been forced to create a distraction, only just managing to make away with a cloak in the commotion.

After sprinting down the acropolis steps, Danae quickly washed herself in a horse trough in a nearby stable yard, then donned the novice's cloak. She allowed herself a moment to enjoy the luxurious softness of the material against her skin, then let the flow of people guide her through the city. They were all going to the same place.

From what she'd gathered, there were only two ways in and out of Athens. One was the walled passageway to Port Phalerum, the other was the gate now towering before her. She ducked behind the canopy of an olive-seller's cart and tugged her pale-blue hood down over her face. If she was right, Queen Phaedra and the Pythia candidates would pass this way to leave the city.

She didn't have long to wait.

A block of guards marched down the road, parting the traffic, and through the now clear passage processed several more guards on horseback and two ornate carriages followed by three wagons stamped with the Athenian twelve-pointed sun.

The procession came to a halt, and Danae glanced between the carriages. One must contain the novices, the other Queen Phaedra. She had no idea which was which. Her attention was drawn by a bone-rumbling creak as the city gates began to open. Pulse quickening, she turned back to the carriages.

She had almost reached the first when a pair of hands clamped down on her shoulders. She spun around to face a scowling guard.

'Where do you think you're going?'

'I ... I'm late,' she blurted. Heart palpitating, she drew herself up. 'I'm a candidate.' She held the cloak tightly closed around her tunic, hoping the guard wouldn't notice her tattered sandals.

'Why aren't you with the others?'

'I wanted to say a last goodbye to my sister.'

The guard's eyes narrowed. Danae's mind raced, searching for anything that might help convince him. Then she remembered the man she'd followed the day before and prayed with all her soul that he was indeed a high-ranking officer.

'I'll be sure to let my father know how helpful you've been.'

He frowned. 'Who's your father?'

Danae puffed out her chest. 'Aristides.'

The guard's eyes widened with recognition, and her heart leapt.

'Yes,' she pressed. 'And if I'm left behind, he will be furious.'

The groove between the guard's brows deepened. He did not move.

Mouth dry, Danae took a step towards him, lowering her voice. 'What's your name?'

'Cyrus.'

She reached for his hand, the other holding her cloak closed over her tunic. As her fingers touched his skin, she fluttered her eyelids.

'I sense great things for you, Cyrus. The Goddess of Wisdom whispers to me from Mount Olympus.' She closed her eyes as though straining to hear. 'General.'

The guard stared at her for three more agonizing heartbeats, then turned to knock on the window of the second carriage and opened the door.

'In you go,' he said gruffly, not meeting her eye. 'And thank you.'

As he helped Danae into the compartment, bile surged into her throat at the thought of the blasphemy she'd just uttered.

She was greeted by three startled faces. Before anyone could speak, she was sent tumbling onto the floor as the carriage jolted forward. The inside was lined with sumptuous cushions in a myriad of colours, on which the three chosen novices were reclining. She'd never been anywhere so luxurious. Not even lying on a soft, sandy beach was as comfortable as this.

A chorus of 'May the Twelve see you and know you' echoed from the girls. At eighteen, she was by far the oldest. She put the two on the right at no older than fifteen and the youngest only looked around thirteen. From the carriage floor, she made the sacred gesture in return, praying that back in the Temple of Athena she had moved too quickly for any of the novices to remember her face.

'Who are *you*?' asked the girl on the right, the colour rising in her pale-pink cheeks. Her blue eyes swept disapprovingly over Danae's flyaway hair as she tucked her own silky blonde strands behind her ear.

'Last-minute addition.' Danae pushed herself off the plush upholstery.

The middle girl's brow creased. Her skin was russet brown, and she had a soft face framed by a cloud of black curls. 'The high priestess never mentioned you. Why haven't you been studying with us?'

'I'm from a town outside the city,' Danae said quickly. 'It took me a while to get here.'

'I don't believe you,' said the blonde girl.

Danae fought to remain calm. 'Do you really think the guards would have allowed me in if I wasn't a candidate?'

The blonde girl gave her a scouring look. 'What does your father do?'

'He owns an olive grove.'

The girl made a disparaging sound in the back of her throat. 'I thought they only chose the daughters of nobility to be novices.'

Danae shrugged. 'I'm special, I guess.'

The blonde girl still looked unconvinced.

'What's your name?' asked the curly-haired novice.

After a beat Danae said, 'Carissa.'

The girl smiled. 'I'm Dimitra.' She nodded at her blonde companion. 'That's Olympia.'

'And I'm Lyssa,' said the youngest of the three. Her copper skin was peppered with an explosion of freckles, and she had large green eyes that reminded Danae of a frog.

Her lips twitched. 'Nice to meet you all.'

'We were just talking about visions,' said Dimitra. 'I haven't had one yet but I'm sure I've heard the voice of Athena –'

'Of course you have,' cut in Olympia. 'Or you wouldn't be here.' She was still eyeing Danae with suspicion. 'They used to only let daughters from the best bloodlines be candidates. They must be getting desperate.'

Danae's cheeks flushed. Olympia would probably faint if she found out she was actually sharing a carriage with a fisherman's daughter.

'The current Pythia isn't from nobility,' said Lyssa in her high, reedy voice. 'She's the daughter of a silk merchant.'

'Shut up, Lyssa.' Olympia folded her arms and stared out of the window.

The Pythia was the priestess who translated the prophecies of the oracle. It was the most sacred appointment in all of Greece. There had been only one Pythia in her lifetime, but Danae knew she was chosen from a selection of virginal novice priestesses, sent from all the major cities.

'Have you ever had a vision?' Dimitra leant forward.

In her mind's eye, Danae saw the tree sprouting from Alea's heart, its branches lowering a golden apple towards her.

She was spared answering by a deep grating sound. The girls scrambled to the windows. The city gates were closing behind them.

Danae sat back and for the first time since arriving in Athens, felt like she could breathe freely. She'd done it. She was on her way to Delphi. Her hand went instinctively to Alea's brooch.

'The Pythia must be sick,' said Dimitra. 'Why else would they be gathering novices to replace her? She can't even be forty yet. Surely it isn't her natural time to pass into the Underworld?'

'What would happen if she died before a successor is chosen?' asked Danae.

Dimitra shrugged. Even Olympia didn't have an answer.

The girls lapsed into silence, and for a while Danae watched the open plains and patches of forest roll past. Soon tiredness weighed heavily on her. She tried to stay awake but, lulled by the rocking motion of the carriage and the soft embrace of the pillows, her eyelids drooped, and she joined her companions in sleep.

Danae woke to the jolting motion of the carriage coming to a halt. The light was fading. She must have been asleep for hours. She looked out of the nearest window and saw rugged hills sloping away from the road. The terrain was even sparser than before, with only the occasional tree appearing between tufts of rough grass and cracked, dusty earth.

There was a knock on the carriage door, then it creaked open. A guard leant in and placed a tray of food onto the cushions between them, followed by a jug and four cups.

Danae stared. The tray was laden with figs, a bowl of honey, cured meats, cheeses and sweet cakes. It took all her restraint not to shovel everything into her mouth at once. Instead, she forced herself to mirror her companions and pick daintily at the meal. Days of hunger roared inside her, nearly drowning out the taste of the first few bites. She dunked a fig into a pot of honey, then groaned with pleasure as the sweetness burst over her tongue. Dimitra laughed and passed her a cup of water. She drained it in one.

'You look familiar.' Lyssa was staring at Danae. 'Have we met before?'

'No, I don't think so,' she replied in what she hoped was a nonchalant tone.

Lyssa shrugged. 'Maybe you've just got one of those faces.'

'Well, common people do all have a look,' said Olympia.

Danae fantasized about grabbing Olympia's blonde hair, dragging her out of the carriage and rubbing her face into the dirt.

'I think it's a good thing Carissa's here,' said Lyssa. 'The new Pythia should be chosen on talent, not birth.'

Olympia snorted. 'You don't know what you're talking about. Next, you'll be saying we should choose our kings. Ridiculous.'

'Why not? Father says Theseus is running Athens into the ground.'

'Careful,' Dimitra placed a hand on Lyssa's arm and glanced at the door. 'You shouldn't repeat things like that, ever. You could get your father in trouble.'

There was another knock. Lyssa twitched and looked worriedly at Dimitra, who squeezed her hand.

The guard opened the door. 'I've been instructed to escort you to the, ah . . .' he cleared his throat, 'toilet facility.'

One by one they stepped down from the carriage. Their procession had pulled in off the road for the night. The other carriage was ahead of theirs, and the three wagons stood behind them.

'What are the wagons for?' asked Danae.

Olympia laughed. 'Gold of course, for the treasure house.'

'All three of them?' Her mind crumbled as she tried to envisage how many villages three wagons' worth of riches could feed.

Olympia stared at her incredulously as though she'd just asked what the sun was. 'Where did you say you were from again?'

They were interrupted by their guard calling for them to follow him. Danae turned away from the others and pulled her cloak tighter around her. She must stop asking foolish questions.

A couple of tents had been erected beside the vehicles, presumably for the guards to sleep in as they didn't have a wagon of their own. The girls trailed past them to an area where a sheet had been stretched between two trees, masking a shallow, freshly dug ditch.

'I'm not going behind there.' Olympia's face contorted in disgust.

'You're welcome to find somewhere else,' said the guard.

Olympia looked around at the scrubland's evident lack of shelter and pursed her lips.

The guard and the novices waited on the other side of the makeshift divide while Danae relieved herself. As she emerged, she heard someone whimper. She glanced around and saw Phaedra, arms pinned to her sides by another guard, as she was bundled back into her carriage. For a moment the queen's face lingered at her window after the door was slammed behind her. Their eyes met. A shiver trickled down Danae's spine.

His task complete, the queen's guard walked over to theirs.

'What's happened now?' asked the novices' guard.

'She's mad,' the other muttered. 'Just tried to grab my weapon. She was trying to . . .' He made a slicing motion across his throat.

The novices' guard shook his head. 'Don't envy you.'

Lyssa, the last to relieve herself, emerged from behind the sheet.

'Right, I'd better get this lot inside,' said the novices' guard. 'Come on, girls, back we go.' He nodded to the other. 'Good luck.'

The man grunted. 'I'm going for a piss.' He disappeared behind the curtain.

As they walked back, Danae's eyes lingered on the queen's window, but Phaedra had retreated into the darkness of her carriage.

By noon the following day the trees had thickened out and rolled over the undulating landscape in a blanket of green. As they began the ascent into the mountains, other travellers joined them on the road, and soon they were part of a steady stream of wagons and carriages, and the occasional rider on horseback.

'I can see it!' Lyssa squealed.

They all rushed to the window, just as the carriage curved around the sloping peak of Mount Parnassus. Tumbling down the mountainside, bathed in shafts of sunlight, was the holy city of Delphi.

It wasn't nearly as large as Athens, but it was majestic. A stone statue of Athena, arms open wide to welcome pilgrims, presided over the city gates. Due to the steep incline of the land, Danae could see inside the walls. The sanctuary of Apollo, which housed the oracle, was nestled in the centre. She could tell this was the temple by the giant likeness of the God of the Sun standing above it, cast in gold, his shining curls crowned with laurel leaves. Further up the mountain, carved into the sloping rock, was the theatre and gymnasium. A procession of pilgrims flowed through the city, treading the road all must take, the sacred way that led to the oracle.

As they drew closer to the gates, Danae's fingers went again to Alea's brooch. She held the weight of it in her hand and remembered her father pressing it into her palm. It was not much of an offering compared to the wealth around her, but she hoped it would be enough.

Maroon-cloaked guards flanked the entrance gates, their shining bronze armour dazzling in the sunlight. She stared out of the window, eyes flitting over the many pilgrims on foot, until Olympia pulled the curtains closed.

'It isn't proper for the commoners to see us.'

Danae was tempted to rip them back open, but she forced herself to sit back and wait. Soon she would be with the oracle, that was all that mattered.

The road tilted beneath the carriage, and with the incline Danae's pulse gathered speed. She was almost there.

Suddenly, the carriage came to a standstill, and she heard the clink of armour.

Their guard opened the door. 'By the command of Apollo, all must walk the sacred way.'

The chatter of the crowd was drowned out by the blood pounding in her ears as Danae stepped down from the carriage and huddled together with the other candidates. She looked about for Phaedra, but a group of maroon-cloaked guards clustered around them, forming a human shield between the novices and the pilgrims. Her senses were smothered by bronze armour, musty cloaks and cries of 'Make way!' as they climbed, hurrying to keep pace with the guards. Her fingers brushed Dimitra's, and the girl grasped her hand. She was glad of it.

Her breath came sharp and fast by the time the guards stopped walking. They peeled away to reveal the sloping entrance to the Temple of Apollo and formed a line behind the girls, pushing the pilgrims back.

The sanctuary of Apollo was fashioned in a similar design to the Temple of Athena in Athens, with towering columns crowned by a slanting roof and painted friezes detailed with gold leaf.

A woman emerged from the shadow of the pillars. She seemed to float as she descended, her deep crimson robe rippling over the stone. It was cinched at the waist with bronze brooches of laurel leaves, her head covered by a translucent veil of the same colour crowned with a headdress of golden coins.

'The Pythia has requested the novices enter one at a time. Who will be the first?'

Danae expected Olympia to jump at the chance of being first to be presented to the Pythia, but now the moment had come, nobody moved.

'I'll go,' she said quickly, the thought of returning home a shining beacon in her mind.

'Good luck, Carissa,' whispered Dimitra and gave her hand a final squeeze.

Danae glanced behind at the guards holding back the crowd of pilgrims. Her stomach hollowed as she looked at the sea of desperate faces beyond the armoured men. If she'd come on foot, it would have taken an age to get through all those people.

Her heartbeat reached a crescendo as she turned back to the priestess and walked up the stone ramp towards the temple entrance. Even though they were hidden, she could feel the woman's eyes boring into her. She tugged the pale blue cloak tighter around her ragged tunic. Another priestess emerged from the darkness within, and wordlessly the women beckoned her into the gloom, flanking her as she stepped out of the sunlight into the cool shade of the sanctuary.

Unlike the Temple of Athena, the entrance led not into an open hall, but into a low stone passage. She flinched as the doors slammed shut behind her. After the clamour of the sacred way, the corridor was eerily quiet. All she could hear was the beat of her own pulse and the clinking of the priestesses' jewellery. Scented braziers smoked at intervals along the walls. As they walked, the priestesses seemed to flicker in the dancing light, as though they were visions and not really there at all.

She felt like she'd been walking for hours when they finally descended a narrow staircase. At its base, a door loomed out of the shadows. It was fashioned from oak and surprisingly plain. One of the priestesses twisted the iron latch, and it creaked open. The other placed a hand on Danae's back and pushed. She stumbled into the chamber of the oracle and heard the door bolt shut behind her.

The room was suffocating.

Danae coughed as smoky vapours burned the back of her throat. Four bronze dishes filled with smouldering incense nestled in each corner of the chamber. Their light licked up the cavernous walls, casting wavering shadows across the domed ceiling. A crevasse ran the length of the room, splitting the floor in two, sulphurous smoke curling from its depths.

The oracle.

Her thoughts melted together as though someone had poured hot oil over her brain. She blinked. She had to hold on to why she was there. She needed the oracle to explain what had happened to her and, if she was cursed, give her a cure.

A figure emerged through the vapour. It was hard to tell where the Pythia began and the haze ended. Tendrils of smoke wove through her long, lank hair. She was dressed in a plain white robe, and, unlike the other priestesses, no jewels adorned her body. She was painfully thin. Pallid skin hung from her cheekbones and red-rimmed eyes stared out from shadowy sockets.

In the dizzying smoke, Danae fumbled to unclasp the owl brooch from the underside of her tunic, then proffered it to the Pythia.

'This is for you. I know it's not much ...' Her voice sounded muffled and distant. 'But I need your help. There's something wrong with me ... I think I might be cursed.'

The Pythia's hand closed around hers. Danae glanced down. The woman's knuckles looked like pearls nestled in a bed of crumpled silk. Her grip was surprisingly firm.

'I made a tree grow out of my sister's chest.' It felt important to explain. 'She was already dead, but ... it had golden apples ...' she trailed off, her tongue thick and clumsy.

The Pythia placed a skeletal finger over Danae's mouth. Paper-thin lips stretched into a smile over wizened gums.

'Come, novice,' said the Pythia. Her voice crackled like dry leaves underfoot.

She led Danae forward, until they were standing at the very edge of the fissure. She pushed Danae to the floor, then moved to stand behind her. The Pythia gripped her scalp and shoved her head down over the oracle.

'Breathe.'

There was something inside the crevice. Something smooth and shining, like a great black eye, covered in a web of cracks. And there, at its heart, was a chip, as though one piece was missing.

'Touch it,' whispered the Pythia, 'and tell me what you see.'

Danae felt the urge to explain that she wasn't really a novice, but instead found herself reaching forward until her fingers connected with something smooth and hard.

For a moment, she felt nothing but the vapours pounding

against her skull and the acrid taste of sulphur in her mouth. Then, there was an intense tugging sensation down her arm. She couldn't move. She tried to cry out, but her muscles seemed locked. Then the ground beneath her disappeared.

Darkness pressed against her eyes. Then she realized she had no eyes at all. She was immaterial, suspended outside her body in a vast emptiness. For a terrible moment it felt like she was the only living thing in existence. Then a single thread of light danced across the void. She watched it scamper away, then somehow without hands, caught it before it could disappear. Her consciousness was absorbed into the thread, and soon more strands appeared, swimming through the darkness towards her. They wove together and found other clutches of threads, until she was part of one great, interconnected web of glowing strands.

She saw shapes she recognized: a blade of grass, an ear of wheat, a beetle, a seagull, a galloping horse. She could feel the pulse of all their lives flowing through the tapestry, ever changing, ever weaving as energy travelled from a dying body to a new life at the moment of its conception. As she darted through them, she realized the threads *were* life itself. And she a spark racing along the network of creation.

Then she stopped.

Before her was an apple tree, sketched by the ever-moving life-threads that cycled through it. She couldn't see its bark, or the colour of its fruit, but she knew, with absolute certainty, that this was the same golden apple tree that had grown from her sister's heart.

There were figures moving around it. Twelve spectres in hooded cloaks. Then eleven stepped back as one moved closer, raising their arms to touch the trunk. The figure's threads began to flow into its bark, and slowly the cloaked phantom dissolved into the tree. Suddenly, the tapestry around Danae bubbled. The life-threads bulged, then became hands, reaching, grabbing, tearing at the fruit. The remaining figures were dragged down and consumed until nothing stood between the tree and the gluttonous fingers.

A scream swelled inside her, but she had no mouth to release it. They were going to destroy the tree. She could not let that happen.

The pressure became so intense she thought she would explode. Then the tree ignited. Its threads burst into flames and blazed so brightly it was blinding. But she couldn't look away; she had no head to turn or eyes to close. The hands cringed from the burning fruit, but they couldn't escape the inferno. Nothing could.

She watched, while everything burned.

15. The Last Daughter

Pain forked across Danae's skull. Something hard pressed against her face. It took her a moment to realize it was the floor. She was back in her body, inside the chamber of the oracle.

Her thoughts blazed, flames ghosting her vision. It felt like she'd touched the mind of a god.

Something was different. Her head still spun with the heady scent of the room, but the air was cooler, clearer. Then she was yanked off the ground and as the room tilted the right way up, she saw the stone floor was now coated with a fine black powder and tiny pieces of obsidian rock.

The oracle was gone.

The walls of the sanctum were cracked, and a scar ran along the floor where the crevasse containing the oracle had been. It was sealed so tightly, no vapours could escape.

She became aware of voices and movement around her. She twisted to see an armour-clad guard holding her arms behind her back. Four more guards in maroon cloaks rushed in through the now open door, swords drawn, all pointed at her. Behind them was a priestess of Apollo. Then she noticed the Pythia being held against the wall by a sixth guard.

'I don't understand,' Danae shouted. 'Tell me what the vision means!'

The Pythia laughed, her hoarse cackle echoing around the walls. The guard holding her smothered her mouth, then dragged her from the chamber.

'No!' Danae struggled, but her guard held her tight. 'Please help me!'

Sobs heaved her chest, her mind still a cacophony of burning gold. She'd come to Delphi believing she would be cured. She never dreamed her curse would destroy the oracle.

The cell was damp and devoid of sunlight. The only light trickled in through a grate in the door from a wall-mounted brazier in the corridor outside. It was completely bare and stank of stale human waste.

Danae knew she was underground. She hadn't felt the warmth of the sun since they blindfolded her, then marched her at swordpoint from the inner sanctum. She could feel the weight of the city pressing down on her. Every part of her revolted at being below, like she was a dead thing buried in the ground.

She stayed sprawled where they'd thrown her for some time and forced herself to relive what had happened.

She'd touched the oracle. It had shown her a vision: the tapestry of light, the tree, the strange hooded figures, the reaching hands, and her burning them all. While experiencing it, she'd felt so powerful. Now, the image horrified her. She didn't know how she had done it, but she knew she had destroyed the oracle.

The shriek of wood grating on stone pulled her away from the vision and back to the cell. She shuffled away from the door until she smacked into the wall. A priestess stood in the doorway, silhouetted in the flickering brazier light. Four armed guards fanned out behind her, two carrying flaming torches. They shut the door and flanked the entrance, while the other two grabbed Danae's arms. She had no strength left to fight them.

Slowly, the priestess moved towards her and knelt, placing a small wooden box on the ground. She undid the clasp and opened the lid.

A hiss issued from inside the box. Despite the cold, a trickle of sweat ran down Danae's back. The priestess reached inside and drew out a snake. Danae would have screamed if her throat hadn't been locked with fear. The serpent's scales were blood red, and a black diamond crowned its flat head, repeating down the length of its body. It moved lazily, winding its way around the priestess's fingers, clinking her gold rings.

A high-pitched ringing exploded in Danae's ears. She squirmed.

'Keep her still.' The priestess moved forward.

Finally, Danae found her voice. 'No, please! I didn't mean to. I'm sorry, please don't . . .'

The guards tightened their grip.

'It's just a little scratch.' The priestess spoke as though she were soothing a frightened child.

The rough stone wall raked Danae's back as the priestess lowered the snake, and pain jolted through her forearm. The guards let go, and by the time she blinked, the priestess was fastening the lid of the box.

Danae looked down at the two red pinpricks swelling on her skin. The priestess sank back on her heels and peeled the veil away from her face. She was beautiful, her skin golden, her irises so dark they were almost black.

Danae sagged against the wall.

So, this was how she would die. Perhaps it was for the best. She would see her sister again. If she was allowed to enter the Asphodel Meadows after what she'd done.

'How long does it take?'

The priestess tilted her head. 'What do you mean?'

'The poison.'

She laughed. It sounded like the tinkling of bells. 'That was just to relax you.'

Danae stared at her. She did feel calmer, like she was floating in a warm summer sea.

'What is your name?'

'Danae.'

'Where are you from, Danae?'

'Naxos.'

The priestess smiled.

'That's a long way from here.' Her voice was like honey. Danae could have listened to it all day. 'How did you get to Delphi?'

The edges of the room were soft; she hadn't noticed that before. They blurred into each other, like she was inside a giant egg.

'A cheese boat. They took me to Athens as a slave.' She grinned. 'But I got away. I slept in a tree, then Athena gave me a cloak and I . . .' She frowned. There was something itching at the back of her mind.

'Go on.' The priestess leaned forward.

'The oracle . . . I can't go home without a cure for my . . . my . . .'

The priestess watched her intently. 'Who helped you?'

'My Pa . . .' Her eyes drifted out of focus, and the priestess morphed into her father. Tears ran down his weathered face, trickling into his beard.

The priestess snapped her fingers, and her father's face dissolved. 'Who helped you get inside the oracle?'

'The . . . ?' The itching became gnawing, like there was a fly in her brain.

'King Theseus sent you, didn't he?'

It was hard to focus on the priestess's words, the drone was so distracting.

'How did you do it?' The priestess was standing now. 'How did you close the crevasse and destroy the oracle?'

Danae's limbs went slack, and she began to shudder uncontrollably.

The priestess let out a sharp sigh and floated the veil back over her face. She picked up the box and turned to the guards.

'We won't get any more out of her for now. Do not let anyone enter this room. Understand?'

Danae slid to the floor, streaks of red and gold dancing across her vision as the guards bolted the door behind them.

Danae had no idea how long it took for the snake's venom to work its way out of her system. Hours might have passed, or even days. She had no way to mark time in her sunless, windowless cell. After the convulsions ravaged her body, she passed out. When she came to, there was a cup of water and a stale hunk of bread next to her. For some reason, they wanted to keep her alive.

She felt untethered, adrift in a sea of fear. For the first time in her life, she couldn't see a way out. She leant back against the wall, the cold rock connecting her to something solid.

When she was little, her father had taught her how to mend fishing nets. They would sit for hours on the hut floor, clumps of netting spread out in front of them. He showed her the trick of methodically running each section through her fingers so she would never miss a join. When mending was needed, he bent her fingers around the needle, fashioning them into the correct hold. 'Loose and nimble', he used to say. The flax had to be darned just so. Even one small hole could ruin a day's fishing. If the links were too weak, the strength of the shoal would break them.

She lifted her empty hands and ran through the pattern

like it was a dance. It was comforting to retreat into muscle memory. A place where she didn't have to think or feel.

The lock clicked. Instinctively, she grabbed the empty cup and thrust it out in front of her, despite having no idea how she could use it to defend herself.

The door creaked open. A guard in full helmeted armour entered the room. He looked like he was going into battle. Her fingers dug deeper into the wooden cup.

'You're to come with me,' he said in a gruff voice.

She didn't move. They were going to torture her. That's why they'd let her live.

The guard edged a hand to the pommel of his sword. 'Now.'

In the face of his blade, she slowly rose to her feet, the useless cup tumbling from her hand.

'Lose the cloak.'

She hesitated. 'Why?'

'Take it off.'

She undid the clasp and reluctantly let the novice's blue cloak slide to the floor. It had, briefly, been the most expensive thing she'd ever owned. Well, stolen.

Impatiently, the guard grabbed her by the arm and dragged her out into the empty corridor. He marched her swiftly through a labyrinth of tunnels. The cells seemed endless. Door after door punctuated the catacombs. She wondered why a city dedicated to worship needed the capacity to hold so many prisoners.

'Where are you taking me?'

He didn't answer, but his stride quickened. Fear bubbled in her throat. She had to jog to prevent herself from tripping as he hauled her along. Two more guards came around the bend from the opposite direction. Her guard's grip tightened around her arm. The men nodded and passed them by.

She was breathing hard by the time they came to a thick wooden door, secured by an iron lock. With his free hand, the guard drew a ring of keys from his belt. They jangled together as he slid the first one into the lock.

It wouldn't twist.

He dropped Danae's arm and tried the next, then the next, swearing under his breath as the bolt didn't move. There was something different about his voice; it didn't sound as deep as it had done in the cell.

She stepped away from him. 'Who are you?'

The metal bar slid back with a clink. The guard didn't have time to reply as voices came echoing down the corridor. He yanked open the door. Sunlight blinded Danae as he pushed her up a flight of steps.

'Run!'

She hesitated for a heartbeat, then her legs jerked into motion.

She squinted against the glare, her eyes adjusting to the brightness of the outside world. She was in a small courtyard at the rear of one of the treasure houses that lined the sacred way. Manicured cypress trees and bronze statues were positioned at precise intervals in front of the high walls, and mosaics swirled within uniform squares on either side of a gravel walkway.

She barely had time to take it in before her rescuer was behind her. He slammed and locked the door, then slipped his hand into hers and pulled her across the courtyard to the wall.

When they reached it, he dropped her hand and threw himself against an empty plinth. To her surprise it toppled under his weight and smashed on the ground, revealing it to be hollow. There was a hole in the base of the wall behind it, where the bricks had been removed, just large enough for an adult to crawl through.

'Go!' He removed his sword from his scabbard belt.

She didn't hesitate this time. Heart thumping, she flung herself to the ground and crawled through the hole, ignoring the pain as the stone grazed her knees. She emerged the other side and found herself in a bustling street. Only the official buildings, dedicated to worship or hoarding offerings, were made of stone, but the holy city was swollen with a patchwork of wooden stalls and dwellings that had sprung up around them, selling goods to present to the oracle, or offering food and shelter to waiting pilgrims.

Danae barely had the time to take it all in before a sword clattered at her feet and the helmeted head of her rogue guard followed.

He was halfway through when he was suddenly yanked back. Danae lunged forward and grabbed his hands, gritting her teeth as she tried to pull him towards her.

'Let go,' he grunted.

'What?'

'Do it!'

She released him. There was a crash on the other side of the wall.

Her rescuer scrabbled forward and dragged himself through the gap. But before he could get to his feet, a hand lunged through the crack and clamped around his ankle.

Danae bent down and grasped the sword. It was so heavy she could barely lift it. She tried to jab the attacker's arm but ended up swinging the blade dangerously close to her rescuer's head.

'Holy Tartarus, watch it!'

He kicked out, but his assailant clung on like a limpet. Then he whistled.

A moment later, a mass of fur hurtled towards them and launched itself at the hand. There was a cry from beyond the wall and the now bloody arm retreated.

'Good boy, Lithos,' her rescuer panted as he straightened up.

The scruffy dog barked and jumped up at his master, tail wagging. He was a strange little creature with rugged chestnut fur, white paws and only one eye. The guard gave his pointed ears a hasty scratch.

'I'll take that.' Danae's guard grabbed the sword and once more took her hand. He grinned at the startled expression on her face. 'Come on, you're not safe yet.'

Just as the face of a furious guard emerged through the hole, the three of them disappeared into the crowd.

They pelted through the winding streets of Delphi. Danae's rescuer pulled her down narrow roads lined with colourful canopies, makeshift bathhouses and imposing official-looking buildings. After the amount of running she'd done in the past week, she should be used to it, but by the time they ducked under the awning of a wine merchant's shop, she was wheezing like an old goat. The proprietor didn't so much as blink as a guard, a dog and a ragged girl piled into his establishment.

They hurried past stacks of amphorae of all shapes and sizes. Danae's guard brushed back a faded curtain at the rear of the shop and tugged her through. There was a small room behind, filled with a few more dusty amphorae and a battered desk scattered with scrolls.

Her rescuer set about rolling back a hessian mat and lifted a hidden trapdoor beneath, but Danae was distracted by a marking sketched in charcoal on the wall above the desk.

An apple tree.

Burning branches seared through her mind. She stumbled back. The rogue guard threw his sword down through the hole, then paused on the edge of the trapdoor.

'I'll explain everything once we're safe, but you need to trust me.'

Lithos scampered past Danae and leapt down into the cellar. There were voices behind her. Someone had just entered the shop.

Her options were limited. Whoever this man was, he'd freed her from almost certain death. And he'd promised her answers.

She lowered herself through the hole.

The trapdoor closed, and she was momentarily blind. Then a candle flickered into being, throwing a ghoulish light on the helmeted face of her rescuer. They were in a tiny cellar with walls of packed earth and just enough room to stand up in. It seemed empty, save for a few amphorae and a pile of blankets that Lithos had already curled up in.

The rogue guard set the candle down on the floor and pulled off his helm. He sighed and ran a hand through his short hair. His tawny-beige complexion was flushed pink, and his hazel eyes danced in the flickering light.

Now the rush of the escape was over, Danae finally noticed the ill fit of his armour; the breastplate that was too long for his torso and the over-tightened sword belt.

'You're a criminal, aren't you?'

Her rescuer raised an eyebrow.

'What other kind of man would spring a prisoner from the gaol?'

'I am no man.'

'Oh . . .' Danae's brow creased. 'I thought . . . because of the armour. So, you're a woman?'

'I am no woman either.' At her confused expression, the guard's mouth stretched into a lopsided smile. 'Not everything fits into a box. I'm Manto.'

They continued to peel off the rest of their armour. Underneath they wore a simple brown tunic. 'We can't stay here long. Nicolau upstairs is one of us, but the guards will be searching the city, especially this close to the sanctuary.'

From the shadows, Manto rolled out a large amphora, stuck their arm inside and tugged out a bundle of black fabric followed by a bag.

They proffered Danae what appeared to be a long black dress, then stripped off their tunic and shoved on a matching black robe of their own. Then they pulled out a knife.

Something inside Danae snapped. She was tired of running, tired of being afraid, tired of not knowing what was happening to her.

'Stop!' She balled the fabric in her fists. 'You promised me answers, now tell me what in Tartarus is going on?'

Manto stared at her for a moment, then bobbed their head like a servant would to their master.

'Of course, sorry. I need to cut your hair so we can both disguise ourselves as seers.'

Danae eyed the knife with alarm. 'You want to do *what* to my hair?'

'You'll be less recognizable. Seers often come to Delphi, so it will allow us to move freely.' Manto's mouth curled into another crooked smile as they held up the knife.

Danae chewed her lip.

'All right.'

Manto set to work, clumps of thick brown hair falling around Danae like leaves blown from a tree. When they were finished, she tentatively lifted her hands to her head and explored her crop. The nape of her neck felt strangely cold. She'd never been particularly fond of her hair. Her mother always told her it was difficult and unsightly, but it had been hers. The further she travelled from Naxos, the more she felt herself crumbling away, like the stones of the sea-buried temple eroded by the tide.

'Put the dress on,' Manto prompted.

Danae self-consciously slipped out of her tattered tunic and squirmed into the dress. It tied at the waist and under her breasts like the robes of the priestesses of Athena. It wasn't as soft as the novice's cloak but compared to her old tunic it felt like silk.

She stared down at the midnight fabric and was suddenly uneasy, but was quickly distracted by Lithos trotting over from his nest of blankets to sniff her discarded hair.

She eyed the dog warily.

'He won't bite.' Manto scratched the coarse fur behind his ear. 'Well, he won't bite you.' They moved towards the trapdoor. 'We can't stay here. We need to get to the safe house before nightfall. Then I promise I'll tell you everything.'

Manto jumped and pushed back the door with a muffled clunk. The sudden gust of air blew out the candle. They lifted Lithos up, then turned to Danae.

'I just want to say . . . it's an honour.'

Danae's brow creased, but Manto had already hauled themselves through the trapdoor.

Manto was right. No one paid either of them much attention as they navigated the streets of Delphi in their obsidian robes. It was an unspoken rule that only seers wore black. Danae tried not to think about what the penalty would be if they were caught in the disguise. That would be the least of her problems if the guards of Apollo found her.

As the incline of the city rose, the buildings grew shabbier. She twitched whenever she heard a clink, expecting soldiers to burst around every corner.

'No one will bother you here,' Manto whispered. 'Unless you've got something worth stealing.'

By the time they'd climbed high enough to leave the stone buildings behind, night had crept over the city. Below them, Delphi sprawled down the slope of Mount Parnassus, a mass of painted roofs, coloured awnings and twinkling brazier lights. Above them was the gymnasium.

A ramshackle collection of wooden buildings clustered around the base of the stadium's seating. They walked past the dwellings until they came to one with old sacking pulled across the windows. Candlelight glowed from within. A couple of people came and went, hoods dipped low over their faces. Two women sat on barrels outside, their chests bare, dresses pooled around their waists. Lithos ran up to one of them. The woman bent down and fussed over him, scratching the fur behind his ears.

'Busy tonight, Hetaria?' Manto called.

Hetaria sighed. 'Same as ever. Be better if there was a war on.'

'Like a general, do you?'

'I like what they pay.' Hetaria swept her heavily kohl-rimmed eyes over Danae. 'What's wrong with this one? Never seen a pair of tits before?'

Danae flushed.

'Not the best pair in the city,' Manto replied.

Hetaria's shoulders twitched with pride and she fought back a smile. 'Flattery will get you nowhere, now piss off before you scare away my customers.'

So much for Delphi being the centre of religious piety.

'Do the officials know about this place?' asked Danae.

Manto laughed. 'Oh, they know. They don't do anything because it's good for business. Pilgrims got to have something to do while they're waiting to see the oracle. The officials take their cut, of course. Lithos, come!'

Lithos scampered away from a drunk man who was attempting to feed the dog from his cup. They continued through one of the arched entrance passages onto the gymnasium's arena. Up close, Danae could see the structure had been left to seed. Moss had grown between the slabs and several of the bricks were crumbling.

'Almost there.' Manto bounded across the dusty ground to a metal grate set into the middle of the first three rows of seating. With a grunt, they heaved it open to reveal a passageway chiselled into the stone.

Her heart sank; she was going back underground.

Manto tapped the stone. 'This was made back when they used to do lion baiting. Had to keep the animals somewhere before the show. Now it's where the forgotten people go. The dark underbelly of the holy city. Welcome to the safe house.'

The hollow beneath the gymnasium seating was surprisingly spacious. Once Danae and Manto were through the rock passage, the walls widened into a large cavern of packed earth. They were greeted by around thirty faces, illuminated by a central campfire. A hole had been carved in the ceiling to let the smoke escape, but the room was still stiflingly smoggy. The sharp tang of bodies caught in Danae's throat, and she coughed.

'You'll get used to the smell,' said Manto.

A small boy of about eight years ran over and flung his arms around Manto's waist. He only had one hand.

'I'm hungry!'

'Didn't you get anything today?'

The boy shook his head sorrowfully.

'That's not true!' said a girl of roughly the same age as she scurried up behind him. 'A pilgrim gave him an apple, I saw.'

Manto smirked, produced a couple of biscuits and proffered them to the children. The pair grinned, snatched the victuals and ran back to the warmth of the campfire.

Danae's eyes were drawn to a girl even younger than the first two children. She wore a coarse tunic of old sacking, and a man was feeding her broth from a rough wooden bowl. There were two raw stumps where her hands should have been.

Manto caught her gaze. 'Penalty for thieving.'

A lump swelled in Danae's throat. 'Who are they?'

'Pilgrims who've slipped through the cracks, orphans, desperate people with only their bodies to sell, those hiding from the iron law of Apollo. The usual waifs and strays.' Manto placed a hand on Danae's shoulder. 'Come on.'

They led her over to a far corner away from the fire. It was colder, but more private. As she sat, it dawned on her that, like the Maenads, Manto hadn't once spoken the sacred greeting. In her village that would be like forgetting to breathe. Not saying it implied you had something to hide from the gods and would bring years of bad luck on your family. Or so everyone believed.

'Don't worry, I haven't told anyone who you are. Only the Children of Prometheus know.'

'Prometheus . . . the Titan?' That couldn't be what Manto meant. The Titans were the embodiment of evil.

'No, my uncle Prometheus.' Manto raised an eyebrow. 'Yes, Prometheus the Titan.'

The crease between Danae's brows deepened. 'Why would they know who I am?'

Manto laughed. Their mirth quickly vanished when they took in the expression on her face. For a moment they looked worried, then their eyes sharpened with realization.

'You're right. At this moment I am the only member who knows that the last daughter has come. Finally.'

Danae's suspicions were confirmed. 'I'm grateful you saved me, I really am . . . but I think you made a mistake.'

Manto frowned. 'Mistake?'

'You've rescued the wrong person.'

Their pointed face hardened. 'Are you not the one who broke the oracle?'

'Well . . . yes.'

Manto sighed. 'Thank fuck. You had me worried there. Do you know the amount of work that went into getting you out?' They fixed her with the intense stare of someone trying to solve a particularly complex puzzle. 'You know . . . you're not what I expected.'

No, she supposed she didn't look like the sort of person who had the power to destroy Apollo's oracle. Whether it was the smoke, or the hours of running, she suddenly felt intensely lightheaded, and the edges of her vision began to crackle.

'You all right?' Manto's voice sounded far away. 'When did you last eat?'

Danae shook her head sluggishly.

Manto disappeared for a moment, then returned with something that looked like a rodent on a spit, although it smelt delicious. Lithos howled, then sat bolt upright, his white-tipped tail whipping the ground.

'In a moment,' said Manto. 'Our guest needs to eat first.'

Danae took the spit and sank her teeth into the meat. It tasted a bit like goat.

Manto pulled a small amphora from their bag, popped the cork with their teeth and took a swig.

'Perks of knowing a wine merchant.' They watched Danae eat for a few more moments then said, 'Leave some for the person who saved your arse.'

'Sorry,' Danae mumbled and handed over the remains of the meal. She licked the grease from her fingers and sighed. She felt a lot more human.

Manto tore off a few strips and threw them to the patiently sitting Lithos, then devoured what was left on the carcass.

'I didn't mean to do it.'

'Umph?' Manto mumbled through a mouthful.

'The oracle,' Danae whispered. 'I don't know how I broke it, or why I keep having visions of a tree with golden apples. I only came to Delphi to be cured.'

Manto threw the bones to Lithos then took another swig of wine. 'You don't need to do that.' They wiped their mouth on the back of their hand. 'We can talk freely here. So, what's next?'

'Next?' It still felt like she and Manto were speaking different languages.

'The grand plan.' Manto's eyes sparkled. 'To liberate us from the gods.'

Danae gasped and instinctively recoiled. She expected Manto to suddenly drop dead or a thunderbolt to come crashing through the roof. But nothing happened.

She eased herself to her feet. 'Thank you for rescuing me and for the food but I really need to go.'

Manto lunged forward and grabbed Danae's wrist. She tried to pull away, but Manto held her tight, desperation etched across their face.

'You can't forsake us now. So many have died so the prophecy, *your* prophecy, could survive. You're our only hope.'

Danae yanked her arm away. She could feel the eyes of the people around the fire on her back.

'You've got the wrong person,' she hissed. 'I'm Danae, a fisherman's daughter from Naxos. I don't want to liberate us from the gods and I'm going home.' She straightened up.

Manto stared at her as though she had just shattered their world.

'You don't know who you are,' they whispered.

'I just told you who I am. Goodbye, Manto.' She turned to leave.

'They'll kill you.'

Danae hesitated. 'I can sneak past the guards.'

Manto barked a hollow laugh. 'I'm not talking about the guards. I'm talking about the gods.'

16. The Wrath of Apollo

'You're wrong.'

Manto downed the rest of the wine and threw the empty amphora to the side.

Danae did not move. 'If the gods wanted me dead, I'd be on my way to the Underworld by now . . . wouldn't I?'

'That's what they want you to think.'

Danae opened her mouth then closed it again. Everything Manto said was infuriatingly vague.

'I'm going to need something stronger.' They reached into their bag and pulled out a pipe and a small pouch of herbs. 'Don't go anywhere.' Lithos whined as Manto lit the pipe from the fire, then sat down again and took a deep drag. Smoke curled from their lips. It had a sweet, earthy quality.

'I was a child when they took my father. The last thing he did was make me swear I'd become the watcher and when I found you, I was to help you at all costs.' They shook their head. 'What a fucking disappointment.'

Danae tried to keep the irritation out of her voice as she knelt on the ground, pressing her fists into the earth. 'I'm sorry about your father. But I have no idea what you're talking about. I came to Delphi to be cured of a curse. I don't know how I destroyed the oracle or who the Children of Prometheus are.'

Manto looked at her as though she'd just said she didn't know who Zeus was.

'The Children of Prometheus are the enlightened outlaws who follow the teachings of Prometheus, the liberator of mankind. We fight for knowledge and free will. And it is our sacred duty to preserve the Titan's prophecy and facilitate the coming of the last daughter.' They pointed their pipe at Danae. 'You.'

She swallowed. Every child in Greece grew up hearing the story of the Titanomachy and the Titans' eventual defeat at the hands of the Olympian Twelve. She could see her mother now, sat by the hearth, smoothing her tunic as she prepared to tell the tale.

Before mankind walked the earth, the Twelve Gods were locked in a cosmic battle with the Titans. The stars wept and the heavens rang with the terrible cries of war. It seemed like the destruction would never end, for both sides were strong and fairly matched. But then Prometheus betrayed his evil brethren, telling Zeus of their secret encampment in exchange for his freedom. The gods staged an ambush while the Titans slept and threw their enemies down into the depths of Tartarus, a prison from which they could never escape. The war was won, bringing peace to the earth. As a gift for his new lord, Prometheus fashioned the first man's body from river clay, and Zeus breathed his divine spark into him, creating mortal life. But by nature, Prometheus was devious. Ever seeking a way to gain power, the Titan stole one of Zeus' thunderbolts and gave it to the kings of men, so they might revolt against their creator. But they were weak, and even in possession of a holy shard of lightning they were no match for the might of Olympus. The rebellion was quashed, and as punishment Zeus chained Prometheus to the highest peak of the Caucasus Mountains at the end of the world, forever to be tormented by an eagle ripping open his stomach and eating his liver, only for it to grow back and be devoured again the next day.

'What's the prophecy?' Danae whispered.

Manto took a drag. Smoke twisted from their mouth as they spoke. '*When the prophet falls, and gold that grows bears no fruit, the last daughter will come. She will end the reign of thunder and become the light that frees mankind.*'

The hairs on Danae's arms prickled, as if an unseen breeze had blown over her skin. She shuddered and pushed the feeling away.

'Why do you think it's about me?'

'You broke the oracle.'

'It could be referring to a different prophet.'

Manto fixed her with a sardonic stare. 'Ah yes, because oracles are common and people destroy them all the time. And what did you say earlier about a golden apple tree?'

Gold that grows bears no fruit.

Danae pushed the words from her mind. 'It's a coincidence.'

'There are no coincidences. Ask the fates.' Another lick of smoke curled from Manto's lips. 'You are the last daughter, whether you like it or not.'

A weighted silence fell between them.

'Does everyone in Delphi know what happened to the oracle?' Danae whispered.

Manto snorted. 'Of course not. You think the priestesses of Apollo would want the world knowing a fisherman's daughter walked right into their sacred oracle and destroyed it? Think of the coin they'd lose.'

'Then how did you know?'

Manto's mouth twitched. 'What do you think I've been doing all these years, sitting on my arse? I know people. The ones no one notices. The ones they send in to clean up.'

Danae repeated the prophecy in her mind. *When the prophet falls, and gold that grows bears no fruit, the last daughter will come. She will end the reign of thunder and become the light that frees mankind.*

'What does the prophecy mean?'

Manto slumped against the earthen wall, their eyes red from the effects of the pipe.

'Not sure about the fruity bit,' they chuckled. 'But the rest pretty much means you're going to storm Olympus, kill Zeus and free us all from the tyranny of the bastard Twelve.'

Danae flinched. 'You can't . . . don't say things like that.'

'Why not?' Manto gestured broadly around the cavern. 'I've blasphemed at least three times since we've been here, and I haven't been struck down. Let me tell you something about the gods – they want us to believe they can read our thoughts and hear everything we say, but it's a lie.' Manto slouched even lower. 'Who was your patron deity on Naxos?'

'Demeter.'

'Right. I bet you all slaved away to produce offerings and pay her temple tithe. But despite all your devotion, all your piety and sacrifice, people still died and starved and joined the Missing, and your goddess did fuck all about it. The gods aren't as powerful as people think.'

Nauseating cracks appeared in Danae's reality.

'You know what's funny.' Manto was practically horizontal now. 'I thought you'd be this fierce warrior with a magnificent plan – a female Heracles. But look at you. The fates have a sick sense of humour.'

As Manto spoke, their thumb slipped from the barrel of the pipe, and Danae spotted a familiar symbol captured in flaking paint.

The golden apple tree.

She pointed. 'That's the tree, the one from my visions.'

Manto held the pipe close to their face, then lowered it and grinned at Danae. 'The tree of knowledge. Those teeny golden apples symbolize the gift of truth Prometheus gave us. That's what my father told me, anyway. The Children of

Prometheus draw it places so we know who to trust and where . . .' Manto yawned, 'we'll be safe.'

Gold that grows. Burning hands reaching for golden fruit.

'Are there many of you?'

Manto shrugged. 'I've got a handful of contacts in the holy city. Sometimes I receive instructions, but I don't know who from. The Children guard their anonymity. It's how we stay alive.'

Danae stared at the ground, her head whirling with disoriented thoughts.

When she looked up, Manto's eyes had closed, and the pipe had tumbled into their lap. Lithos trotted over and nudged the smouldering barrel away from their robe, then curled up against them.

She could leave now, find her way to a port and sail back to Naxos. But she was the girl who'd destroyed the oracle. She couldn't risk bringing such danger back to Naxos.

As much as she wanted to run from Manto and whatever sacrilegious schemes they were involved in, they had saved her from almost certain death. Perhaps these Children of Prometheus could help her too.

There might be hope of a cure after all.

Danae was jolted awake by Lithos barking. The fire had died to ash, but an orange light shone through the passageway. She became aware of other noises outside, crashing and screaming. The air smelt acrid and bitter. Above them, the ground rumbled, and clumps of earth fell from the ceiling.

'Out, everybody out!' Manto was already on their feet, bag slung over their shoulder. They turned to Danae. 'Come on.'

Manto and Danae joined the crush of people piling through the passageway. Danae nearly fell as the earthen walls shook with the force of another collision. Once free of the tunnel, they ran across the arena, stones rolling into their path from the crumbling seats above. They ducked through an entrance and, once clear of the gymnasium, Danae's legs stopped moving.

Billows of black smoke boiled up from the burning city. A light appeared in the sky, a streak of fire searing through the darkness to explode into the buildings below. Then came another and another.

'Lithos! Lithos!' Manto cast around frantically.

They were answered by a gruff bark, and the dog pelted towards them. Manto gathered him in their arms and stared up at the sky.

'He's here.' Their voice shook like the rocks at their feet.

As Danae looked up, she realized there was something at the centre of the roiling clouds. A dark shape formed of more than smoke. Then the wind blew, and for a moment the tendrils parted. He was so far away, she only caught a glimpse of wings and gold before the blackened sky swallowed him again, but it was enough. He looked just like his counterpart standing guard over his temple.

Dread seeped through her. Apollo.

As she stood, petrified, another fireball crackled into being from where the clouds shrouded the god. It hurtled towards them and crashed into the roof of one of the brothel buildings. A moment later, a man staggered from the doorway, screaming as the flames melted his skin like wax.

'Hetaria!' Manto's glassy eyes reflected the fire spreading from one wooden structure to another. In moments the entire row was blazing. There was no way anyone inside had survived.

The screams were terrible. Liquid terror coursed through Danae's veins. She felt like she could do nothing but stand there and watch the city burn.

'This can't be because of me . . . it can't . . . it . . .'

'Come on.' Manto hoisted Lithos under one arm and grabbed Danae's hand with the other. 'I swore I'd protect you and I'm not going back on my word.'

They ran past the smouldering brothel houses just as another blast hit the gymnasium. It collapsed in on itself, belching a cloud of dust into the fiery air.

The streets were thick with people fleeing their homes. Some were weighed down by piles of belongings, others hadn't even put on their sandals. The air was so dense with smoke, Danae could barely breathe. Manto pulled her through the burning streets, both of them tripping and skidding over a sea of lost belongings and broken pottery. Half blind and head pounding from the smog, Danae clutched Manto's hand like it was a lifeline.

Eventually, they hurtled out onto the sacred way. The stone buildings that a day ago had looked so grand and pristine were blackened and crumbling. A plethora of burnt body parts protruded from the rubble. Those that could still run were fleeing the city. Pilgrims, priestesses, guards and citizens alike, all flocked to the gates. Danae and Manto were carried forward by the crush of people, out of the city onto the road at the base of Mount Parnassus. Here the crowd forked, some hurrying left around the base of the mountain towards Athens, others running in the opposite direction.

'What's that way?' Danae shouted, pointing right.

'Port of Cirrha.'

She looked back at the sprawl of burning buildings on the mountainside. The flames ignited an anger deep inside her that had grown with every misfortune, every struggle unaided, every prayer unanswered. The gods didn't care about mortals at all. Her family were good people, and the Twelve had done nothing while they were beaten into the ground by pious cruelty. Where were the gods when the villagers shunned them, when Arius was taken, when Alea drowned herself?

And now Apollo would raze an entire city just to eradicate one person.

As she watched Delphi burn, the wall of adamant that stood between her and the prophecy crumbled away. Manto was not the only one who believed Prometheus' words were about her. The gods did too.

She was the last daughter.

17. Flight

As Danae stared at the burning city, the flames licked away the last of her resistance, leaving the truth gleaming like bones on a funeral pyre. The power that had awoken in her the day she found Alea's body was no curse. It was fate. Her future was tied to Prometheus' prophecy. And with that rush of realization, a voice spoke. It was inside her and yet not hers. It came from the part of her that knew things she did not yet understand.

This is only the beginning. You cannot hide from your destiny.

A thrill rippled through her body. She let it take her, and for a heartbeat she flew above her fear. She felt as though she was dissolving, while at the same time becoming part of something larger that she couldn't quite comprehend.

Then the reality of their situation came flooding back. Manto's network of Children of Prometheus members in Delphi had been destroyed. They had said it themselves: the rest of the organization guarded their anonymity. There was no one left they knew who could help her.

No mortal.

She turned back to Manto. 'Is it true that Prometheus is chained to the highest peak of the Caucasus Mountains at the end of the world?'

They nodded. 'That's what my father said.'

Danae drew a deep breath. 'He made the prophecy, and I think he might be the only one who can help me fulfil it.' She looked down the right fork of the road. 'You say that way leads to a port?'

Manto nodded.

'Then let's find ourselves a boat.'

It didn't take Danae and Manto long to reach Cirrha. The town was a small cluster of low stone buildings, built on a protruding leg of Mount Parnassus. After the last row of houses the cliff fell away to a sheer drop below. The port itself was only accessible by deep, wide steps carved into the rockface.

Woken by the commotion, the inhabitants of Cirrha emerged from their homes to see a flood of people pouring through their little town. Most ran back inside and bolted their doors. Those who stayed to stare at the burning sky were absorbed by the throng and dragged with it.

Danae heard the screams before they reached the cliff. People were spilling into the ocean as the crush of bodies forced too many onto the steps. Manto tucked Lithos under one arm and grabbed her hand.

'Whatever happens, don't let go.'

She nodded. Then a dash of crimson darted across her vision. She scoured the crowd ahead and spotted the red dress of a priestess. The woman's veil and headdress were gone, her dark hair pulled loose. Something about the tilt of her head made the tendons in Danae's neck clench. As though the priestess could feel her gaze, she turned.

It was the woman who'd interrogated her with snake venom.

The priestess's eyes met hers and ignited with recognition. The woman dived against the current, fighting her way towards Danae. She tried to turn back, but was penned in by the tightly packed bodies.

'Manto,' she shouted, 'the priestess!'

Just as the woman's fingers stretched close enough to

touch her, they all reached the top of the steps. Manto lunged at the priestess but was shoved to the side by the crowd, and Danae's hand was wrenched from theirs. With a grunt of triumph, the woman latched onto the fabric of Danae's dress. She tried to prise her off, but her grip was hard as iron.

'You did this,' she snarled and yanked Danae towards her, then faltered as her heel slipped over the lip of the first step. She fell, dragging Danae with her, and they both tumbled across the steps below.

Danae heard Manto call her name as she was trampled under a stampede of feet. Through the rush of legs, she saw the priestess crawling towards her. Then Manto dropped Lithos and hurled themselves through the mass of bodies towards the woman. The priestess let out a guttural roar as their knife sank into her thigh. She grabbed Manto by the hair and dragged them towards the edge of the steps, knocking several people, screaming, into the sea.

'No!' Danae yelled, fighting her way towards them.

Manto disappeared over the edge. Then Lithos was at the priestess's neck, a wild mass of teeth and claws. The woman thrust her arms up to protect her face and lost her balance. She teetered for a moment, then Lithos' attack tipped her back and she fell, still fighting with the fierce little dog as she tumbled towards the rocks below.

Danae crawled to the edge of the step and there, clinging by one hand, was Manto, their other clamped around Lithos' tail.

Lightheaded with relief, she grasped their arm and pulled them both up. Manto bundled Lithos into their arms, and together they all crawled through the crush of people towards the inner wall, flattening themselves against the rock while bodies battered past.

'Are you all right?' rasped Danae.

'I'm alive.' Manto managed a smile.

'Thanks to Lithos.'

In response the little dog proceeded to lick the grime from Manto's face. They squeezed him tight then turned to Danae.

'Come on.'

The pink of dawn cracked through the burnt crust of night as Danae and Manto reached the bottom of the steps and ran towards the port. Several ships, laden with fleeing pilgrims, had already left their moorings. The pair joined a clamouring group trying to board a merchant vessel. The ship's captain stood in front of the gangplank, physically restraining people from climbing aboard.

Manto elbowed their way to the front. 'We're seers! Let us through.'

The captain's head twitched in their direction. Then the crowd surged, almost toppling the man into the sea. He clung onto the mooring post and unsheathed a long knife, sweeping the blade through the air like a sickle.

'If anyone shoves me again, no one boards my ship!'

The first clutch of people backed into the row behind, chattering with desperation.

'Who said they were a seer?' the captain called over the racket.

'Us!' Manto pulled Danae through the throng, Lithos tucked under their arm.

The captain's brow creased as he took in their filthy faces, tattered black robes and the ragged dog.

Manto drew themselves up to their full height. 'The Twelve see you and know you. I am the Seer Melampus of Mycenae. This is my apprentice, Daeira.' The lies rolled effortlessly off their tongue. 'We were in Delphi on the orders of King Eurystheus. I guarantee our master will reward you generously for our safe passage home.'

'All right,' said the captain. 'You two can go aboard, but the mutt stays here.'

Manto's eyes flashed. 'How dare you. This creature is sacred to Apollo.'

If it weren't for the severity of their situation, Danae would have laughed.

The captain's eyes narrowed. 'It's only got one eye.'

'So do the fates.'

Danae could hear the blood thumping around her skull as the captain appraised Lithos. As though playing his part, the dog lifted his head and gave an imperious bark.

'Hm.' The captain pressed his lips together. 'Go on, then.'

He moved aside to let them hurry up the gangplank, leaving cries of outrage in their wake.

The ship was so crowded, people were packed like sardines onto the platforms at either end. There was barely an inch of wood that wasn't filled with soot-covered refugees. Behind them, Danae could hear the captain shouting that there was no more room.

'Dion!' the captain called to the helmsman as he hurried up the gangplank. 'Get us out of this gods-forsaken place.'

As he jumped down between the rowing benches, two crew members hauled in the plank. There were screams from those who'd climbed on after him, as they tumbled into the sea.

Once they were both ensconced on the stern deck, Manto turned to Danae. 'End of the world is it then?' They smoothed Lithos' fur as he curled up between their legs.

'You don't have to come with me.'

Manto snorted. 'You're not getting rid of me that easily. I made a promise to help you fulfil your destiny. And after seeing how clueless you are, I don't like your chances of reaching the Caucasus Mountains without me.'

Danae offered them a tired smile.

'You know,' an idea glowed on their face. 'To reach Prometheus we'll have to cross the Black Sea.'

'Yes?'

'That's where my father is.'

'I thought your father was killed?'

'No, he was exiled somewhere along the coast of the Black Sea. If we can find him, I know he could help us.'

Hope sprouted wings in Danae's chest. For the first time, light chinked through the cloud of terror that had clung to her since the oracle's vision. There was someone out there who understood what was happening to her. She might have to travel to the end of the world, but she would find answers. And she didn't have to do it alone.

She curled her hands into fists. One day, when all this was over, she would see Naxos again.

PART TWO

18. Birds of Prey

The rising sun glowed on the passengers' ashen cheeks as they stared at the chaos they'd left behind. The Port of Cirrha writhed with people screaming for ships to carry them away from the burning city. Danae was grateful she could no longer see their faces. The wreckage of Delphi was hidden behind Mount Parnassus, but the sky still blazed with raging flames, and thick clouds of smoke billowed into the dawn.

She forced herself to look away from the devastated mainland. The tension in her shoulders eased as she glanced around the ship. Nowhere could she see the red robe of a priestess of Apollo or the maroon cloak of a guard. Besides that, it was difficult to gauge anyone's status under the layers of torn, ash-blackened clothing. All of them, high and lowborn alike, were crammed onto the same vessel, fleeing the wrath of the Sun God.

With each length of the ship the rowers put between them and Cirrha, Danae's lungs expanded. She had escaped. She was free.

From what she'd gathered listening to a conversation between the captain and the helmsman, not all the crew had made it aboard. Only five men were spread across the six rowing benches.

The captain clambered between the oarsmen and made his way to the prow of the ship. He squeezed himself up on the platform, so all could see him, and cupped his hand around his mouth.

'Listen, everyone! My name is Erastus and I'm the captain

of this ship. We don't usually ferry pilgrims, so you're all lucky to be on board. Do not – I repeat – do not touch any of my stock.' He wiped his brow. 'Look, it's been a terrible night for us all. If there are any men able to row, make yourself known to Dion.' He pointed at the wiry helmsman stationed at the steering oar. 'If we're granted a fair westerly wind, we will arrive at Corinth in around two hours. From there you make your own way.'

His announcement made, he jumped down to the middeck and hurried along the benches to speak in a hushed voice to Dion.

Danae turned to Manto. 'Have you got any money in that bag?'

Manto frowned, stuck their arm in and foraged around. 'I think there's a few obols in here . . .' They paused, their brow wrinkling. They glanced around the platform then pulled out something palm-sized, wrapped in a scrap of brown cloth. Carefully, they lay the object flat on their hand and unwrapped it.

It was a piece of obsidian rock. The sunlight glinted off its sharp edges. Through the haze of her memory, Danae pictured the oracle's chamber and something black and gleaming, lying just beneath the cracked lips of stone.

'What is it?' she whispered.

'It's a prophecy stone.' Manto quickly wrapped it back in its cloth. 'My father used to divine from it. I've been waiting to give it to you.'

'It can tell the future?' Danae stared at it as Manto carefully pressed it into her hand. 'Have you ever divined from it?'

'No,' Manto said quickly. 'My father told me never to touch it with my bare skin, only keep it safe and give it to the last daughter.'

As Danae's fingers closed around the stone, she felt a tingling sensation through the wrapping. 'How do I use it?'

A smile tweaked Manto's lips. 'By doing exactly what my father told me not to.'

Danae began to peel back the cloth.

'Not here.' Their hands closed around hers. They looked around again and took back the stone, careful to keep it covered. 'Why don't I keep it safe for now.' Manto slipped the stone back into their bag.

'Haven't you ever been tempted?'

There was a pause before Manto replied, 'I keep my promises.'

After that they both sat in silence for a while, the murmurs of the other passengers and the crash of the sea wrapping around their thoughts.

'What's your father like?' Danae asked.

Manto smiled. 'He's . . . eccentric. I think you'd like him. He doesn't care much for society's rules. He believes that foresight should be for everyone, not just those who can afford it.'

'What happened to him?'

Manto sighed and looked up at the sky. 'When I was young, we used to travel around Greece. My father would trade a prophecy for a bed and a hot meal. One day he saw a vision in the stone and said we had to go to Delphi, and that he was to become the watcher and wait for the last daughter. He thought he could keep on telling the future in the holy city, but the priestesses . . .' an edge crept into Manto's voice, 'they didn't like someone giving away what they charged for. Eventually they came for him.'

'I'm sorry.'

'Don't be.' Manto looked at her with fire in their eyes. 'We're going to tear down the whole fucking pantheon.'

*

Lithos was growling. Danae sat up and rubbed her face. The warmth of the sun had lulled her into a stupor.

'What is it, boy?' Manto stroked the dog's back, but his teeth remained bared, his hackles raised.

Nothing seemed untoward as Danae glanced across the ship, then back at Manto, who shrugged. All around them was calm, empty ocean. She tilted her head to the sky, shading her eyes against the glare.

Three specks of black blotted the sun. For a moment she thought they were gulls, but as she watched, the shapes grew larger. They appeared to be heading for the boat.

Then a woman shouted.

Next to her, Manto was already standing, Lithos barking beside them. The men stopped rowing. Passengers and crew stumbled to their feet, staring at the dark shapes heading towards them.

Danae's heartbeat slowed then rapidly sped up again. They were too large to be birds, larger even than eagles, and their shape was all wrong.

The ship had become eerily quiet. She looked around for the captain and saw his jaw fall slack. Then people began to scream. As quickly as the fire had ravaged Delphi, panic spread through the boat. Some passengers threw themselves into the water, others fell to their knees, muttering desperate prayers to Poseidon, God of the Sea.

The creatures were nearly upon them. Up close, they were the stuff of nightmares.

Vast leathery wings spread from their lithe, scaly bodies, and their long, muscular legs curved into taloned feet. There was something eerily human about their snarling faces, matted hair and the breasts that sagged from their chests. But their keening shrieks were the cries of predators closing in for the kill.

Manto grabbed hold of Danae's arm, their nails digging into her skin.

'Harpies.'

The three hounds of Zeus. His personal weapons of vengeance.

Icy terror sluiced through her, and for a heartbeat she saw her own fear reflected back in her friend's eyes. Then it faded, to be replaced by a calm deeper than the ocean that held them. They took hold of Danae's shoulders and pressed their forehead against hers.

'I know you're scared, but you must believe me, you are the last daughter. You are the hope of mankind. Find Prometheus and take down the whole lot of those Olympian bastards.' They drew back and squeezed her arms. 'If you see my father, tell him the watcher kept their promise.'

Before Danae could reply, Manto pushed her over the side of the ship.

Unprepared for the fall, she hit the water chest first. She floated for a moment, dazed and breathless, blinded by the salt. Then she twisted onto her back, gasping, unable to fill her stinging lungs.

Somewhere above, she heard Lithos barking and Manto shouting, 'Tell your master, the end has begun. I am the reckoning!'

Danae blinked frantically, trying to clear her vision. The creatures loomed over the boat like engorged bats, their wings shrouding what was happening from sight. All she could see were glimpses of flailing limbs and slashing claws.

She knew then what Manto had done for her. They were both of a similar age and appearance, especially now Danae's hair was cut short and they wore matching seer's robes. The harpies would think they had got what they came for. Her instinct was to swim back to her friend, but even if she tried to climb back up to the deck, she would never reach them in time. And Manto's sacrifice would be for nothing. Fighting every urge to cry out and return to the ship, she lay still, floating like a dead thing in the water.

The sounds from above chilled her to the core, screams mingling with unearthly shrieks and the ripping of flesh. Then, just as swiftly as they'd appeared, the harpies rose into the air and flew off towards Cirrha.

Spluttering, her mouth full of seawater, she struck out towards the ship. Her nails scraped the underside of the boat as she attempted to climb back on, but her fingers kept sliding down the greased hull. She looked up as red blossomed into the water around her. Streams of blood were dribbling down the side of the ship.

Frantically scouring the hull, she caught sight of a ladder of pegs bolted into the bow. She swam towards them, her limbs shaking as she clambered up and dragged herself over the side.

The deck was carnage. The blood seemed endless, still pumping from freshly dismembered bodies. Captain Erastus lay next to her feet, his steaming guts spilled between the benches. Then she heard Lithos whimpering and forced her legs to move over the collection of broken limbs. It didn't take her long to find Manto. They were crumpled where they'd been standing, their chest a gory mess of flesh and bone, the little dog beside them, his fur flecked with blood. She fell to her knees, the water from her sodden tunic muddling into the wine-dark deck.

The harpies had ripped out their heart.

'Manto . . .' Tears burnt rivets down her salt-crusted cheeks. 'I'll tell your father. I promise.' She pulled Manto's body into hers, rocking them as sobs shuddered through her.

She felt as though she was looking down on the ship from

above. Everything was smaller, as if the boat was just a toy bobbing on the surface of a pool. She could see herself, a little figurine on the deck. She knew she had to go on, but there was pain down there, so much pain. Up here, there was only endless sky. She could just float away and never look back.

You do not run, you fight, said the voice.

She returned to her body with a jolt. A surge of nausea clenched her stomach as she looked down at Manto. The weight of their sacrifice was crushing. She didn't know how she would be able to bear it.

She didn't have a choice.

'They will pay. I will make them pay,' she whispered to Manto's corpse.

Danae carefully wrapped Manto's body in the fabric of their robe. The contents of Manto's bag had remained secure, and after removing it from them, she fished two obols from its depths and tucked them into the blood-soaked folds. The coins should have been placed on Manto's eyes, but she wanted to make sure they weren't lost, or Manto's soul would have nothing to pay the ferryman and be left stranded on the banks of the Underworld.

While she worked, those who'd survived the attack by jumping in the water clambered back on board. There weren't many of them. Only two of the crew remained. Dion, the helmsman, and an oarsman whose left arm had been clawed through to the bone.

The colour drained from the helmsman's face as he took in the disembowelled captain and realized that, by default, he was now in charge.

'Right . . .' He looked at the blood-slicked deck and scattered body parts. 'I need everyone who's able to wrap the dead.'

A young mother, her child's face buried in her skirts, cried out, 'What if they come back?'

They won't come back, Danae thought. *They think they got what they came for.*

'I hear you,' said Dion. 'But we can't row with –'

'We're an open target out here!' shouted a merchant who'd been the first to throw himself overboard.

The child began to wail.

'Poseidon, why have you forsaken us?' His mother sank to her knees, clutching her sobbing son to her chest.

'We can't leave them like thi– stop!' Dion lunged towards the merchant, who'd grasped an oar and was frantically rowing, sending the boat in a futile curve. As he struggled with the man, the helmsman began to breathe heavily. He backed away from the flailing merchant and sank down onto a rowing bench, clutching his chest and looking thoroughly overwhelmed.

Danae glanced up from Manto's body. The boat had descended into chaos. Something had to be done.

She rose to her feet and shouted, in what she hoped was an authoritative voice, 'Be quiet, all of you!'

Silence fell. Even the child's crying reduced to a whimper.

'Who are you?' the merchant asked, taking in her black dress and short hair.

'She's a seer,' breathed Dion as he pushed himself off the bench.

Now she had their attention, what in Tartarus was she going to say? Like the seer in Athens had done, she tilted her face towards the sky and rolled her eyes back. The line of blasphemy was so far behind her it was no longer visible. But if the gods already wanted her dead, what harm would a little false divination do?

A single cloud floated across the sun, sparing the boat

from its glare for a brief moment. She raised her hand and pointed.

'It is a sign! The gods' rage has been sated and we have all been spared by our virtue. But we must honour Poseidon and give the dead to the sea.'

A tense pause stretched across the ship, then the young mother shouted, 'Praise the Lord of the Ocean, praise him!'

While Danae was speaking, the child had spotted Lithos. He detached himself from his mother and walked across the deck to tentatively pat the dog's ears. In return Lithos licked his hand. The child smiled.

Danae's eyes met Dion's, and the helmsman inclined his head, then took back command.

'There's a canopy stowed under the helm platform and spare sail tarp, we can use that.'

Wrapping the bodies was stomach-churning work. Loose guts slipped through their fingers like eels, and the stench grew increasingly pungent in the heat. When their task was finally complete, they stood back, breathing heavily, arms and clothing drenched in blood.

'Will you say the rights?' Dion asked.

As the helmsman, the merchant and the other two women began to heave the wrapped bodies over the side of the ship, Danae cleared her throat. She'd heard the words so many times but had never been the one to say them.

She raised her middle finger to her forehead. 'May the Twelve see you and know you, may the Keres spread their wings over you as you walk the path of judgement. May your souls find peace across the final river.'

'Go with the blessing of the Twelve,' murmured the others.

Danae felt a lump settle at the back of her throat as she watched Manto's body bob away on the glinting waves.

Her vision blurred. She never got to see Alea buried. She

should have been there, should have helped her mother wash and anoint her sister's body, should be mourning with her family.

While the others observed a moment of stillness, soundless tears tumbled down her face.

After the silence, Dion climbed up onto the stern platform. The heat was stifling now, with no wind to offer a breath of relief. He considered the unfurled sail and sighed, then pointed to the merchant.

'You take the top right bench. And you the middle right.' He placed the injured oarsman behind the merchant, then sat himself on the top left bench.

'I can't row,' said the wounded man through gritted teeth.

'You've got one good arm, haven't you? Use that.'

The man glared at Dion's back, then sank onto his designated bench.

The helmsman turned to Danae and the other two women. 'I'm sorry to ask, but we'll never get to shore, just the three of us.'

'We can row,' Danae said quickly. The other women nodded.

Dion gestured for the mother to share a bench with the injured man, and Danae and the blue-cloaked woman took the bench opposite. The child sat against the stern deck, Lithos curled in his lap.

They grasped the oars, and Dion called, 'Follow my count, one, two, one, two . . .'

Danae's palms ached. She could already feel blisters forming. There was nothing to look at, nothing to distract her from the pain of rowing, except the sparkling blue on blue horizon.

She glanced at her companion. The woman's face was

obscured by her hood, her pale fingers decked with rings. One, on the fourth finger of her left hand, was dazzling. It held the largest sapphire Danae had ever seen, set in a bed of diamonds. The woman winced every time they pulled their oar.

'It will hurt less if you take them off.'

The woman looked at her, and Danae caught a glimpse of her rowing mate's face. There was something familiar about the shape of her jaw and tilt of her nose. The woman seemed skittish and avoided making eye contact. Danae couldn't blame her after what they'd just been through.

'I can row alone for a moment.'

The woman nodded and Danae took over as she slipped her rings into her cloak pocket. 'Thank you,' she said as she clutched her section of oar again.

If the jewels weren't enough, her accent confirmed it. This woman was nobility.

From behind her blue hood, their eyes finally met, and Danae's mind sparked with recognition. It must have been written on her face, because the woman muttered, 'Please, I don't want anyone to know who I am.'

Danae was suddenly cold despite the heat and exertion of rowing. Out of all the people in Delphi, she had ended up on a bench with the Queen of Athens.

'I won't say anything.' She hoped she was unrecognizable from the last time Phaedra had seen her in her novice's disguise.

'Thank you.' The queen's words were stilted by the effort of rowing.

A few more strokes of the oar fell between them.

Danae stole another glance at the queen. She was so like her sister. From what Ariadne had told her back on Naxos, she wondered if Phaedra even knew her sister was still alive.

She bit her lip. She knew it was risky, but she had to say something. She wouldn't be able to live with herself if she didn't.

'I've met your sister, Ariadne.'

Phaedra's hands jerked from the oar, sending their shaft bashing into the man in front.

'Middle left!' Dion shouted. 'Keep rhythm!'

Fumbling with sweat-slicked hands, Danae and Phaedra regained control of their oar.

'You are mistaken.' The queen's voice was all edges. 'My sister died a long time ago.'

'I promise you, Ariadne is alive and well on Naxos. She lives with a collective of women, the Maenads. She's happy.'

Phaedra was silent. Danae looked across and saw the front of the queen's cloak was stained with tears.

'Theseus told me she was dead. All those wasted years.'

'You still have time.'

Phaedra shook her head. 'There are some things you cannot come back from.'

'I know only one, death.'

The words came with a sharpness Danae hadn't intended. Phaedra's head snapped towards her. She bit the inside of her cheeks, but she couldn't stop her thoughts from tumbling out.

'I would give anything, everything, to see my sister again. But she's in the Underworld, and I will have to wait a lifetime. You could go to Ariadne now and live with her for the rest of your days. Don't waste the time you have left.'

They continued to manipulate the oar in silence, their laboured breathing the only sound between them.

'I'm sorry,' Phaedra said eventually. 'About your sister.'

Danae didn't trust herself to speak. She returned to gazing at the gleaming shards of sunlight skipping across the water.

She wondered how long it would take her to reach the end of the world. Guilt twisted her stomach. She'd made a promise to Manto, yet without them she had little hope of finding their father. She didn't even know his name. And ever constant, the words of the prophecy lay heavy in her heart.

Prometheus was her only hope.

19. New Beginnings

'Land ahead!'

There were sighs of relief from the rowers. Despite hours of aching limbs and raw palms, they redoubled their efforts. Danae stared at the green-flecked hills of Corinth materializing on the horizon. She'd never been so happy to see land.

The port of Corinth was a similar size to the one at Cirrha. Rows of bobbing merchant ships, like their own, crowded the edges of the single jetty. Dion bounded from his bench, calling for them to withdraw their oars, then carefully steered them into an empty sliver of water. As Danae helped Phaedra haul in their oar, she noticed the handle was smeared with blood. She winced as she uncurled her fingers and looked down at her cracked palms.

Dion leapt onto the jetty. He called to the merchant to toss him the rope and set about tethering the ship to the mooring pillar. Once the plank was lowered and the rest of the passengers were on land, they gathered around Dion like sheep.

'Well then . . .' The helmsman rubbed his head. 'I'm going to find the harbour master and tell him what's happened.' He looked at the wounded man, who'd turned a worrying shade of green. 'You'd better come with me and find a healer.' He backed away from the rest of the group. 'The rest of you can make your own way. Ah . . . I'm sure the port officials will help you get home.'

Fat chance of that, thought Danae.

'Dion,' she called after the helmsman.

He looked around.

'Thank you.'

He cleared his throat and nodded before walking on. The others glanced between her and the helmsman, then traipsed off after Dion. Only the boy lingered, looking back at Lithos as his mother pulled him away.

'Go on,' said Danae.

The little dog barked, then ran after the boy, his white-tipped tail wagging.

She looked past the white-stone buildings of the harbour to the town beyond. Her hand tightened on the strap of Manto's bag as she wondered what she should do next. Then she realized Phaedra was still standing beside her.

'What's Naxos like?' The queen was staring out across the sea.

'It's the most beautiful place in the world.'

'Is it your home?'

'No,' Danae said quickly. 'Just a place I visited once.'

Phaedra smiled. 'I don't think I'll be going back to Athens after all.' She looked expectantly at Danae. 'We could travel together. I don't have any coin, but I think I have enough jewellery to buy our passage.'

Danae's heart felt heavy. She desperately wanted to say yes, to sail back to Naxos and see her family. But she knew she couldn't go home.

'I can't. There's somewhere else I must go.'

One day, when she was certain the wrath of the gods would not follow her, she would walk the dusty path to her hut again.

Phaedra nodded and slipped her hand into her cloak pocket. She pressed something into Danae's palm. It was the sapphire ring.

'I . . . I can't take this.'

'If you don't, I'll throw it in the ocean. I don't need it any more.'

The two women stared at each other. Danae's resolve broke first and she reluctantly took the ring.

'Thank you.'

Phaedra smiled. 'It is nothing compared to the gift you've given me. Goodbye . . . ?'

After a beat she said, 'Daeira.'

'Goodbye, Daeira. May the Twelve ever watch over you.'

Danae watched the Queen of Athens walk away down the jetty. Phaedra wouldn't know it, but her parting words left a chill in the air. She looked towards the ocean one last time, slipped Phaedra's ring into her bag, then set off towards the town.

Manto had done their best to convince the Twelve that she was dead. That would hopefully buy her some time. Her seer's disguise was a good one, but she was currently caked in grime, sweat and blood. If she was going to talk her way aboard a ship sailing for the Black Sea, first she would need a bath.

Corinth was a town somewhere in size between that of Delphi and Danae's village on Naxos. The official port buildings soon gave way to humbler stone dwellings. Women, their hair bound up in scarves, swept their porches while children played petteia in the middle of the street. Despite being a direct sailing route to and from Delphi, the people of Corinth seemed to exist at a more relaxed pace than in the larger cities. Danae was relieved. Her body trembled from days of running and fearing for her life. She knew there was a chance the harpies could realize their mistake and come back for her, but she needed a moment to gather herself or she would collapse.

She paused to watch a potter sculpt a clay bowl outside his stall. Deep red vases and amphorae detailed with black and white paint were stacked to the side of him, many adorned with likenesses of Heracles and his heroic deeds. On some he was fighting the many-headed hydra, on others he was felling the Erymanthian boar, and on a row of vases at the front, he was wrestling the Nemean lion. The great beast roared as the hero squeezed its neck between his massive arms. In this last image, Heracles wore nothing but a small kilt.

'Five obols for those.' The potter winked, after muttering the sacred greeting. 'That design is very popular with the ladies.'

'Oh.' Danae swiftly returned the gesture and shook her head. 'I'm not buying. I'm actually looking for a bathhouse. Do you know if there's one nearby?'

It felt strange now, touching her forehead with her middle finger.

The potter looked disappointed but inclined his head down the road. She hurried off and was relieved when she turned the corner and saw a dolphin mosaic set into the stone above a curved doorway. She ducked through the entrance and found herself in a large vestibule, women passing through a doorway to her right and men through an identical one to the left. A sturdy oak table was positioned against the far side and a bored-looking man was slumped behind it. She stank of dried blood and sweat, but thankfully her black dress hid the worst of the stains.

You're a seer, she told herself. *Act like it.*

Steeling herself, she held her head high and marched up to the desk, then said the sacred greeting.

The proprietor's eyebrows crept up his forehead as he took her in.

'A private room or the communal baths?'

'Private room.'

'Scented oils?'

'Yes.'

The proprietor smiled obsequiously. 'Good choice.'

Danae shoved her hand into Manto's bag and rooted around for coins. She placed two obols on the desk.

There was a pause.

'And the rest?'

Her brow creased. She had no idea how much a bathhouse cost, having only ever washed in the river back home.

'The price is one drachma.'

One drachma for a bath! That much coin could have fed her whole family for a month.

'What if I don't have the scented oils?'

The man pursed his lips. 'Four obols. *Two* will buy you half an hour in the women's communal baths.'

She'd been planning on washing her robe and inspecting the prophecy stone. She could do neither in a communal bath.

'Wait.' She delved back into the bag to see if there were any more coins she'd missed on her first sweep. Her fingers brushed Phaedra's ring. She hesitated, imagining it was worth far more than one drachma, but having no other way to pay, dropped it on the desk between them.

The proprietor's mouth fell open. He looked at Danae, then the ring, back at Danae, then the ring again. He picked it up like it would shatter at any moment and turned it slowly between his fingers.

'Beautiful,' he breathed.

'One hour, private room, scented oils. I will not be disturbed. And my change, of course.'

The man cleared his throat. 'Of course.'

He opened a chest on the table to his right, drew out a purse of coins and placed it in front of Danae.

She pulled the purse towards her. It was heavy. She peered in and had to stop herself screaming at the sight of around fifteen gold drachmas. More money than her father made in a whole year. More than her life had been worth at the flesh market. She fought to keep her face calm as she stowed the purse away in her bag.

The proprietor snapped his fingers, and a slave girl with mousy hair and pale, freckled skin hurried over to them.

'Take our esteemed guest here to our best room.'

The girl bowed and headed off down the right-hand passage. Danae followed her, the weight of the coins bashing opulently against her thigh.

They headed through the main walkway towards the women's communal baths, then veered off down another corridor. A mosaic of blues in every hue swirled in the pattern of waves along the wall. Their footsteps echoed around the quiet passage, joined by the occasional tinkle of laughter and ripple of voices from other private rooms.

At the far end, the girl led Danae through a curtained archway into a room dominated by a large pool sunk into the floor. Light poured in from three small windows carved into the thick stone just below the ceiling, illuminating the murals of dancing sea nymphs painted on the walls. A stone bench jutted from the right-hand side. On it were rows of glass bottles filled with different shades of amber liquid.

Danae twitched as the girl stepped towards her. She backed away.

'May I help you undress?'

'No,' she said quickly. 'I can do it myself.'

The girl's face betrayed a flicker of surprise. 'As you wish.'

Danae eased off her sandals, watching the girl walk around the pool to the collection of bottles.

'Which oil would you like?'

Danae hesitated. She didn't know what any of them were.

'We have laurel, marjoram, iris, cardamom, sandalwood –'

'The last one.'

She had no idea what it smelt like, but anything would be an improvement on her current scent. Slowly, she placed her bag on the floor while the girl poured an oil, the colour of the sun, into the water.

Then the girl padded around the edge of the pool and held out her hands. 'I can wash your dress while you bathe?'

'No.' Danae wrapped her arms around her chest, acutely aware of how dirty and bloodstained her clothing was. She noticed, then, the scars that circled the girl's thin wrists.

'Here.' Danae opened her bag and drew out the purse of coins.

The girl backed away.

'I want to give you something.'

The girl shook her head. She looked scared. 'I'll get in trouble.'

'All right.' Reluctantly, Danae placed the purse back in her bag. 'I'd like privacy please.'

The girl bowed and stepped behind the curtain into the shadow of the passageway.

Danae shrugged off her dress. She dropped it in the bath, then waded into the water down stone steps carved into the side of the pool.

She gasped. It was warm, like the sea at the height of summer. She inhaled the spiced, steaming air as the oil coated her skin. Rubbing her face, she sighed as the tight crust of salt was washed away. Then she ran her hands through her short hair to dislodge the dirt. Its length still felt alien to her, but she had to admit it was much easier to wash.

A rust-coloured cloud seeped into the water around her dress. After cleaning herself she gathered it in her fists and scrubbed, wincing as the friction stung her raw hands. Once she'd washed out all the blood and dirt she could, she wrung out the fabric, then climbed out of the pool and draped it over the stone bench. Hopefully it would dry by the time she left. Dripping across the floor, she retrieved her bag, placed it on the side of the bath and slipped back in.

Carefully, she drew out the prophecy stone and placed it on the floor. She peeled back each side of the fabric wrapping until the obsidian shard lay naked, shining in the light of the bathhouse room. As she leaned closer, she thought she could hear whispers coming from inside the stone. She was afraid to touch it and yet she was compelled to. As her hand hovered over it, her fingertips began to ache.

The whispers grew louder. They were men's voices. Then she realized they weren't coming from the stone. The words 'Athens' and 'ring' carried down the corridor.

Danae leapt out of the water, hastily rewrapped the prophecy stone, shoved it back into her bag, then tugged on her wet dress. She slung her bag over her shoulder and grabbed her sandals with the other hand. There was no time to put them on.

She ducked through the curtain, almost colliding with the slave girl. They looked at each other for a moment, then the girl's eyes darted towards a narrow passage that led away from the entrance hall.

Danae ran until she reached the end of the corridor, skidding to a halt outside a small wooden door. As she opened it, steam billowed in her face. In the room beyond, vast iron tubs with fires lit beneath them were stationed at intervals along the floor and rows of folded laundry were stacked on shelves at either side. Red-faced women in stained aprons leaned over the vats, stirring the contents with large wooden sticks.

She hesitated for a moment, then darted forward, ignoring the women's cries as she sprinted out of the bathhouse.

She pelted through the streets, every few moments glancing behind her to make sure she wasn't being followed. Her wet dress clung uncomfortably to her body, restricting her movements. Then a flash of blue at the end of the street sent her pulse racing. Without waiting to find out if it was the cloak of an Athenian guard, she dived through the doorway of the nearest shop.

Spools of fabric were stacked along the walls in rainbows of silk, linen and wool. She paced to the back of the room and, keeping an eye on the door, pretended to examine a length of green cloth.

'May the Twelve see you and know you. A seer in my shop. Now that's not something that happens every day.'

Danae whirled around. An ancient woman was peering up at her through rheumy eyes.

'Oh, you're soaking wet.'

Danae glanced down at the puddle around her bare feet.

The old woman shook her head. 'I'll never understand you mystic types. Still, who am I to question those who speak to the gods.'

Danae was barely listening, tensing with each shadow that passed the door.

'Not even a cloak to keep you warm . . .' She tutted at the sandals in Danae's hand. 'Those look like you've run across half of Greece.'

'What did you say?'

The old woman shrank back. 'I'm sorry, I only meant –'

'A cloak.' That was exactly what she needed. A large, hooded cloak. 'Do you have one in black?'

The shopkeeper looked relieved. 'I'll have to check in the back.' She scurried under a drape at the rear of the shop.

After a few scrapes and bangs, the old woman re-emerged with a pair of long strapped leather sandals and a folded pile of fine black woollen fabric.

'Thought you might like these as well.'

She lay the sandals down and Danae slipped her feet between the woven leather. They fitted perfectly. As she bent down to tie up the straps she admired the fine craftsmanship, stitching so delicate you could barely see it, yet they felt much sturdier than her old sandals.

The shopkeeper unfurled the obsidian cloak and swung it over Danae's shoulders. She fastened the neck with a copper clasp.

'Come,' she grabbed Danae's hand and pulled her towards the front of the shop, where a large bronze mirror hung on the wall.

Danae glanced worriedly at the door, then stopped as she caught sight of herself.

She didn't recognize the woman in front of her. She'd only ever caught glimpses of her reflection in still rock pools. Her family and the village had effectively been her mirror. She looked so much older than the child she'd been on Naxos. Draped in the black folds of the cloak, she was every stitch a seer. Her breath fluttered in her chest. Her short hair drew out a whisper of Alea in her cheekbones. She was still the image of her father, but it was a comfort to know that she carried her sister in her bones.

'Well?' the shopkeeper asked.

'Yes.' Danae smiled. 'It will do.'

Her purse several coins lighter, Danae emerged onto the street, the hood of her cloak pulled over her face. She had to find Prometheus, but she had no idea which way the Black Sea was. What she needed was a map.

A bell tolled as she walked away from the shop. A step later, she flinched as the door slammed shut behind her. She looked back to see the old shopkeeper heave a wooden board over the window. By the time she turned back around, the street was deserted. Doors that had previously been open were bolted, and iron locks had been slid across the painted shutters. Her frown deepening, she walked back to the fabric shop and rapped on the door.

'Hello, what's happening?'

The shopkeeper did not answer.

Clutching her bag, she broke into a run and turned a corner to find herself in a large square lined with eateries. Despite the tantalizing smell of roasted meat filling the air, there was not a soul to be seen. The establishments had closed in such a hurry, the tables outside were still strewn with half-eaten plates.

A laugh rippled across the square. Danae's head snapped towards it.

Four people leant against the wall of a modest kapeleion, hidden in the shade of its tattered green awning. They all had cups of wine in their hands and did not seem in the least bit concerned that everyone else appeared to have fled. The tallest of the group was a man with ivory skin peppered with freckles and hair the colour of fire. To his left was an older man with sun-leathered cheeks and a slight build, and next to him was a youth who looked around Danae's age, with a broad, rosy face and ears that stuck out beyond his mop of chestnut curls.

But it was the fourth member of the group that held Danae's attention. A woman. The only females that frequented kapeleia on Naxos were women of the night, but this person looked more accustomed to providing pain than pleasure. Her ochre skin was laced with pearly scars, and she was dressed in battered silver armour that looked as though it had been beaten to follow the contours of her lean body. A bow and quiver of arrows were strapped across her chest, as well as at least three knives that Danae could see. Her companions were just as heavily armed.

Danae had barely taken two steps towards them, when a cry that sounded like the slaughter of a thousand lambs ruptured the air.

She backed away and flattened herself against the bricks of an eatery as something vast slithered out from a street on the far side of the square.

Danae's mouth stretched in a silent scream.

An obsidian, serpentine body wound across the stones. The creature had no legs, only long double-jointed arms ending in vicious talons that scraped along the ground as it dragged itself forward. Danae was violently reminded of the harpies at the sight of its bulbous head, which looked like a diabolical amalgam of a woman's and a snake's. Ropes of long matted hair hung past its undulating neck, and vertical eyelids blinked across yellow irises and black, slitted pupils. Its flat nostrils flared, and a mouth cut from cheek to cheek, peeled open to reveal two rows of fangs. The creature's sickly eyes roved across the square and settled on Danae.

It slid towards her with terrifying speed.

Then something leapt from the roof of a building to her right. All she could see was a mass of fur before the serpent-creature snarled in pain and twisted back on itself.

She gaped. A lion stood upon its tail.

No, not a lion, a man wearing the animal's hide.

He looked like a god, his golden-brown skin gleaming like the fur upon his back. He knelt astride the beast, his sword buried deep in its thrashing tail. He was dressed in nothing but a kilt, his powerful torso bare save for the lion hide draped over his shoulders, the animal's head crowning his own. Below it was a face Danae knew well, despite never having seen it in the flesh. An arrestingly handsome face that would have been a replica of his divine father's, were it not for the scar that sliced his cheek from his eyebrow to the bone of his strong jaw.

Heracles' ocean-blue eyes met hers, and Danae was sure her heart stopped beating. Then he wrenched his sword free of the monster's scales and swung it to meet the talons swiping towards him. The creature shrieked as the hero cleaved its fingers straight through the bone. An arc of blood painted a dark rainbow across the sky, then splattered onto the square along with the severed digits.

Incensed, the creature bared its fangs and lunged at him, milky venom dripping from its teeth. He leapt to meet it, lowering his head so his impenetrable lion hide collided with its mouth, while thrusting forward and burying his sword in its throat.

Teeth shattered; wine-dark blood sluiced from the creature's mouth as it thundered to the ground with a last rattling shriek.

Heracles jumped down from the trunk-thick body and wiped his sword against its scales as though he'd done little more than fell a tree for firewood.

Danae remained fused to the wall as he approached her, only moving when something prickled against her thigh. She glanced down. Heat was pulsing into her skin from something inside her bag.

The prophecy stone.

'Are you hurt?' The hero's voice was honey and thunder all at once. He stood before her, his cerulean eyes scanning her for injuries.

'N-no.'

A slight crease formed between his brows. His lips parted as though he would speak again, just as the woman outside the kapeleion shouted, 'What took you so long?'

Heracles' attention snapped to her. He grinned, his blue eyes sparkling as he strode towards the group.

'Thanks for the assistance, you lazy bastards. You'd better have at least got me a drink.'

The woman tossed an empty cup to the side and shrugged. 'I got thirsty waiting.'

The older man rolled his eyes.

The youngest held out his cup. 'You can have mine.'

The hero took the wine, just as the kapeleion door cracked open and the barkeeper peered through the gap. He beheld the monster lying in the square and cried, 'Heracles has slain the Lamia!'

'Here we go,' said the hero and downed the contents of his cup.

Wood creaked on its hinges, and faces emerged in doorways and windows. Tentatively at first, the people of Corinth crept from their homes. When they saw Heracles and the bloody carcass of the Lamia, the dam of fear erupted, and people flooded into the square, clustering around the hero like ants to an overripe fig.

'Now where is that boy . . .' The flame-haired man spied his prey and stalked over to a younger man – nobility by the looks of his clothing – loitering at the edge of the adoring crowd.

'Drinks for everyone on Polyphemus!' He clapped the lad on the back.

The gathered Corinthians cheered while the young noble scowled.

The flame-haired man laughed. 'That will teach you to bet against the greatest hero who ever lived.' He steered him towards the kapeleion. 'Come on, you wouldn't want to keep all these people waiting for a drink now, would you?'

Danae watched them go, her breath still raw and heavy. She slid her hand into her bag and curled her fingers around the prophecy stone. Even through its cloth wrapping she could feel it pulsing. Like a heartbeat.

Through the wonder and amazement and sheer blood-boiling terror, when she watched Heracles slay that beast she had felt a deeper truth, free of logic or reason. And the same voice that had awoken in her outside Delphi had spoken again, whispering one word.

Fate.

20. The Lion

As the daylight faded, the crowd finally dispersed and traipsed back to their homes. In the end it took ten men to drag the Lamia's corpse from the square. The stones were scrubbed, but the tinge of its dark blood remained, staining the slabs.

From conversations she'd overheard, Danae gathered the monster had emerged from a cave in the hills above Corinth a few months prior and would periodically venture down to the town to steal children and feast upon their flesh. The town's soldiers had proved no match for the Lamia, so resorted to keeping watch and sounding a warning bell whenever the creature was spotted. In their desperation, the people had sent word to Greece's greatest hero. And he had answered their call.

Heracles and his companions remained at the kapeleion to eat and drink their way through the rest of the young noble's purse. Danae lingered too, sitting at a table in the corner, within earshot of Heracles' group.

She didn't know what she was doing. She should have found a map, left Corinth and been on her way to the Black Sea by now. But she could not silence the echo of the voice that was hers and yet not hers.

Fate.

The hero was important to her quest. She just had to find out why.

Her hands nudged the cup of wine she'd been nursing for the last hour, as the barkeeper placed a candle on her table. He gave her a strange look but said nothing. A seer's coin was as good as any other. Her eldest brother, Calix, once told her barkeepers prided themselves on guarding the secrets of their patrons just as much as the quality of their wine.

She watched him move over to Heracles' table with another candle. The hero sat a good head taller than his companions, his eyes crinkling with amusement as the red-haired man talked animatedly. At the climax of the story, Heracles let out a laugh that echoed round the kapeleion, and the woman snorted out a poorly timed gulp of wine and pounded the table with her fist, while the younger man slapped her vigorously on the back. They'd all had a lot to drink.

It was strange to see the hero like this, sat amongst a group of ordinary people, sharing wine like he was one of them. She'd always imagined Heracles to be more god than mortal. A man of dignity and power, a miniature version of his father.

Zeus, the God of Thunder, the creator of mankind, the deity she was prophesied to destroy.

'It's a fool's errand,' said the flame-haired man loudly.

'I don't know,' said the older man. 'Apparently, this Jason has already gathered quite a following. They're calling themselves "the Argonauts", after the ship King Pelias has had specially commissioned.'

'Ridiculous name,' muttered the woman.

He ignored her. 'Apparently it's the fastest vessel ever made.'

'I don't care how bloody fast it is,' said the flame-haired man. 'Even if a strong headwind blew us all the way, it would take most of the year to get across the Black Sea. Colchis is at the end of the world. Let's go home to Mycenae.'

Danae sat up, straining to catch the next words.

'Mycenae isn't home,' said Heracles darkly.

'The last labour that bastard Eurystheus sent us on was a joke.' The woman drained her cup and slammed it down on the table. 'Stealing cattle? Who does he think we are, farm-hands?' Then she added quickly, 'No offence, Hylas.'

The young man shrugged. 'We did have to kill a giant first. And there's nothing wrong with being a farmhand.'

'That's the spirit.' The red-haired man slung an arm around Hylas' shoulders.

Danae had always assumed Heracles undertook his heroic deeds alone. But, she supposed, even a hero needed backup.

'I hear Ancaeus, the bearskin warrior, has already pledged himself to the Argonauts,' said the older man.

The woman laughed. 'Warrior, my arse. He probably skinned the first beast he found dead in the woods.'

'Let's settle this.' The flame-haired man looked to Heracles. 'We could either go on a needlessly lengthy quest for some mythical golden fleece or go back to Mycenae, where there are warm beds and women waiting for us?'

The hero stared into his cup.

'Well?' prompted the woman.

After a stretch of silence, Heracles looked up from his wine. 'I have no appetite for Mycenae or Eurystheus' demands. We join Jason and these Argonauts.'

The red-haired man sighed but made no attempt to argue.

Danae's mouth was dry. They were going to the end of the world. This was it, the feeling like eels in the pit of her stomach. The fates must have drawn her to Heracles for this reason. Now all she had to do was convince the hero to take her with them. She gulped down the last of her wine and rose to her feet, wiping her sweaty palms on her cloak.

'Heracles!' Someone called across the kapeleion.

Danae shrank back into her corner as a man came striding towards the hero's table. From his blue cloak and armour, she recognized him to be an Athenian guard. She pulled her hood down lower over her face.

The guard and Heracles evidently knew each other well. After exchanging the sacred greeting, the hero rose to grasp the man's hand and slap him on the back, the force of which nearly sent the guard crashing into the table.

'Leander, what in Tartarus brings you to Corinth?'

With a flick of his cloak, Leander sat at the table, forcing the older man to move along the bench. He leant in and lowered his voice. Danae was forced to lip-read to determine what he was saying.

'You've heard about Delphi?'

The others shook their heads.

Leander sucked in a breath. 'The entire city's been razed to the ground. Balls of flame fell from the sky.'

All merriment vanished from the listeners' faces.

'What?' Hylas' voice was barely a whisper.

'Who would dare invade the sacred city?' asked the older man.

Leander stretched out a dramatic pause. 'They're saying Apollo himself.'

'Impossible,' said the woman. 'Why would Apollo destroy his own city? His oracle?'

Leander shrugged. 'It's not for us to question the will of the gods.'

The silence was heavy. Danae felt nauseous as the smell of burning flesh came unbidden into her memory.

'Join us for a drink?' asked Heracles.

Leander shook his head. 'Can't, I'm on official business.' He looked around again and leant in even closer. 'Our queen's gone missing. She was in Delphi when it all happened, but we know she got out. Found her wedding ring in a bathhouse a few streets away from here.' He shook his head. 'Theseus will lose his mind, and I'll probably lose my head if I return to Athens without her. Don't suppose you've seen anything?'

Heracles shook his head. 'We're just passing through.'

Leander sighed. 'Well, I'd leave tonight if I were you. The city's going to be flooded with pilgrims before long. They'll have nowhere to go.' He pushed himself up from the bench. 'Right, I'd best be on my way.' He inclined his head, then left the kapeleion in a flare of blue.

'You heard him,' said the flame-haired man. 'Let's go before those bloody pilgrims get here.'

Danae watched them leave, rushed to the doorway and peered out into the square. After making sure the guard was nowhere to be seen, she slipped after them.

She followed Heracles and his companions to the outskirts of the town. The rich darkness of night had swept over Corinth by the time they stopped at a stable.

She crouched down behind a large juniper bush and watched the older man pay the stable owner while the others saddled up their mounts. At the turn of each new street, she'd told herself this would be the moment she would introduce herself, but everywhere the hero went, admirers were drawn to him. This was her last chance. Once they were on horseback, she would never be able to keep up with them.

She'd almost summoned the courage when she felt the cold kiss of a blade on her neck.

'Get up.'

Slowly, Danae rose to her feet. She hadn't even heard the woman steal up behind her.

'Move.' The knife pressed into her jugular as the woman marched her out from behind the bush. 'Told you there was someone following us.'

Danae fought to keep calm as the others stared at her. 'Unhand me, if you want to live.'

The flame-haired man laughed. The blade jiggled against her skin as the woman caught his mirth. Evidently these warriors were not as easily cowed by her disguise as the ship's captain at Cirrha had been.

Despite the knife, Danae lifted her chin. 'You dare mock a messenger of the gods?'

There was a pause. Then Heracles said quietly, 'Let her go.'

The woman withdrew her weapon.

Danae's pulse quickened as Heracles dropped the reins of his horse and walked towards her. He was so powerful, and yet he moved with the grace of a panther.

'You were in the square.'

She was grateful for the poor light as her cheeks turned the colour of a ripe fig. Heracles' eyes were startlingly blue. Everything around him seemed to disappear under the weight of all that ocean. She dug her nails into her palms to focus.

'I received a vision from the gods. It led me to you.'

The woman tensed beside her, but Heracles said, 'Go on.'

She had one chance to convince him. She bit the inside of her cheeks and tasted blood. It helped. As the metal tang swirled around her mouth, she thought of how easily Manto had lied to Captain Erastus.

'I was trapped in a labyrinth. I couldn't find my way and was sure I was lost. Then, I saw a great lion. It led me through the maze and showed me the way out into the light. I did not know what it meant until I came here. When I saw you in the square, I recognized you.'

'Everyone recognizes me.' It was a fact, stated without arrogance.

As she looked up at him, she noticed a dark curl had escaped from the jaws of the lion hide to twist against his temple. She hadn't thought it possible, but he surpassed his likenesses painted on pottery and stone. He was the most beautiful man she'd ever seen. Doubt began to weaken her resolve. Perhaps she'd imagined the prophecy stone burning her side when he appeared, perhaps she was nothing more than a delusional girl caught in the thrall of his fame.

'The lion had blue eyes. Your eyes. I have felt the will of the gods and I know destiny's voice when it speaks. I am to accompany you on your journey across the Black Sea.'

'She's been spying on us!' The woman's knife returned to Danae's throat.

'Atalanta.' Heracles' voice was the thunder before a storm.

Atalanta glared at Danae, but she lowered the blade.

'Above all things we honour the gods.' Something danced behind his eyes and she wondered if he was being entirely truthful. 'What is your name, seer?'

'Daeira.'

'Daeira.' The way Heracles spoke the name sent a shiver down her spine. 'You may travel with us for now, and we will see if your company proves useful.'

'Heracles –' Atalanta began, but the hero raised a hand to silence her.

'I have made my decision.' Heracles gestured to his companions. 'This is Telamon.' He pointed at the flame-haired man, who winked. 'Atalanta.' The woman sheathed her knife in a strap on her thigh, still smouldering with mistrust. 'Hylas,' the younger man smiled, 'and Dolos, our healer.' The grey-haired man frowned, as though he didn't quite know what to make of her. 'They're not bad company and occasionally come in handy in a fight.' Heracles' eyes twinkled. 'But despite what you've heard it's not all guts and glory.'

The corners of Danae's mouth twitched.

'And yet you don't see our faces on the amphorae,' said Telamon, as he swung himself onto a dappled mare.

'I'm not taking her.' Atalanta spat on the ground and kicked her horse into a trot.

'You can ride with me,' said Hylas.

As he lifted her up, it suddenly occurred to Danae that she'd never ridden a horse before. Trying to slide on as gracefully as her dress would allow, she clamped her legs either side of the animal's torso and clutched the saddle so tightly her knuckles turned white. It couldn't be that dissimilar to riding a donkey, just faster and with further to fall.

Hylas slung himself up in front of her in one deft motion.

'All right back there?'

'Fine,' Danae said through clenched teeth.

'You're right to hold on tight.' Hylas grasped the reins. 'Heracles likes to ride fast.'

Tall cypress trees blurred past, their ghostly bodies smudging into a continuous streak of grey. Danae clung to Hylas, the wind whipping her face and tearing at her cloak. Once she overcame her initial fear of falling, she found riding exhilarating. Galloping was what she imagined flying felt like.

Heracles led them off the main road away from the town, forging a path across the open scrubland. After a while she smelt a change in the air. The cool trace of a sea breeze. She took a deep breath, enjoying the taste of salt on her tongue. Then a strip of silver glimmered on the horizon, and the Bay of Corinth appeared before them.

She shivered. Manto's body was out there somewhere in all that water. She hoped they'd found their way to the Asphodel Meadows. Perhaps they'd met Alea there. The thought brought her a whisper of comfort.

In front of them, Heracles slowed. Hylas tugged the reins and brought their horse to a steady trot.

'We'll camp here for the night,' said the hero. 'Get a few hours' sleep before dawn.'

They stopped on a bank of rough grass near the bay.

A collection of stone ruins stood stark against the moonlit sky. All that was left was a circle of jagged slabs, like the crumbling crown of a long-dead giant.

Hylas dismounted and lifted Danae down from the saddle. As her feet hit the ground, pain shot through her legs. She stumbled.

'You all right?'

'I'm fine.'

'You'll get used to it. The first day of riding is always the worst.'

'I know,' she lied.

His mouth quirked. 'Of course you do.'

Once the horses were tethered to a nearby crop of trees, they sat on the dusty ground inside the remnants of the ancient structure. Dolos produced some bread and cured meat from his saddle pack, and they ate for the most part in silence, without a fire. Danae pulled her cloak tightly around her as a chill breeze whistled through the old stones.

'We should send word to Eurystheus once we reach Iolcos,' said Dolos. 'He won't be happy that we've disobeyed his command.'

Danae wondered why Heracles took orders from the King of Mycenae, but she didn't dare ask. Her place travelling with th hero and his companions was already precarious.

Heracles took a swig from a waterskin. 'The old goat will find out where we've gone soon enough.'

Dolos' lips parted as though he were about to disagree, then he pressed them together again.

At the risk of sounding naive, Danae asked, 'Who is Jason?'

'Good question.' Telamon looked at Dolos.

'I only know what was sent out in the decree,' said the healer. 'King Pelias of Iolcos has commissioned a ship, captained by this Jason, to sail to Colchis and retrieve the golden fleece. I imagine he must be a seasoned sea captain.'

'A lot of effort for some old sheep fur,' said Atalanta.

'Yes, well,' said Dolos. 'That old sheep fur is said to grant prosperity and unnaturally long life. Pelias has promised a hefty amount of gold to anyone who helps Jason retrieve it.'

'So, Pelias fancies himself a god,' said Hylas.

'Don't all kings?' There was a bitter edge to Heracles' voice.

For a few moments no one spoke.

'How long will it take to get there?' asked Danae.

'Three days, I'd say,' said Telamon through a mouthful of bread. 'Two if we push the horses.'

'The sooner the better,' said Atalanta. 'Don't want them leaving without us.'

'They'll wait for me.' Heracles got to his feet. 'We should get some rest. Whose turn is it to keep the first watch?'

'I'll do it.' Danae was eager to make a good impression.

Heracles gazed at her, his eyes lingering on her face as though she were an intricate mural. Then he nodded and said, 'The seer's proving her worth already.'

Heat prickled her cheeks. She fought the urge to grin.

'Atalanta, relieve Daeira after a couple of hours.'

Danae caught Atalanta smirking at Telamon, and her smile faded. She had the unsettling feeling she was going to wake up to a knife in her face.

'Don't mind Atalanta,' whispered Hylas. 'When I first joined the group she kept threatening to gut me in my sleep.'

'When did she stop?'

'She still does it on occasion.'

'Great,' muttered Danae.

'She's all right once you get to know her. She could have turned out a lot worse, given she was raised by wolves.'

Danae's eyes widened. Hylas smiled. 'Only until she was six, then a group of hunters took her in.' He glanced at the warrior. 'Most loyal person I know. Sleep well, Daeira.'

She watched him walk over to their horse, wishing he was the one relieving her watch.

The rest of the group made makeshift beds against the stones with blankets from their saddle packs. They all kept their weapons close. Atalanta slept with her quiver in one hand, her bow in the other. Heracles set himself up away from the rest of them, behind the trees where the horses were tethered. Dolos watched him go, then took his healer's pack and followed him.

Cocooned in her cloak, Danae sat with her back to one of the stone slabs, looking out across the sea. She waited until Telamon was snoring and the others' breathing had calmed, then delved into her bag and drew out the prophecy stone.

She felt its pull before she'd finished unwrapping it. Its jagged edges shone so brightly it looked as though it was made of hardened moonlight.

She took a breath, then touched it.

21. Unseen Enemies

On Naxos, Danae had once gone swimming in an inland lake. Afterwards, her mother had to prise over a dozen leeches off her body. She'd felt every single one of their little mouths sucking her blood. The sensation she experienced now, as she touched the prophecy stone, was similar. But instead of her blood it was like the stone was drawing out her very life force, and she could suddenly see threads of glowing light rushing from her fingers into the obsidian rock. She tried to pull her hand away, but she couldn't let go.

It was the same sensation she'd had when she touched the oracle in Delphi. Her vision blurred, and she felt as though she was falling into darkness. Then she was suspended once more outside her body in the empty void, but this time there was no shining thread to grasp onto, no tapestry of life to weave a vision. Just nothingness. Panic swallowed her whole. All the while she could feel herself weakening. It felt as though the stone was going to suck her dry until there was nothing left.

With a great effort she managed to wrench her fingers from the rock. It fell to the ground and rolled between her feet. Her skin covered in cold sweat, she turned to the side and vomited.

When she looked up, Atalanta was awake and staring at her.

For a heartbeat she was transfixed, like a mouse caught in thrall to a falcon. Then she forced her gaze downwards and hastily wiped her mouth. She steeled herself for an onslaught of questions or the sting of a blade at her throat, but when she looked back, the warrior's dark eyes were scanning the land beyond their encampment, an arrow notched in her bow.

Danae blinked, trying to calm the breath surging in her chest. She lowered herself to the ground and slowly, with the edge of her sandal, nudged the prophecy stone between the folds of her dress. Careful not to let it touch her skin, she wrapped it in its cloth and slid it back into her bag.

Turning away from Atalanta, she curled her knees into her chest and whispered to herself, 'Oh, Manto, what in Tartarus have you given me?'

Danae was woken by a hand on her shoulder. Someone hovered over her, the dawn shining through a cloud of chestnut hair. Her mind still hazed with sleep, for a moment she thought it was Santos.

'Time to go,' said Hylas.

Danae grabbed her bag and pushed herself to her feet, glancing shamefully at the pile of vomit next to her. She'd been able to stow away the prophecy stone without question, but she knew she'd by no means got away with it. She had a feeling Atalanta wasn't remaining silent about what she'd seen out of kindness.

She understood now why Manto's father told them never to use the stone. Even after a few hours of sleep, she still felt drained from her brief contact with it. And yet he'd instructed Manto to give it to her. There must be a way of mastering it. When she could be certain she wasn't being watched, she would try again.

Dolos handed round a light breakfast of biscuits, washed down with a few gulps of water.

'Remind me again why I'm not in a feathered bed being fed grapes by a serving girl?' Telamon grumbled as he cricked his back.

'Seer,' said Heracles as he packed his saddle bags. 'What do the omens say waits for us at Iolcos?'

Danae's eyes met his, and her heart contracted like an anemone under a prying hand.

'A fresh start.' She hoped that was broad yet intriguing enough to placate whatever Heracles was hoping to hear.

A crease formed between the hero's brows, his ocean-deep gaze still fixed on Danae. She had to remind herself to keep breathing.

Then he turned his face to the bay. 'Good. That's exactly what we need.'

Hylas was wrong. The second day of riding was far worse than the first. Danae's entire body ached, pain radiating through muscles she didn't even know she had. She ground her teeth as Hylas urged their horse into a gallop and tried to keep her eyes fixed on the expanse of sea to their left.

They hugged the coast for a few hours, riding close to the sandy dunes that eventually rose into jagged cliffs. When the terrain became too rocky for the horses, Heracles led them inland across open fields and eventually onto a wide, well-trodden road.

Danae watched Atalanta riding ahead, her dented armour gleaming, her braids streaming in the wind. She had thought the Maenads wild, but they were tame compared to her. There was a fierceness in the warrior born of mountains and ravines, of living life on a blade's edge. It both thrilled and terrified Danae. Perhaps Hylas had been teasing her, but she could imagine Atalanta as a child, running with her wolf pack and howling at the moon.

The group was forced to slow by midday and let the horses rest from the unrelenting sun. They dismounted by the side of the path, where the trees were thickest, and took shelter under the leafy canopy. While Telamon fed the horses, they took the opportunity to rest themselves, and Dolos handed round a lunch of berries and more biscuits. Danae watched Heracles pace back and forth, then remove his lion hide. Her eyes traced the scars across his muscled back as he took himself away from the group to the dappled shade of an oak tree. The others slid him sideways glances but said nothing.

Danae took advantage of the hero being out of earshot and whispered to Hylas, 'Why does Heracles take orders from the King of Mycenae?'

Hylas licked the berry residue from his fingers. 'The same reason most people take up their professions . . . coin.'

Danae's lip curled. 'I don't believe the greatest hero in Greece works for a king he clearly dislikes just for coin.'

Hylas shrugged. 'You're a seer, surely you can just gut a rabbit and read its entrails or eat sacred cow dung and the mystery will be revealed to you.'

'Are you making fun of me?'

Hylas looked at her with a face so sombre he could have been at a burial. 'I would never make fun of one who speaks to the gods.'

Danae couldn't tell if he was teasing her.

'You're right. I could use my gift if I wished, but it would save a lot of time and effort if you just told me. And if you do, I'll put in a good word for you . . .' She glanced upwards.

Now it was Hylas' turn to look as though he couldn't work out if she was mocking him. He glanced over his shoulder, then said softly, 'He was ordered to, by the oracle at Delphi. That's all I know.'

There was something he wasn't telling her. She was about to press him further when Heracles strode over, a scowl etched across his brow.

'We should head east, bypass Creon's kingdom altogether.'

Danae was about to ask why, then she caught the expressions on Atalanta's and Telamon's faces.

'That would add on at least a day's riding,' said Dolos. 'At the speed we've been going, I don't think the horses have it in them.'

Heracles ran a hand through his thick mahogany hair and continued pacing. Then he turned abruptly and strode towards his stallion.

'Heracles.' Dolos rose to his feet.

'We leave now.' The hero strapped his lion hide to his saddle so the head was covered. 'You want to get there quickly? Then we'd better get a fucking move on.' He swung himself onto the steed, his powerful limbs tight with tension.

Atalanta and Telamon shared a weighted look before shoving down the last of their victuals and securing their saddles.

'Fine,' said Dolos with the resignation of a parent placating a stubborn child. 'We'll go now, but the horses must walk, or we'll knacker them before we reach Iolcos.'

Heracles' expression darkened but he said nothing.

In silence they mounted the horses and continued at a slower pace along the road.

'Where are we?' Danae asked Hylas as the trees began to thin and she glimpsed golden fields of barley in the distance.

'Just outside the city of Thebes.'

Once, on one of Philemon's visits to Alea, he had brought a map. It was the one occasion she'd been happy to stay in the hut while he fawned over her sister. He'd spread the scroll across their table and pointed out the route he and his father sailed to Athens, and the surrounding cities of Eleusis,

Eretria and Thebes. She'd gazed in wonder at the land sketched out on the parchment and pictured herself journeying between the lines of ink. From what she could remember, Thebes was north of Athens. Her aching bones were vindicated; they'd already come a long way.

'I grew up not far from here, on the other side of those hills.' Hylas pointed beyond the barley fields. His face softened as he gazed in the direction of home.

'How did you come to travel with Heracles?'

She'd wondered this when she'd been sitting listening to them in the kapeleion. Dolos was a healer, which would be invaluable given the hero's line of work, and Telamon and Atalanta looked like seasoned fighters, but she couldn't imagine Hylas tussling a many-headed hydra or brawling with a bloodthirsty giant.

'Not much to tell. Heracles and the others stopped at my uncle's farm on their way to capture a giant boar that was terrorizing Erymanthia. Heracles asked if I wanted to come with them and here I am.'

She thought of the hostility she'd received before being allowed to join their group and sensed there was more to the story, but her desire to find out more about Heracles outweighed her curiosity.

'Why was he so keen to take another route?'

'That's just Heracles. He can be impatient sometimes.'

After another hour of riding, the forests on either side of the road became dense again. With no views of the surrounding countryside to distract her, the ache in Danae's thighs became so uncomfortable, she had to shift every few moments. Rearranging herself, she accidentally kicked the bag she'd attached to the saddle. Worried about losing the prophecy stone, she leant over to make sure it was secure.

As she straightened up, an object whistled past her head. A heartbeat later, pain spiked through her ear and something warm trickled down her neck.

She barely had time to register what had happened before Heracles twisted in his saddle and spun a dagger into the branches of a tree on the opposite side of the path. There was a wet thud, a moan, then a man tumbled from the branches, the blade wedged in his throat.

Danae stared at the body, her breathing shallow. She'd half expected to see the blue cloak of an Athenian guard, but the man bleeding out in front of her was dressed in a humble tunic with a dark strip of cloth wound around his face.

She didn't have long to recover from the shock. Men surged from between the trees on either side, all dressed similarly with their faces obscured, clutching an eclectic assortment of weapons.

Telamon unsheathed his sword and Atalanta drew her bow, an arrow poised at her cheek in the space of a heartbeat. They worked in harmony, Telamon slashing and stabbing the nearest attackers, while Atalanta picked off the ones lurking in the foliage. The ground around their horses soon turned red.

Danae scrabbled around for her knife, while Hylas pulled their horse away from a man wielding a sickle.

Heracles threw his reins to Dolos and slipped from the saddle. Unarmed, he moved amongst their attackers, crushing their weapons as though they were blades of grass. Danae gaped as he grabbed a sword in his fist, the metal crumpling under his grip, while he punched the man who held it. With a sickening crack, the man sank to the ground, his head lolling from a broken neck. The others faltered, staring at Heracles in slack-jawed horror.

Hesitating was a mistake.

The hero darted forwards with the speed of someone half his size. There was a pop as he wrenched a man's arm from its socket, while at the same time shattering another's pelvis with a kick. While Danae clung to Hylas, uselessly waving her knife, Heracles felled a dozen men in moments. Two dropped their weapons and turned to run, but the hero grabbed each of their heads and smashed them together, showering the path in fragments of skull and brains.

Suddenly, the sky seemed to slide forwards as Danae was pulled off the horse. An attacker had a fistful of her cloak and was dragging her along the path. Winded, she tried to swing her blade in front of her, but the man grabbed her arm, forcing her knife down towards her chest.

Then Hylas was soaring through the air above them. He must have leapt from the saddle, drawing his dagger at the same time. He landed on his feet, his blade sinking into the back of Danae's attacker. Blood dribbled from the man's mouth and he toppled over, dead before he hit the path.

She propped herself onto her elbows. Bodies littered the ground around her. After what Heracles had done, most of them barely looked human.

Atalanta and Telamon brought their horses around. Neither of them had even broken a sweat. Hylas held out a hand and lifted Danae to her feet. She was glad he didn't let go straight away. Without his arm, she didn't know if she would have remained upright.

'Any injuries?' called Dolos as he trotted over with Heracles' horse in tow. The healer looked down at Danae. 'Are you all right, Daeira?'

'Fine,' she said, wiping the blood from the front of her dress. 'Who were they?'

'Bandits,' said Heracles as he climbed back onto his steed. 'People aren't as respectful of your kind in these parts,' said Telamon to Danae. 'Coin is coin no matter how holy the purse.'

'It's the temple tithes,' said Hylas. 'People are starving and desperate.'

'Well, I had fun,' said Heracles. 'Shall we?'

Hylas lifted Danae back onto their horse, then remounted himself. Heracles trotted out in front of the pack and they set off, leaving the dead bandits strewn behind them.

The hero donned his lion hide once more, lifting the roaring head over his tousled curls. As he turned his back to her, Danae's eyes traced the breadth of his shoulders, the contours of his muscular arms as he clenched the reins. He was so magnificent part of her couldn't believe he was real.

'Are you sure you're all right, Daeira?'

Her gaze snapped up. Heracles was looking over his shoulder, his cerulean eyes clouded with concern.

She must have been staring. Searching for a distraction, she glanced back at the slain bandits. 'Shouldn't we bury them?'

Amusement hooked the corners of Heracles' mouth. 'We'd still be digging graves back in Erymanthia if we buried everyone we killed in a fight.' He turned back to look at the path ahead.

All their souls, lost forever on the banks of the Styx. She tried not to think about it.

'It sounds callous,' said Hylas. 'But you'll get used to it.'

Danae swallowed. She hoped not.

'Where did you learn to fight like that?' she asked.

'My father. He was a soldier.'

'What does he do now?'

Hylas let out a soft sigh. 'He died. There was a war, like there always is. My mother joined the Missing when I was young, so when my father didn't come back, my aunt and uncle took me in. They needed another pair of hands on the farm, so . . .' He shrugged.

She thought of Arius, the smell of his head and the sound of his robust little laugh.

'I'm sorry.'

'It's just life. Worse things have happened to many. And look where I am now.'

Danae smiled. 'My brothers would be so envious. When we were little, Calix insisted he was going to be a hero when he was grown. He used to make Santos dress up in a heap of Pa's old fishing nets and pretend . . .' She stopped herself.

Hylas reminded her of the boys she'd grown up with. Open, honest, sun-ripened fisherman's sons. But he was a stranger, and she didn't know if she could trust him.

'Have you seen them, your family, since you became a seer?'

'No. Once we take the sacred oath we can't go back.' It was true, or it would have been if she really was a seer. Danae hoped with all her soul that it would not be the same for her.

The road sprouted branches, feeding the towns and villages that lay nestled in the nooks of hills and swathes of woodland. The landscape became increasingly wild. Great chalky mountains reared into the sky, populated by herds of mountain goats. The rougher the terrain and further from civilization they travelled, the more Heracles relaxed, until the thundercloud that had hung over him as they passed Thebes dissipated.

As the horses trotted through a wild grove of poplar trees, the hero shouted back, 'Telamon, tell us a joke.'

There were grumbles from the rest of the group.

'For the love of the gods –'

'– don't encourage him –'

'– I'd rather listen to Hylas sing.'

Hylas delved into his saddle pouch and threw a nut at Atalanta.

Unperturbed, Telamon cleared his throat. 'Did you hear the one about the soldier from Sparta? A fellow says to him, "Lend me your sword as far as Phrygia," and the Spartan says, "I haven't got one that long, but I've got something else that is."'

There was a collective groan. Heracles alone let out a deep chuckle.

'Your jokes are terrible,' called Atalanta.

'Like you could do any better.'

The warrior arched an eyebrow. 'A widow is standing by her husband's grave. A woman approaches and says, "Who is it that rests in peace?" The widow says, "Me, now he's dead."'

Danae laughed, a genuine mirth that rumbled from her gut and shook her shoulders. Atalanta glanced back, a flicker of surprise briefly softening her brow.

As the sun dipped towards the horizon, Heracles led them off the road altogether, urging the horses into a gallop across an expanse of dry, shrub-peppered earth. He seemed to know the lay of this land like the creases of his palm. Clouds rolled in from the west, absorbing the light from the sinking sun. By the dying rays, Danae could just make out a crop of dwellings in the distance, nestled in the lower ledges of a small mountain.

She felt disorientated as they joined the rocky path that snaked up towards the village, lost in a sea of earth and stone. She wondered how she would ever find her way back to Naxos. She banished the thought as quickly as it came; she had a long way to go before she could think of returning home.

The mud-brick huts of the little village were painted white, reflecting the last of the sun. As they approached the first clutch of dwellings, people emerged from their doorways. Children in homespun tunics peered out between their parents' legs. From their expressions, it didn't look like they were used to visitors.

The group carried on up the mountain path until they reached the centre of the village. A small stone well was sunk into a patch of relatively level ground, and a few shops were scattered between the ramshackle dwellings. Danae recognized a blacksmith's workbench outside one and a domed brick stove outside another that she assumed was the village kapeleion. A couple of men were sat outside drinking. They eyed the newcomers with suspicion.

The group dismounted and followed Heracles' lead as he tied his horse to a post beside the kapeleion. An elderly man with a full grey beard and a rounded back brushed aside the faded curtain that hung over the doorway.

'Good to see you again, Dru,' said Heracles.

'Ah! I wondered if you'd ever come through these parts again.' Dru's voice was surprisingly hearty.

'May the Twelve see you and know you.'

The old barkeeper returned the sacred gesture. 'You'll be wanting a bed then?'

'And food, if you have it.'

Dru nodded. 'Leave the horses here, I'll get Evan to tend to them. Evan!'

There was a clang from inside. A gangly boy came crashing through the curtain, almost knocking into Dru. His eyes widened at the towering height of Heracles and bulged still further at the sight of Atalanta in her silver armour.

'Here you go, lad.' Dolos took an obol from his purse and tossed it to the boy. Evan's face stretched into a toothy grin.

'Wine, food and bed, in that order,' said Heracles.

Dru nodded and sent Evan scurrying to fetch the victuals, then beckoned them inside.

It transpired the kapeleion was also Dru's dwelling. The single room was strewn with straw, barrels were stacked against the far wall, and a single mat lay under a small window on the left.

Dru delved into a wooden chest and busied himself unrolling another mat. Then he straightened up and spread his arms wide.

'Beds for the ladies; I'm afraid you men will have to take the floor.'

Telamon stood in the doorway, arms folded. 'This, over the palace at Mycenae?'

Heracles shot him a withering look. 'Dru, I apologize for my companion's rudeness. Telamon used to be a prince and never quite got over it.'

The flame-haired man feigned a wounded expression. A myriad of questions whirled through Danae's mind. If she had to place Telamon's origins, she would never have guessed royalty. He swore far too much for a start.

Dru smiled graciously. 'Any friend of Heracles is a friend of mine. Come, you must be thirsty after your travels. We have a couple of fresh barrels from Epirus. Lovely vintage, I'm told.'

After stowing their packs inside, they followed the barkeeper back out into the square. The men who'd been drinking outside had made themselves scarce and Dru bustled around until he'd located enough mismatched stools.

As they sat, Evan emerged, carrying a tray of cups and a couple of jugs of wine. Dolos emptied a pouch of coins into Dru's hand as Atalanta downed the first jug in one go, then set about pouring the rest of the wine. She left Danae's cup empty. Biting back a comment, Danae reached for the second jug at the same time as Hylas. Their fingers bumped, and he withdrew his hand, mumbling an apology while she sloshed wine into her cup. When she looked up, she caught a gleam in Telamon's eye. She'd been teased enough by her brothers to know what would come next.

Before Telamon had a chance to speak, she said, 'So, was being a prince too much like hard work or were the silk sheets not soft enough for your liking?'

A spark of amusement cracked Atalanta's scowl.

'She bites!' Telamon took a gulp of wine. 'Oh, that *is* nice.' He turned back to Danae. 'Who could resist the call of adventure, the promise of a blood-slicked sword and a chance to *royally* shove it to one's father . . .' He looked around the table expectantly.

Atalanta groaned and drained her cup.

Danae raised her wine to her lips. She spluttered.

'It's not mixed!'

'And?' said Atalanta, the tilt of her jaw daring Danae to continue.

Her mother said that drinking wine without mixing it with water was barbaric. But she wasn't on Naxos any more. She swallowed and took another sip of the strongest wine she'd ever tasted.

'All the better for it.'

The salivating scent of roasting meat wafted over from the outdoor oven. Dru was sizzling strips of what smelt like lamb on the open flames.

'Gods, that smells good,' said Hylas.

Evan returned to the table, a bowl of olives in one hand and a loaf of bread in the other, then went back for more wine as Dru shuffled over and set down a plate of steaming meat on the table. They abandoned the bread and fell upon it. The lamb was tender and smoky from the fire. Danae couldn't remember the last time she'd had meat so succulent. Atalanta skewered a strip with her dagger, eyeballing Danae as she ripped it with her teeth. Wilting under the warrior's gaze, Danae glanced down at her food.

'Seer, why don't you tell everyone about that rock you carry.'

The hairs rose on the back of Danae's neck. She knew she had to tread carefully, was all too aware that these people probably wouldn't hesitate to kill her if they found out she was deceiving them. And yet, the fire of confrontation burned in her belly.

'I consulted the omens last night – there are objects I have that help me do this – and I saw something. Something that concerns you, Atalanta.' The warrior's eyes narrowed. 'I didn't want to alarm you, but perhaps it's best if you are prepared.' She knew she should stop, but she couldn't help relishing the rapt silence that had fallen over the table. 'A sickness will come upon you. Your mouth will dry and no water will quench your thirst. Your stomach will churn and your head will pound as though a hoard of wild boar are trampling through your skull.'

A muscle pulsed in Atalanta's jaw. 'You're lying.'

'I swear on the Styx I am not.' Danae's face was grave. 'I've watched you drink at least a jug and a half of wine already. I guarantee, tomorrow your headache will rival that of a farmer after his wedding night.'

The silence that followed was filled with the sizzle of lamb fat.

In a heartbeat Atalanta was on her feet, stool upended in the dirt, her knife stretched over the table, poised at Danae's throat.

'You're a liar! I see you!'

'Sit down, Atalanta,' Heracles pulled her away from Danae. 'Learn how to take a joke.'

Telamon chuckled. 'I like this one.'

Atalanta sat slowly, her eyes searing into Danae as she took a long, deep drink.

'I've heard the people of Colchis drink the blood of their enemies,' said Hylas.

'Poor bastards,' said Telamon. 'They must be desperate for a decent libation. Perhaps we should take an amphora of this wine with us and trade it for the fleece.'

Atalanta flicked her gaze to him and snorted, then reached for the wine jug.

Danae's shoulders loosened as the conversation trickled back to a steady pace, but she knew she'd been lucky.

She just had to anger the wolf.

Danae woke suddenly. She propped herself up on the mat. The room was dark. Everyone else appeared to be asleep. Telamon was snoring loudly and next to him, Heracles lay on the straw-covered floor, head resting on his lion hide, his scarred brow creased. In sleep he looked younger, softer. She mapped the sharp angle of his jaw and the shape of his mouth, marvelling at how beauty and power were sculpted together into the lines of his face. A shiver ran down her spine. A face so like his father's.

As she watched him, a dash of movement flickered past the window. Careful not to wake Atalanta sleeping beside her, she slipped her hand into her bag and rose, clutching her knife.

Silently, she padded out into the moonlight. The night was still, and the square appeared empty, save for the sleeping horses. Then she heard the crunch of a stone underfoot. Shaking off the lingering haze of the wine, she hugged the wall of the kapeleion and crept around the side. Edging forward, she peered around the corner. Behind the hut was a dirt track that continued up the mountain. There was something large on the path where the road twisted. She squinted, trying to make it out in the darkness.

It was a cart, its bulky contents covered by a tarpaulin. A jet-black horse was harnessed to the front. She glanced around, then darted across the path and concealed herself in the shadow of a protruding rock. As the cart inched forward, a limp arm fell free of the cover. The driver turned, as though sensing her gaze, and she stifled a gasp.

A pair of red eyes glinted beneath the charcoal hood.

Icy fear flooded her veins. For a moment she was paralysed, then the sound of footsteps drew her back. Someone else was on the path. A shadow, distorting the scenery it passed through. Another shade. It was carrying something. Someone. A shudder ran through her as she realized it was Evan. The boy appeared to be unconscious.

She could hear Arius crying as though he were right in front of her, his pitiful wails searing through her mind.

She would not let them take another.

The screaming intensified inside her skull, ringing in her ears until her whole body vibrated with noise and fury. She leapt from behind the rock, knife raised and charged towards the shade holding Evan. As her feet hit the path, the ground shook, sending rocks cascading down the mountain. The shade spun around to face her. It dropped Evan, its crimson eyes widening in fear.

Anger radiated out of her. She could feel it pulsing into the ground through the threads of light shooting from her feet into the earth. It was happening again, the strange power inside her was erupting, but she didn't care. All she wanted was to inflict as much pain as possible on the creatures that had destroyed her family.

The cloaked shade driving the cart didn't wait. It cracked its whip and urged the wagon upwards around the bend as Danae continued to shake the earth. The second shade fled after it, its camouflaged body near impossible to follow. But she doggedly pursued it, tracking its blurred outline along the road. Then the quake loosened a large rock above the path. The second shade twisted, its crimson eyes flashing in the moonlight ahead of her as the boulder crashed into it and the shade tumbled down the mountain out of sight.

'Daeira!'

She turned and saw Heracles, sword in hand, standing on the track behind her, legs braced against the shaking ground. At the sight of him, the thrumming inside her stopped and the earth stilled.

She was stunned to see that despite the chaos she had somehow left a clear path through the rubble.

Heracles was staring at her, a strange look in his eyes. Then the others appeared behind him, weapons drawn. They paused as they took in Danae, the unconscious boy and the rock-strewn path. Dolos was the first to move and rushed over to Evan.

'Drugged,' said the healer as he lifted the boy's eyelids.

A sudden weakness washed over Danae and her legs sagged beneath her. She staggered, teetering on the edge of the track. Dolos ran over and caught her before she fell.

'Easy now.' He gently guided her to the ground.

'Shades . . .' she muttered, 'with a cart. I think they've taken people. They tried to take Evan. You can't see them, but their eyes –'

'You don't have to explain,' said Dolos. 'We know about shades.'

'Which way did they go?' asked Telamon.

Danae pointed up the path. Without hesitating, Telamon, Hylas and Atalanta set off after them.

Heracles remained. He hadn't taken his eyes off her. Concern and intrigue swirled in his ocean-blue gaze. And something else, something like hunger. She wished she knew how long he'd been standing there. How much he'd seen.

She had to be more careful. Whatever strange power was growing inside her, she must keep it hidden until she reached Prometheus.

22. Heroes and Masters

'My boy!'

A woman, her cheeks streaked with tears, rushed over to Evan, who was hanging like a rag doll in Heracles' arms. Dru also looked stricken.

'He's alive,' said Dolos. 'I'm a healer and I can help him, but we need to get him inside.'

The entire village was awake. Many had fled their homes, fearful of their shaking walls collapsing in on them. Danae felt a twinge of guilt: her earthquake could have brought the whole village crashing to the ground. She was unsettled by the tiny part of her that found that exciting.

At that moment, Telamon, Atalanta and Hylas appeared from behind the kapeleion. Danae turned, hope swelling in her chest at what they might have found, but Telamon shook his head and said breathily, 'We couldn't catch the cart.'

A cry echoed through the square. A young man was running from hut to hut. 'My wife! Has anyone seen Bia?'

Heracles re-emerged from Dru's hut. The villagers surged towards him, clamouring for answers.

'Listen!' His voice thundered across the square, but still they would not be quiet.

'The gods have cursed us!' moaned a grey-haired woman.

Danae stepped forward. 'The gods have not cursed you. I'm a seer, I know the will of the Twelve. Poseidon will not shake your village again.'

That silenced them.

Heracles shot her an appraising look. 'Go back to your homes. You are safe now.'

'But my wife!' The young man sank to his knees in front of the hero. 'Please, you have to help me find her.'

Heracles gazed down at the man, his eyes misting as though he'd gone somewhere far away. 'She's gone, I'm sorry. There's nothing to be done.'

'No, no!' The man grasped the hem of Heracles' kilt. 'Please help me. You're Heracles! You can find her.'

The hero detached himself and ducked into Dru's hut.

Danae's heart ached as she watched the man sobbing into the dirt. She turned and ran into the hut after Heracles.

She placed a hand on the hero's arm. 'Can't we do something? We could wait for daylight and follow any tracks left by the cart –'

He turned, his blue eyes hard as ice. 'If I tried to track every person who'd joined the Missing I would not be the legendary Heracles but a ghost hunter. I can't save everyone.'

'But isn't that the point of being a hero?'

For a moment he looked so flushed with rage, she was sure he was going to strike her, but when he spoke his voice was quiet.

'We leave for Iolcos at dawn. If you want to track that cart, you're on your own.'

He turned away and left her standing there, disappointment heavy in her chest.

They left at first light. Evan was still not awake, but Dolos assured his mother he should recover once the effects of the drug wore off. No one was in the mood for conversation as they saddled up the horses and took the track that led down the other side of the mountain.

Heracles forced them to push the horses even harder than the previous day. They raced across the border into Thessaly, where they left the mountains behind and were greeted with lush green fields and vineyards. They stopped once, briefly, to let their mounts drink, then Heracles drove them on again and didn't slow until the earth gave way to sandy dunes and the sea broke over the horizon.

Danae could hear the roar of a crowd before they reached the crest of the hill. Heracles held up a fist, and they pulled up the horses to look down over the beach. A stadium had been erected, the central seats covered by an emerald canopy. A huge crowd was spread out on either side, cheering a group of men that stood between the stadium and the ocean. They appeared to be taking part in some sort of athletic trials. One man ran forward and let a discus fly. It sailed almost the entire length of the stadium before crashing into the sand just in front of a smouldering altar with the carcass of a large animal still burning on its coals. The crowd went wild.

Beyond the beach, floating in the shallows, was the most magnificent ship Danae had ever seen. It was a penteconter, smaller than the warships of Athens, with only a single row of oars punctuating its seamless hull, but it was so sleek, she found it hard to believe it had been crafted by a mortal hand. A white sail was coiled to its mast and a painted figurehead presided over the prow. Hera, Queen of the Gods. She swallowed the bitter taste in her mouth.

Heracles turned to the group. His lips twitched into a smirk. 'Let's give them something to cheer about.'

With a roar that rolled down the dunes, he urged his steed onwards. Danae clung to Hylas as they bolted after him, Atalanta and Telamon adding their voices to the hero's cry. The crowd turned, and their screams reached an ear-splitting crescendo at the sight of Heracles in his famous lion hide.

As they drew closer to the stadium, the chant of, 'Heracles, Heracles!' reverberated through Danae's bones.

On the central platform a sumptuously dressed man rose to his feet and spread his arms wide. From the gold band glinting across his brow, she assumed he must be King Pelias of Iolcos.

At a gesture from their king, the crowd quietened.

'Welcome, Heracles! May the Twelve see you and know you. We are honoured by your presence.'

Heracles drew up his horse and dismounted. A servant in a green tunic ran forward to take his reins. The hero bowed deeply and touched his finger to his forehead.

'King Pelias, the honour is mine. My companions and I offer our service on your quest to retrieve the golden fleece of Colchis.'

A young man detached himself from the group of athletes and ran towards Heracles. His skin was deep brown, as were his eyes, set in a delicately handsome face.

'By the gods, you came!'

Heracles looked him up and down. 'You are?'

'Jason, captain of the *Argo*.' The man beamed, exposing a row of dazzlingly symmetrical teeth.

Heracles looked as surprised as Danae felt. She'd expected Jason to be middle-aged and grizzled by years of sea taming. But he looked only a few years older than her, with not a single battle scar on his lithe limbs.

A hulking figure walked up behind Jason. It was hard to tell where the brown fur of his bearskin ended and his own hair began.

'Ancaeus.' Heracles nodded. The bearskin warrior did the same.

'Peleus!' Telamon dropped his pack and ran to embrace a

man with sun-blushed skin and rust-coloured hair. 'You bastard, what are you doing here?'

'Telamon.' Peleus drew back and grasped Telamon's face in his hands. 'No one told me my little brother was coming along for the ride.'

The two men embraced again, then Peleus grabbed Telamon in a headlock and rubbed a fist into his hair.

'That explains a lot,' said Atalanta.

'Who do we have here?' Jason smiled at Atalanta with the full force of his charm.

'These are my companions,' said Heracles. 'Warriors who've fought by my side throughout my labours. This is Atalanta, Telamon, Hylas, Dolos, our healer, and the seer, Daeira.'

'Fantastic, we're in need of a healer.'

Despite the joviality of Jason's greeting, Danae noticed a gleam of ice in his eyes as his gaze slid past them to the royal box.

'You're not suggesting these women come with us?' A bald man with a livid scar that sliced the tanned skin of his skull eyed Danae and Atalanta disparagingly.

'It's bad luck,' growled his twin brother. If it weren't for the first man's scar, Danae would not have been able to tell them apart.

Atalanta sighed, reached into her pack and pulled out an apple. She threw it to Hylas, who caught it one-handed, drew back his arm and let the apple fly. The fruit soared into the air, far above the gathered warriors. Atalanta watched its progression for a moment, then lazily slung her bow from her shoulder and drew an arrow to her cheek. A breath later two apple halves fell to the sand.

She turned to the scarred twin and held out her bow. 'Your turn.'

Jason laughed and stepped between them. 'I see you ride with a talented group, Heracles. You've missed our competition, but there is no need to test your skill.' He turned to the crowd. 'Heracles and all who travel with him are welcome aboard the *Argo*.' He looked up at King Pelias. 'With your permission of course, Majesty.'

Danae sensed a tinge of mockery wrapped around that last word. Pelias' eyes flickered in response, then the king inclined his head.

Jason turned to Danae. 'The omens will surely be in our favour with two seers in our ranks.'

Her stomach clenched.

From behind the array of warriors emerged a thin man in a black robe. His hair was cut so short, she could see the outline of his skull.

'Idmon, meet Daeira.'

Danae bowed, squeezing her fists so her hands wouldn't tremble. 'May the Twelve see you and know you.'

Idmon touched his forehead and returned her bow, his beady eyes never leaving her face. She swallowed. Her disguise suddenly seemed a lot less infallible than it had before.

After an excessive amount of ceremonial waving, King Pelias bid them farewell. The last of the crowd dispersed, and the thirty chosen Argonauts were left alone on the beach.

They settled around a large campfire in front of the ghostly structure of the stadium, passing skins of wine between them.

Jason got to his feet and looked around at his crew. 'Argonauts, I'm honoured that all of you here tonight have pledged to join me on the greatest voyage ever sailed. Some of you know each other already, but for those that don't, let me make some introductions. We have one legend among us, whose reputation needs no preamble from me.' Jason bowed to Heracles, then gestured to the bald-headed brothers beside him.

'Castor and Pollux, otherwise known as the diabolical twins. You wouldn't want to face these two in the boxing ring.' The men grinned. Danae noted Castor was the one with the scar. Jason pointed at the bearskin warrior. 'Ancaeus, the bane of any monster in the Peloponnese.' Atalanta snorted. Either Ancaeus didn't hear her, or he pretended not to. Jason continued, 'Tiphys, our navigator and the finest sailor in all of Greece.' He nodded towards a wiry man with copper skin and a long silver beard. Danae's heart ached. He looked a little like her father. 'Orpheus,' Jason pointed at a round-faced man with apricot cheeks and a lyre resting on his lap, 'a musician whose voice is sweeter than a lark's –'

Heracles interrupted him. 'And you?'

Jason faltered. 'I'm Jason, the captain –'

'Yes, I know your name. But what have you done?' Heracles gestured around the fire. 'Like you said, I know by reputation most of the people here. But before this voyage, I'd never heard of you. And you're damned young to be a captain.'

There were a few mutterings of agreement.

Jason forced out a laugh. 'You're right. I am young to captain a ship.' He paused. 'I am the rightful king of Iolcos.'

'What?' Telamon looked at his brother, Peleus, for confirmation.

'It's true.' The firelight illuminated the hunger in Jason's eyes. 'I was living as a shepherd when I received a message from Hera, the Queen of Heaven herself, telling me of my birthright. I came to Iolcos to claim my throne.'

A muscle twitched in Heracles' jaw.

'Let me get this straight,' said Telamon. 'You marched up to King Pelias' gate, told him you were going to take his kingdom and in return he put you in charge of a crew of the deadliest warriors in all of Greece?'

'Not quite.' Jason smiled. 'At first, he wanted to have me executed. But he was ordered to let me put together this expedition by his priestesses. If I return with the golden fleece, I will be given my crown by divine decree. You see, my destiny is written by the fates. By joining me on this quest, you will all cement your reputations for centuries to come.'

'*If* you return.' Heracles threw an empty wineskin to the ground. 'Clever move on Pelias' part. All this makes him look like a pious and generous king. Not to mention powerful, gathering all of us together at his command. It's a dangerous voyage, all he has to do is wait for tragedy to strike.'

The charm slipped from Jason's face. 'I'm surprised you, of all people, doubt the will of the gods. Hera's, in particular.'

Heracles remained silent, glowering into the fire.

'How about we hear that legendary voice of yours?' Ancaeus said to Orpheus.

'Yes.' Jason clapped his hands, seemingly glad of the distraction. 'Music!'

The musician smiled dreamily and lifted his lyre, cradling it as if it were his lover. As he began to play, a shiver ran over Danae's skin. His voice was like the first breath of dawn, the rush of a tumbling river, and the pounding of horses' hooves charging into battle, all at once.

> *In the beginning, before first light*
> *Before cities and temples and law took flight,*
> *The earth was broken, wild and dark,*
> *The Titans' rule left its evil mark.*
>
> *This is how it came to be,*
> *The life we tread from dawn 'til eve,*
> *The Twelve who watch over us all,*
> *The sun, the stars, the earth and sea.*

The gods descended from on high,
Zeus, most wise, let his thunder fly,
The Twelve battled fierce and strong,
But despite their power the fight was long.

This is how it came to be,
The life we tread from dawn 'til eve,
The Twelve who watch over us all,
The sun, the stars, the earth and sea.

The Twelve defeated their treacherous foe,
Imprisoned them in the fires below,
Then Zeus made man and led his kin,
To rule from Olympus and keep us from sin.

This is how it came to be,
The life we tread from dawn 'til eve,
The Twelve who watch over us all,
The sun, the stars, the earth and sea.

And now we are forever blessed,
The Titans bound in Tartarus,
The gods watch over from above,
Forever praised, worshipped and loved.

By the time he had finished, Danae's cheeks were wet with tears. She wasn't the only one. Even Atalanta hadn't remained dry-eyed. Orpheus blushed and laid his lyre carefully across his lap.

'Gods,' breathed Telamon, 'a talent like that is more dangerous than all of ours put together.'

*

They set sail with the dawn tide.

Once the Argonauts had clambered aboard the *Argo*, they hung their shields over the side of the ship and tucked their belongings under the rowing benches. It transpired there was only one cabin under the prow deck, and it was nearly full to the brim with supplies for the long journey. There were crates of salted meats, biscuits, barrels of olives, skins of wine and packs of furs to stave off the chill when they reached the Black Sea. It was going to be cold at the end of the world.

Danae squeezed her bag next to Hylas' pack and climbed up to the prow deck with Idmon. Everyone else, bar Tiphys and Jason, was seated at the oars. To even out his strength, Heracles was given an entire bench to himself.

But the crew didn't have to row just yet. A strong northeast wind breathed into the sail and with Tiphys at the tiller guiding the steering oar, the *Argo* cut through the water like a freshly sharpened blade.

'Orpheus! Sing us a song to see us on our way,' called Jason.

The musician climbed off his bench and sat himself on the edge of the prow platform, his feet drumming a rhythm on the wooden planks.

The beat was strong, and the song's lyrics told of a great battle and courageous fighters, yet a lilt in the musician's voice revealed a reservoir of longing. It touched a part of Danae still too raw to be brought into the light. Telamon was right, his was a dangerous talent indeed.

She stared out at the open water, the breeze whipping her short hair. She'd made it this far; now all that stood between her and Prometheus was the ocean. She'd always felt more comfortable on water than land. This was where she belonged. She thought of what her father had said to her the day she left

Naxos. She wondered if he was out on his fishing boat at this very moment. Perhaps they were riding the sea together.

Idmon appeared beside her. He wrapped his long fingers around the side of the ship, so close to hers they almost touched. She fought the urge to move her hand away.

'The Twelve see you and know you, sister of the all-seeing eye.'

She'd never heard that additional part of the greeting before.

'You are young to be holy counsel to a man such as Heracles.'

She touched her forehead and replied, 'Age is no quantifier of ability.'

He shifted his weight closer towards her. He smelt of altar smoke and something sour, like long-curdled milk.

'How old *are* you, child?'

'Old enough to know the will of the gods.'

'Of course.' He smiled obsequiously. 'Under whom did you train?'

She let the question hang in the air for a moment then met his gaze, her face calm as the cerulean sea.

'One could almost be forgiven for thinking you are questioning my place on this voyage.'

With satisfaction, she watched his features squirm into a mask of mortification.

'Never, sister.'

He turned and walked briskly to the other side of the deck, leaving Danae alone. She moved her hands and saw her nails had made two rows of crescent indents in the wood.

They had barely sailed a league before the sky darkened.

'Jason!' called Tiphys. 'I don't like the look of those clouds.'

Danae followed the navigator's gaze and saw thick grey

clouds rolling in from the west. They were moving fast and soon swallowed the sun. The air chilled.

From what she knew of sea storms, the old navigator was right to be worried.

'Idmon,' called Jason. 'You said we'd have fine sailing to Troas.'

'The omens indicated we would, Captain,' said Idmon. 'I'm sure the clouds will pass.'

'My arse they will,' said Telamon. 'That's a storm coming.'

Then a rumble of thunder came, and a fork of lightning cracked the sky. Orpheus stopped playing and clutched his lyre to his chest. Soon, dark clouds boiled above the ship. The wind picked up, and the sea frothed, tossing the *Argo* between swelling peaks. Danae and Idmon climbed down to the mid-deck and braced themselves against the wall of the prow platform.

'The omens are in our favour, it will pass,' yelled Idmon. He sounded a lot less certain than before.

'Pull in the oars and sheath the mainsail!' called Tiphys.

'Shit.' Jason clenched his jaw as rain pelted the deck. He pointed at the twins. 'Castor, Pollux, do what he says!'

The twins abandoned their benches and battled their way across the swaying ship. They started to undo the sail knots, then a sharp gust ripped the sodden rope from Castor's fingers, and the untethered sheet flapped violently in the wind.

They were going to lose the sail. Danae had seen it happen on her father's boat, when they'd been caught out in a flash storm.

'It's going to rip!' she shouted.

The rope was writhing like a possessed serpent, the half-tethered sail screeching under the pull of the wind. Without thinking, she launched herself across the deck. Rain and saltwater blew like grit into her eyes but as the rope whipped back, she threw herself forwards and caught it. The friction burnt her palms, but she held on, crashing down between the rowing benches.

Then a blast of wind caught the sail. She was thrown into the air, her screams lost to the raging storm. Something gave way in her left shoulder, and pain seared through her arm, but she held on. She was tossed across the ship and just as she was about to fall into the iron embrace of the sea, something clamped around her legs.

Heracles had one arm around her thighs and his free hand clasped the end of the rope.

'Let go!'

She obeyed, her left arm hanging useless as she slid down Heracles' torso. She fell back between the rowing benches, where Hylas caught her and Atalanta and Telamon fought to secure the sail.

Dolos climbed over the benches towards her. 'Your shoulder's dislocated,' the healer shouted above a surge of thunder. 'This is going to hurt.'

He grasped her left arm by the bicep and pulled. A wave of nausea ripped through her as her shoulder popped back into its socket with a sickening crunch. She stared up through the driving rain, sagging with relief as Heracles and the others clambered back onto the mid-deck, the sail now bound to the mast. The storm had become so violent, Tiphys had even abandoned the steering oar.

'Argonauts, brace yourselves under the benches!' yelled Jason.

Danae clung onto the sodden wood either side of her as the rest of the crew scrambled to find a hold. All they could do was ride out the storm and pray they survived.

23. A Bargain

Danae looked up into a now clear sky. A gentle breeze fluttered over her face, barely lifting a hair. Not one cloud remained, as though the storm had been but a passing nightmare. Her raw skin and aching bones told her otherwise. It was a miracle the ship had survived intact.

She unfolded herself from under the bench and straightened up. The *Argo* was caught on a strip of reef in front of a long expanse of beach. Creamy sand stretched away from turquoise shallows into a dense tangle of greenery. Trees with long, layered trunks that rose into a crop of feathery leaves stood tall above the jungle. Large brown nuts, almost the size of her head, nestled below their fronds. In the distance a lone mountain, its ridges carpeted in emerald foliage, reared against the sky. The vegetation was unlike any she'd seen before. How far had the storm carried them?

She flinched as birds and creatures she didn't recognize chirruped to each other from the depths of the jungle. She tried to place them, but their strange voices were so unlike the gulls, larks and kestrels of home. The air was different here too, heady and sweet like syrup.

'Where in Tartarus are we?'

Atalanta's salt-crusted head appeared from behind the next bench. Telamon and Hylas emerged beside her, then the rest of the crew began to stir, unfurling themselves from the nooks they'd wedged themselves into during the storm.

'Argonauts!' Jason shouted as he clambered unsteadily onto

the prow deck, a deep gash across his forehead. 'If I call your name, say "aye". Ancaeus?'

'Aye.'

'Castor?'

'Aye.'

'Pollux?'

'Aye.'

'Orpheus?'

'Aye.' The musician sounded stricken. Danae looked across the deck and saw him cradling his broken lyre.

As the rest of the crew answered their names, Danae heard a groan behind her and twisted around. Her heart sank as she watched Tiphys climb onto the stern deck and run his calloused hands over the shattered planks. The mast had snapped in two and smashed through the wood, the steering oar lost to the sea.

'The figurehead!'

Looking back towards the prow she saw that the carved likeness of Hera was another casualty of the storm. Idmon stared at the splintered wood, his face pale, and declared, 'This is a terrible omen.'

'I hope she's at the bottom of the ocean,' murmured a deep voice.

Danae turned to see Heracles standing behind her.

'How's the arm?' His gaze swept over her, lingering on her shoulder.

She rotated the joint. It hurt, like the rest of her, but she could move it.

'Fine.'

'Good.' He looked at her so intensely the ship seemed to disappear into his eyes.

The breath swelled in her chest. Then his next words expelled it.

'What you did was incredibly foolish.'

She was stunned. She'd saved the sail from tearing. He should be thanking her.

'I was trying to help. I *did* help. I stopped the sail –'

'Don't ever risk yourself like that again.'

Before she could reply, he turned away and clambered across the sloping benches.

Dolos appeared beside her, clutching his healer's bag. 'Are you hurt?'

'No,' she snapped. At the healer's expression she added, 'My arm's fine. Please go and help the others.'

'Daeira?' called Jason.

'Aye!'

Dolos searched her face for a moment, then turned and made his way between the benches calling, 'Anyone who's injured, put your hand up. I'll come to you.'

Suddenly she remembered her bag. She tugged it out from where she'd wedged it under the bench and was relieved to find the purse, knife, pipe and prophecy stone were all there, and despite being sodden, nothing was broken.

'Anyone seen Iphitos or Augeias?' asked Jason.

The Argonauts looked at one another and shook their heads.

As the loss of their crewmates sank in, there was a shuddering creak, then the ship slid to the right, sending several of the men tumbling to the deck.

'Abandon ship!' Tiphys yelled as the *Argo* shifted again, groaning like a dying animal.

The crew didn't need to be told twice and set about hoisting themselves over the side into the shallows.

As Danae waded out of the water onto the beach, she turned to look back at the *Argo*. Where the ship had scraped the reef, a deep tear, nearly the full length of the starboard side, had ruptured the hull. A leaden weight settled in her chest. Wherever they were, they wouldn't be leaving anytime soon.

'Tiphys,' Jason called, walking over to the navigator. 'What is this island?'

Tiphys shielded his eyes against the sun as he peered up towards the mountain. 'No idea, Captain. The storm can't have blown us more than a hundred leagues. I know most of the islands in the Aegean but this . . .' He shook his head. 'The climate, the trees . . . strange, very strange.'

He was right. It was as though the god that had blessed this island with life had grown bored with the flora and fauna of Greece and decided to experiment with something completely different. Even as they spoke, Danae spotted a wiry creature with soft white fur, a long tail and a face like a human child swinging between two tree trunks at the edge of the jungle.

Jason looked strained. He turned to the remaining crew, now congregating on the beach. 'Listen up! As you can see, the *Argo* has suffered badly in the storm. We will need to make repairs before we can continue our voyage.' He glanced at the jungle behind him. 'Luckily it seems we've landed on an island with plenty of wood. Heracles, Ancaeus, you start felling trees. Castor, Pollux, scout the island for –'

Jason stopped speaking mid-sentence, his mouth continuing to move like a fish out of water, as he sank to his knees and keeled over to lie unconscious on the sand.

There was a collective clink as the Argonauts drew their weapons, casting around for their unseen enemy. Then, one by one, they fell. Danae caught a dash of movement between the leaves. She threw her hands into the air and ran towards it.

'Stop, we mean no harm!'

Something stung her. She lowered her arms and saw a dart tailed with a small white feather protruding from her forearm. Before she could rip it out, her muscles went slack and she fell face first into the sand.

When Danae came to, it felt as though someone had cracked open her skull and scrambled the insides like an egg. Her vision was hazy, but she could tell she was still on the beach. The turquoise sea stretched out before her, the broken *Argo* wallowing in the shallows. The sun had arced along its course to the west and was much lower than it had been when they came ashore. She must have been unconscious for hours.

She tried to move her arms and couldn't. She was bound to something hard and scratchy. As she shifted, pain lanced through her shoulder. Biting the inside of her cheek to distract herself, she twisted her fingers to explore her restraints. The knots wouldn't budge. They were nothing like the bindings her father had taught her, but whoever tied them knew what they were doing.

She saw no sign of their attackers. The rest of the crew were dotted along the sand, tied to the trunks of tall trees at the edge of the jungle. Heracles was slumped around one near her, darts peppering the bare skin on his chest, arms and legs. Evidently, the hero hadn't been easy to take down. She spotted Jason further along, a cluster of darts protruding from his jugular. Brow creased, she looked down at her own body. Lodged in her arm was a single feather. That explained why she was the only one awake.

She felt movement behind her. Someone else was tied to the same tree. Craning around, she saw a long dark braid trailing over the back of a silver breastplate.

'Atalanta,' she hissed.

The warrior moaned. Then Danae noticed a sliver of iron glinting by Atalanta's feet, half buried in the sand.

'Atalanta!'

'What the fuck do you want?'

'By your feet, the sword.'

Atalanta grunted, then stretched forward. Her toes had almost reached the hilt when a sandalled foot, with a dagger sheathed between the straps, stepped down on the blade.

Danae's eyes travelled up the amber legs of a tall, muscular woman clad in a leather tunic. An assortment of weapons was tucked into her belt, including a dart pipe, whittled from what looked like bone. Her head was shaved at the sides and the remaining hair was plaited into a thick rope that fell down her back. An array of tiny animals, also carved from bone, was woven into the plait. The woman placed her hands on her hips and a smile, sharp as a whetted blade, cracked her mouth.

Behind her, more similarly dressed women emerged from the bushes, stalking between the unconscious Argonauts. All of them were heavily armed.

Danae redoubled her efforts to break her bindings, but they held fast. As she struggled, she felt a stinging sensation around her wrists as though whatever was tied around them was laced with something unpleasant.

The first woman flipped up the sword with her foot, caught the handle and pressed the blade into Danae's chest.

'Why have you come to my island?' Her voice was deep and husky, her accent unlike any Danae had heard before.

'We were wrecked.' Danae's tongue was still clumsy from the effects of the dart. 'The storm . . . smashed our ship.'

The woman pushed the sword to biting point through the fabric of Danae's dress. 'You've come to pillage us.'

'If that were true, you'd be dead,' said Atalanta.

Danae could feel the warrior trying to break her bonds. She wasn't getting anywhere either.

'Come on,' growled a blonde woman with lightly tanned skin and high cheekbones. She was standing over Heracles' unconscious frame wielding an axe. 'Let's finish them.'

Danae had to think, buy them some time. She looked around for something, anything to distract their captors. Her eyes fell on the darts peppering Heracles' skin.

'You kept us alive,' she blurted. 'We've been here for hours. If you wanted to kill us, why wait?'

The sword remained at Danae's chest, but the woman hesitated. She glanced at Heracles. 'Your leader killed two of my hunters before he succumbed to the phármakon.'

'He's not our lead – he was defending himself.'

'Only cowards drug their enemies,' growled Atalanta.

'Hypsipyle,' said the blonde woman impatiently. 'Why do we wait? He killed our sisters.'

Hypsipyle's face was almost impenetrable. But Danae could tell there was something holding her back from giving the order.

'You want something from us.' She hoped with all her soul she was right.

With a grunt, the blonde woman swung her axe over her head. Both Danae and Atalanta cried out as the double blade sang through the air.

'Peta.'

The axe came to a halt just above Heracles' neck. Hypsipyle removed the sword from Danae's chest and turned towards her hunter, eyes burning with fury.

'I did not give the order.'

The two women stared at each other, like two rival predators circling the same fallen prey. With a snarl, Peta swung her axe away from Heracles' body and stalked off across the beach.

'No one harms them until I give the word,' shouted Hypsipyle.

The hunters glanced at each other then took a reluctant step back from the unconscious Argonauts, their weapons still raised.

Hypsipyle rounded on Danae. 'What are you to them?'

She frowned, surprised by the question. She was still light-headed from the dart. 'I . . . I'm their seer.'

Hypsipyle's eyes narrowed.

'I divine omens and relay the will of the gods.'

'You are their mantis.'

'Yes.' She had no idea what Hypsipyle was talking about.

'They listen to you?'

'Yes,' she said again, with more conviction than she felt.

'And you.' Hypsipyle pointed the sword at Atalanta. 'You fight with them?'

Atalanta spat onto the sand. 'I would give my life for the man your dog tried to kill.'

Thankfully Peta was too far away to hear the insult. Danae clenched her jaw. The last thing this situation needed was the warrior's temper.

Hypsipyle appraised them both for a long moment. 'Maybe I can make use of you after all.' She cut Danae's bindings with her sword. 'Make a move towards a weapon and I will kill you. Understand?'

Danae nodded, aware of the knife nestled in her bag.

Once free of her bonds, she rose unsteadily to her feet. Whether it was the effects of the dart or the strangely viscous air, she couldn't quite shake the fog that had settled into the creases of her mind. A worrying predicament, given she had to negotiate for all their lives.

She was distracted by her itching wrists. Angry red welts circled her skin. She glanced down at the discarded bindings lying in the sand. They appeared to be fashioned from vines with black, mould-like spots. She rubbed her skin and looked warily at the hunters scattered around the beach.

Hypsipyle prodded her with the sword. 'He is not your leader?' She gestured at Heracles.

'No.' Danae pointed to Jason.

Hypsipyle's eyes roamed over the captain's unconscious form. '*This* one?'

She nodded.

Hypsipyle marched her over to him. 'This is the deal I offer you. Our homes were damaged by the storm. You will repair them for us, then we will allow you to take wood from the island to mend your ship. Break your word and we will kill you. Your leader and your men must agree to these terms.'

Danae didn't trust her, but what choice did she have? She nodded.

Hypsipyle crouched down and pulled the darts from Jason's neck. Then, she took a small bottle of amber liquid from a pouch on her belt and wafted the contents under Jason's nose. His eyelids fluttered. Then he struggled like a new-born lamb, his legs flapping uselessly against the sand.

Hypsipyle placed a firm hand on his thigh.

'W-what have you done to me?' Jason slurred.

'I am Hypsipyle, Queen of Lemnos. We bound you to protect ourselves from those who come uninvited to our shores.' The other hunters were looking at the Argonauts with sullen, mistrustful eyes. 'Tell me who you are.'

Jason pulled himself up against the tree trunk. 'I am Jason, captain of the *Argo* and rightful king of Iolcos.' He looked as though he was going to be sick.

Danae was suddenly reminded of how young he was. For all his bravado and confidence, he was a boy playing at being a captain, in charge of warriors far older than him and hardened by years of bloodshed.

Hypsipyle moved her face closer to his. 'This is what will happen, Jason. I will wake your men, and you will stop them from attacking us.' She glanced at Heracles. 'If you fail, you all die. Understand?'

Jason nodded.

'Good.' She straightened up, staking her sword into the sand and folding her hands over the pommel. 'Tell him the deal, mantis.'

Danae relayed the bargain Hypsipyle had offered.

Jason stared at her while she spoke. When she finished, he said quickly, 'I accept. I swear to the gods, we will do as you ask and I will keep my men in line. Then we will repair our ship and leave your shore.'

Hypsipyle smiled, cut Jason free and gave the order to her hunters to revive the crew. Begrudgingly, the hunters lowered their weapons. They moved among the unconscious men with vials of the amber liquid.

The Argonauts didn't come round quietly. As soon as they woke, most strained violently against their bonds, swearing at the hunters. The Lemnians shouted back and raised their weapons.

'Listen to me, Argonauts!' Jason shouted. 'I have made a bargain with these women –'

'I'm not agreeing to anything,' growled Pollux.

Ancaeus spat at the hunter nearest him.

Jason raised his arms in a placating gesture. 'I will explain! Please, calm yourselves . . .'

He was interrupted by the crack of splintering bark. Danae spun around to see Heracles rip the tree he'd been tied to from the sand and toss it across the beach, his bindings shredded on the ground. Chest heaving, he glanced down at his muscled torso and pulled fistfuls of darts from his skin.

Danae's throat tightened. The hero's pupils were swollen, his eyes crystallized with hatred.

Silence rippled across the beach. Then the hunters charged.

Heracles swatted them away like flies. He grabbed one woman by the throat, crushing her windpipe, while punching a hole straight through the chest of another. Jason just stood there, gaping at what was happening.

'No!' Danae shouted, running towards Heracles as he backhanded another couple of hunters, sending them crashing into the undergrowth.

She skidded to a halt as the hero swung around to face her and she was hit by a wave of fear. His handsome features had morphed into something terrible. He didn't look human.

'Heracles, it's all right, they're not going to –'

A dart embedded itself in Heracles' neck. The hero snarled, pulled it out and looked around for the woman who'd shot him. She dropped the pipe, but Heracles grabbed her before she could run. Screams tore across the beach as he ripped off the woman's arms one after the other.

Danae froze, unable to look away. Something inside him was broken. He was going to kill them all unless someone stopped him. As though answering her call, her limbs began to thrum with energy.

Use your power, said the voice. *You can save them.*

But after the mountain village, could she risk revealing herself again?

Another hunter shrieked as Heracles caught her.

Danae's nails bit into her palms. She couldn't stand by and watch more people die.

She closed her eyes.

Breathe, said the voice.

She listened, her lungs inflating like a pair of bellows. And then she felt it, like the clouds parting to reveal the sun: the power of the life-threads running through her veins. She hadn't known how she'd accessed the energy before, but now she understood. It was her life force, always there inside her, waiting.

Bending the threads to her will, she gathered a clutch of glowing strands and pushed them out of herself into the earth. The ground quaked. Trees vibrated, and birds rose from the shuddering jungle like sparks escaping a bonfire. No one was left standing.

Jason, Heracles and the hunters scrambled back up, gazing around in shocked confusion. Fighting the sudden weariness that threatened to drag her to the sand, Danae raised her arms to the sky.

'The Lord of the Sea and Shaker of the Earth has spoken to me!' she called. 'Poseidon, in his wisdom, demands peace.'

24. The Daughters of Artemis

The gods, the great unifiers. Whether inciting love or fear, they could always be relied on to hold an audience captive.

For what seemed like a lifetime, no one spoke. Then Idmon the seer cried out, 'Lord Poseidon, we hear you!'

Who better to blame for shaking the earth than Poseidon, God of the Sea and master of earthquakes?

The hunters were like a clutch of crabs, scuttling side to side, unsure of what to do. Hypsipyle's face was pale. The queen was staring at Danae. So was Heracles, but after what she'd seen him do, she didn't dare meet his eyes.

'What does he want from us?' asked Hypsipyle, her voice trembling.

'There will be no more bloodshed.' Danae paused. Her head was spinning. 'He brought us to this island to help each other.'

The Argonauts looked as shaken as the hunters, many staring at her as though seeing her for the first time.

Then Heracles came striding towards her through the blood-churned sand. Could he tell she was lying about hearing Poseidon speak? Was he going to pull her apart too?

Her fear bled away as he fell to his knees at her feet, and when he gazed up at her, she saw with relief that his pupils had returned to their right size. There was a knowing in his gaze, as though they shared a secret. He took her hand and pressed his lips to her skin. Even after he drew away, she felt their imprint linger.

'I will honour the wishes of my uncle.'

Hypsipyle's eyes widened. She muttered something inaudible to Peta.

'I too will uphold the will of Poseidon, as shall my men,' said Jason, quickly. He glanced at the bound Argonauts, who all nodded. Many still looked dazed after the quake.

'My hunters and I will do the same,' said Hypsipyle. The queen pointed at a couple of women, who set about freeing the rest of the Argonauts. 'We will take you to our town, but first we must tend to our dead.'

'Let us help you,' said Jason.

'No.' The queen's voice was sharp as flint. 'Your men will not touch them.'

The Argonauts clustered together while Hypsipyle and several of the hunters collected their fallen sisters.

'Some of us should remain with the ship,' said Tiphys.

'No one stays.' Peta appeared behind them. 'All must come.'

Castor squared up to her. 'I don't take orders from you.'

'No.' Jason put a hand on his shoulder. 'But you do from me. And I say we all go.'

Castor scowled and shrugged him off.

A vein pulsed in Jason's temple. 'Look at it, the *Argo* isn't going anywhere. Do you wish to anger the gods further?'

Tiphys shook his head, and no one else made any further arguments.

'Follow me,' said Peta.

As they traipsed after her, Danae glanced back. Heracles and Dolos were lagging behind the others. The hero's head was bowed, and the healer was whispering fervently in his ear. She wondered what sort of man the fates had tied her to. The more time she spent in Heracles' company, the more unpredictable he seemed to become.

'Stay close to the hunters,' said Peta. 'The jungle is not kind to strangers.'

'It's not the only one,' muttered Telamon.

The women led them through a path hidden amidst the tangle of branches. Danae tried to commit the route to memory, but it was useless; every twist looked the same. They had no way of getting back to the ship without the guidance of the hunters. The thought weighed heavily in her chest. The further they travelled from the *Argo*, the further she grew from finding Prometheus.

After shaking the earth, her body felt brittle, like a piece of coral beached on baking sand.

Her foot caught on a rock and without the strength to steady herself, she tumbled forwards.

Hylas caught her before she hit the ground.

'I'm fine,' she said reflexively, secretly grateful for his sturdy frame behind her.

'I bet it's tiring,' he slipped his arm through hers, 'communing with the gods.'

'Yes.' They walked in silence for a few steps, then Danae found herself saying, 'To be honest there's still a lot I don't understand.'

'I can imagine. I'd be scared shitless if I heard the voice of Poseidon.'

The hint of a smile hooked the corners of her mouth. 'It can be a shock, especially if it comes when you're indisposed.'

Hylas paused for a moment. 'Don't take this the wrong way, but you're not what I expected a seer to be like.'

'Young?'

'Funny.'

Danae's smile widened. 'It helps with the crippling exhaustion.'

A comfortable beat fell between them.

'I used to wish I could do things other mortals couldn't.

But travelling with Heracles ... it seems like it can be very lonely.'

He had no idea how right he was.

'I don't think many people can fight like you can.'

Hylas laughed. 'With enough practice anyone can learn. I could never do what you do.'

Ahead of her the twins muttered as they walked. She overheard the words 'easy pickings' and 'need a good fuck'. She glanced at the pairs of hunters flanking the Argonauts. Thankfully none of them seemed to have heard. She had a feeling their truce would not be easily maintained.

As they delved further into the jungle, dark leaves closed in above their heads. The air was even thicker here, moist and cloying. Beady eyes, like clutches of black pearls, stared out at them from the undergrowth. The tree trunks were wound with creepers and covered in green moss so luminous it almost glowed. Danae flinched as a bird erupted from the foliage, its feathers the colour of a blazing sunset, and watched it soar through the vines above.

It felt like they'd been walking for hours when Danae spotted a structure up ahead. As they drew closer, she saw the outline of a hut built around the trunk of a tree, a good twenty feet off the ground. The same green moss that covered the trees coated the roof and walls, blending with the jungle around it. A walkway stretched from the decking to another hut and then a whole network of dwellings came into focus above her.

As they progressed below the patchwork of tree huts, the storm damage became evident. Torn walkways hung between broken branches, and planks of fallen decking were strewn across their path. But despite the debris, the majority of the huts seemed intact. Having seen how capable the hunters were, she wondered why they needed to enlist the Argonauts to carry out the repair work.

Shards of sunlight broke through the canopy above, then the group poured into a clearing. Dominating the centre ground was a vast effigy, constructed of hundreds of branches twisting together to form a depiction of Artemis. The Goddess of the Hunt stood at least fifteen feet tall, a wooden bow and arrow drawn at her cheek.

Up ahead Atalanta faltered. The muscles in the warrior's shoulders clenched as her gaze lingered on the goddess. She flinched when Telamon touched her arm, then shrugged him off, stalking ahead.

Behind the statue was a large circular building made entirely of wood, the domed roof covered with dried fronds. The doorway was hung with fur pelts, and stuffed animal heads were mounted along the front of the building. What looked like a deer with twisted horns was nestled between a large cat with striped fur and protruding fangs and a creature with a face of leathery skin surrounded by thick black fur.

'Come,' Hypsipyle called. 'Feast with us in the Hunters Hall.'

Unease gripped Danae's spine as she followed Jason and the others inside. It was strange; all hostility seemed to have vanished. Hypsipyle was treating them like honoured guests, rather than strangers who'd just killed several of her hunters.

The hall itself was dominated by a smoking fire pit underneath a hole in the ceiling. A large boar was already roasting on the embers, as though the hunters had been expecting company. Smaller stuffed animals lined the walls. Birds with electric-blue wings were pinned as though captured in flight, and lifeless snakes coiled up the wood, their eyes replaced with yellow beads. They were so well preserved, Danae was almost sure she saw one of them move.

Hypsipyle turned her attention to the doorway, and Danae looked around to see another woman enter the hall. She was tiny and much older than the others, her loose white hair flowing beyond her waist. She looked around the room, and her eyes, green and mysterious as the jungle, lingered on Danae.

'This is Polyxo,' said Hypsipyle. 'Our mantis.'

Polyxo held a cup to the sky, her features blurred by the smoke curling from the roasting pit. Danae's eyes had not left the old woman since she entered the hall. She did not look like a seer, but that didn't make her any less dangerous. Danae licked the sweat from her lips. She was becoming increasingly light-headed from the intense heat of the fire.

'The first cup I give to Artemis, may we forever hunt in her light.' The old woman's voice whistled like wind across an open plain. 'We pledge ourselves to you, blessed Parthéna, now and 'til our ghosts cross the final waters of the Styx.' With a flick of her wrist, Polyxo poured the honey-coloured liquid from her cup onto the dried fronds that layered the floor.

The Argonauts sat around the fire pit, hunters dotted between them. Danae heard Atalanta mumble something to Telamon about a waste of good drink. She hesitated before lifting her own cup to her lips, wondering if it might be laced with whatever drug had coated the darts. But the wine the hunters drank had been poured from the same jugs, so she took a sip. It coated her mouth with a cloying stickiness, but she found herself draining the cup and wishing for more.

A stream of women appeared through the pelt-covered doorway, carrying woven bowls piled high with a vibrant array of fruit and vegetables. The food was bursting with flavour. After a few mouthfuls, Danae became aware of how hungry she was. She helped herself to a slice of something soft and orange. It was so juicy it almost slipped through her fingers, and when she bit into its flesh, sweetness exploded over her tongue.

'Mmmm!' Dolos moaned from across the fire, tucking into a steaming pile of mushrooms mixed with delicate purple flowers. 'These are fantastic, what are they cooked in?'

The girl who laid down the bowl smiled coyly, before scurrying away to fetch another tray of food.

Hypsipyle stood. 'It is our custom that the hunter responsible for killing the beast carves the first slice.' She fondled her braid as she spoke, the bone figurines clinking together. She had the most talismans of all the hunters. 'But tonight, the honour of the first cut is yours, captain of the *Argo* and rightful king of Iolcos.' She handed Jason a long, bone-handled blade and a two-pronged fork.

It was incongruous how effortlessly Hypsipyle slid into the role of fawning hostess. She seemed like an entirely different woman to the commanding warrior they'd met on the beach.

Danae was distracted as a plate of mushrooms was placed in front of her. She absentmindedly popped one in her mouth, then another, and another. Dolos was right, they were delicious. Earthy, sweet and spicy all at once.

With some effort, Jason pushed himself to his feet. As he stabbed the fork down into the crackling skin of the boar, a bead of sweat trickled down his nose.

The thought crossed Danae's mind that something was not as it should be.

A woman appeared behind her and filled her empty cup with more of the sweet wine. As she leant forward, her loose hair tumbled in a floral-scented cascade, brushing Danae's shoulder. The woman swept it over the nape of her neck and when she drew back Danae found herself looking into a pair of round eyes rimmed with thick lashes. She realized she was staring and blushed. A smile played across the woman's mouth as she moved along to fill Hylas' glass, her gaze still lingering on Danae.

'Your Majesty,' Jason licked the meat grease from his fingers, 'will the men of Lemnos be joining us?'

A shadow passed over Hypsipyle's face. 'There are no men of Lemnos.'

Jason looked confused. 'They've left the island?'

'They have left, but not by ship.' Hypsipyle drained her cup, then held it out to be refilled. 'It is a tale that requires more wine.' The woman who had served Danae ran over to refresh her queen's drink. Hypsipyle took a deep draught, wiped her mouth, then began.

'Lemnos was once a happy place. The women hunted, the men farmed, and the elders cared for the children. Everything was as it should be. One day, the queen led the hunt into the jungle, as she did each dawn. Her mantis begged her not to go. "No killing must be done today," she said. But the queen, eager to taste the excitement of the chase, did not listen.

'The hunters were climbing the mountain when she saw it. The most beautiful creature she'd ever laid eyes on, a hind so bright its fur shone like gold. What a prize, she thought, her eyes round as suns. She raised an arrow to her cheek, and with desire guiding the shaft, it sang true and found its mark. The hunters returned home with the slain beast, their high spirits echoing through the jungle. But when they reached the village they found the men lying on the ground, their eyes staring up at a sky they would never see again. They were dead, all of them, even the young boys. For the creature had been sacred to Artemis, and in her fury the goddess had taken what was sacred to the hunters.'

Hypsipyle wiped her cheeks. 'Now we dedicate ourselves to honouring the Parthéna, and devote our lives to repaying that one, terrible mistake.'

Danae could picture the scene. Men falling from their tree-top homes, their lifeless bodies crashing to the ground below, their families screaming. A crease formed between her brows. She knew first-hand how vengeful the gods could be, but if that was within their power, why hadn't she been struck down in Delphi? Why had the harpies been fooled into believing she was dead? As she turned the puzzle over in her mind, she pushed another handful of mushrooms into her mouth, licking the purple petals from her fingers. Gods, they were good.

Jason lay a hand on Hypsipyle's arm. 'You poor women.'

Hypsipyle smiled tearfully and caressed Jason's hand with her long fingers.

Danae's eyes drifted across the pit. Many of the Argonauts were now talking to the hunters, loose-limbed and relaxed. Ancaeus had pulled a serving girl onto his lap, the woman giggling as she toyed with the fur of his bearskin. Atalanta was fondling the talismans in Peta's hair, while the hunter described the kills that earned them.

Someone was missing, but she couldn't work out who. The harder she tried to remember, the more insubstantial the thought became until it faded from her mind altogether.

She looked up through the open smoke hole. The sky was dark and flecked with stars. The feast must have been going on for much longer than she'd thought.

She'd always believed what her mother had told her, that Apollo's sun chariot dragged all the colour from the world at the end of the day, only returning it again at dawn. But here the sky was filled with swathes of indigo and navy, obsidian, mahogany and deepest green all swirling around the most dazzling stars she had ever seen.

She reached for Hylas' hand.

'Look up,' she whispered. 'The stars are dancing.'

She glanced down at his face, then her gaze was drawn to something behind him.

Polyxo was staring at them, eyes bright, a sinister smile stretched over her wizened lips.

25. Vines and Venom

When Danae woke, everything around her was misty. She threw her arms out in front of her and was relieved when her fingers connected to fabric. She began to panic again when she couldn't find an opening. It was like she was cocooned in the web of a giant spider. Then a pair of hands appeared through the curtain, drawing it back to expose the girl who had served Danae wine at the feast. An amused expression played across her full mouth as she pulled apart the swathes of material and tied them back to reveal the insides of a small wooden hut.

'It's for the konops.'

Danae stared at her. The girl made a buzzing sound then slapped her arm.

'Oh, the mosquitoes?'

The girl cocked her head and looked at Danae as though she were an ignorant but adorable animal.

Danae didn't know how she'd got here. The last thing she remembered was gazing at the night sky through the smoke hole in the roof of the Hunters Hall. And Polyxo, watching her. She shivered, then looked down and saw her black dress was gone and she was now clothed in an animal-hide tunic, like the women of Lemnos wore.

'How did I . . . Where are my clothes?'

The girl laughed shyly and glanced up at Danae through her thick lashes. 'You took off your dress last night because you were hot.' She gestured to Danae's new tunic. 'This will be better for the jungle.'

'Right,' Danae said slowly, disconcerted by the gaps in her memory. The wine must have been stronger than she thought.

Crawling out from the nest of furs, she saw the fabric surrounding her was bound to the roof of the hut and fell all the way to the ground, covering almost a third of the tiny room. The floor was strewn with dried fronds and part of a tree trunk bulged through the right-hand wall. She tried not to think about how high up they were.

She was relieved to see her dress and cloak were folded neatly in a corner and her bag lay next to them. She scurried over and pulled it towards her. Everything was there.

She shoved her seer's clothing into her bag and slung it over her shoulder.

'Here.' The girl sat on her heels, holding out a woven plate. 'I made you breakfast.'

Danae took the dish, broke off a piece of omelette, sniffed it, then nibbled tentatively. It was stuffed with the same violet flowers the mushrooms had been dressed in the night before.

'Mmm,' she mumbled as the flavours danced across her tongue. She shovelled the rest into her mouth.

The girl smiled indulgently, like a mother watching her child eat.

'Thanks,' Danae said through a mouthful. Then she frowned. 'I don't know your name.'

'Sofia. You're Daeira.'

She must have told her last night. Thank the gods she hadn't given her true name.

She set the empty plate on the floor and licked her fingers. 'I should find the others.' Hopefully, one of the Argonauts remembered more of the night than she did.

Sofia slipped her silky hair behind her ears. 'Most are sleeping, but everyone always gathers in the clearing when they wake.'

Danae moved towards the doorway. 'Thanks for the omelette.'

She shuffled out onto the platform. Looking down, she saw a tangle of vines and branches but no obvious way of descending. The walkways only seemed to stretch between the tree huts.

'How do I get down?'

Sofia smiled, picked up a husk from the corner of the hut and dipped her fingers into the milky substance within. Danae recognized it as a nut from the tall trees on the beach. She recoiled as Sofia stretched out a hand, daubing her skin.

'You'll need this first.'

She backed away, roughly rubbing the substance off her arm.

Sofia laughed, then proceeded to massage it over her own honey limbs. 'Coconut salve. It protects us from the vines.'

Danae glanced down at her wrists. The welts were still visible from where the vines had bound her the day before.

Tentatively, she crawled forward and held up her arm, letting Sofia spread the salve over her skin. It felt cool and smelt sweet and creamy. She had a sudden desire to eat it. When Sofia reached her legs, Danae blushed, but Sofia didn't seem to notice.

Once both their limbs were completely covered, Sofia placed the husk back inside the hut and grabbed hold of one of the many vines that trailed down from the canopy above.

'Watch first.'

She wound the vine around one leg then stepped off the platform. Danae peered over the edge as the girl glided down to earth, gripping the loop with her feet to prevent herself from falling. She landed on the ground with the grace of a gazelle, then looked up at Danae.

'Your turn.'

Danae grabbed onto a nearby vine and wound it around her leg like Sofia had done. She took a nauseated glance at the ground, clenched her jaw, then stepped over the edge. She fell to a shuddering halt just below the hut. The half-digested omelette flipped in her stomach as she clung to the vine.

'Use your feet!' called Sofia.

She bit back a retort about how ridiculous it was not to have a ladder, then slightly loosened her fingers. To her surprise, she began to slide slowly downwards. She grinned. It *was* as easy as Sofia made it look.

Then her foot slipped, and she tumbled through the air, the vine tangling around her ankle. With a painful jolt she came to a halt, dangling just above the ground. Sofia's face loomed above her, biting her lip to stop herself laughing. She pulled a knife from her belt and cut Danae loose. Danae thumped to the ground in a heap, but only her pride was wounded.

'Any other way up or down?' she grumbled as she unwound the vine from her ankle.

Sofia shook her head.

'Right,' she said darkly.

'You will learn. Children can do it.' Sofia helped Danae to her feet. 'Or we can winch you down in a bucket like an old woman.'

'I'll get the hang of it,' Danae mumbled, brushing leaves from her tunic. Then she caught the glint in Sofia's eye. A joke. Despite herself, she smiled.

She eyed the knife in Sofia's hand. 'Does everyone here carry a weapon?'

A faint line appeared between Sofia's brows, as if she didn't quite understand the question. 'Never leave the hut without a knife. Everyone knows that.'

As she spoke, Danae was distracted by a movement in the trees ahead. Ancaeus crawled out of a nearby hut and straightened up on the adjoining platform. A beautiful raven-haired woman joined him and began rubbing salve into his bare limbs.

As she watched him, Danae became aware of the jungle moving around the hut. It was dreamlike with the vibrant colours and sweet, heady air. A butterfly the size of her hand flew past, cherry-red swirls winking on its wings. She turned her head to follow its path until Sofia's fingers slipped between hers.

'Come,' Sofia said gently.

As they walked, serenity washed over Danae in undulating waves. She was content for Sofia to lead her through the sea of moss-covered trunks. The ground felt softer than back home. She looked down at her feet and the springy, luminous moss that cushioned her sandals. It was so intensely green, it made all other greens look like a weak imitation of this true colour. She must have stopped moving because a moment later Sofia gently tugged her hand.

More Argonauts began to appear from the tree huts. Danae laughed as Telamon attempted to descend on a vine, lost his grip and fell to earth with a thwack, cursing all the way down.

Watching him brought back a memory. A story about a golden hind and men tumbling, dead, from the trees.

'When did all the men die?'

Sofia stopped walking, her pretty face crinkling into a frown. Then she pointed into the undergrowth. 'Look.'

Danae followed her finger and saw a tiny frog crouched on a leaf. Its skin was bright yellow with splashes of black, like dark vinegar poured into a dish of olive oil.

'That is a dart frog. Polyxo uses their skin to make the phármakon.'

Danae stared, mesmerized. 'It's beautiful.'

'Don't touch.' Sofia's eyes were wide and serious. 'Don't touch anything unless I say it's safe.'

Danae could have gazed at the frog for hours. But there was something nagging her, something lingering on the tip of her memory. Then it was gone.

Sofia placed a hand on her cheek. 'The island gives to those who know her ways and takes from those who don't. I want you to be safe.'

Danae found it hard to concentrate on Sofia's words, entranced by the movement of her lips.

'Promise you will do as I say?'

'I promise.'

By the time they emerged into the clearing, the wooden structure of Artemis was drenched in sunlight. Orpheus sat at its base, surrounded by a group of women all working on his broken instrument. He glanced up, smiling dreamily.

'These lovely women are helping mend my lyre.'

Danae grinned back at him.

'Daeira!' Dolos waved at her from the edge of the clearing, where he was standing with Polyxo. 'Look at this!'

Her fingers slipped from Sofia's and she ran over to them. Polyxo was kneeling on the ground, rootling around in the undergrowth. As Danae approached, the old woman sat back, a white flower with a long black root clasped between her gnarled fingers.

'Isn't it brilliant?' said Dolos, with the exuberance of a child discovering a colourful lizard.

Danae stared at the little flower, so delicate it looked like its petals were flecks of foam that would dissolve at any moment.

'We call it moly,' said Polyxo. 'The antidote to poison. By

distilling one petal you can create a draught that relieves the drinker of all their pain.' She pointed to her heart.

'Fascinating,' breathed Dolos.

'Help me.' Polyxo reached for the healer's arm. 'Girl, take my basket.'

Danae picked up the wicker basket laden with various plants. She glanced around the clearing, looking for Sofia, but the girl was gone.

'Where did Sofia go?'

She turned back to find Polyxo watching her.

'Collecting lotus flowers. That is her task. She's a good girl, Sofia, you will learn much from her in time.'

'Oh, we won't be here long.' Even as she spoke, the words surprised her. It was as though, until that moment, she'd completely forgotten their quest. *Her* quest. The prophecy. Prometheus. The hope of one day returning home.

She glanced at the groups of Argonauts now dotted around the clearing. It didn't look as though much repair work was being done on the tree huts. Telamon and Peleus were lying on the grass while islanders hand-fed them berries. Castor and Pollux were re-enacting one of their famous boxing matches for a rapt group of women, and even Tiphys seemed to be distracted enough to have forgotten the *Argo*.

The feeling that someone was missing returned with intense pressure at the back of her skull.

Polyxo slipped her hand around the crook of Danae's elbow.

'Help me back to my hut, will you?'

Danae glanced at Dolos, but he was already distracted by the intricacies of a spider's web. Polyxo pulled her away and steered her firmly towards the Hunters Hall.

'Shouldn't we be mending the huts?'

'Plenty of time for that.'

Danae frowned. Her headache was getting worse. 'What did you mean about Sofia's task?'

Polyxo leant heavily on her arm. 'We all have our tasks.'

'Why does Sofia have to pick lotus flowers?'

Polyxo shook her head. 'So many questions. Did you have breakfast?'

Danae nodded.

The old woman squinted at her but said nothing more. They walked together in silence past the Hunters Hall, towards a small hut like the ones nestled in the trees, but this dwelling was built on the ground.

Polyxo let go of Danae's arm, pushed back the animal hide that hung over the doorway and shuffled through. Danae followed her and was immediately hit by an onslaught of musk and spice. Polyxo's hut was like an apothecary. Every available surface was covered in woven bowls and wooden boxes of various dried plants and herbs. The bodies of stuffed animals hung from the low ceiling, and blocks of insects, preserved in amber resin, clustered on the shelves.

'What are those?' Danae reached towards a jar filled with black-feathered darts.

'Don't touch!' Polyxo slapped her hand away. 'Prick yourself on one of those and you'll be dead before nightfall.'

She stared at their tiny needled ends. They looked so small, so harmless.

Suddenly, one of the stuffed birds moved. Danae lurched back, nearly falling over a stack of crates as the buzzard flexed its tawny wings.

'Don't mind Glaux,' said the old woman, delving into a clay jar and feeding the bird a maggot. 'Now, pass me that.'

As Danae proffered the basket, she noticed a piece of jewellery on the workbench. It looked like a small gold medallion, a bow and arrow stamped into the metal, its chain wrapped around a tiny piece of parchment. Polyxo snatched it and tucked it into her tunic pocket.

'Tell me, child.' The mantis drew a bowl towards her, containing the flaked remains of a shredded snakeskin. 'What did he sound like?'

'Who?' Danae was captivated by the motion of Polyxo's hands as the old woman mashed the scales with a pestle.

'The Lord of the Sea. What did he sound like when he spoke to you?'

The beach. The lie. She had forgotten.

'Angry.'

'How did his words come to you?' Polyxo dipped a finger into the bowl and licked it. She added a pinch of herbs.

Sweat was pooling at the gathered waist of Danae's tunic. 'I just heard him, inside my head.' She was starting to feel nauseous, the sticky heat and muddle of aromas adding to the pounding inside her skull.

'Hmmm.' Polyxo set down the pestle and her hand drifted to a tiny bottle containing a milky liquid.

Then the sound of a horn blasted through the air. Danae backed away, a set of claws from one of the stuffed birds catching her scalp. She cried out, ducking away from its talons.

'The hunters have returned,' said Polyxo.

'I should go,' Danae mumbled, not waiting for a reply before stumbling through the doorway and breaking into a run.

She sprinted around the side of the Hunters Hall and felt a rush of relief when she spotted Hylas in the clearing.

'Daeira.' He beamed as she approached. 'I've been looking for you.'

'Hylas,' she said breathily, 'do you remember what happened last night, after the feast?'

A line formed between his brows.

'It's all a blur. I remember sitting around the fire and then . . . I just woke up in one of the tree huts –'

At that moment, the hunters came streaming into the clearing. Hypsipyle was striding at the helm, a horn pressed to her lips. Behind her, carrying a large boar trussed to a pole, were Atalanta and Peta.

Jason emerged from behind the effigy of Artemis, walked straight up to Hypsipyle and kissed her on the lips. The queen dropped her horn and pressed her body into his, raking her fingers through his hair.

Danae glanced around. No one seemed shocked by the display, as though the pair were a long-married couple. When they finally drew apart, Hypsipyle took Jason's face in her hands.

'Your warrior earned her first talisman today. Atalanta brought down the boar with a single arrow.'

Atalanta was beaming.

Hylas leant into Danae and whispered, 'Where is her armour?'

How could she not have noticed? Gone was Atalanta's silver breastplate, replaced by the same leather tunic the other hunters wore. She'd even shaved her head to the temples and her braids were woven into a single plait.

'She never removes her armour. In all the time I've known her, I've never seen her without it.'

Danae watched Atalanta basking in the praise of hunters and Argonauts alike as they clustered around her. The lines permanently etched between her brows were gone. Danae realized it was the first time since joining Heracles' group that she had seen Atalanta genuinely smile.

Heracles.

The edges of her vision began to pulse. He was the one

who was missing. She looked around the clearing but couldn't see the hero's towering frame anywhere.

'Have you seen Heracles?' she whispered to Hylas.

He blinked. 'Not since . . . I can't remember.'

Another cheer surged from the hunters. Hypsipyle clasped Atalanta's hand in hers and raised it to the heavens. 'Tonight, we celebrate the newest hunter of Lemnos!'

Danae looked around at the Argonauts. All of them wore the same glazed grin. Why was no one working on the tree huts? Where was their urgency to repair the *Argo*? Why was no one looking for Heracles?

She clutched Hylas' arm. 'We need to find him.' She turned, her eyes searching the depths of the jungle, and cupped her hands to her mouth. 'Heracles!'

Then Sofia appeared beside her, a basket in the crook of her arm.

'Sofia, we need your help.' Panic was beginning to bubble in Danae's stomach. 'Heracles is missing.'

'I'm sure he'll turn up.' She smiled and held out a lotus petal. 'They taste good fresh too.'

26. An Unexpected Gift

Danae stretched her limbs, then reached out and brushed the mosquito curtain aside. Sofia was waiting to greet her with breakfast. She had the strange feeling she'd woken like this many times before, and there was something important she should be doing, but when she tried to remember, the thoughts slipped through her memory like sand.

She rubbed her face, unable to clear the mist from her mind.

'I think . . . I need to go . . .'

Sofia held out an omelette stuffed with lotus petals.

'You can't go anywhere on an empty stomach.'

It smelt delicious, and suddenly Danae realized that she was starving. She bolted down the omelette, and as she ate the tension in her shoulders eased. She was being foolish, there was nothing to worry about.

'Your task is fishing,' prompted Sofia as she began massaging coconut salve into Danae's skin.

'Yes.' A smile drifted across her face. She was good at fishing.

Sofia nodded and handed Danae her bag.

'Have you got your knife?'

Danae stepped onto the platform and reached for a vine. 'Of course,' she said as she wound it around her thigh, then stepped over the edge.

She moved along the familiar path, hidden to those who did not know the ways of the jungle. The luminous moss held the memory of each footstep she'd imprinted the day before and the day before that. How many times had she walked this way? She couldn't remember. But that didn't matter, it wasn't important.

In no time at all she stepped out into the clearing. She waved to Telamon and Peleus as they passed, carrying a couple of wooden crates. They must be on their way to harvest the mango trees in the southern part of the jungle. That was their task.

She headed straight to a low, square structure on the opposite side of the Hunters Hall to Polyxo's hut. Brushing aside the animal pelts hanging across the doorway, she stepped into the armoury. Walking past the rows of wall-mounted bows, swords and axes, she reached up and grabbed a simple wooden spear and a wicker basket. Armed with the tools for her task, she turned to leave, but something caught her eye. A forgotten thing, small and white, lying on the floor in the corner of the armoury.

A dart pipe.

The faintest crease appeared between her brows as she stooped to retrieve it. There were carvings whittled into the bone, prayers to Artemis to bless the speed and accuracy of the darts. One of the hunters must have dropped it. They were the only ones permitted to carry them. She should give it to Hypsipyle, that was the right thing to do.

But even as the thought percolated in her mind, her hand slipped the pipe into her bag. She would return it later. No need to delay her task.

The water sang to Danae through the network of trees, drawing her along a path she sensed rather than saw. She had the feeling she hadn't always been useful. But now she was. She listened and moved with the jungle. It was satisfying to be part of something larger than herself.

She emerged onto the bank of a wide river that wove a

torrent of blue through the trees. She tucked the basket under her arm and, spear in hand, leapt onto a large boulder that split the current in two.

Her feet planted solidly on the familiar rock, she set down the basket and loosely cradled the spear in her fingers. A man's face floated into her memory, kind and sun-worn. The man who'd taught her to fish. A dull ache spread across her chest at the thought of her father. Then, as quickly as it had come, the pain faded, and his likeness melted like morning dew. Nothing that came before mattered now, all she had was this moment.

She waited for her breathing to slow, until all she could hear was the pulse of the river. Then she gazed down into its depths, waiting for the flicker of a fin.

There.

The spear pierced the current, straight and true. It sliced through the water and stuck fast into the riverbed. She peered down and her heart skipped as she saw a large silver fish pinned below the surface.

She squatted to keep her balance and tugged the weapon free, the fish still impaled, and pulled it clear of the water. Then she yanked the fish from the spear and held on tight as it twisted in her hands. It was at least three times the size of a red tunny. Polyxo and Hypsipyle would be pleased. She dropped the still-twitching fish into her basket and wiped her brow.

She delved into her bag, searching for her knife to bring the fish's life to a quick end. But instead, her hand brushed something hard and cloth-wrapped. As she drew it out, her palm began to tingle.

The prophecy stone. She had not thought about it in so long.

Heat pulsed through her hand and through the stupor

fogging her mind she heard the voice, so faint it seemed to be calling from the other end of the world.

You are the last daughter! You are the last daughter!

As she gripped the stone the voice grew louder, and memory, nauseating and overwhelming, crashed over her. She staggered, knees jarring as she hit the rock.

She stared at the cloth-covered stone, then at the fish still jerking limply in the basket. What was she doing? She had to gather the Argonauts and get back to the ship.

'Daeira?'

She shoved the prophecy stone back into her bag and spun around. Hylas was standing on the bank, a netted sack stuffed with coconuts slung over his shoulder. He'd grown a scraggly beard. When had that happened? Her hands flew to her own hair and discovered that her crop had grown over her ears and halfway down her neck. Despite the warmth of the island, the cold arms of fear wrapped around her. They must have been on Lemnos for months.

'What are you doing?' Hylas cocked his head.

There was something wrong with his face. Something other than his new facial hair. His pupils were huge, consuming his irises with gluttonous darkness.

'You're not doing your task.'

Her mouth was dry, the back of her neck clammy with sweat.

'Yes I am, look.' She tilted the basket towards him, revealing the fish. Hylas stared at it and blinked. It was horrible to watch him, as if a stranger had stolen his skin.

'What did you just put in your bag?'

He walked to the edge of the bank, as though he was going to jump and join her on the boulder. Danae scrambled back, lost her balance, and crashed into the water.

The shock of the fall robbed the breath from her lungs.

She broke the surface, gasping for air, while the river carried her downstream. She struck out to swim to the bank, but the river twisted, flowing into a much larger, faster-flowing channel of water. Hylas was shouting from the bank, but his voice was soon drowned out by the roaring current. It took all of her strength to keep her head above water as it tore at her limbs. The river was shockingly cold and blasted away the last of the haze clouding her mind.

She had been drugged. Polyxo, Hypsipyle, Sofia had all lied. They had no intention of letting the Argonauts leave the island.

Bruised and battered, she tumbled through the water, trying but failing to grasp hold of anything that would halt her progress.

Suddenly, the end of the river came rushing towards her.

No, not the end. A waterfall.

She barely had time to brace herself before she was falling, the weight of the water crashing behind her.

Sunlight prised her eyelids apart.

Wincing, Danae eased herself onto her elbows. From the pain lancing across her ribs, it felt like she'd broken them all. Drawing shallow breaths through the ache, she took stock of her surroundings. She was lying, half submerged, on the bank of a lagoon. Despite the torrent that hurtled down the mossy rock face from the river above, the water was calm. It lapped gently at her torso as if it had been disturbed by nothing more than a tumbling stone. Then she noticed the cloud of red blossoming into the blue around her. Clenching her teeth, she heaved herself further up the bank, her sodden bag that she miraculously still had dragging alongside her.

Nausea lurched up her throat as she looked down at her legs. A shard of her left thigh bone had broken through the skin, her blood pumping thick and fast into the water. Tentatively, she prodded the flesh near the crest of bone. She felt nothing. That was bad, very bad.

When they were children, Santos had broken his arm diving from the cliffs on their beach. She'd only been seven, but she remembered the waxy pallor of her brother's face as her father pulled him from the water. She'd thought him so brave for not crying. But later, back at their hut, his screams echoed to the sun and back when their mother reset the bone. The shock of the fall delayed the pain, but when it finally came it was all-encompassing.

She tried to move her leg and found she could not. Hauling herself onto the bank had been taxing enough, there was no way she'd be able to get back up the waterfall.

Hylas would have gone for help. He wouldn't abandon her. But his mind was lost to the effects of whatever the islanders were drugging them with. She couldn't count on him. He might not even remember what had happened.

She had to do something quickly or she was going to bleed to death.

Her trembling fingers slipped over the wet buckle of her bag as she searched for her knife. Blade in hand, she cut a long strip of leather from the hem of her tunic. Gasping at the pain in her ribs, she reached down and tied it as tightly as she could above her broken thigh bone. The stream of blood slowed to a trickle. That at least might buy her some time.

Then the full weight of reality crashed over her. She was alone on a hostile island, mortally wounded, and those who could help her were drugged out of their minds.

A swell of panic erupted into a sob. She was going to die on this island, and Manto's sacrifice would be for nothing. She would be left to rot unburied, and so her soul would be condemned to wander the banks of the Styx for all eternity.

She would never meet Alea in the Asphodel Meadows or see any of her family ever again.

Tears rolled down her cheeks as her memories leaked out like the blood pumping from her leg. The smell of the goat pen, her mother making cheese, her father walking up the track, his nets slung over his shoulder. Alea, by her side, her sister's fingers woven between hers. The joy of it hurt so much she thought it might kill her before the wound did.

'Hades,' she moaned. 'Please let me see her again, just for a moment.'

A deep, body-crushing ache was beginning to spread up her thigh. She waited. The river rushed, the birds chirruped, and insects clicked their wings. But the ruler of the Underworld did not reply. She should know better by now. The gods couldn't hear her. And even if they could, they wouldn't help.

'Fuck you,' she whispered.

There was a rustle behind her. Slowly, she turned her head.

A pair of yellow eyes loomed from the undergrowth, followed by the head and sinewy shoulders of a black panther. She almost laughed. Death had come quicker than she expected. Then she noticed the shudder of the creature's movements, the ragged wheeze of its breath, stilted with pain just like hers.

The large cat eyed her warily as it dragged itself towards the lagoon. Now it had fully emerged, she could see three broken arrows protruding from its hide, two in its left flank and one between its ribs. Rivets of dried blood matted its fur.

She knew then it wouldn't hurt her. There was no point. They could each sense the other was dying.

The panther slumped down beside her, its face almost at the water. It turned its head and fixed her with its yellow gaze. There was a stillness to its sun-like eyes. Something like acceptance. After a while their shallow breathing fell into a rhythm. They were together, she and this creature, at the end. She was not alone.

She blinked. She thought she'd seen a flicker in the panther's eye. A tiny thread of light dancing through its iris. It must be her blood-starved mind conjuring illusions. But then she saw it again.

The panther let out a low, guttural moan. She reached across and placed a hand on its fur, just below the arrow wound. It looked at her, then closed its eyes for the last time.

She could suddenly see threads of light weaving beneath the panther's fur. Then the creature's hide became translucent. She could make out every vein, every muscle, every sinew the threads ignited with life. She could see them in her own arm too, ribbons of light darting under her skin.

They were the same glowing threads that made up the tapestry of life in the oracle's vision. The same life-threads she had cast into the ground to shake the earth.

Hunger roared inside her, a desperate need to consume the energy beneath her fingers. Some of the panther's life-threads were already leaving, fleeing into the ground. She couldn't let any more escape.

Breathe them in, said the voice.

Concentrating on the tingling in her palm, she took a breath and willed the panther's life-threads into her hand. She shuddered as streaks of light shot up her arm and energy flooded her veins. Her vision exploded with clashes of colour and light. She felt as though she was not a whole thing at all, but a collection of tiny moving parts, small as a glint of sunlight and large as the ocean, all at once. She was made of energy, of joy, of pure ecstasy. The air tasted sweeter than honey, and there was no pain. She couldn't even remember what pain felt like.

Perhaps she was dead after all.

Then the sound of her ribs knitting together confirmed she was very much alive.

She looked down at her body and gaped. The bone in her leg had moved back beneath her skin and her torn flesh was healing. Once the process was complete, she tentatively moved her leg. It was as though it had never been broken.

Sucking in deep lungfuls of air between her freshly mended ribs, she pushed herself to her feet. A ripple of laughter escaped from her chest. Her body barely ached.

She sobered at the sight of the dead panther. Sinking down beside it, she placed a hand on its fur. It was cold, and she knew that its warmth was now in her. Its parting gift was the only reason she was still alive.

'Thank you,' she whispered.

She didn't know where animals went when they died; they didn't have an Underworld like mortals. But she hoped wherever it was, it was at peace.

She stood and set her sights on the waterfall. She had to get back to the Argonauts. Gods know what the Lemnians were planning to do to them.

She set off at a run around the edge of the lagoon and when she reached the base of the shallow cliff next to where the water tumbled into the pool, she began to climb. The moss-padded rocks would have floored an inexperienced climber. But she had been clambering over the sea-slicked crags of Naxos since she could walk.

She'd almost reached the upper bank when she saw something she had not noticed before.

It looked like there was a cave behind the waterfall. She stretched out an arm and thrust her hand behind the torrent. Rather than brushing stone, her fingers met air. She almost fell as she leant forward, her arm pinwheeling through the rush of water into nothing.

Bracing herself, she inched across the rocks and stuck her head through the cascade. Behind the waterfall was a passageway. She squinted through the gloom. What looked like a burnt-out torch was lying on the stone floor below.

Go inside, said the voice inside her mind. It was louder than before, as though it had been fed by the panther's life force.

She paused for a heartbeat, then clambered back down to the ground and leapt through the stream of water.

She skidded on the stone floor, before tumbling to the ground with a wet slap. Pushing herself to her feet, she looked around for the torch. Picking it up carefully, so as not to dampen the end, she held it against a dry section of wall. Then she took out her knife and struck it against the rock. Eventually, she was rewarded with a spark. She blew, hoping there was still some flammable liquid left on the hessian-wrapped tip.

The spark stuttered, then a tiny flame licked across the end of the torch.

She lifted it high, illuminating a rough passageway hewn from striped layers of rock. Accompanied by the crash of the waterfall and the dripping of her clothes, she took a step towards the darkness.

27. Cave of the Fathers

The passage seemed to go on forever. Danae shivered. It reminded her of being in the catacomb prison beneath Delphi.

After a while, she noticed markings on the stone wall. Lifting her torch, she realized that what she'd first taken for cracks were figures drawn onto the rock. They were simply sketched, but she could tell they were mortals. The artist had used the striped gradient in the rock as margins, and each strip contained a different scene. There were groups of hunters chasing deer and boar, clusters of farmers gathering crops, and a collection of people with their arms raised above their heads. They might be singing, dancing or worshipping, she couldn't tell. The stick-like bodies were all pointing in the same direction, with their heads tilted upwards. She carried on along the corridor, her pace quickening.

Suddenly, the rows of people fell away and drawn on the ceiling, spanning across the ribbons of rock, were twelve figures much larger than the rest. They too had their hands outstretched. She lifted the torch higher.

The light spilled across twisted branches. There was no colour to the apples that hung from the tree's boughs, but Danae knew its inspiration had been laden with golden fruit.

The torch slipped from her fingers. It hit the ground with a sizzle and died. For a moment she was alone in the darkness, her heart threatening to break through her newly mended ribs. Then her eyes became accustomed to the gloom, and she realized the passageway ahead was more grey than black.

She ran forwards, arms stretched out in front of her, desperate to reach the daylight. But when she came to the end of the tunnel, she found herself not outside, but in a vast cavern.

A bank of smooth rock stretched out before her, leading down to a mirror-flat pool. There was something unsettling about its stillness. Not a single leaf or fish rippled its surface. It seemed completely devoid of life. Even the air was stifling and stagnant. The light she'd seen filtered down from an opening far above in the rock ceiling. It illuminated the water with a sickly yellow glow and shone onto a mound of earth that rose from the centre of the pool.

For a moment she thought she was hallucinating.

Rising up from the little island was a tree. At first she thought it was the one sketched on the roof of the passage behind her. The one she'd seen grow from Alea's chest. The one burning in the oracle's vision. Then she realized it could not be. Its branches were not twisted or bowed low with golden apples, but were smooth, like silvery arms reaching towards the light.

It was dead.

Large white stones were clustered around its trunk, and, instead of fruit, bodies hung from its skeletal branches. Fighting her revulsion, she drew her knife and waded into the pool, shattering the reflection. She could smell them now, the stench of putrid flesh melting from the corpses. They had been there long enough to rot, but not enough to completely dry out.

She fought down the bile that rose in her throat and climbed, dripping, onto the mound of earth. With another sickening jolt, she realized that what she'd mistaken for stones was a pile of human skulls. It was hard to tell the age of the corpses. Some were almost completely skeletal, the remnants of flesh still clung to others, and a few still had short strands of hair attached to their scalps. Their clothing was varied too. Many were wrapped in leather kilts, similar to the tunics the Lemnian women wore. Others were draped in colourful robes.

Then she noticed a dart pipe belted to the kilt of one of the bodies. She staggered away from the tree.

The men of Lemnos.

She recalled Hypsipyle's glistening eyes when the queen spoke of their men being struck down by Artemis. But this was no burial chamber. These men had been killed at different times and, given the discrepancies in their clothing, she guessed not all were from the island.

The Argonauts were in grave danger.

She was about to turn back when she saw a hand protruding from behind the mound of skulls. An unusually large hand.

Skulls toppled into the pool as she raced around to the other side of the tree. When she saw who lay there, she fell to her knees on the cold earth.

The strength had been leached from Heracles' body. He was curled up like a child against the trunk, his cheeks hollow, his eyes sunken, and more white-tipped darts peppered his bruised, wasted limbs. How long had he been like this?

As she looked at the hero, Alea's sea-bloated face rose from his waxy pallor. Tears blurred her vision. She couldn't go through this again, it would break her.

Then Heracles' right eyelid twitched. Feverishly rubbing the moisture from her eyes, she leant over his face.

'Heracles?'

A whisper of breath passed between his lips, but he didn't move. She said his name again and shook him. Still he did not stir. Biting her lip so hard she drew blood, she tried splashing water on him, slapping him, but nothing would rouse him. Frustration forced its way out through her throat into something between a scream and a moan.

There had to be something she could do.

She placed her hands on his chest. If she could heal herself, perhaps she could heal others. She drew a deep breath, called for the life-threads rushing around her body and gathered the strands into her hands. Her fingers throbbed as the power built to a climax. Then she pushed, an intense tugging sensation dragging down her arms as the life-threads left her body.

She was hit by a wave of tiredness and thought it had worked; then a rush of energy surged back up her arms as her life-threads returned to her.

She cursed and sat back, pressing the heels of her palms into her eyes. What good were her healing powers if she could only save herself? She was nothing but a parasite.

She lowered her hands and looked down at Heracles. Self-loathing was not going to save him. She set about removing the darts from his body and stowed them away in her bag. They might come in useful.

'I'm going to get Dolos.' She squeezed his hand. 'I'll get you out of this, I promise.'

The last thing she wanted to do was leave him, but the healer would know what to do.

The sky was inked with twilight by the time Danae returned to the clearing. As she stepped through the trees, she saw a small crowd had gathered outside the Hunters Hall.

'Daeira!'

Sofia slipped through the tangle of bodies and ran towards her. Danae stopped as the girl flung her arms around her.

'I was so worried.'

Anger bubbled in her stomach, but she forced herself to remain calm. She knew it was imperative she play the part of drugged, dutiful islander to gain access to Dolos.

'I'm fine,' she smiled.

Over Sofia's shoulder, Danae saw Hypsipyle striding towards her, Polyxo hobbling in the queen's wake.

'Where have you been?' asked Hypsipyle.

'I was doing my task. But I slipped and fell in the river. I must have hit my head because I woke up on the bank and the sky was darkening, so I came home.'

Sofia raised a hand to Danae's cheek. 'I'm glad you're safe.'

Despite herself, Danae flinched. Hurt flickered over Sofia's pretty features.

'We thought you were lost to the jungle.' Hypsipyle's voice was honeyed with concern.

She was good, she was very good.

'I'm sorry to have caused trouble. I hope all these people aren't here for me.'

Hypsipyle smiled. 'No. There is to be an announcement, but that will come later.' She placed a hand on the small of Danae's back. 'Go with Polyxo, she will check you over.'

'I'm fine, really.'

She saw Dolos in the crowd and tried to catch his eye, but the healer didn't look her way. She cursed inwardly. She had to take him to Heracles before it was too late.

Then Polyxo grabbed her arm with a claw-like hand and steered her towards her hut.

You could destroy her in a heartbeat, said the voice.

Danae swallowed. It scared her because she knew it was true.

Polyxo pushed her through the doorway of the hut with surprising strength. Danae ducked to avoid colliding with the preserved animals dangling from the ceiling. As she straightened up, she noticed a row of amber bottles stacked on a shelf on the right-hand wall, identical to the ones the hunters used to revive the Argonauts on the beach.

'Sit,' said Polyxo.

Danae pulled up a stool. Immediately, Polyxo's prying hands were running through her hair, feeling her scalp for bumps.

'You hit your head?'

'No, yes . . . I'm fine.' She chewed the inside of her lip. She didn't have time for this, she had to get Dolos.

'Somewhere you'd rather be?'

Danae shook her head, forcing a dreamy smile across her face.

Finished with her head, Polyxo moved on to her left arm and lifted the limb into the air. 'Not a scratch,' the old woman muttered.

This was taking too long.

Looking around the hut, Danae spotted a jug of water on the workbench. Polyxo bent down to inspect Danae's legs and she seized the opportunity.

She didn't know if this would work. She'd only used her life-threads to heal herself or manipulate the earth, and that was the result of an emotional outburst, not a conscious choice. But she had to try.

Danae summoned a stream of shimmering life-threads from their flow around her body, concentrated on holding them in her mouth, then blew.

A gust of air, with the strength of a sea wind, tore from her lungs across the hut. The jug fell, cracking as it hit the workbench, liquid contents spilling over the wood.

Polyxo cried out and scurried over to salvage her stock. Danae took her chance, reached up, grabbed a couple of bottles of the reviving potion and ran from the hut.

She sprinted across the clearing, her body thrumming with the realization of what she'd just done. If her power could manipulate earth and air, what other elements might she be able to master?

When she arrived at the Hunters Hall, the last of the Argonauts and hunters were piling in for dinner. She glanced over her shoulder, but it seemed Polyxo had not pursued her. Dolos would be inside by now. Slowing to a walk, she blended with the crowd and slipped into the hall.

She spotted the healer near the entrance, already tucking into his meal. She tried to catch his attention, but he just smiled lazily at her, then returned to his food.

Clenching her jaw, she skirted around the edge of the hall and crouched behind him.

'Polyxo needs you.' She had to get him away from the hunters before she could tell him about Heracles.

'Coming,' Dolos mumbled. He shoved another handful of mangos tossed with lotus petals into his mouth before rising to his feet.

Danae's eyes bulged.

She looked along the table. Jason was draped across Hypsipyle's lap while the queen fed him slices of the orange fruit, making sure he ate the lotus petals soaked in its juice. She consumed none herself. As Danae watched, she realized none of the islanders were eating anything that contained lotus petals, only the Argonauts. The omelettes Sofia gave her for breakfast every day were stuffed with the purple flowers. Now she thought about it, there wasn't a meal she'd eaten on Lemnos that didn't contain lotus.

'Come on, it's urgent.'

She grabbed Dolos' arm and steered him outside before anyone could question where they were going. As soon as they were clear of the hall, she broke into a run, dragging him into the jungle.

'We're going the wrong wa—'

'Sorry about this.' She punched him in the stomach.

The healer doubled over, splattering half-digested mango across the tree roots.

Despite dispelling the lotus petals, he still looked dazed, so she pulled an amber vial from her bag.

Dolos backed away from her. 'What are you doing?'

Popping the cork with her teeth, she grabbed the healer by the tunic and held the reviving liquid under his nose.

She had no idea if this would work. She'd only seen the liquid revive those who'd been put to sleep by the darts. But she had to try something. She released Dolos and watched him closely as he leant against a nearby tree, his face scrunched in discomfort.

The moments stretched on, and when she could wait no longer, she said, 'Dolos?'

The healer looked up at her. Relief swelled in her chest as she watched his pupils shrink back to their normal size.

'Do you know where you are?'

'Yes,' he said slowly. 'An island . . . Lemnos?'

'Do you remember how we got here?'

The healer frowned. 'A shipwreck . . . We were ambushed . . . What have they done to me?'

'They've been drugging us. I think it's the lotus flowers. I'll explain everything but right now we have to go. Heracles is hurt.'

Dolos' face tightened with worry. 'I'll need my healer's kit.'

Once they had Dolos' bag, Danae led him through the jungle and told him everything that had happened since she fell into the river. Everything except the panther's sacrifice.

'Are you sure you're all right?' The healer looked at her with concern once they reached the waterfall.

'I'm fine, just a bit bruised,' she lied.

'You're incredibly lucky.' Dolos peered over the edge. 'A fall like that could kill, or at least break some bones.'

'This way. Be careful, it's slippery.'

She began the descent towards the mouth of the waterfall. The sun had abandoned the sky, and the climb was twice as treacherous in the dark, but they couldn't delay. Each moment they wasted might be Heracles' last.

Danae landed on the bank and waited for Dolos to catch up before leading him through the waterfall. With no torch to guide them, they took each other's hands, stretching out their free fingers to brush against the passage wall.

'So, you think the women of Lemnos killed their menfolk and brought them here?' asked Dolos.

'Not just their men by the look of the clothing. And some of the bodies are more recent kills. Maybe sailors who came to the island by chance, like us. I don't know what the Lemnians are planning, but I think we're all going to end up rotting in this cave if we don't do something.'

'I wish I knew exactly how long we've been on this damned island.' Dolos' voice was strained. 'How long he's been down here.'

'I think it's been months. If he wasn't a demi-god, he'd surely be dead by now.'

Dolos was silent.

Eventually, the ghostly light appeared ahead of them. The healer dropped Danae's hand and ran through the darkness towards it. She followed him, their breath chasing the sound of their footsteps as they emerged onto the edge of the pool.

It was a clear night, and the silver moon illuminated the grotesque scene below. Dolos barely slowed at the sight of the tree, crashing through the water, not stopping until he was by Heracles' side.

The healer unfurled his pack. His usually steady hands trembled as he wafted a pouch of herbs under Heracles' nose.

The hero's eyelids fluttered open, then closed again.

'Can I help?' Danae couldn't bear how useless she felt.

'His head,' Dolos said, retrieving a vial of blue liquid from his pack. 'Prop it up.'

She shuffled round and eased the hero's head onto her lap.

'Heracles, it's me.' Dolos gently prised open the hero's lips. 'You need to drink this.'

He poured the potion into Heracles' mouth. The hero gagged.

'He's choking!' Danae tried to turn him on his side, but Dolos pushed her back.

'He's got to drink it, it's the only thing that will help.' He tilted Heracles' head back, forcing the liquid down his throat. 'Swallow! Gods damn you, swallow!'

Danae's heart was in her mouth. Heracles sounded like he was drowning. Then he gulped. Relief seeped through her as the hero sucked in a lungful of air. She grinned, hastily blinking the moisture from her eyes.

Dolos wiped his forehead, and the pair of them helped Heracles prop himself up onto his elbows. He looked blearily from the healer to Danae, then took in his surroundings.

'Have another,' urged Dolos, handing him a second vial. Heracles downed the contents in one and smashed the bottle on the ground. He pushed himself to his feet, grabbing onto the tree for balance.

'You need to be careful,' said the healer, leaping up to steady him. 'We don't know how long you've been without your tonic . . .'

Heracles pushed him away. 'Just tell me how to get out of this gods-forsaken place and who I need to kill for putting me here.'

28. Fire and Fury

Danae stared at Heracles' back. His muscles were rippling like sand under the weight of an ocean tide, and his wasted frame appeared to strengthen with every step he took through the jungle. The divinity in his father's blood must be potent. The divinity she somehow had to destroy.

Ahead of them, Dolos held up a fist.

'We're almost back at the clearing.'

'Good,' muttered Heracles. He had barely spoken to either of them since the cave.

'I think it would be wise if you stay here for now,' said the healer.

'I'm coming with you.' Heracles' eyes were hard as sapphires.

Danae placed a hand on his arm. 'You will have your vengeance. But the Argonauts are drugged and would be defenceless if we attack now.'

Heracles' brow darkened.

Danae glanced at Dolos. 'Do you trust us?'

The hero's eyes swept over her, then the healer. He placed a hand on Dolos' shoulder.

'I trust this man with my life.'

Dolos' eyes crinkled to the corners of his face. He clasped Heracles' arm in return.

'Then wait for our signal,' said Danae. 'Together, we will free the crew and get off this damned island.'

'What did you give him?' Danae whispered as she peered through the tangle of vines to the clearing beyond.

Dolos didn't answer.

'That blue liquid?'

The healer remained silent.

'If it's some kind of reviving potion we could give it to the Argonauts –'

'No,' Dolos said sharply. He paused for a moment. 'It's merely a health tonic, to support his demi-god constitution. It would do no good to a mortal.'

Danae glanced back into the depths of the jungle, where Heracles crouched a few trees behind them. 'For a moment there I didn't think he was going to agree to wait for us to drug the hunters.'

A strip of moonlight fell across Dolos' face, illuminating a wry smile. 'Despite appearances sense can, on occasion, prevail with him.'

Danae wiped a bead of sweat from her brow, her stomach writhing. Her hand twitched to her bag, where the freshly tipped darts were stowed. It had been Dolos' idea. After the healer had almost trodden on a dart frog, he'd painstakingly rubbed the tips of the darts Danae had salvaged across the creature's yellow and black skin. Using the pipe she'd found in the armoury they planned to knock out the hunters. But they didn't know how potent the raw poison would be or how long it would render a person unconscious. And with their limited number of darts, there was no room for mistakes. Even with Heracles' fists, they would be no match for the hunters if they caught wind of the attack.

The image of rotting bodies and gleaming skulls flashed across her mind.

'I pray the gods look kindly on us tonight,' Dolos whispered.

Danae swallowed the lump in her throat. Part of her wished she still believed in prayer. It would be a comfort.

But she knew better. They were in the hands of the fates, not the gods.

She could still feel it, fainter now, but it was there. The power lingering beneath her skin. She'd thought about using it, of course she had. But it would involve revealing herself to Dolos and Heracles. Rumbling the earth and blaming it on Poseidon was one thing, but she couldn't hide behind the gods forever, and if Heracles found out the true extent of her powers . . . she didn't want to think about it. The screams of the hunters he'd attacked the day they arrived on the beach were forever burnt into her memory.

Finally, the pelt covering the entrance of the Hunters Hall was drawn back, and people spilled out into the clearing. Danae frowned. The Lemnians and Argonauts weren't dispersing to their huts as usual but lingering around the giant structure of Artemis.

Then the crowd turned to the doorway, and a hush descended on the clearing. Hypsipyle and Jason emerged, silhouetted against the dying flames of the fire-pit. Hypsipyle reached across the space between them and took Jason's hand in hers, thrusting their arms up towards the moon.

'Tomorrow, by the glory of Artemis, the blessed Parthéna, I shall take this man as my husband.'

A foolish grin was plastered across Jason's face. The crowd erupted with cheers, surged forwards and lifted the couple onto their shoulders. A sea of hands reached to touch them, as though their joy was infectious. Danae turned to Dolos, but before she could speak the healer cried out in shock.

A lime-green snake had dropped from the trees above and was winding around his neck. Heracles surged forward and grabbed it, tossing its coiling length into the undergrowth.

But the damage was done.

Beyond the tree line the crowd fell silent. The hunters turned towards the jungle, reaching for their weapons.

So much for a stealth attack.

For a heartbeat, Danae, Dolos and Heracles looked at each other. Then the hero ripped through the foliage, torn vines trailing behind him as he lunged at the hunters.

Danae's heart dropped through her stomach. Fingers clumsy in her haste, she rushed to undo the straps of her bag. 'Take this.' She pulled out a bottle of reviving liquid and shoved it into Dolos' hands. 'Wake the others. I'll take out as many hunters as I can.'

Dolos nodded and dived into the throng.

While the islanders scattered and the Argonauts floundered in confusion, the hunters closed ranks, forming protective rings around Hypsipyle and Jason while backing into the Hunters Hall. Heracles followed them, knocking through islanders like a bull thundering through a field of barley. His strength wasn't what it had been when they'd arrived on the island, but even so he wielded the power of four men combined.

Through the chaos, Danae saw Telamon and Hylas running towards the armoury. From their panicked faces, she gathered Dolos had revived them. But their path was soon blocked by three hunters, who emerged from the armoury swinging axes.

She sprinted from the cover of the jungle and sheltered behind the effigy of Artemis. Fumbling a dart into the stolen pipe, she lifted it to her lips and blew towards one of the hunters outside the armoury.

The dart fell short.

Cursing, she reloaded. She was too far away.

Breathe, said the voice.

She panicked for a moment, then forced herself to focus

on the air in her lungs and felt for the pulse of her life-threads. She was swollen with them, her own piece of life's tapestry engorged with the panther's threads.

She lifted the pipe to her lips and locked eyes on her target. She blew again, and this time, glowing threads streamed behind the dart as it shot through the air. No one else seemed to be able to see them. The first hunter fell. She fired another and another. The other two hunters dropped their weapons and slumped to the ground.

Telamon and Hylas stared in confusion at their fallen attackers.

'You can thank me later,' said Danae as she appeared behind them.

'Daeira!' Hylas threw his arms around her. She pulled away, light with relief as she looked into his eyes, bright with their familiar warmth.

'I would ask you to fill us in, but we appear to be in a battle.' Telamon retrieved the hunters' axes and threw one each to Danae and Hylas.

A splintering crack signalled that Heracles had punched through the wall of the Hunters Hall.

'Now that's more like it!' Telamon shouted and launched into the fray.

Danae looked down at the axe in her hand. It was so heavy. She'd never held a weapon like this before.

A cascade of screams rang out from the Hunters Hall.

'You'll be fine,' Hylas said quickly. 'Just keep your stance strong and aim for the head. Come on.' He sprinted after Telamon.

Danae gripped the axe shaft so tightly her knuckles turned white.

'Strong stance,' she muttered, then ran after him.

As she raced towards the Hunters Hall, she saw Dolos was

making quick work of reviving the Argonauts. Ancaeus roared as two hunters rushed him, breaking one's arm with his bare hands and gutting the next with her own sword. Behind him, Pollux and Castor fought like twin hurricanes, their bloody fists dripping in Lemnian blood. On the far side of the clearing, Danae caught sight of Atalanta staggering away from Dolos. The warrior stared about, wild-eyed, then sprinted towards the armoury.

'Daeira!'

Danae spun around and saw Sofia running towards her. She raised her axe between them as the girl skidded to a halt.

'Get away from me.'

'Daeira, please,' Sofia stretched out her hand, 'come with me, it's not safe.'

'You killed the men, didn't you?'

Sofia's eyes widened.

'I've seen the cave.'

Tears ran down the girl's cheeks. 'It wasn't us; Artemis killed them.'

Danae's fists tightened on her weapon. 'Don't lie to me.'

'We drugged them, but Artemis drained their lives, I swear.'

Danae faltered. 'Drained?' She thought of the panther, of the life-threads she had sucked from its dying body.

Sofia's lips parted, but instead of words, blood oozed from her mouth. She fell to the ground, an arrow protruding through her abdomen. Atalanta stood behind her, bow raised.

'You're welcome!' the warrior shouted before launching back into the fray.

Danae sank down beside Sofia, her limbs trembling. Alea's body surged violently into her mind: her misted eyes, the seaweed tangled in her curls, her bloodless lips.

Danae felt herself fragmenting, but she forced her shaking hand to Sofia's face and nudged the girl's eyelids closed. Then she picked up her axe and ran after Atalanta.

She spotted the warrior, sending arrows flying into the crowd, felling hunters and islanders alike.

'Atalanta!'

The warrior ignored her and latched another arrow. Danae dodged round Orpheus as he and a hunter clashed blades across her path.

'Atalanta!' Danae shouted again, grabbing the warrior's arm. Atalanta snapped around, the tip of an arrow barely a hair's breadth from Danae's face.

'You can't just massacre the islanders.'

Not even a flicker of emotion cracked the warrior's gaze.

'We don't know if they were all involved. And those that were might have valuable information.'

Disdain spread across Atalanta's face. 'They lied. All liars deserve to die.' She turned and continued to send arrows into the throng with deadly accuracy.

Danae backed away, ears ringing with the clash of bronze and bone. Islanders' bodies littered the clearing. Many hadn't found the safety of the jungle in time. They weren't hunters and stood little chance against the rage-fuelled Argonauts. This wasn't how it was supposed to be. These people had lied to them, drugged them, but they didn't all deserve to die.

As Danae looked around, she saw the Argonauts had casualties too. Idmon, the seer, was lying on the ground, a spear protruding from his gut, his sightless eyes staring at the stars.

She was distracted by a hunter hurtling towards her with a broadsword. Just in time she swung up her axe and blocked the woman's blade from cracking her skull. The hunter swung again, and this time her sword hit the axe's handle, biting into the wood. Danae tried to reach for her life-threads but was too distracted to concentrate. The hunter snarled and pushed her sword, shoving Danae back until she collapsed, pinned under the weight of both their weapons.

Darkness began to press against the corners of her vision. Her chest was screaming, the weight of the axe crushing her. Then the hunter's eyes were drawn to something behind her. The woman's face fell slack and she let go. Scrambling back, Danae twisted to see what was happening.

Heracles was striding from the hall, dragging Hypsipyle by the neck. Jason staggered after them, his face bloody. From his glazed expression, it looked as though he had not yet been revived.

The hero threw Hypsipyle to the ground.

'I'm going to enjoy killing you, witch.'

'No,' moaned Jason.

'Pathetic.' Heracles kicked him as he reached towards his bride. 'Dolos! Revive our *leader*.' Then he turned his attention to the Queen of Lemnos. 'Only a coward drugs their enemies. You are spineless by deed, and I will make you spineless by nature.' He reached for her.

'Wait!' Hypsipyle stretched out a bruised arm between them. 'To kill me in our holy clearing, before the eyes of Artemis,' she reached towards the wooden effigy, 'would be a sin against the gods.'

'Fuck the gods.'

Stillness rang across the clearing.

'You dare dishonour your father?' whispered Hypsipyle.

A terrible smile spread across Heracles' face as he grasped her tunic and lifted her into the air. 'I don't give a damn about my father.'

Danae stared at him. She would never have imagined the hero harboured anything other than love for Zeus.

Then something small bounced off Heracles' impenetrable lion hide. He dropped Hypsipyle and stooped to pick it up. Even in the moonlight Danae could make out a black feather. One of the deadly poisoned darts she'd seen in Polyxo's hut.

One by one, the Argonauts started to fall. Blood thumped through Danae's veins as her head whipped round, searching for the culprit. Pollux tumbled to the ground, then his twin, Castor. Telamon sank to his knees beside his fallen brother, Peleus. Then she noticed a wisp of silver hair disappear behind the Hunters Hall.

Polyxo.

She dropped her axe, it would only slow her down, and sprinted after the old woman. As she drew closer to the hall, Polyxo's face appeared around the corner, a dart pipe pressed to her lips. Danae sped up, pumping her arms with all her might. Then someone grappled her. She crashed to the ground, the air punched from her lungs. Gasping, she looked up, but Polyxo had disappeared.

'Shit!' She pushed herself away from her attacker. It was Hylas. 'What the fuck are you doing?'

He didn't move. 'Daeira . . . I feel strange.'

Then she saw the black dart lodged in the side of his neck. She ripped it out, throwing the cursed object as far away as she could. Hylas' brow was already clustered with cold sweat.

'She would have . . . hit you,' he slurred.

Tears blurred Danae's eyes. 'It's all right, you'll wake up in a few hours.'

'Ahh . . . sorry to miss . . . the fight.'

She forced herself to smile. 'You've earned the rest. I'll see you when you wake up.'

She felt his body go slack.

For a moment, there was nothing. No sound, no moon, no earth. Then she roared until her lungs ached to draw breath. All she wanted was to destroy.

You know what to do, said the voice.

She rose to her feet and summoned the power of her life-threads, throwing a surge of them through the hole Heracles had smashed into the side of the Hunters Hall.

The fire-pit in the middle of the hall exploded. In moments, flames as tall as trees were licking up the sides of the building. Lemnians and Argonauts alike ran for the protection of the jungle. Heat billowed from the broken mouth of the hall, and soon the inferno had spread to the armoury. The fire feeding her rage, Danae sent another stream of life-threads into the burning hall and whipped the flames towards the wooden statue of Artemis. It caught alight instantly, and the effigy began to eat itself, crumbling as it burnt.

Polyxo's buzzard soared into the sky, flying away from the old woman's hut. In the light of the fire, it looked like there was something metallic glinting on its breast.

Then a flicker of movement drew Danae's attention back to earth. The hunched figure of Polyxo was stumbling across the clearing towards the jungle.

She walked towards her without hurry, her eyes cold and bright as stars.

The old mantis was crawling by the time Danae reached her, dragging a salvaged bag of potions along the ground. Her face was covered in soot, and she spat out blackened phlegm as coughs racked her body. She looked up as Danae came to stand in front of her.

'You . . . did this.'

'Yes,' Danae's voice was hard as iron.

'On the beach, it was you who shook the earth.'

'Yes.'

The old woman grabbed her foot. 'Please don't kill me.'

She withdrew her leg in disgust. 'I don't drug and murder people, unlike you.'

Polyxo laughed. It was an ugly sound, muddled with pain. 'You know nothing, child. Our men took and took until our bodies were broken.' She coughed up another lump of phlegm. 'Artemis knows, she set us free.'

'Sofia said she drained the men, what does that mean?'

'You already know.' Polyxo smiled, revealing bloody teeth. 'You reek of power. Just like her.'

'No.' Danae backed away. 'I'm nothing like her.'

She became aware of screaming, the smell of scorched wood and charred flesh. She looked at the burning hall and was transported back to Delphi, to standing on the mountainside outside the flaming city as the horror of Apollo's vengeance washed over her. But this time, the destruction was hers.

She turned back to Polyxo, but the old woman had disappeared.

29. Ash and Salt

Dawn wandered listlessly over the island.

Danae sat on the beach, looking out at the *Argo*. The mast had been restored, a new steering oar fashioned, and the ship's hull was a battered patchwork of freshly stripped wood. Heracles stood beneath the prow, hammering the last few planks into place. The crew had worked through the night to repair the vessel, with the hero bearing the brunt of the labour.

After the fire ravaged the village, victory had come swiftly. Once revived, Jason regained command of the Argonauts, and at his order, they rounded up the rest of the hunters, executed them and piled the bodies on what remained of Artemis' burning effigy. But it was a sullen and subdued crew that now carried the weapons, food and animal pelts they'd pillaged across the beach to the ship. No one seemed to be able to look the others in the eye. The fiercest fighters in Greece weren't used to the shame that accompanied powerlessness.

By some miracle, in all the chaos, it seemed no one but Polyxo had seen Danae start the fire. The old mantis had vanished into the jungle and not been spotted since. After confronting her, Danae had been engulfed by a weariness that seeped into her marrow. She felt empty, like she was just a sack of mindless flesh and bone. Part of her hoped it was temporary. Part of her didn't.

Perhaps it was a blessing, given what had happened.

Polyxo's words echoed around her skull, taunting her.

You reek of power. Just like her.

For the first time, she wondered if she was more monster than saviour. How could she ever hope to become the light that frees mankind if all she did was destroy?

'It is time,' called Jason.

Danae slowly pushed herself to her feet and wiped the sand from her dress. She'd changed back into her black seer's robe. It felt fitting for what she had to do.

The crew set down their loads and flocked to their captain.

She turned to face the seven bodies laid out on the beach, wrapped in furs from the Lemnian stores. She took the obols from Jason's outstretched hand and placed a pair on each of the fallen Argonauts' eyes. When she was done, Jason nodded, and she lifted her arms to the sky. Even that small movement taxed her, but she didn't let the strain show.

'May the Twelve see you and know you. May the Keres spread their wings over you as you walk the path of judgement. May your souls find peace across the final river.'

'Go with the blessing of the Twelve,' murmured the crew as they bowed their heads.

Danae lowered her arms, and in silence, Heracles, Telamon and Atalanta set about digging graves in the sand. The warrior had removed the bone talismans from her hair and was once more in her silver armour. She had not spoken a word to anyone since they burnt the hunters.

Danae felt a hand on her shoulder. She turned, and a breath of feeling returned to her chest.

Hylas smiled at her. 'Obol for your thoughts?'

She shook her head. 'None worth buying.'

From the ruins of Polyxo's hut, Dolos had salvaged a bunch of moly. Armed with the herb and the contents of his healer's bag, he'd been able to concoct an antidote for those hit by the poison darts. Those felled by sword and axe were not so fortunate.

Hylas' gaze travelled past Danae to Hypsipyle. The queen was bound to the trunk of a coconut tree, like the Argonauts had been the day they arrived. Jason had an ironic sense of justice.

'Do you think they would have killed us?' Hylas asked.

'Probably. They killed all those other men. They left Heracles in that cave to be sacrificed to Artemis.'

Once the battle was won, she'd told the crew what she'd learned from Sofia and Polyxo, save what the old mantis had said about her. She had to believe she'd saved the Argonauts, that she'd had no choice but to unleash her powers. Even so, she couldn't prevent her mind wandering to the charred bodies of the islanders who hadn't escaped the blaze. She'd done that.

'I know I shouldn't question the gods but . . .' Hylas paused. 'Why would Artemis kill all those men?'

'Because the gods are cruel.' Danae only realized she'd said the words out loud when Hylas turned sharply to look at her. 'But just,' she added quickly. 'Like you said, it's not for us to question their ways.'

When the last man was buried, Jason marched across the sand to the woman who would have been his wife. He stopped in front of Hypsipyle and squatted to her eye level. The crew paused what they were doing to watch.

He lifted her bruised chin. 'Now you get to watch me sail away and live out the rest of your gods-forsaken life knowing I got what I wanted from this pathetic little island.' He spat the last words into her face.

Jason navigated the world with the confidence of a man who knew he was right. He believed he was chosen by the gods. He believed he was special. And to a man like that, there was nothing more humiliating than being bested by a woman.

Hypsipyle parted her cracked lips. 'What a big, brave man you are.'

Jason's face twitched. He stood up and for a moment, Danae thought he was going to walk away. Then he unsheathed his dagger and in one smooth motion, slit Hypsipyle's throat. Her eyes bulged as blood washed down her front, sluicing onto the sand.

The crew were silent as Jason thundered back down the beach.

'What are you looking at? Get back to the ship!'

'He's unravelling,' whispered Hylas.

He's not the only one, thought Danae, as she watched Heracles climb aboard the Argo.

Hylas shook his head. 'It doesn't bode well for us.'

'No,' she muttered, 'it does not.'

'I see Imbros!'

Tiphys crouched on the stern platform, shielding his eyes from the sun. A patchwork of maps fanned out around him. Danae knelt opposite, fingers splayed across the parchments, tethering them to the deck. The old navigator was squinting at a verdant island piercing the horizon to the port side of the ship.

Jason jumped down from the prow deck and clambered towards them over the rowing benches. 'How far off course are we?' His eyes were bruised from lack of sleep. They had been sailing for two days straight.

Tiphys stared down at his maps. 'I cannot say for sure, Captain. There's no record of Lemnos anywhere. But if that *is* Imbros, I'd say about a week. Not counting the time we lost on the island.'

From their collective hair growth, it was estimated the Argonauts had spent at least four months on Lemnos.

'Fine,' Jason grunted as he climbed up to the stern deck, 'clear this up and get us back on track.'

'Impossible,' muttered Tiphys, poring over the swirls of ink. 'How can an island the size of Lemnos not be recorded on a single map?' He lowered his face closer to the parchments. 'There's only one thing for it; I'll have to draw it on myself.' He glanced up at Danae. 'Fetch me ink and quill, will you?'

'Enough!' Jason seized a fistful of maps and thrust them in Tiphys' face. 'If you mention that damned place again, I will throw these overboard.' He tossed the scrolls at the navigator, then swung around to face the crew. 'No one is to speak of that island, that's an order. And why in Tartarus have you stopped rowing?'

As Jason stormed back to the prow deck, Danae and Tiphys scurried to rescue the maps from flying overboard.

'Thank you,' said Tiphys quietly.

As the navigator eased the parchments from her arms, she looked down at the last map trapped below her knee. She was about to roll it up when something caught her eye.

There it was, barely larger than a thumb print. Her home.

Naxos was so small, so far away. She stared at it for a moment, then her eyes travelled east. Past the jaws of the Black Sea, the map grew sparse. There was hardly any writing, just the outline of the land and, at the very edge of the page, a row of peaks. The Caucasus Mountains, where Prometheus was imprisoned.

The mountain where her destiny waited.

Danae woke to a sky pricked with stars. She lay on the deck, staring at the night, until the sound that had roused her caught her ears once more.

Someone was crying.

Silently, she rolled onto her side. Beside her, Atalanta's silver breastplate was trembling. As she watched her weep, the warrior's vulnerability held her still. After a breath of hesitation, she eased closer and placed a hand on Atalanta's arm.

The warrior stiffened. Immediately, Danae realized she had made a terrible mistake, and waited for the inevitable squeeze of hands around her throat. But to her surprise, instead of pushing her away, Atalanta's body melted.

Danae edged forward, until the warrior's armour pressed against her chest. Atalanta still did not pull away. Her hair smelt of oak wood, salt and something sweet like honeysuckle, and despite the cool night air her skin was warm as sun-baked stone.

Danae had slept this way with her sister more times than she could count, but this was different. She was very aware of all the places their skin touched. A thrill of pride whispered through her that Atalanta allowed her to be this close.

They stayed this way, the curve of their bodies pressed together, until Atalanta's breathing calmed.

Then the warrior peeled back and wiped her face. 'Tell anyone and I'll kill you.'

'I know,' Danae whispered.

Atalanta rolled away and Danae's gaze lingered on her back, watching the moonlight pool in the creases of her armour.

For three days the sun reigned unchallenged in the sky, and a strong north-easterly wind bloated their sail.

Danae sat with Hylas on his rowing bench, the pair eating their lunch rations. She paused, a piece of bread halfway to her mouth, as Hylas began to dissect a fig. He grasped the base in his fingers and carefully peeled it apart from the stem until the fleshy insides splayed out like a bloom.

'Where did you learn to do that?'

'You ask the strangest questions.' He laughed at the intensity in her gaze. 'It's how I've always eaten them. It makes it last longer.' He popped a piece on his tongue. 'Unlike some, I like to savour my food.'

Danae looked down at her hands. Her sister was the only other person she'd known to eat a fig that way.

'Will you do something for me?'

Hylas swallowed his mouthful. 'Depends what it is.'

'Will you cut my hair?'

Despite hating it when Manto first hacked off her curls, she'd become used to her crop. She felt freer without her tangled mane, and no seer worth their coin would let their hair grow past their shoulders.

'I'm only asking because I don't trust any of the others not to make me look ridiculous. And you grew up on a farm, so you'll know what to do.'

Hylas chuckled. 'Are you comparing yourself to a sheep?'

She glared at him. 'Will you do it or not?'

'Of course I will.'

He followed her to the stern deck. Tiphys raised an eyebrow as they settled down behind him but said nothing.

She sat with her back against the side of the ship so her hair would fall into the sea, with Hylas working around her. She'd been right to ask him. He was gentle and careful with his knife. But she couldn't help laughing at the concentration on his face when he knelt in front of her, tongue poking between his teeth, to make sure he was doing an even job.

'You won't be laughing when I make you look like the twins.'

'Don't you dare!' She could see Castor and Pollux's bald heads glistening in the sunlight on the mid-deck.

Behind them, Telamon, Atalanta and Heracles were playing

a game of petteia. The hero's face cracked into a jovial smile as he slapped Telamon on the back for winning a round.

'Did you hear what Heracles said on the island during the fight . . .' She twisted to look at Hylas. 'When he was about to kill Hypsipyle?'

Hylas looked blank.

'About the gods? His father?'

He hesitated. 'Yes.'

'Have you heard him blaspheme like that before?'

Hylas turned her head back so he could continue cutting. 'We shouldn't talk about it.'

'Does he not fear the gods?'

'Of course he does.'

'It didn't sound like it.'

'You don't know him.' There was an edge to Hylas' voice she hadn't heard before. 'Everyone thinks they do because they've heard the stories, but he's so much more than just his father's son. He's been through a lot, more than most could survive without going mad, and still he sees the best in people. He gives them a chance when no one else will.' Hylas stood and handed her the knife. 'It's done.'

Before she could thank him, he turned and walked away across the deck. Her eyes lingered on his back for a moment before returning to Heracles.

A kernel of thought that had been planted in the battle on Lemnos sprouted roots. If Heracles really did dislike his divine father, perhaps he would be glad to see an end to Zeus' reign. Perhaps he might even help her bring about the King of Heaven's downfall.

She barely dared to hope, but perhaps they were destined to find Prometheus together.

30. Spoils of the Sea

'Land, starboard side!'

Startled by Tiphys' voice, Danae slipped from where she'd been leaning on the prow rail, gazing into the marbled sea. An uneventful two weeks had passed since the *Argo* left Lemnos, with little for her to do but stare at the empty ocean.

Jason appeared beside her as a bank of rock came into focus through the haze, nestled in the fingers of a large bay. Danae squinted. What she'd first taken for a cliff face now appeared to be the yellow stone wall of a vast fortress.

'If my eyes don't lie,' said Tiphys. 'I'd say that's Troy.'

'Yes,' Jason breathed excitedly. 'Priam's kingdom.'

As they watched the shore, a fleet of ships emerged from a harbour in the shadow of the fortress wall. Their crimson sails were emblazoned with white suns overlayed by crossed black tridents, and gilded figureheads spearheaded their prows.

'The royal fleet!' said Jason. He turned to Danae, his eyes dancing. 'It is not widely known, but Prince Paris of Troy himself spent much of his youth as a farmhand, oblivious to his true parentage.'

'Perhaps it is a sign, Captain,' said Danae. It did no harm to occasionally stroke his ego.

'I am sure of it.' Jason's face shone with unbridled hunger as he turned back to gaze at the Trojan ships. 'One day, I will stand at the prow of my own fleet, my crest imprinted on the sails. Who knows – gods willing – in time Iolcos might not be the only kingdom under my command.'

As he spoke, Danae thought how dangerous it would be if a man like Jason wielded a power like hers.

After sighting Troy, the *Argo* left the waters of the Aegean, and sailed towards the inland sea of the Propontis through a passage known as the Hellespont. Danae stood on the stern platform, staring at the rocky dunes and rearing hills rippling past to her left. Shielding her eyes from the sun, she squinted for any dwellings or glints of metal. To her right, Jason did the same. After their encounter on Lemnos, they had become a wary vessel, and the Hellespont was the perfect location to ambush an unsuspecting ship.

But as the hours trickled by and the *Argo* sliced through the channel unhindered, the knot of tension between Danae's shoulders began to melt. The rugged banks and beaches appeared completely deserted.

'How long 'til we clear the channel?' Jason asked Tiphys.

'A few hours yet, Captain.'

Jason tracked the movement of the sun across the bleached sky. 'We'll drop anchor as soon as we reach the Propontis. We don't have much daylight left.'

'Aye, Captain.'

'Look there, a ship!' Orpheus had abandoned his oar and was pointing ahead.

Heading towards the *Argo* was a single-mast sailboat about two-thirds the size of their penteconter. No shields flanked her sides, and the oiled hull bore no markings save the wear of the sea's tongue.

'They look like fishermen!' called Ancaeus.

The bearskin warrior was right. As the vessel drew nearer, Danae could see nets trailing from the side of the ship. The five men aboard waved their sea-weathered arms, grinning at the Argonauts.

'Might be worth seeing if they've got stock to trade, Captain,' said Tiphys.

'An excellent idea,' Jason replied. 'Argonauts, haul in the oars!'

The captain bounded down to the mid-deck, and Danae followed him, already salivating at the prospect of fresh fish. As they drew closer, she could see an array of crates and nets strewn in the belly of the tub.

She stopped and as calmly as her now thundering heart would allow, sidled over to Hylas.

'They aren't fishermen,' she murmured.

A string of confusion hitched his brow.

'The nets, look at them, all tangled together. Trust me, no fisherman would ever keep his netting that way.'

He held her gaze for a moment, then gave an almost imperceptible nod. Their faces masking into smiles, Danae and Hylas moved along the boat, whispering to Atalanta, Telamon, Peleus and the others. Jason was leaning over the side of the *Argo*, beckoning to the fishermen to steer towards them. When Danae reached Heracles, the hero's lips twitched into a smirk.

'At last, some entertainment.'

'Do you have fish to trade?' Jason yelled across the narrowing stretch of water between their ships.

'We have a lot of fish!' A bearded man in a worn brown tunic nodded enthusiastically.

Danae's chest bubbled with anger. She thought of how carefully her father tended his nets, the hours he spent weaving, darning and folding them. The fishermen of Naxos cared about their craft, they respected the sea and the creatures that dwelt in her depths.

She forced herself to grin at the imposters while moving closer to Jason. 'They're not fishermen,' she whispered.

The captain's face fell. 'What?'

The ship was so close now, Danae could see the whites of the strangers' eyes. She continued to smile through aching cheeks. 'Keep them talking, but we should be ready –'

It was at that moment the five supposed fishermen heaved over the crates on their deck to reveal another half-dozen men all armed to the teeth.

'They're fucking pirates!' shouted Atalanta with glee.

The pirate who'd been conversing with Jason caught a curved sword, thrown to him by another man, and pointed it at the *Argo*. 'Kill them!'

The Argonauts did not need to wait for Jason's command to dive for their weapons. Danae backed away from the side of the ship as the pirates rushed to leap aboard. Without even having to summon them, her life-threads clustered to her throbbing fingertips, aching to be released.

Save the crew, urged the voice. *They need your help.*

It was too risky; there were so many bodies crowded onto one small stretch of ship. She would be exposed, and besides, it looked as though the Argonauts were doing just fine without her.

Telamon and Atalanta had boarded the pirate vessel and were merrily gutting the men left behind. They could not have been more different; Telamon was all grace and technique, as though he was dancing at court, whereas Atalanta fought like she drank, furiously and with an unholy appetite. Yet there was a rhythm that sang in both their bodies when they battled together, an awareness of each other's patterns that could only be learned by years of fighting side by side.

Back on the *Argo* the rest of the crew were bludgeoning,

maiming and – in the case of an overzealous Ancaeus – decapitating the pillagers who'd dared step foot on their ship. The twins, Pollux and Castor, hadn't even paused to take up their weapons and were smashing their way through the pirates' skulls like they were pottery.

Her back to the stern platform, Danae watched pirate blood spray over the deck. Then her eyes found Heracles. He stood at the other end of the mid-deck, leaning against the prow platform, his arms folded. A smile shadowed his mouth as though the pair of them were watching gladiators in a stadium, performing for their pleasure.

She scowled at him. He could end this tussle in a heartbeat, why was he just standing there? Even if he only donned his lion hide, the sight of it would probably be enough to scare the attackers back to their ship.

Then a pirate came careering towards her, sword in hand. His tunic was sliced open, his gut a bloody mess. He lunged at her with the reckless violence of a man with nothing left to lose.

It was inevitable. She could not stop it. Her power expanded inside her, igniting her skin with tingling energy as she reached for the man. He was dying, she could feel it, just as she had done with the panther; she could see his lifethreads seeping out through his wound. She wanted them. She needed them.

Then Hylas dived between them. He parried the man's sword with a blow that sent the weapon clattering to the deck and in one smooth motion drove his blade into the soft flesh between the pirate's neck and shoulder. Danae felt the man's death like a limb had been ripped from her body. All that wasted power.

A moan slipped from her lips.

'Did he hurt you?' Hylas put a hand on her arm, his eyes sweeping over her.

Danae managed to regain enough control to shake her head. Beyond him the fight was already over, and the Argonauts were busy heaving the pirates' bodies into the sea.

'They've got wine!' Back on the pirate ship, Atalanta had prised open one of the locked crates to reveal it packed to the brim with amphorae. 'A shitload of wine!'

Danae had never seen the warrior look so happy.

When the Hellespont finally opened into the sea of the Propontis, the *Argo* dropped anchor in the shadow of the jagged Phrygian cliffs. The crew crowded onto the mid-deck under an indigo sky dappled with stars. Spirits were high after their victory over the pirates, fuelled by the contraband wine they'd decanted into drinking skins.

'I've heard,' said Telamon, grinning at the twins, 'that your sister is the most beautiful woman in all of Greece.'

'Which one?' said Castor. 'We have five.'

'Five beautiful sisters?' Atalanta's mouth curled into a smirk. 'Nice.'

'You know which one.' Telamon wagged his finger. 'Married to . . . oh, what's his name . . . King of Sparta.'

'Helen,' said Pollux, with the resignation of someone who'd answered the same question many times before.

'That's the one!' Telamon took a swig of wine. 'This is what I want to know . . . is she *really* as beautiful as everyone says? Rumour has it she's actually,' his eyes slid to Heracles, 'the big man's half-sister.'

'Telamon, enough,' said Heracles.

Telamon looked offended. 'I just want to know if the God of Thunder fucked their mother.'

Atalanta laughed. The twins glanced at each other, then lunged at Telamon. The three tussled together on the deck until Heracles grabbed the brothers and hurled them across the benches.

Unbidden, Alea stole into Danae's mind. Her sister lay on their pallet, her legs curled into her chest, weaving a piece of their father's fishing flax into a bracelet. She always used to lie like that. Danae would say she looked like an upended beetle. Then Alea would flap her legs to make Danae laugh.

She blinked away the memory. Despite locking her sister away, Alea kept escaping. Sometimes she appeared smiling, sometimes her eyes were cold with blame, and sometimes she was a sea-bloated corpse rotting on the sand.

'Orpheus!' called Jason. 'Sing us a song.'

The musician obliged and took up his lyre. He sang of his mountain village and Eurydice, the girl he'd left behind. It was a beautiful melody, sweet and tender, the lyrics full of longing and the hope of returning to her a worthy man.

The music faltered as an empty skin hit Orpheus in the face.

'Read the ship, lad!' shouted Ancaeus. 'Play something cheerful.'

Orpheus paused, swept wine droplets from his cheek, then began to pluck his strings so fast his fingers blurred.

> *There was once a maiden, young and fair,*
> *Light of foot and light of care,*
> *She danced through the grass, she danced through the trees,*
> *She danced like a flower kissed by the bees.*

Abruptly, Heracles grabbed a wineskin and took himself off to the stern deck. Danae watched him go, her brow creased, before Orpheus' tune lured her attention back to the benches.

> *She came to a river, wild and wide,*
> *The water called, she did not hide,*
> *She unpinned her hair, she unpinned her dress,*
> *And with eager feet, met river's caress.*
>
> *Oh poor maiden, young and fair,*
> *She'd stepped into a centaur's lair,*
> *A dreadful brute, all lust and greed,*
> *On maiden flesh did love to feed.*
>
> *But as the creature grabbed his prey,*
> *And maiden feared her final day,*
> *The lion came!*

'The lion came!' cheered the crew.

> *Tall as an oak, as broad as an ox,*
> *The son of Zeus, quick as a fox.*
>
> *Charging forth in his crowning mane,*
> *He brought the centaur a storm of pain,*
> *And the maiden cried —*

'The lion came, the lion came!' Danae shouted with the rest of them.

> *And he slay the beast in his father's name.*
>
> *So pleased was the maiden that then and there,*
> *She lay on the bank, let down her hair,*
> *And the maiden roared full and true,*
> *Oh, lion come, as I come for you!*

The lion came, oh, the lion came,
Lover of maidens no mortal can tame,
The lion came, oh, the lion came,
All praise to Zeus, the lion came!

The Argonauts erupted with cheers. Orpheus stood and, lyre at his side, bowed to the crew.

'Now, that's more like it!' shouted Ancaeus as he pounded his bench.

Danae looked back to Heracles sitting on the stern deck, a lone silhouette against the dusky sky. She picked up a skin of wine and climbed across the benches.

'Thought you might need another.'

He turned, his eyes lingering on her face before accepting the drink. He took a swig, then handed it back to her. She drank too. She realized it was the first time she'd ever been alone with him. Well, as alone as it was possible to be on a twenty-crew ship. The thought sent a little flutter through her chest.

'Not a fan of your songs?'

The hero reached for the wine again. 'I've heard them all before.' He shot her a wry smile. 'And however tuneful, they're not always entirely accurate.'

She wanted to ask which part wasn't accurate but felt heat rising in her cheeks at the thought, so instead said, 'Why didn't you fight the pirates?'

For a moment he looked taken aback. 'I would have thought that obvious.'

Danae refused to let him make her feel foolish. 'If you'd put on your lion hide and made it known the mighty Heracles was aboard, they'd never have fought us. You could have saved a lot of bloodshed.'

'Is that always the best outcome?'

'Yes.'

Heracles did not contradict her, but his expression made it clear he didn't agree. She took another drink.

'Educate me.'

His smile gleamed in the moonlight. 'The fight is what bonds soldiers. The Argonauts are not just warriors by trade, it's in their bones. Victory sustains them as much as food and water. After Lemnos they needed a win. A win that was theirs, earned by their blades, not delivered to them on a platter by a demi-god.' He took back the wine. 'And I need a day off every now and then.'

'How do you live with it . . . all the death? How do you stop each kill reminding you of those you love who've . . .' She did not trust herself to continue.

His gaze softened and for a moment, she thought he would reach for her, but instead he said quietly, 'Time and familiarity. Death has become a companion I walk beside each day. But there are some deaths that weigh more heavily than others.' A shadow passed over his face. 'All we can do is make sure we're strong enough to carry them.'

There was pain there, beneath his chiselled exterior that looked so like one of his father's statues.

'I never thanked you. For what you did in the cave.'

'It was nothing.'

'You saved my life.'

A bout of raucous laughter bubbled from the mid-deck. They both glanced back to see Hylas cajoling Atalanta into dancing with him. The pair made Danae think of a mountain goat attempting a jig with a bear.

Heracles laughed. 'He's a good lad, Hylas.'

'Yes, he is.'

'I've grown very fond of him.'

She could tell he meant it.

'Is that why you let him join you on your travels?'

Heracles pierced her with those startlingly blue eyes. Then he turned back to the sea. 'Not entirely.' The lines of his face deepened. 'I was put in charge of an army. I was young, and the king was foolish. He saw only my strength and none of my immaturity. I was eager to prove myself, but I wasn't ready. I made a bad decision, led my men into an ambush. Many were killed, including Hylas' father.' He paused, staring at the water. 'The boy was wasted on that farm. I felt like I owed it to him to take him with me.'

Silence settled between them. Heracles lifted the wineskin to his lips and drank deeply.

'I'm sure it wasn't your fault.'

His jaw tightened. 'It was, and I must never forget it.' His pain was so close to the surface she could almost grasp it. 'I have done terrible things, and all of them were my fault.' He shook his head. 'People think they want power, but they have no idea. It eats you until there is nothing left.'

As she watched him, her fear melted away. She wished she could tell him she understood. Instead, she reached for his hand. He looked at her, scarred brow creased in surprise. Her skin prickled, her stomach pulsing with nervous energy. Holding his gaze was like falling into an endless sky. There was something else in his eyes, something beyond the guilt he was drowning in. The faintest spark in the darkness. Was it hope?

'You know you can trust me, Daeira,' he said softly.

The feeling she'd had in the square in Corinth returned with a vengeance. She was as certain as if it were written in her bones: they were destined to walk the same path towards Prometheus.

'Heracles . . .' she began.

'You're missing all the fun!'

The moment shattered as Telamon appeared behind them and slapped a hand on both their shoulders.

'Peleus and I have been teaching the men to dance, *properly*. Believe it or not, Ancaeus is surprisingly good.' He straightened up, looking at them expectantly. Heracles sighed, heaved himself up and followed Telamon.

Danae lingered on the stern, the salt wind buffeting her hair, the hint of a smile imprinted on her lips.

31. Stranger Lands

The beach was only visible once the *Argo* sailed past the jutting cliffs that shielded it from the ocean. The land behind was dominated by sparse, mountainous earth and the occasional smattering of woodland. An isthmus cut a pathway of sand out from the far side of the shore into the water. At its end, a mound of rocks reared out of the waves.

'Tiphys!' Jason stalked the length of the ship to stand beside the old navigator. 'What is that land?'

Tiphys wiped sweat from the sun-ploughed rivets on his forehead. 'Territory of the Doliones, I believe.'

'Friendly?'

'Can't say I've heard either way.'

Jason was quiet for a moment, his brow heavy with thought.

'Daeira.' He turned to where Danae stood on the prow deck. 'As our only remaining seer,' his tone implied this to be her fault, 'consult the omens and tell us if it's safe to land.'

She'd been dreading this moment. She was going to have to use the prophecy stone.

'Captain, we're down to our last waterskins. The barrels are all dry,' said Tiphys. 'We really need to go ashore –'

'Drop anchor!' Jason cut across the navigator. 'We wait here until our seer tells us it's safe to land.'

Danae glanced at Tiphys. The navigator was staring at her, silently pleading.

'I'll need privacy.'

Jason drummed his fingers on the rail. 'Fine, you can use the store. But be quick about it.'

Danae stepped into the musty confines of the cabin, moved a clutch of swords, and sat down between two bundles of furs. She placed her bag in front of her and took out the prophecy stone.

Carefully, she set the obsidian stone on the floor and unwrapped it. She stared at it for a moment, let out a breath, then stretched out her hand and touched it.

Instantly, she felt an intense tugging sensation. She could see her life-threads being sucked from her fingers, but she fought her instinct to try to hold them inside her and let them rush into the stone.

Suddenly, the room lurched, and she was hurtling into darkness. Then she was floating, disembodied, in the void of nothingness. She concentrated, fighting the sensation that she was slowly dissolving into the emptiness around her.

Is it safe to land?

She had no idea if her question had been heard. She didn't seem to have a mouth to speak it with. Then a glowing thread darted across the darkness, just as it had in her vision from the oracle. She became one with it, flowing along the tapestry of life until she came to a stretch of land shaped just like the beach in front of the *Argo*. Then, without any will of her own, she was drawn to the isthmus. She was no longer part of the picture but looking down on the scene from above. She watched the threads move like someone was constantly re-sketching the image in ever-moving lines of light. She drew closer and saw something imprinted on the isthmus that did not wash away as the tide lapped over it.

Three sets of handprints.

She was pulled out of the vision by the creak of the cabin door opening. She jerked her hand away from the stone. It felt as though someone had reached into her skull and yanked her out by her sinuses. She breathed through the nausea then shot a murderous look at the doorway.

Jason stood in front of her.

'I need an answer.'

'These things take time.' She flicked the hem of her dress over the stone.

'I am the captain of this ship.' Jason moved towards her, his left eye twitching. 'You are *my* seer.'

She cringed away from him.

At her expression, he faltered. 'Please.' He ran a hand over his face. 'I need the omens to be good.'

He was desperate. Lemnos had nearly cost him everything and they were about to run out of water. There was nothing in the vision that seemed obviously ominous, but she had no idea what it meant. Three sets of handprints could be anything.

'We should land on the beach.'

For a wild moment, he looked like he was going to kiss her, then he turned and launched himself onto the deck shouting, 'The omens are in our favour! We land!'

She carefully wrapped the prophecy stone and stowed it back in her bag with unease in her heart.

Danae strode up the beach, her sandals crunching on the fine stones. The shore appeared deserted. A bleached cliff face guarded most of the mainland from view. Apart from a peppering of hardy shrubbery there wasn't much in the way of vegetation. Everything about this place was sharp and inhospitable. There was even a dry, brittle quality to the air. She was glad of it after the soporific effects of Lemnos. She needed to keep a clear head.

The crew were all standing, and there were no darts in sight, but still her body sang with tension. She took a deep breath and felt for the energy of her life-threads. They answered her call, thrumming to the surface of her skin. It was comforting to test her connection to her power in case the vision turned out to be a warning after all.

She looked over at the isthmus, then her eyes were drawn to a collection of objects floating in the sea. The shapes were too angular to be seaweed. She went over to investigate and noticed there were more littered across the beach. When she reached them, she could see they were the planks of a ship, ripped apart and splintered.

'Argonauts, to me!' Jason thrust his sword into the rough sand, and the crew clustered around their captain, weapons in hand. He pointed to Ancaeus and three other men. 'You four, take the empty barrels and find fresh water.' He turned to the twins. 'Castor, Pollux, scout the area. The rest of you, set up camp on the beach. We stay one night, then we'll be on our way.'

Danae hurried over to Jason. She kept her voice low. She had, after all, just claimed the omens were favourable. The last thing she wanted was to induce panic.

'Captain, there are what appears to be parts of a shipwreck further up the beach. Perhaps it would be wise to leave as soon as we've gathered supplies.'

Jason frowned. 'You said the omens were good.'

'Yes, but . . .' She wanted to say he hadn't given her much choice, 'divination is not a precise art.'

From beyond the cliffs, a flock of birds scattered into the sky.

Jason looked at her with disdain. 'Ships are wrecked all the time. It might even have been the same storm that caught the *Argo* months ago.'

Gods the man was infuriating.

'Jason!'

They both turned to see the twins running back towards the ship. Someone was chasing after them along the beach.

'Fall back, protect the *Argo*,' shouted Jason.

The Argonauts formed a barrier around the ship and raised their weapons. Danae positioned herself between Hylas and Telamon, drawing a clutch of life-threads into her fingertips.

'They don't look armed,' said Dolos, squinting at the figure.

'I'm not waiting to find out.' Atalanta notched her bow.

Then Heracles broke formation and walked towards the stranger.

'Heracles, get back here!' Jason called.

The hero didn't stop. As the person drew nearer, Danae could see it was a man dressed in a ragged green tunic. He was indeed unarmed, his limbs flailing with frantic energy as he ran towards them.

He fell to his knees in front of Heracles, heaving for breath as he uttered the sacred greeting. His feet were bleeding.

'Please, I need your help.'

He was painfully thin, his pale skin covered in bruises. Danae noticed a freshly stitched gouge on his right arm.

'What happened here?' asked Heracles.

Jason pushed his way forward. 'I am Jason, captain of the Argonauts. I am the leader of this crew.'

The man's eyes darted between Heracles and Jason. 'My people, there are barely any of us left. You look like you know how to fight, please help us.'

Another flock of birds soared into the air, their cries echoing off the rocks. They were getting closer to the beach.

Jason's frown deepened. 'Who attacked you?'

The man didn't answer. Shaking like a flame in the wind, he turned back to Heracles and grabbed the hem of his kilt.

'I've risked my life coming out here. Look at me!' He spread his arms wide. 'They invaded my town. Most of my people are dead. They've destroyed every ship that's landed here. They're going to kill us all.'

Heracles took the man by his arms and pulled him to his feet. 'This terror of which you speak, it's not human, is it?'

The man trembled. 'They are monsters the like of which you've never seen.'

'Oh, I doubt that.' A smile curled Heracles' lips. 'Monsters happen to be my speciality.'

The stranger took in the hero's stature and the lion hide draped over his head and shoulders. His mouth fell open. 'I thought I must be mistaken but . . . you're really him!'

The hero grinned.

Jason looked at Danae. She could sense he was looking for reassurance. Ever so slightly, she shook her head.

'Back to the ship!' yelled Jason. 'Now!'

'No, please!' The man reached towards Heracles. 'I have a family.'

Danae's heart ached for him, but they had to leave. Dread seeped through her skin. They should never have landed here in the first place. The omens were clearly against them, and she was a fool for saying otherwise.

Heracles remained where he was as the crew began to wade towards the *Argo*.

'Heracles,' said Danae.

He turned, his eyes burning with blue fire. There it was again, the pain she'd seen on the ship. He paced past her, towards the *Argo*.

'Argonauts!' he shouted at the crew climbing aboard. 'Why did you come on this quest? For glory? For riches? Or to flee like cowards at the first sign of danger? Yes, we've been humiliated and lost good men, but we are still the greatest warriors in all of Greece. It is not in our blood to run. We were forged in the heat of battle, it's what we were born for.' He fixed his gaze on Jason. 'You want your voyage to be legendary, *Captain*? I know a thing or two about that.' He turned back to the crew. 'Let's kill some fucking monsters!'

There was silence as Heracles' challenge hung in the air.

Then Telamon thrust his sword into the sky and roared. He was swiftly followed by Atalanta, Hylas, Peleus, Ancaeus and the twins, until the entire ship was clamouring.

A stony weight settled in Danae's stomach as she looked at Jason. The captain was still. He made no effort to regain control of his crew. Perhaps he knew it would be futile now their blood was up.

Tears streaked the stranger's hollow cheeks, but he raised a finger to his lips and frantically gestured for the Argonauts to be quiet.

'Thank you, thank you! But we must hurry, they will have heard you.'

'Good,' said Heracles.

'There's too many of them. Please come with me; I couldn't live with myself if I sent you to face them unprepared. We must go, quickly.'

Heracles appraised him for a moment, then placed a large hand on his shoulder. 'Come then, take us to your people.'

They travelled by ship, skirting along the beach. The stranger told them not to leave the *Argo* beached on the shore, otherwise it would be destroyed.

'My name is Cyzicus,' he said, once they were aboard. 'You wouldn't believe it to look at me, but I am the King of the Doliones.' He raked a hand through his filthy hair. 'You can moor your ship to the rocks at the end of the isthmus, it will be safe there. The creatures never venture beyond the beach. I will explain everything once we're inside.'

Jason ordered the crew to do as he said. Sweat trickled between Danae's shoulders as she clambered down from the *Argo* onto the wave-slicked rocks. She couldn't shake the gnawing feeling this was her doing. The prophecy stone had tried to warn her, but she didn't recognize it as a warning, and now the Argonauts were about to fight a deadly foe they knew next to nothing about.

'Follow me,' Cyzicus called from further along the rocky outcrop. Then he ducked out of sight.

The Argonauts climbed after him, one by one disappearing behind the rocks. When Danae reached the spot she saw an opening, invisible until you were upon it. Easing through the gap, she found herself in a tunnel. Green veins of algae snaked over the walls. It was steep and treacherously slippery, the rock echoing her breath back to her. She flattened her hands against the damp stone for stability and descended. A familiar tightness bound her chest as the daylight faded behind them. Perhaps it was her imagination, but the rock passage felt like it was growing narrower. She closed her eyes and forced herself to breathe.

Gods, she hated being underground.

Finally, a glimmer of light silhouetted the outlines of the crew ahead, and they stepped out into a cave. Danae looked up. The ceiling stretched high above her, jagged with the underside of the rocks they'd just climbed over. She tried not to think about the weight of the ocean pressing in around them. The steady drip, drip, drip of seawater punctuated the air and glistening stalactites lengthened down to kiss their stalagmite sisters stretching up from the floor.

Clustered around the stone structures were people. About forty or so men, women and children, all bedraggled like

Cyzicus. They reminded Danae of the forgotten citizens of Delphi, forced to hide in the cracks to stay alive. Their faces flickered in the weak light of several bronze dishes holding stuttering candles, filling the cave with a stifling smokiness. Despite the few pieces of ragged material stretched between the stalactites for shelter, everything was wet and smeared with algae. Even the Doliones' faces looked green. Many shied away from the strangers who'd invaded their sanctuary. A few of the men drew their weapons.

'Doliones!' shouted Cyzicus. 'Do not be afraid, these warriors are going to help us fight the Earthborn.' He stepped aside. 'And look, the mighty Heracles is among them! The gods have not forsaken us. Zeus has sent his son to our aid!'

The Doliones lowered their weapons, eyes glistening with wonder. Danae wouldn't have thought it possible, but she felt even more wretched than before.

'Why the long face?' Hylas whispered. 'The omens are good.'

She avoided his gaze.

A stout woman with deep-brown skin and hair flecked with grey came pacing towards Cyzicus, as fast as the slippery floor would allow.

'Cleite, my love!'

Cleite slapped him across the face.

'You foolish man.' Her voice shook with fury. 'How could you go out there on your own without a weapon?'

Two small children appeared behind her skirts. She glanced down at them and placed her hands protectively around their shoulders. Dark circles puckered her eyes.

'Did you once think about your girls? About me? About your people?'

Cyzicus rubbed his cheek, then bent down and took his

daughters in his arms. 'I know, it was foolish to go unarmed. But when I saw these warriors on the beach, I couldn't miss the opportunity to recruit their help.'

Cleite pressed her lips into a hard line. She looked at the array of strangers standing in her cave then said to Cyzicus, 'I suppose they'll need feeding.' She turned to the Argonauts. 'We've not much, but a hot meal is the least we can do if you really are going to help us.' She turned away muttering, 'Gods save us all.'

Danae noticed a wooden structure snaking up the rock wall to the ceiling. A rickety ladder, constructed from what looked like driftwood, rose up to a small platform.

'Is that how you saw us?' she asked Cyzicus.

He followed her gaze and nodded. 'There's a crack between the rocks above sea level. You can see most of the beach from up there. We wouldn't have survived without it.'

'How did you find this place?'

'My friend Theo discovered it when we were boys. It was our secret sanctuary for many years.'

His grief rose like flotsam on the sea of his thoughts. Danae hoped the Doliones had been able to bury their dead.

'These warriors are the best fighters in all of Greece.' Hylas appeared behind them. 'I've seen Heracles take out a dozen men at once and creatures five times his size. If anyone can help you, he can.' He placed a reassuring hand on Cyzicus' shoulder.

Cyzicus' brow smoothed and the same hope that glowed in the faces of his people now shone in his.

'I'm counting on it.'

When the food was ready, Cleite called the Argonauts over to the far side of the cave. She gestured for them to sit, while she spooned what smelt like fish stew into clay bowls.

'It's not much, but it's the best I could do under the circumstances.'

'My lady, you do yourself an injustice.' Dolos slurped from his bowl. 'This is the finest soup I've tasted in years.'

Cleite's cheeks glowed, and she busied herself with passing steaming bowls to the rest of the crew. A soft smile tugged at Cyzicus' mouth as he watched his wife work. From the little she'd seen of them, Danae thought theirs was a marriage born from love. A rare and precious thing.

'Now, Cyzicus.' Heracles set aside his empty bowl. 'Tell us everything you know about these creatures.'

The King of the Doliones grew grave. 'They are abominations. Like huge bears with six arms and their claws . . .'

Danae didn't hear the rest of the description.

Six arms. Six hands. Three sets of handprints. This must be what the stone had been trying to show her. The vision had been a warning after all.

'Numbers?'

'We believe just over a hundred. They invaded us about a year ago.'

'Is their skin hard to penetrate?'

Cyzicus nodded. 'Their fur is unnaturally tough, but their bellies are soft like a man's. We call them the Earthborn. We've managed to kill several with spears through the gut.'

'Their sleeping habits?'

'They sleep at night and hunt during the day.'

'Any other weaknesses?'

'Not that we know of.'

'So, what's the plan, Heracles?' Jason sat slightly apart from the others. It was the first time the captain had spoken since they'd descended into the cave. 'If these Earthborn are as strong and as plentiful as Cyzicus says, even you won't be able to match them in a direct attack.'

'We have fighters too,' said Cyzicus. 'I have fourteen soldiers and a dozen more capable men.'

Jason laughed.

'We could ambush them at night,' said Telamon. 'Stake out their nest.'

Atalanta nodded. 'With bows we could take them out at long range.'

Cyzicus shook his head. 'We've tried. Even with arrows, we can't get near enough without them knowing we're there. We believe they have a heightened sense of smell.'

Danae's brow creased as they continued to toss ideas between them. The fighters would need to mask their scent for an ambush to work. Submerging themselves in the sea would do that, but then the monsters would see them when they came up for air. Unless . . .

'What if the Earthborn couldn't smell or see us?' she said.

'What are you thinking?' asked Heracles, his eyes sparkling with intrigue.

'If the men were fully submerged in the sea, it would mask their scent and keep them hidden. My sister and I once played this trick . . .' She could feel Jason's eyes boring into her, but she continued, 'We hid on the beach under water, breathing through hollow reeds to hide from our mother. What if we were able to draw all the Earthborn down to the isthmus? Our fighters could hide in the water on either side of the sand – where it's deepest by the rocks – and ambush the creatures once they're on it. Then you'd be rid of them once and for all.'

'It's a brave idea,' said Cyzicus. 'But there are so many of them, we couldn't draw them all onto the isthmus.'

'You wouldn't need to. Atalanta and anyone else who can use a bow could hide aboard the *Argo* and take out the ones left on the beach. Heracles,' she glanced at the hero, 'could lure them down from their nest and entice them to follow him onto the isthmus. He's the strongest by far, and his lion hide would protect him from stray arrows.'

'A seer and a strategist.' The edge in Jason's voice could have cut bronze. 'There is no end to your talents, Daeira.' He turned to Cyzicus. 'Do you have a supply of reeds lying about this cave?'

Cyzicus shook his head.

Jason shot Danae a hollow smile. 'Why don't you help Cleite with the children and let the warriors plan the battle.'

In that moment, she wanted nothing more than to conjure a wind and slam Jason into the rocks.

'The pipes!' Hylas jumped to his feet. 'Sorry...' His cheeks flushed as everyone stared at him. 'It's just, when we left Lemnos,' he glanced nervously at Jason, 'I took the dart pipes. I thought they might be useful. They should just give us enough depth to breathe through them under water.'

'How many?' said Atalanta.

'Twenty.'

'You clever bastard.' Telamon slapped the younger man on the back.

'Looks like Daeira's plan might work after all,' said Heracles, his mouth quirking into a smile.

The sight of it sent a flutter through Danae's stomach.

'How will you get the beasts to follow you?' asked Jason, petulantly.

'Leave that to me,' said Heracles. The hero rose to his full, towering height. He was still slimmer than he had been when Danae first saw him in Corinth, but standing before her now he looked like a god.

'Doliones,' his voice boomed across the cave. 'I know you have suffered. But you need fear no longer. We are the scourges of evil. Where men fear the fires of Tartarus, monsters fear us.' The Argonauts began to stamp their feet and bash their weapons against the rocks. 'We will turn the sea red with the blood of the Earthborn, and never again will they darken your shores!'

The Argonauts roared. Many of the Doliones joined them, thrusting their fists into the air. Danae noticed a man holding a small baby. A sudden pain struck her chest. She pictured Arius in the child's chubby cheeks. The boy's father was weeping silently, staring at Heracles as though he was salvation incarnate.

The crew had belief on their side, and although they didn't know it, they had her power. Perhaps the omens *were* in their favour. Perhaps the vision had been a symbol of the six-handed Earthborns' destruction.

Perhaps, against the odds, they might just win.

32. Into the Mist

The viewing platform creaked as Danae flexed her legs. She stretched her eyelids, blinked, then returned her face to the crack in the rock.

The gritty beach sparkled as dawn swelled over the horizon, a gentle breeze wafting through the gap in the stone. It was calm. Too calm. As if the sea was bracing itself for what was to come.

Atalanta and the Argonaut bowmen had boarded the *Argo* under the cover of night. To a man, the Doliones soldiers had pledged to fight. Most of them submerged themselves with the remaining Argonauts on either side of the isthmus, breathing through the dart pipes. Dolos had insisted on testing the pipes first, to make sure there were no residual smears of phármakon inside the barrels. The last thing they needed was for half their force to pass out underwater.

Heracles had left just before first light, and Danae had watched him scale the shallow cliff with dread in her heart. She didn't know why she was so worried. If anyone could look after themselves in a fight, it was Heracles.

The platform wobbled, and she turned to see Hylas heaving himself onto the decking.

'I've been ordered to stay behind with the second wave.'

'Jason's orders?'

Hylas shot her a weary look.

She shook her head. 'The man's a fool. You should be out there with Telamon, Ancaeus and the others. You're one of our best men.'

Hylas looked down at the planks, his cheeks reddening as they always did when she paid him a compliment. She turned back to the crack. Still no sign of Heracles returning. He should have been back by now.

'You don't need to worry about him. I've seen Heracles face far worse things than a bunch of six-armed monsters. This will be sport for him.'

'I'm not worried,' she lied. 'I just hate waiting.' She shifted to peer through the crack again. 'I wish you could see more of the isthmus from here.'

'May I?'

She made what room she could for Hylas to shuffle in beside her. There was barely enough space for them both on the platform, and their bodies pressed together as he leant in.

She looked at him squinting through the crack. The hours spent on the rowing benches had drawn out the freckles on his cheeks. His ears, always pinker than the rest of him, poked through his chestnut curls. She remembered how it had felt, watching him slip away under the influence of the poison dart. She couldn't explain why, but she felt like they were made of the same clay, like there was a grain of Naxos in him. He didn't even know her real name, but when she was with him, she felt like Danae. It was comforting to know that despite everything that had happened, she was still in there somewhere.

'I'm glad you're not dead.'

He turned to her. They looked at each other, but neither spoke. The silence grew thick as honey, then suddenly he leant forward and pressed his lips to hers. Instinctively, she jolted back, cracking her head against the cave wall.

The colour drained from Hylas' face. 'I'm sorry . . . I . . . I misunderstood.'

Danae didn't know what to say. The platform seemed to shrink in size with each moment she couldn't muster words.

There was a roar beyond the cave. They both lurched towards the crack, and Danae pressed her eye so hard into the gap, the rock cut into her skin.

Heracles was charging along the beach, clanging a bronze shield with his sword. Was that blood on his blade? She couldn't tell at this distance. The hero was running towards the isthmus, kicking sprays of pebbles in his wake. She waited, the breath locked in her chest, but the Earthborn did not appear.

'Why aren't they following him?'

She leant back to let Hylas look, sagging in disappointment. Her plan had failed.

Then Hylas tensed. 'I can see them!'

She pushed against him and looked through the crack.

The Earthborn poured over the cliff in a wave, like huge rats surging from a cesspit, their coarse fur glistening like oil in the morning light. Cyzicus hadn't done them justice. Their faces bore the snarling snouts of bears, but that was where the similarity ended. Their movements were grotesque, bodies jerking as they scuttled on elongated arms like spiders, their claws scoring rivets in the rock. When they reached the beach, they transferred seamlessly onto their thick, muscular legs and towered above even Heracles.

There were so many of them.

'Shit, I can't see the isthmus,' said Danae.

The Argonauts should have leapt from the water by now. Fear began to leach out of her skin. She had to know what was happening.

'Fuck Jason,' she said as she dived across the platform and lowered herself down the ladder.

'What are you doing?' asked Hylas.

'Helping our crew. Are you coming?'

He hesitated, then climbed down after her.

They hit the ground running, slipping between the stalagmites as they raced towards the entrance.

'Stop!' Dolos called after them. 'Jason hasn't given the signal!'

But his words echoed down an empty passageway. Danae and Hylas were already clambering out of the cave.

The Argonauts and Doliones had leapt from the water, their weapons clanging as metal met claw and the sea around the isthmus ran red. From the heaps of bristly bodies lining the sand, it looked as though the ambush had been a success. There were still several Earthborn on the beach, but Heracles stood as a mighty gatekeeper, felling the creatures as they surged towards their kin trapped battling the Argonauts and Doliones on the isthmus.

The hero slashed down and in one motion sliced two arms off an Earthborn that had lunged towards him. The beast howled, waving its useless stumps, as Heracles swung his sword back around and drove it deep into the creature's gut.

He was in his element. He looked like the Heracles Danae had always pictured from her mother's stories. The hero who was unstoppable.

At that moment, a slew of arrows shot over their heads and rained down on the Earthborn left on the beach. With a swell of satisfaction, Danae saw at least a dozen fall.

'What in Tartarus is that?' said Hylas.

She looked up, squinting against the sunlight.

Curling around a mountain in the distance, like a snake coiling around its prey, was a tendril of dense fog. She watched it quickly blanket the land in an opaque grey mist. Her frown deepened. It was moving unnaturally fast. It didn't come from the ocean, yet it raced like it was driven by a stormy sea-wind. And it was heading straight for the beach.

Despite the heat of the rising sun, her blood ran cold.

The gods had found her.

It happened so fast. Danae could do nothing but watch as the fog enveloped the cliffs then advanced on the beach. In moments no one would be able to see who they were fighting.

There was a nauseating crack from the isthmus as an Earthborn smashed open the skull of a Doliones soldier like it was a melon, while the man was distracted by the rolling mist.

Hylas unsheathed his sword. 'Fall back! Fall back!'

But it was too late. Danae looked to the end of the isthmus just in time to see Heracles, up to his sword hilt in the innards of an Earthborn, be swallowed by the fog. The rest of the men froze as the mist consumed them.

Behind her, the fighters of the second wave came pouring out of the tunnel and scrambled down the rocks.

'Stop!' Her words fell unheeded as they disappeared into the mist and Hylas plunged in after them.

'Shit.' She hesitated for a heartbeat, then followed him.

The silence hit her like a wall of stone. The noise of battle sounded very far away, like she was underwater. She shivered. The fog was cold with the promise of death. It was so thick it rendered her almost blind. She stretched out her arms. Her limbs looked ghostly, fingers fading into the mist in front of her. Was that an Argonaut moving ahead, or an Earthborn?

She fought down the fear that threatened to choke her. She had to stop them, or the fighters would be slaughtered.

Something loomed out of the mist towards her. Realizing too late she'd forgotten a weapon, she threw her arms over her head and braced herself for the rake of an Earthborn's claws.

'Gods' bollocks, I nearly killed you!' Telamon stood over her, his sword barely a handspan from her arms.

Heart still palpitating, she straightened up. 'Have you seen Hylas or Heracles?'

'Can't see anything in this damned fog.' He grasped her by the shoulder. 'Do you know why this is happening? Is this the gods' doing?'

Before she could respond, a claw slashed through the mist above them. Telamon pushed her out of the way and swung his sword to meet the Earthborn's talons. She rolled across the sand, losing sight of them both as they disappeared into the fog. She came to a halt bashing into something on the ground. At first, she thought it was a fallen Earthborn, but as she leant over the body, she realized what she'd mistaken for its fur was Ancaeus' bearskin. The Argonaut's face was slack, eyes misted as the air around him. Danae felt something warm and wet pooling around her hand.

Part of her was transported back to the bay of Corinth and the sight of Manto's mangled corpse. But another part knew now was not the time for guilt. With each battle, each death, this part of her grew louder. She closed Ancaeus' eyes, swiftly whispered the prayer that would send him to Elysium, then took his sword and stepped over his body.

With her vision blocked, every cry, grunt and clash of metal took on its own distinctive note. But she was listening for something else.

She stopped, the rough sand crunching beneath her feet as she raised Ancaeus' sword. Someone was nearby. She could hear their breath, slow and steady, devoid of the panic around them. The hairs on the back of her neck prickled.

Trust your power. The voice was calm, confident, certain.

She knew what she must do. She dropped the sword and felt for the energy surging through her veins. She took a step forward, then another. The outline of a figure came into focus. It was wearing golden armour, topped with a blue-plumed helm, unlike the kind worn by any soldier or general Danae had ever seen. From the neck down, it covered the figure's entire body, down to gauntlets that capped their fingers.

Suddenly, the figure raised its arms, golden gauntleted hands piercing the mist. Danae flung out her own arms and cast her life-threads into the fog. The wind howled like a thousand wolves as she whipped the air into a torrent, slicing a path of clarity through the mist. As it recoiled and daylight poured in, she caught a clear glimpse of the figure, their golden armour so dazzling they shone like the sun itself. There was something familiar about the face beneath the helm, but she had no time to rack her memory, as the figure was sent sprawling backwards onto the sand from the force of her gale. She advanced, but the figure raised its arms once more, and the mist surged back around them. The golden stranger must be controlling it. Danae redoubled her efforts and drove the fog back for a second time.

But the figure was gone.

Danae whipped the wind left and right, clearing swathes of the isthmus, but the golden stranger had vanished. Roaring in frustration, she turned her efforts back to banishing the rest of the fog. Had the being fled? If it was powerful enough to conjure an all-consuming mist, why would it run from her?

She had no time to dwell on it. Despite having cleared a good deal of ground, she still couldn't see Hylas or Heracles. Her vision was crackling at the edges. She knew she didn't have much strength left; she'd drained her life-threads dangerously low. The wind required much more energy than the fire on Lemnos.

Her next gust uncovered Jason, blindly battling an Earthborn. The captain was in the process of wrenching his blade from the belly of the beast when Danae's wind blew the mist away. He stared around wildly, swinging his sword as the creature tumbled to the ground. Then, out of the retreating fog behind him, someone lunged forward. Jason spun around, driving his blade upwards.

Cyzicus stumbled into the light. Danae dropped her arms and stared in horror at the King of the Doliones impaled on Jason's blade. Jason's mouth moved wordlessly as Cyzicus slumped onto the sand.

Danae tried to reach them, but her legs buckled. She'd overspent herself. She didn't know her limits yet and had used too many life-threads.

A scream pierced the air. Cleite was standing on the rocks at the far end of the isthmus, her mouth stretched open long after the sound had left her throat. Then she half slipped, half ran down the rocks, pausing only to take up the sword of a fallen Doliones.

She hurled herself towards Jason. 'Murderer!'

Jason tugged his sword from Cyzicus' chest and parried her blow.

'I couldn't see him, I –'

Cleite swung at him again. Jason pushed her back, but she continued to throw herself at him.

'Doliones, your king is slain! Murdered by this monster in man's flesh! Avenge my husband, kill them all!'

All around the now clear isthmus, the Doliones soldiers retreated from the few remaining Earthborn and turned towards their queen. They saw Cyzicus slain and Cleite rounding on Jason. Like wildfire, her wrath leapt from man to man, igniting them all. Despite having to defend the isthmus against the remaining Earthborn, several of the Doliones turned on the Argonauts. These people had promised to save them, but instead had murdered their king.

Jason locked blades with Cleite. They struggled for a moment, but his strength outweighed hers, and with a shove he sent her crashing to the ground.

'Argonauts, back to the ship!' he yelled, while sprinting along the isthmus towards the rocks where the *Argo* was tethered.

Danae clenched her teeth and managed to heave herself onto her knees. Then an Earthborn came charging towards her, ropes of spittle flailing from its gnashing jaws.

The next moment, she was lifted from the ground. Hylas slung her over his shoulder and ran along the stretch of sand. He slowed as he reached the rocks and attempted to clamber one-handed towards the *Argo*. She could feel his muscles straining and lungs heaving. She was slowing him down.

'Leave me,' she croaked.

'Never.' Hylas tightened his grip around her waist.

Argonauts scrambled past them, pursued by incensed Doliones and raging Earthborn.

'Heracles!' Hylas shouted as the hero's huge frame appeared beside them, battering away two Earthborn as they clawed their way up onto the rocks. 'Help her.'

Danae became weightless in Heracles' arms. He bounded across the last stretch of rock and passed her up to Atalanta, who stood ready with the rest of the archers to haul the fleeing crew members aboard. The warrior dropped her onto the deck and stretched an arm back to Hylas, as Heracles leapt over the side of the ship.

Danae grasped a bench and heaved herself upright. Atalanta pulled Hylas up to the ship's rail, and Danae's eyes met his. The feeling that blazed from him hit her like a sudden summer storm. She wondered how she'd never seen it before.

He loved her.

An Earthborn reared up from the rocks. The surprise had barely registered on Hylas' face by the time two sets of blood-smeared claws closed around his torso. To her credit, Atalanta held on, but she was no match for the beast's strength, and her fingers slipped from Hylas' as the creature yanked him backwards.

Before the scream had left Danae's chest, Heracles launched himself overboard and ran across the rocks after them.

Jason, seemingly oblivious to what had happened, leant over the stern, feverishly undoing the tether. 'Row!' he yelled, as the rope slithered free of its knot. 'Gods damn you, row!'

The remaining crew rushed to take up the oars.

'Heracles, Hylas, we can't leave them!' Telamon shouted.

Jason's eyes were wild as he glanced back at the shore, still crawling with Earthborn and enraged Doliones. 'I'm not risking the rest of the crew for two men.'

'But Heracles –' Tiphys began.

Jason pushed the navigator aside and grabbed hold of the tiller. 'If you want to live, row!'

The men didn't need to be told a third time. The mist had turned the tide of the battle, and with the Doliones now on the attack as well, they knew the fight was lost. The Argonauts grabbed the oars and pushed the ship away from the rocks. Atalanta launched herself at Jason but was brought thudding to the deck by Pollux before she could reach him.

Telamon drew his sword. 'Jason! Order them to turn back, or I will make you.'

Without a word, Dolos sprinted across the deck, his healer's bag secured across his torso, and dived into the sea. There was a clash of metal behind Danae as Castor's blade met Telamon's, but her gaze stayed with Dolos as he swam back to the rocks that moved further and further away with every heartbeat.

She desperately wanted to follow the healer. But she didn't move.

She remembered now where she'd seen the face of the golden stranger before. In a city far away, cast in a likeness over eight times her size.

Athena.

She, a mortal, had conjured a wind that knocked a goddess of Olympus to the ground. Not only that, Athena had fled rather than fight her. The Twelve were not untouchable after all.

When the prophet falls, and gold that grows bears no fruit, the last daughter will come. She will end the reign of thunder and become the light that frees mankind.

She saw Delphi: the burning bodies, the screams of terror, all those people massacred and unburied. She had a chance; she could stop that from ever happening again.

You know what you must do, said the voice.

Tears streamed down her face. She had to stay with the *Argo*, no matter who got left behind. Her destiny was greater than her desires, greater than the sum of every person aboard the ship. Reaching Prometheus had to come above all else. And no matter how much it hurt, she couldn't let anything, or anyone, stand in her way.

PART THREE

33. Revelations

'You're a pathetic excuse for a captain, Jason!' Telamon's face was redder than his hair. 'You're a parasite, a leech, a maggot on a steaming pile of shit! I wouldn't piss on you if you were burning to death!'

Atalanta sat in silence beside him, her glower more cutting than any of Telamon's insults. Both were bound by the ankles and wrists, tied to iron rings in the wall of the stern deck. In the end, it had taken five men to restrain them.

The land of the Doliones was far behind them, but Telamon was unrelenting. Danae was amazed he still had breath in his lungs. And that no one had gagged him.

Jason was rowing with the men. The captain didn't have much choice. After fighting the Earthborn the Argonauts were down to fourteen crew, two of whom were currently tied up. Danae's position as seer saved her joining the rowers, and with Tiphys at the tiller, there were only ten men spread across the benches.

Danae sat on the stern deck, staring unfocused at the waves. She was grateful she'd been left alone. She felt brittle as glass after conjuring the wind. No matter where she looked, she saw Hylas' face as the Earthborn dragged him away.

She told herself she was too weak, that she wouldn't have had the strength to swim back to the shore. But no matter how fervently she rallied her excuses, the truth stood like a colossus against her. She could have followed Dolos, but she chose to remain on the ship.

How strange that a lump of obsidian rock knew her nature

better than she did. Three pairs of handprints: Hylas, Dolos and Heracles.

'King of Iolcos?' spat Telamon. 'What a fucking joke. Heracles was our real leader. You just cost the Argonauts our best man. He was a true hero. He went back for Hylas, he'd have done that for any of us, and what do you do? You abandon them! Heracles is a living legend, and you are nothing!'

'Stop rowing!'

The men hauled in their oars as Jason climbed over his bench to face the crew.

'The time has come for the truth.' His chest was heaving, and his palms bled. He hadn't built up callouses like the rest of them. 'I hoped it wouldn't come to this. But you all deserve to know. We have endured more than bad luck on this voyage.'

Danae's head snapped towards the rowing benches.

'The storm, Lemnos, the mist, all in defiance of the omens. The gods have been punishing us, because of one of the Argonauts.'

Her stomach dropped through the deck. How did he know?

Jason took a breath. 'Heracles is not the man you think he is.'

She froze.

'He has committed a blood crime –'

'No!' Atalanta writhed against her bonds. 'I'll kill you, Jason. I'll kill you!'

The captain ignored her outburst. 'He was ordered, by the sacred oracle at Delphi, to cleanse his soul by performing twelve labours for King Eurystheus of Mycenae.'

'Jason, I swear on the Styx –'

Jason's voice rose above Atalanta's cries. 'His *heroic* deeds are nothing but ordered penance and by joining this mission he is in violation of his agreement with King Eurystheus, and therefore the decree of the gods as passed down by the oracle. I believe we are being punished for his actions.' His words sounded rehearsed. 'I had hoped I would never have to reveal this. I thought he would be an asset to our cause, but he has brought nothing but death and destruction upon this ship.'

'You bastard,' growled Telamon.

'What crime did he commit?' whispered Orpheus.

'Jason, please. Don't do this.'

Stunned, Danae looked at Atalanta. She'd never heard the warrior speak so softly. She must be desperate.

The captain's handsome face was a mask of regret, but he couldn't quite hide the glint of satisfaction in his eye. 'Heracles murdered his wife and children.'

The ship swayed in silence. Danae wanted to scream at Jason, call him a liar, but the truth was written on Atalanta and Telamon's faces.

I have done terrible things, all of them my fault.

Jason must have known all along and held the information back until he needed to sway the loyalty of the men.

She thought of her little nephews, of her brothers who as children wrapped themselves in goat hides pretending to be the hero, of all the people who listened to the tales of mighty Heracles and believed anything was possible.

By toppling their idol, Jason may have won back the crew's allegiance, but he must be able to see what was plain to her. By killing the hero in Heracles, he had killed the dream of what they could become.

Danae sat down next to Atalanta and proffered a skin of wine she'd pinched from the store cabin.

The warrior snatched the vessel between her bound hands, pulled the cork with her teeth, and drank like her life depended on it.

Beside her, Telamon's head was slumped on his chest. 'We should have abandoned ship with Dolos,' he murmured.

Atalanta offered him the wine. He shook his head.

'Tell me what happened,' said Danae.

Atalanta glared at her.

'I don't want to judge him until I've heard the truth.'

'Just tell her,' said Telamon. 'What's the point in hiding it now?'

Atalanta sighed heavily through her nose. Danae waited.

'Heracles lived in Thebes as a lad. Even before he had hair on his balls, he'd made a name for himself. So, King Creon decided to put him in charge of the army. Long story short, a neighbouring city tried to invade, and Heracles defeated them. As a reward, Creon gave him his daughter, Megara, as a bride.'

Pressure was building in Danae's chest. That explained Heracles' unsettled behaviour when they passed close to the city. No wonder he'd been so keen to leave that place.

'He's not to blame for what happened. It's important you know that.'

She could hear the reluctance in Atalanta's voice, the discomfort of edging closer to words she did not want to say.

'Go on.'

'One night, someone drugged him. He went mad. Took a club to his wife and the three boys while they slept. When he came to his senses and saw what he'd done, he tried to kill himself. Dolos stopped him.'

Danae imagined the horror of it. Heracles' wife, his children. The fear on their little faces when they woke and saw their father standing over them wielding a club. All that blood.

'Jason's right. We've had more than bad luck on this voyage.'

Atalanta turned her acid stare on Telamon. 'You can't seriously agree with that prick?'

'It's because of Hera.'

Zeus' wife. Danae's stomach hollowed. 'Why do you think that?'

'I've never told you this.' Telamon shot Atalanta a guilty glance. 'A couple of years ago, I got Dolos really drunk –'

'I don't remember that.'

'You were in some woman's bed.'

Atalanta grunted.

'Anyway,' Telamon continued, 'he became morose and went on about how the gods had ruined Heracles.' He glanced at the sky and lowered his voice. 'Dolos said that it was Hera who drove Heracles mad the night he killed his family, out of spite for being her husband's favourite bastard. And she's had it in for him ever since.'

'So, you think the Queen of Heaven has been attacking the Argonauts to get at Heracles?' Atalanta shook her head. 'Why now? She could have taken him down so many times on his labours. I don't buy it.'

'The gods work in mysterious ways.'

'Fuck that. Something else is at play here.'

Danae should have been worried. But she was pierced through with white-hot rage. Heracles' children were innocents, just like Arius. The gods weren't careless, they were cruel.

You can make them pay, said the voice. *You are the reckoning.*

'How did Jason find out?' The glower Atalanta reserved especially for him returned as she stared at the captain's back. 'I thought Creon hushed it up, and we were the only ones who knew the truth.'

Danae remembered what Jason had said on the beach at Iolcos. Hera told him of his true parentage and set him on the path to reclaim his throne. Perhaps she'd revealed other things too.

They were interrupted by a crash from the rowing benches.

'Hold the oars!' shouted Jason.

Peleus lay crumpled in the footwell.

'Peleus!' Telamon yanked against his bindings. 'Untie me! For the love of the gods, he's my brother!'

A trickle of blood ran out from behind the bench.

'Where's the healer?' Jason looked around. 'Dolos . . .' The name died before it had fully left his lips.

Danae paced across the deck and clambered over the benches. Jason pulled apart the side of Peleus' tunic to reveal two deep gashes across his stomach. His skin was drained of colour, brow beaded with cold sweat.

'Why didn't you say anything?' said Jason.

'Didn't want any bother.' A thin smile twitched Peleus' pale lips. 'It's not that bad.'

Jason looked at Danae. They were all looking at her.

'We need to stop the bleeding.' She racked her memory for anything that might help, and recalled what her mother had done when, as a boy, Calix had torn his thigh open climbing.

'I need cloth.'

She wasn't going to let another Argonaut die. Not if she could help it.

Orpheus ripped the top section from his tunic and handed it to Danae. She balled it between her fists and pressed it against Peleus' wounds. He groaned. Already, the muscles in her arms were spasming with the effort. Curse her weakness.

She replaced her hands with Jason's. 'Put pressure on it.' Then rose to her feet and ran towards the store cabin.

'What's happening?' called Telamon. 'Is he going to be all right?'

She glanced back at him as she ducked into the cabin. 'I'm not Dolos, but I'll do my best.'

Once inside, she leant against the door, head spinning. She took a deep breath, then scoured the room, shoving aside boxes of biscuits, weapons and packs of furs. Her eyes lingered on a skin of the pirate wine. She picked it up and took a swig to calm her nerves, then continued her search. Dolos had a collection of fine needles and thin gut string designed specifically for stitching flesh. She had neither, but perhaps she could improvise.

She emerged from the cabin, the wine in one hand, a tarpaulin needle and twine in the other. Telamon turned almost as pale as his brother when he saw what she was carrying.

'You're not going to . . . with that?'

Danae didn't have time to answer as she rushed back to the benches. Taking Jason's place, she helped Peleus raise his head and held the wine to his lips.

'Drink this, you'll need it.'

Peleus spied the needle in her other hand and took a large gulp. Danae took back the wineskin and splashed the remaining liquid on his wounds and over the needle. From across the deck, Atalanta moaned. It could have been sympathy for Peleus, but it was probably prompted by the wasted wine.

'This is going to hurt.'

Danae bit down on her bottom lip. The pain helped steady her hand as she separated the strands of twine and threaded the needle. Taking a deep breath, she pressed the sides of the first gash together and sank the needle into Peleus' skin.

It wasn't so bad if she imagined she was stitching a fig and the blood was just juice. There was so much juice. She fought down a wave of nausea as an image of Myron, the butcher, elbow-deep in the carcass of a cow, invaded her thoughts.

Please work, she thought with each plunge of the needle.

Peleus' screams ripped through the benches every time she broke his skin. By the time the wounds were stitched, the poor man's voice had reduced to a whimper. Danae sank back on her heels and looked down at her trembling, blood-stained hands. How she'd held them steady, she did not know.

As the men moved Peleus behind the benches and made him comfortable in a bed of furs, she pushed herself up and walked over to Telamon.

'He's stopped bleeding.' She sank down next to him. 'I think he's out of danger for now.'

Telamon nodded, then held her bloody hands in his. 'Thank you.'

She drew them away, mumbling, 'It's the least I could do.'

When night came, and the crew lay down between their benches, Danae remained beside Telamon and Atalanta.

Telamon's head lolled on his chest, gently bobbing as he snored. In her sleep, Atalanta had slid sideways against the stern platform, her bound hands resting on the deck, fingers nestled against Danae's thigh.

The moon was half swallowed by darkness, but it cast just enough light to see by. Danae gazed at Atalanta's face. She would never dare look this long when the warrior was awake. Her features were surprisingly soft without her permanent scowl. She seemed younger than Danae had first thought, perhaps around her twenty-fifth year, like Santos. Her mouth was slightly parted, breath whistling gently between her full lips. She was beautiful, in her own fierce way. She was a woman who could take on a god.

Danae wondered if the night she'd comforted Atalanta had really happened. It felt like a dream. A moment stolen from a world ruled by different stars.

The warrior's eyes snapped open. Danae flinched.

'How long have you been staring at me?'

'I wasn't –'

'Yes, you were.' Atalanta heaved herself up and began rooting around for the wineskin. She winced.

'Are you hurt?'

'No.'

'Show me.'

Atalanta clenched her teeth. Grimacing, she lifted her arms, revealing the tip of a gouge below her right armpit. Mercifully, it didn't look like it needed stitches.

'It's just a scratch. One of those bastard Earthborn got me when I was trying to hold onto Hylas.'

Danae's heart suddenly felt too heavy for her chest.

'Why will none of you admit to being wounded?' she said sharply and reached to undo the straps of Atalanta's breastplate.

The warrior jerked away from her.

'I can't get a good look without removing it.'

'I never take off my armour.'

'You did on Lemnos.' She regretted the words as soon as they'd left her lips.

A beat fell between them.

'I'm sorry. It must have been difficult, being back with a group of hunters and then –'

'You think you're clever, don't you?' Atalanta's eyes grew hard as frosted iron. 'You think the men respect you? The only reason you're here is because of *them*,' she glanced to the heavens, 'but the gods won't protect you, seer, no matter how special you think you are to them.' She gestured to the rowing benches. 'I am faster, stronger, tougher than all those pricks, but I have to prove my worth every fucking day. You want to know why I don't take off my armour?' She thumped her chest. 'This was beaten from the breastplate of the man who murdered my people. Because he was faster, stronger, tougher . . .' She paused, her breath ragged. When she spoke again her words bit like a silent blade. 'Don't ever touch my armour again.'

Danae swallowed, her mouth dry. 'If I don't clean the wound, it will become infected. If it's all right with you, I'd rather you didn't die.'

The two women stared at each other. Atalanta's dark eyes burnt with an intensity that made Danae's stomach writhe, but she did not look away.

'Fine. But the armour stays on.'

'Yes, you made that clear.'

Atalanta's mouth twitched. Danae located the wineskin and, armed with a cloth retrieved silently from the store cabin, she eased herself back down beside the warrior and began to dab the gouge. Atalanta stiffened, but she didn't make a sound, even as Danae pressed against her sore flesh to reach the tip of the wound beneath the armour.

'I'm sorry about your people.'

Atalanta grunted.

'They were hunters too, weren't they?'

'Who told you?'

'Hylas.'

Atalanta was silent.

'I don't love the gods.' Danae didn't know how the grain of truth had escaped, but there it was. 'I channel their will, when they wish me to receive it, but I know that I am just a tool to them, nothing but a disposable mortal.' She didn't try to hide the venom that seeped into her words, hating the half-lie she had to weave.

Atalanta gently moved her hand away.

'Has Artemis ever spoken to you?'

'No.'

Atalanta's frown deepened. 'She used to hunt with my people.'

Danae's heart tripped. 'You've met her?'

'Yes,' Atalanta said with a quietness that betrayed her fear. 'We were her mortals, just like the hunters of Lemnos. She promised no one would touch us, that we were under her protection. Then raiders came to our forest. We prayed to her to save us, but she didn't come. When she did finally return she found all but three of us dead . . .' Atalanta paused, her mind flying somewhere far away. 'After what they did to us, she didn't think we were worth saving.'

The anger that lived beneath Danae's skin singed her blood. She wanted to reach for the warrior, but she knew Atalanta would detest her pity.

'How did you escape?'

'Heracles.'

Atalanta's eyes lifted, and Danae was no longer afraid to hold her gaze.

'Why did you hate me when we first met?'

The moon emerged from behind a cloud. In its radiance, Atalanta's eyes were all ebony and silver light.

'I didn't hate you. I just didn't trust you.'

'But you do now?'

She could barely breathe as she waited for an answer.

'Trust has to be earned. You saved Heracles back on the island. That was a start.'

Danae's heart lifted. 'I want you to trust me.'

Perhaps it was the moonlight, but she thought she saw the ghost of a smile touch the warrior's lips. Her eyes lingered there.

Then Telamon let out a rumbling snore.

Atalanta laughed and grabbed the wineskin from Danae, draining the remaining liquid.

'I'll tell you how to earn my trust.'

'Go on.'

Atalanta leant closer. Danae could feel the heat of her, smell the oak and honeysuckle on her skin. Then the warrior whispered, 'Bring me more wine.'

Danae cricked her neck, her body still stiff from sleep. The light of dawn cast luminous ripples over the inky waves.

'Daeira.'

At his summons, she joined Jason on the prow deck.

'Captain.'

He glanced back at Telamon and Atalanta, still bound to the stern deck. 'I know you travelled with them before the *Argo*. But I am your captain, and they disobeyed my orders on the Doliones' shore.'

Reaching Prometheus was all that mattered, and Jason was currently in charge of the ship that would get her there. Her stomach writhed, but she knew what she must do.

'I am loyal to you, Captain. I have come to believe the fates put me in their path to lead me to you.'

Jason's mouth twitched. 'Good. Then we understand each other.'

She inclined her head and turned to walk back down to the mid-deck, but Jason caught her arm. He pulled her close, his grip firm.

'What did you see, before we landed on the Doliones' shore?'

She looked into his eyes, expecting to see accusation, but instead she found hunger.

'Sometimes, the omens do not offer a clear path. One sign may be favourable for some and not for others. Sometimes sacrifices must be made for the greater good.'

His hand stayed on her arm.

'The Queen of Heaven herself has blessed this quest.' Jason spoke so softly his voice was almost a whisper. 'I know the omens are on my side. At first, I thought losing men was a failure on my part, but now I see that this is exactly how it was meant to be. We are treading the path the Twelve have mapped out for us. You interpret the will of the gods, and I have their blessing. Stay loyal to me, and I will make you my royal seer when I return to Iolcos and claim my crown.'

She felt nauseous, but she made herself smile. 'It would be the honour of my life to serve at your side.'

Jason smiled at her, showing all his perfect white teeth. 'We must reach Colchis, whatever it takes.'

'Whatever it takes,' she replied.

34. My Enemy's Enemy

After another day's sailing, two cliffs towered before the *Argo*. Two vast walls of rock, like a pair of enormous gates, guarding the entrance to the Black Sea. They were so close together, the rising sun looked like an orange squeezed between them, leaking its bright juice onto the stone.

'The Symplegades rocks,' Tiphys called from the stern. 'Otherwise known as "the clashers". They're said to grind anything unworthy that passes between them. It's the only way through to the Black Sea.'

A lone bird flew overhead, soaring between the rocks. The cliffs remained still.

'Any truth in it?' shouted Jason from the prow deck.

'An old fisherman's tale, Captain. Still, best to proceed with caution.'

Jason was quiet for a moment. 'We drop anchor here. Replenish water and food if we can find any, then we press on.'

There was no beach to run aground on. Instead, Tiphys was forced to steer the ship in between the boulders that littered the base of the coast. They were rectangular in shape, like vast bricks laid long ago by giants. Unlike the sheer cliffs at the entrance to the Black Sea, the land slanted upwards away from the water. Steep, but climbable.

'Look!' Orpheus pointed up at a seam of silver that ran through the rust and dark-green shrubbery of the land above the rocks. 'Fresh water.' They only had two full skins left.

A couple of the men secured the mooring rope while Jason gave instructions.

'Don't stray too far from the ship. We fill our barrels and scavenge what food we can but always keep the *Argo* in your sights. And if anyone sees anything, beast or man, do not engage but come straight back to the ship. Tiphys, stay here with Peleus, and *them*.' He glanced at Atalanta and Telamon.

'I need to shit,' said Atalanta.

Jason's perfectly straight nose wrinkled in disgust.

'Yes, Jason, women shit. I can always go right here on the deck.'

Jason looked pained. He loosed a sharp sigh. 'You can go in a bucket in the store cabin. Pollux, untie her.'

As the twin bent down to release Atalanta's bindings, the warrior's gaze met Danae's. She winked.

Danae's eyes widened, but before she could make a sound, Atalanta smashed her forehead into Pollux's nose. He staggered back, blood streaming down his chin, and in the space of a heartbeat the warrior grabbed the knife that had clattered to the deck, slashed through Telamon's restraints and twisted the blade to press against Pollux's neck.

Telamon didn't hesitate. His reflexes honed by years of riding cheek to cheek with danger, he lunged at the other twin, who stood nearby, and swiftly turned Castor's weapon on himself.

'Turn back the ship,' Atalanta hissed.

The rest of the crew were as taut as a freshly strung lyre, their eyes darting between the mutineers and their captain. Jason drew his dagger.

'Don't even think about it,' said Atalanta. 'I will kill him if you don't order the men to sail back.' A fresh bead of blood trickled down Pollux's neck as Atalanta dug the blade into the skin above his jugular.

The bald man growled, but fear flickered through his eyes.

'You would risk all our lives . . .' Jason shuffled back, 'for a child murderer and his lackeys.'

Rage flared in the pit of Danae's stomach, but she didn't move. She had already made her choice.

'Stay where you are,' said Telamon as Jason continued to inch towards the stern.

'As you wish.' The captain grew still. Then he lunged across the last stretch of deck to where Peleus lay in his bed of furs and yanked him upright.

Peleus cried out in pain, clutching his wounded side as Jason pressed his dagger into the man's collarbone. Telamon stiffened, the colour draining from his face.

Jason bared his teeth. 'By the time my count reaches five, you will have both dropped your weapons. Or I will slit his throat.'

Danae's heart thundered against her ribs. Jason might be young and inexperienced, but he'd slain Hypsipyle on Lemnos as easily as drawing breath.

'One, two . . .'

Telamon glanced at Atalanta. The warrior's jaw was set, her eyes two burning coals beneath her scowl.

'. . . three.'

Telamon's blade clattered to the floor. Castor immediately grasped his arms, twisting them behind his back, and brought Telamon thudding to the deck.

Danae's chest twinged at the betrayal etched on Atalanta's face.

'Coward,' she spat.

'He's my brother,' Telamon said pleadingly.

Atalanta turned her molten stare on Danae. She who had stood there and done nothing. She was not as brave as Telamon and looked away, not daring to meet the disappointment she knew waited for her in those dark eyes.

'Four,' said Jason.

'Atalanta,' Telamon begged.

'Five.'

The warrior's blade fell to the deck.

The crew released a collective breath as Atalanta was forced to her knees and a bloody-faced Pollux retied her restraints.

As the twins worked, Jason let go of Peleus and straightened up. The blade in his hand was trembling.

'Pollux, Castor, you stay on board with Tiphys. If the traitors even think about trying to break free, you have my permission to kill them.'

Danae's stomach lurched as the twins grinned at each other.

It was a subdued crew that fetched empty barrels and skins from the store cabin and clambered over the side of the *Argo* onto the rocks. They made their way up the boulders to the ground beyond, carrying the barrels between them. As they climbed, the stone underfoot gave way to tufted earth, littered with lichen-stained rocks. When they reached the stream, Danae made sure to walk further ahead than the others. She squelched down into the mud, cupped the water in her hands and drank. Whether because of the strict rationing aboard the *Argo* or because she'd been drinking stale water for weeks, the stream tasted deliciously sweet. She splashed her face, washing away the salt and grime, then retrieved the skins she'd stowed in her bag and filled them with fresh water.

She glanced behind her, making sure the rest of the crew were occupied, then backed away from the stream and scurried towards the crest of the hill.

She'd been waiting for an opportunity like this, time away from the others to explore her powers. She desperately needed to learn how to harness them properly, especially if another of the Twelve came after her. Whatever Athena's reason was for fleeing, she doubted it would happen again.

She could feel how raw her energy was when she channelled it. When she manipulated her life-threads it was as though she was riding an untamed stallion. The line between control and losing herself was hair-thin. On Lemnos, the power had taken her, not the other way around. She had summoned it on the Doliones' beach, but conjuring the wind had left her drained and defenceless. Rest and food had restored her a little, but her strength was not fully recovered. It was imperative she learn her limits. That, however, would be a challenge without a full reservoir of life-threads to draw upon.

But she had an idea.

From her encounter with the panther, she'd learnt that she couldn't generate more life-threads herself, but she could take them from animals. It wasn't a solution she liked, but she saw no other option. She needed to take on more life-threads before she could use her powers again.

As she walked, she scoured the ground for droppings or prints.

'Where's a lame mountain goat when you need one?' she muttered.

It was unlikely she'd find a creature at the end of its life, like the panther. But if she could catch one, she had her knife to do the deed.

Up on her right, a clutch of boulders had tumbled in on each other, creating a haven of nooks and crannies, perfect for small creatures to nest in. She crept towards it.

Then she slipped on a loose rock and landed heavily on her back, crying out as she fell. So much for a stealthy approach.

'Who goes there?'

She froze. The voice was thin and crackled like sun-baked leaves. It was followed by a clacking sound. Then the end of a spindly piece of driftwood appeared around the edge of the rocks. A moment later, a man came tapping his way towards her.

He was wizened with age, painfully thin and clothed in a filthy black robe. What remained of his grey hair clung in wisps to his skull, and his cheeks were pinched by malnutrition. The skin around his eyes was scarred, and his lids hung loose over empty sockets.

She pushed herself to her feet, saying the sacred greeting. 'Sorry to startle you.'

The old man didn't return the customary gesture.

'You're not the one who brings me food.' He swung his stick out in front of him. 'Longer and longer they're leaving it these days.'

Where had he come from? She couldn't see any dwellings nearby.

'I'm a stranger to these parts. I have no food, but I can give you water.'

'Ahh.' The old man stopped, resting his hand on the rock to steady himself. 'I would be glad of refreshment.'

Danae drew one of the skins from her bag, took out the stopper and placed it in the man's hand. He drank deeply, the folds of his neck quivering as he gulped. Up close he smelt like stale urine.

'This is from the stream.' He wiped his mouth. 'Sweetest water in the world.'

'Do you live here?'

The old man nodded and tapped the rock like it was a prize heifer. Danae walked around and saw there was a much larger opening to the side. As she moved closer, she could see there were carvings etched into the stones. They looked like they had once formed a doorway. This was no rockslide, it was a ruin. She traced the grooves with her fingers, then stopped. Her pulse quickened.

There, chiselled on what would have been the keystone, was the apple tree.

She turned to look at the old man as he shuffled round the rocks. 'Do you know what this place used to be?'

The stranger moved to the entrance with surprising dexterity, feeling the way with his staff.

'I've spent years alone in this ruin. And I've found many things.' He ran his hands over the doorway, then leant back against the stone. 'This was a place of worship. But what I have not been able to discover is who the people that built it were worshipping. There are no sigils of any of the Twelve.'

'This stone here, may I?' She touched the old man's hand. He inclined his head. Gently, she placed his hand on the engraving of the tree. 'Do you know what this symbol is?'

'The tree of knowledge.'

She'd only ever heard one other person call it that.

Fighting to keep her voice calm, she asked, 'Have you come across it somewhere before?'

The old man tilted his head. 'Have you?'

'A few times.' She chose her next words carefully. 'I think it might be important. It might indicate a safe place for certain people that find it.'

Despite his lack of eyes, she had the distinct feeling he was staring at her.

'It might . . . and those that draw it might want to encourage those that recognize it to trust that they share the same belief.'

Something was happening at the back of her mind. A thought trickling like honey, slowly at first, then gaining momentum as it gathered weight.

'There is an ancient one some believe to be misunderstood. One who had a hand in our creation. I believe this to be true. Do you?'

The old man smiled, his remaining teeth stark against his receding gums. 'I do. I believe we are all his *children*.' He lingered on the last word.

Excitement surged through her. This had to be fate. Somehow, in all the vast reaches of land and sea, she had stumbled across a member of the Children of Prometheus.

35. An Eye for an Eye

'Quickly.' The old man gestured her into the ruins. 'It is not safe to talk out here.'

Danae followed him into the collapsed room. A musty pile of rags was heaped in one corner and on the other side was an eclectic collection of objects. Small pieces of rock, shards of bone and a scatter of broken pottery were lined up in neat rows. It looked like he'd been excavating.

'What are you doing here?'

'I was exiled,' he said quickly. 'Tell me, do you have news of the last daughter?'

He didn't look like an agent of the gods, but then how could she be sure?

'What's your name?' she asked.

'Phineus.' The old man leant on his staff. 'But please, friend. I have lived alone all this time, wondering, waiting. Is there news from the watcher?'

Her eyes prickled. 'The watcher is dead.'

The old man jerked as though she'd punched him. He sagged, reaching behind him as he crumpled onto a jutting piece of stone.

'Manto,' he whispered. His stick clattered to the ground as he raised his shaking hands to cover his face.

'Holy Tartarus,' she breathed, realization crashing over her. 'You're Manto's father.' She edged towards him. 'Phineus, I'm so sorry.'

He raised his mangled head. 'Get out.'

She faltered.

His frail voice shook. 'How dare you come here and say my Manto is . . . is . . .'

'I'm not lying.' Danae reached into her bag and pulled out the prophecy stone. She grabbed one of his hands and pressed the rock into his palm.

Phineus tensed, then drew the stone into his chest, caressing its wrappings like an old lover.

'You should not have brought this here,' he said quietly. Then his face spasmed, and the ghosts of tears tumbled from his empty eye sockets. Danae wept too, cracked open by the old man's grief.

When he regained himself enough to speak, he said, 'How did it happen?'

'Saving my life.'

She felt the weight of his guilt like it was her own. He hadn't asked Manto to wait for the last daughter because he didn't love them. He did it *because* of his love for them. So no more parents and children would have to live under the tyranny of the gods.

'Did they suffer?'

Danae saw Manto's final moments. The bloody gash where the harpy had ripped out their heart.

'No, it was over quickly. We were leaving Delphi and our ship was attacked by harpies. Manto pushed me into the sea and distracted the beasts so I would survive. They died a hero. I gave them a sea burial and made sure they had coin for the ferryman.' Her voice grew thick. 'They asked me to tell you that they kept their promise.'

'I don't understand.' Phineus shook his head. 'They would never have left Delphi without . . .' He grew very still.

Danae could not breathe.

'Tell me who you are,' Phineus whispered.

She felt as though she were standing on the edge of a

precipice. She briefly closed her eyes and imagined stepping off the ledge.

'I'm the reason Apollo razed Delphi . . . because I destroyed the oracle.' She finally drew a breath. 'I am the last daughter.'

The old man reached for his staff and, still holding the prophecy stone, pushed himself to his feet, murmuring, 'When the prophet falls, and gold that grows bears no fruit, the last daughter will come. She will end the reign of thunder and become the light that frees mankind.' He pressed the prophecy stone back into Danae's hand, then raised his gnarled fingers to her cheek, mapping the contours of her face. 'I have waited so long. Since my exile, I'd given up hope of ever meeting you, but here you are.'

She lowered his hand. 'There's something I need to tell you. I'm not a warrior, but I can do things – manipulate the threads of my life force and use them to influence the elements. But I'm working off intuition and I've no idea what I'm doing most of the time. If I'm ever going to be ready to take on Zeus, I need to understand what this power is and what I'm supposed to do with it, and why I keep being shown that bloody tree.' She stopped to draw breath.

Phineus lowered himself back onto the rock, his wrinkled face deep in thought.

'You've seen the tree of knowledge?'

'Yes.'

'Tell me exactly how it appeared to you.'

'This is going to sound strange but the first time . . . it sprouted from my sister's dead heart.' Her mouth was arid, but she forced herself to continue. 'Then it appeared in a vision the oracle at Delphi showed me . . . there were figures around it, then all these hands dragged them down and reached for its apples, and I burnt them. I burnt everything.'

'Interesting,' he murmured.

'Do you know what it means?'

Phineus twisted his staff between his palms. 'You have seen a manifestation of the tree at the point of its conception and at its end.' He was silent for a moment. 'Those symbols would suggest a cycle is almost complete. Like the phoenix reborn from the cinders of its old body, you are the embodiment of a new beginning. A world free of the gods.'

She swallowed. 'In the prophecy, Prometheus called me "the last daughter". Why the last?'

Phineus did not reply immediately. 'Perhaps you are the last of your kind.'

'What kind?'

He shook his head. 'That part is not clear.'

Her shoulders sagged with disappointment. Since learning who Phineus was, hope had blossomed. She thought he might be able to give her answers, but instead he left her with more questions.

'It's fascinating,' said Phineus, more to himself than to her. 'You can control your life-threads and use them to affect change outside of yourself in the physical world?'

'Yes.' She was growing impatient. 'But I don't know why or how. I just . . . can.' She paused. 'Wait, you know about life-threads?'

'Of course, they are what power the prophecy stone. I may not be able to see them as you can, but they run through all living things.' As though sensing her confusion he continued, 'All that touch the stone are pulled from their body and taken to the void. Once in that place, all who ask questions are shown the answer woven into the tapestry of life.'

'You could have left instructions. The stone's visions are impossible to understand.'

Phineus wheezed out a dry chuckle. 'If only it were that

simple. It took me years of study to accurately divine its revelations.'

She clenched her jaw. 'I don't have years, the gods are hounding me now.' Then she remembered something. 'Why did you tell Manto not to use it?'

Phineus bowed his head. 'You must forgive me for wanting to protect my child. You will have realized by now that foresight has a price.'

The life-threads that were drawn from her every time she touched the stone.

'I am not as old as I look . . . The stone is an empty vessel of sorts. For it to weave a vision it first needs to be filled with life-threads. I spent years divining prophecies from it, and in return it took years of my life.'

She stared at him in horror. He looked ancient. 'But you told Manto to give it to me . . .'

'You are the last daughter, I thought giving you access to what is to come was of greater importance than the longevity of your life.'

Silence settled in the cracks of the room. Phineus spoke without the hesitation of regret, like he was merely stating he preferred black olives to green. It was then Danae realized that while the prophecy foretold her destruction of Zeus' reign, it did not promise she would survive. She let the weight of that thought sink into her bones.

After a long pause, she asked, 'Did the stone take your eyes?'

Phineus laughed bitterly. 'The priestesses of Delphi did that. Did you know Prometheus' prophecy came from the very oracle you destroyed?'

'No?'

'Much of the story is lost to time. But fragments remain, passed down the generations of the Children of Prometheus.

Long ago, a rock was forged in the heart of the earth. All who touched it were granted visions of the future. It was named the omphalos stone, after the centre of the world from which it was born. Everything you've heard about Prometheus is a lie. His only crime was that he saw the downfall of the gods in the depths of the stone and, for daring to speak the truth, he was strung up on the highest peak of the Caucasus Mountains for all eternity. I do not know how the stone came to be broken, but I do know this: before his capture, Prometheus took one piece of the shattered omphalos stone and gave it to mankind, so the gift of prophecy would be available to all. The gods were not happy with mortals knowing freely what was to come. They have spent centuries hunting the missing piece. The rest of the shards they placed in Delphi and built guarded walls around them, only allowing their priestesses to grant prophecies to those who could pay a mighty price.'

Danae could see it so clearly: the glittering oracle, shards and shards of obsidian stone trapped below the earth.

Another wave of realization crashed over her. The Pythia. No wonder she had been withered before her time after decades of the omphalos stone gorging itself on her life-threads.

'That stone,' Phineus gestured towards her, 'is the last piece. Through the years, it has been passed through the Children of Prometheus, along with the truth. The omphalos stone is the only true source of prophecy. There is no other way to divine the future. That shard is how we've managed to stay hidden from the Twelve. It is how I knew you would come to Delphi in my lifetime.'

This was not the story she'd been told. She had believed, like everyone else, that Prometheus had stolen one of Zeus' thunderbolts and given it to mankind so they might rise up against their creator. But this was an even greater transgression. She thought of the ripple effect Hera's revelation about Jason's parentage had created. It touched the lives of all who travelled on the *Argo*, the islanders of Lemnos, the Doliones, potentially the entire city of Iolcos. So many mortals pulled by her puppet strings. The gift of foresight would give men a weapon against the gods' manipulation. After all, what greater way to start a revolution than allowing people a glimpse of their future.

Carefully, she unwrapped the shard of omphalos stone, making sure not to touch it with her skin. It felt heavier than before. In the light from the doorway its corners looked tinged with red, like it was soaked with the blood of all those who'd carried it.

'So all the seers and priestesses lie about reading the omens?'

Phineus made a noise in the back of his throat. 'They are either charlatans or fools who believe their own delusions. They can no more read the omens in animal intestines than I can fly.'

Phineus' implication weighed heavily on her. If what he said was true, and the will of the gods could not be divined, the priestesses of Demeter had ordered the slaughter of Melia's daughters and all those who'd gone before based on lies. Her hands trembled as she rewrapped the stone and stuffed it into her bag.

'What is the point of feeding my life-threads to this stone if I can't even decipher the visions it shows me?'

'You must learn.'

The finality in his tone struck a chord inside her that had been stretched to breaking point. Before she knew what she was doing, she'd thrown her bag to the ground.

'The Children of Prometheus are a joke. Whispering your secrets to each other, waiting for the last daughter to change the world for you. Do you have any idea how it feels to be told you are destined to kill Zeus, the actual god that created mankind? And to have the rest of the Twelve hunt me like a boar –'

Phineus slammed the end of his staff into the ground.

'Enough!' He drew a breath. 'You and the gods are not so different. They have the power to command the elements, so do you. They are not omnipotent, as they want us mortals to believe, and they make mistakes just like we do. You have a chance to make a real difference, to end the suffering of so many. Here's my advice: stop feeling sorry for yourself, work it out and trust no one. Oh, and don't get killed.'

Danae stared at him, her mouth slightly open.

Phineus twitched his head in the direction of the doorway. 'Ah! Lunch, at last.' He pushed himself to his feet. 'Stay here.' He tapped his way towards the entrance.

Then she heard it too. A rhythmic thumping, growing louder and louder.

Ignoring Phineus, she grabbed her bag and rushed out of the entrance, to see the sky darkened by the vast wings of a harpy.

She shrank back against the ruin, as Phineus staggered around beneath the creature, bony arms reaching for the cloth parcel dangling from its claws.

Her memory of the harpies' attack on the ship was a blur of wings, talons and blood. Her legs threatened to buckle. It felt as though the ground was moving, like she was back on the deck, trapped in the memory of Manto's death.

But she was no longer that terrified girl who'd fled Delphi. She forced herself to look at the harpy. Really look at it. Her eyes traced its arms fused to its leathery wings, the sagging breasts that hung from its scaly chest, the squashed, snarling face and the matted hair trailing down its back. Lastly, she made herself look at its taloned feet, from which sprung the claws that had ended Manto's life.

It was monstrous, yes. But it was just flesh and bone. It could be killed.

The harpy landed awkwardly, like a giant bird, and dropped its load. Phineus fell to his knees, scrabbling for the parcel. How could he? One of these creatures killed his child. Then she realized, he didn't know. He couldn't see the harpy.

She drew out her dagger.

The harpy sniffed the air. Then its grizzled head snapped towards her, indigo eyes narrowed. Danae's fist tightened on the handle of her knife. She could feel the power of her life force thrumming through her, but it was weak. She hadn't replenished her threads.

Snarling, the harpy unfurled its wings, creating a gust of air that knocked Phineus to the ground. Then it launched itself towards her. In the moment before impact, she pictured Manto, standing on the deck of the ship, arms flung wide, nothing to fight with but their belief that Danae would bring about a reckoning that would shake the world.

She sprang towards the harpy. Metal clashed with bone. She twisted on impact, skidding underneath the harpy's talons as she sliced upwards. The creature wheeled around in mid-air, its vast wings propelling it round for another attack. But Danae was ready. She feigned to the right, nicking the beast's thigh with her blade as it descended. It roared and lashed at her, but she dodged again.

Phineus cowered, his hands over his head. 'What's happening?'

She couldn't spare the breath to answer. She darted around the thrashing claws, cutting the harpy's legs where she could. But she was tiring, and each wound fed the harpy's rage. It was learning to predict her movements, and on the next jab talons raked over her shoulder. The pain was excruciating.

She was going to die, just like Manto.

Gasping through the ache, she transferred the knife to her left hand. Instead of dodging the harpy's next assault, she leapt into the air. Swinging her good arm around the creature's scaly neck, she clung on as the harpy flapped into the sky, attempting to throw her off. Its breath was rancid, its pointed teeth gnashing at her face.

With a spasm of pain that almost forced her to let go, Danae stretched out her arm and sliced. The harpy screamed as she hacked at its wing, tearing holes through the membrane. Unable to stay airborne, the beast tumbled down, spiralling back to earth.

They landed with a bone-shattering crack on top of the ruin. The harpy broke the worst of her fall, but the air was pummelled from Danae's lungs, and the entire left side of her body was in a vice of agony.

Then she felt it, the whisper of life-threads leaving the harpy's body. She placed her good hand on its chest and sucked the creature's fleeing life force into herself. She gasped as the sinews in her shoulder knitted together and the pain melted from her bones, just as it had done on Lemnos when she took the life of the panther. Energy raced through her, and she was bright and new again. She could see the translucent strands moving through each blade of grass, the insects that flew from leaf to leaf, and Phineus. He was radiant, a glowing tangle of moving energy.

But something was different. The power rushed through her faster and faster until it felt like her body would break open; it surely could not contain so much life. Everything around her was so bright, too bright, the colours exploding together until she could see nothing but blinding white light.

Excruciating bliss.

Then the world came back into focus. She sat up slowly and looked at the mangled body beneath her. The harpy was dead, and yet she felt no joy. Something had shifted, and she didn't know what. It unsettled her. Perhaps absorbing a life taken by force felt different to taking one that was offered willingly, like the panther's.

She clambered down to the ground, where Phineus sat, calmly eating the bread and cheese he'd unwrapped from the harpy's parcel.

He choked as Danae pressed her blade against his neck.

'Why did that thing bring you food?'

'It was my tormenter,' he spluttered.

She squeezed her knife into his skin. 'Explain.'

Phineus gulped down his mouthful. 'The creature brings food and some days it allows me to eat, others it waits until I've unwrapped the victuals, then attacks . . .'

For the first time Danae noticed the silver scars that laced Phineus' arms.

'Why?'

'It was my punishment . . . from the gods.'

Danae stared at him.

'Do you know what it was?'

Phineus shook his head. She believed him.

'It was a harpy. One of the creatures that killed Manto.'

Phineus stiffened. She waited a moment to let the revelation sink in, then touched his shoulder. 'We must leave now. There are two more of them, they could be anywhere.'

'Is it dead?'

'Yes.'

'Good.' Instead of getting to his feet, the old man placed a knob of cheese in his mouth and resumed chewing. The line between Danae's brows deepened.

'Phineus, you're coming with me.'

He swallowed. 'No, child. I would only slow you down. Besides, I have played my part.' A smile spread across his face. 'It's time I saw my Manto again.'

'You don't have to die,' Danae said quietly.

'Oh, but I do. Sooner or later the gods will come searching for the harpy, and when they do . . .' He paused. 'All mortals must travel to the Underworld. Leave me the dignity of choosing when.'

'Who will bury you?'

Phineus' mouth quirked. 'Don't you worry, I've had a long time to plan for this.'

'I'm not leaving you here.'

'You must.' Phineus spoke with iron-hard resolve. 'Your life is not your own any more, you are the last daughter. Your destiny is all that matters. I can be of no more help to you. But you are not alone. The Children of Prometheus are out there. There are powerful people in our ranks. When the time comes, they will find you. But you must go, now.'

Danae stared at him, then threw her arms around his thin neck and whispered, 'I will be the reckoning. And when my work is done, I will tell the world the part that you and Manto had to play.'

As she drew away, Phineus clutched her hand.

'Before you go, tell me your name.'

She straightened up.

'My name is Danae.'

'Daeira!' called Jason, as Danae clambered down the boulders towards the *Argo*. 'Thank the gods. I was beginning to think you were lost.'

By way of an explanation, she held up a full waterskin.

She'd left the other with Phineus. Another person to add to the list of those she could not fail.

She took Castor's arm, and he pulled her up over the side of the ship. Her wet dress clung to her legs as she landed on the deck. She'd washed off the harpy's blood in the stream. Not for the first time she was grateful that seers always wore black.

Jason turned to address the crew. 'We have a difficult journey ahead. The elements will only grow harsher the closer we come to Colchis.' He looked at Atalanta and Telamon, who were once more restrained. 'I hold no tolerance for mutiny, but we need rowers. I offer you both the chance to swear your allegiance to me as captain. If you refuse, we will leave you here without weapons or supplies.'

Telamon glanced at his brother, lying on his bed of furs behind the rowing benches, and said quickly, 'I pledge my service to you, Jason.'

Jason smiled. 'Release him.' He nodded to Pollux.

Atalanta shook her head, staring resolutely at the deck. Danae's heart drummed against her chest. She couldn't see a world in which the warrior would ever swear loyalty to Jason.

Once free of his bonds, Telamon crouched beside Atalanta and whispered something in her ear. Her head snapped up, and she stared at Telamon with a look so penetrating it could have bent iron. Then her eyes found Danae's.

Silently, Danae begged her with every bone, breath and life-thread in her body to choose life over pride.

Something softened in Atalanta's eyes. She lowered her gaze and muttered, 'I pledge my service.'

Relief cascaded through Danae.

'Louder please, for everyone to hear.'

'*I pledge my service.*'

Jason nodded and signalled for Pollux to release her

too. 'If you disobey me again you will be killed instantly, and your bodies will be tossed into the sea without burial rights.'

It was a heavy threat. Not only death but the promise of eternity spent wandering the banks of the River Styx.

Atalanta and Telamon were silent as they joined the men on the benches. As Danae watched Atalanta take up an oar, warmth spread through her chest. The warrior was safe, for now, and she had the rest of the voyage to win back her favour. Starting by sneaking her extra wine rations that evening.

As they set off, Danae looked to the horizon. The wind was strong, and soon the mainsail was bloated by gusts of salty air, driving the *Argo* onwards, towards the mouth of the Black Sea.

36. Interlude on Thrace

Phineus leant against the stones of the ruin, the last rays of sunlight warming his face. He wondered if he should have been more forthcoming with the last daughter. Divining prophecy was by no means an exact art. One had to be careful, especially when hearing the prophetic vision described second-hand. Whilst he believed what he'd told her to be true, he had remained silent on the other possibilities that had presented themselves. Darker paths swathed in blood and destruction. She would end the reign of thunder, of that much he was certain. But at what cost?

She was right, she was not what he'd expected. He couldn't deny that he'd hoped she would be better prepared, but it was fitting somehow that the champion of mankind should be an ordinary girl who would become extraordinary. Perhaps he'd been too hard on her. It was a mighty burden she carried. But there would be no softness in what was to come.

He took comfort in the knowledge that he'd guided her as best he could. Besides, soon none of it would matter to him. Soon he would join the souls of all those that had come before, in the Underworld. Soon he would be with his Manto again.

His staff was to his left, and the wrappings that carried his last meal lay to his right. He was glad he would meet death on a full stomach. A small mercy. Tucked into the sash of his robe were two coins he'd found in the temple. He had no idea what currency they were. Too small for drachmas and too large for obols, but he hoped they would be enough to pay the ferryman to take his soul across the River Styx.

A disturbance in the air pricked his attention. There was a sound, something other than the usual crash of the tide, whine of the sea-wind and squawking of gulls. He tilted his head to the west and waited.

Soon, his patience was rewarded by the clink and thud of a pair of armoured feet landing on the ground.

Then a laugh, shrill and boyish.

'Oh.' Phineus didn't try to hide his disappointment. 'It's you.'

'Phineus.' The voice sounded petulant. 'That's no way to greet an old friend.'

Phineus reached for his staff, wedged it into the ground and pushed himself up. 'I'd hoped your father would come. But he sends his messenger.'

'You wound me. I thought you enjoyed our chats.'

Phineus was in no mood to be toyed with. Not today.

'If you've come to ask about the omphalos shard, my answer is the same as it has always been. It was stolen from me in Delphi, and I have no idea where it is now. Fly back to your father and tell him he's wasted his time.'

'Oh, I don't care about the stone, and Father doesn't actually know I'm here. Although, I'm sure he'd be very interested to learn how one of his pets came to end up dead on top of your hovel.'

Phineus could hear the smile in the other's voice. That was worrying.

He tapped his stick against the ground. 'I'm deadlier than I look.'

The other laughed again, his voice crackling across two octaves, like a boy's on the cusp of adolescence.

'What do you want, Hermes?'

The laughter stopped abruptly.

'You're no fun today.' The god sighed. 'Father's given my siblings a new game. A hunt. It's turning out to be rather exciting. Uncle Hades has set loose a creature from the Underworld disguised as a mortal girl. Apollo thought he'd got rid of her in Delphi, but somehow, she escaped. Then Artemis received a message from one of her followers on that strange little island of hers saying the girl has godlike powers. Well, we all thought she was exaggerating, but then Athena went to have a look and got the shock of her life. So, tell me, where is she?'

Phineus' fists tightened on his staff. They didn't know. Zeus hadn't told his children who Danae really was. Could it be that the King of the Gods was afraid?

A smile bloomed across Phineus' face.

'You're in a strange mood. Is this what happens to mortals when their bodies shrivel up?' Hermes didn't wait for Phineus to reply. 'Anyway, I don't have all day. She's been here, hasn't she?'

Phineus' smile grew broader.

'Hasn't she?'

'How should I know? I'm blind.'

Phineus flinched at a loud crack next to his ear, and a spray of rock shards hitting his cheek.

'I'm getting bored now. I know she has. That ship she's on stopped here. You won't be so difficult once I tell you which of my siblings wants the information.'

He wanted to be entertained. Phineus knew that tone. He also knew how to prick his visitor's anger. 'Ah, little messenger, doing someone else's bidding as usual. Are the others not letting you play?'

Phineus choked as a gauntleted fist clamped around his neck and he felt the sharp sting of metal cutting into his skin.

'I am a god, you maggot. You will show me respect.' Hermes tightened his grip. 'It's Ares' turn next, and the God of War doesn't like to lose. Now, I'm going to ask you one last time. Has the girl been here?'

I'm coming, Manto, Phineus thought, as he hawked and spat into what he hoped was Hermes' face.

The god released his neck. There was a pause. Then Phineus was pushed violently against the rock. The breath was knocked from his lungs. He wheezed in agony, Hermes' gauntleted hand pressing against his chest, crushing his ribs with unworldly strength.

'Before you die, I want you to know that I'm the one who convinced Father to keep you alive. The harpies brought you food because of me. Every breath you've taken, every dream you've had, every hope, every thought, every shit, has been mine. Goodbye, Phineus, I will forget you ever existed.'

The pain was excruciating. Phineus could barely breathe, but he was no stranger to agony. Then he felt something completely new. He'd lost sensation in his fingers and toes. It was beyond numbness, like his extremities were filling with emptiness. He was diminishing, as though Hermes were pulling his very essence out through his chest.

For the first time in a long time, he was afraid. Only his Manto remained a glimmer of hope as the last of his life-threads were wrenched from his body.

The mortal's corpse crumpled to the earth. It was a shame really. Hermes enjoyed talking to Phineus far more than his self-absorbed siblings.

The god tugged the helm from his head. He looked down in disgust at the spittle smeared on the golden cheekplate. He could already hear his stepmother chastising him. *Foolish boy, the man could have been diseased, how many times do you have to be told?* Hera had such a fear of catching mortal illnesses.

He supposed it was understandable, given how many of her husband's bastard children littered the earth.

Hermes knelt and wiped his helm on the grass. The craftsmanship really was stunning. The flawless gold was detailed with a filigree of ivy, winding up to two leaves that pointed upwards like ears on either side. He only ever took it off when he was alone. He liked himself much better inside his armour.

He barely noticed the extra life-threads whirring through his veins, he'd grown so used to the sensation. But he could still remember the ecstasy of his first time, all those centuries ago. That was a feeling he would never forget.

As he lifted the helm, he caught a glimpse of his reflection in the mirrored gold. The downy hairs on his chin that would never become a beard, the painful spots marring his rose-pale skin. He rammed the helm back over his face. Forever cursed to remain on the edge of boyhood. His father was so cruel. Not a day went by when Hermes didn't wish Zeus had waited before performing the ritual, let him become a man first.

His thoughts were interrupted by a distant screech. The remaining harpies were searching for their sister. He'd better make himself scarce. Besides, Ares would be waiting. He sighed. Returning without information would cost him a beating, but not returning at all would be worse.

Hermes bent his knees and kicked into the air. The metal wings melded to his armoured boots beat rapidly and propelled him into the sky. Flying never failed to bring him joy, and he smiled as he cut through the clouds like a golden spear.

37. Metal Skies

Thirty-two days had passed since the *Argo* entered the iron waters of the Black Sea. Danae knew this because she had been scoring a line on the wall of the store cabin each day before preparing the lunch rations. Each mark scratched was another day closer to Prometheus and discovering the true nature of her destiny.

Under Tiphys' advice they kept to the coastline, landing only when they needed to replenish the ship's store. Jason drove the Argonauts hard, only letting the rowers rest when the wind picked up and they could unfurl the mainsail. The closer they came to Colchis, the more he pushed. The crew pulled the oars from dawn until dusk, not dropping anchor until the starry cloak of night swept over the sky. They slept under the ship's tarpaulin and as soon as dawn broke, took up the oars again.

A chill crept into the air. When the wind blew from the east, it cut to the bone, and even at its height, the sun didn't warm the skin like it did back home. Danae was glad of the extra furs they'd taken from Lemnos. Rowing was tough, but at least the exertion kept the crew warm.

With no time alone to explore her powers, she spent most of her days with Peleus, tending to his wounds. At first, he seemed to be improving. Then came the day she peeled off the makeshift dressing and found his stitches were inflamed, yellow pus oozing between the twine. She hid the last two skins of wine from Atalanta and used the liquid to clean the wounds. But without Dolos' expertise and bag of medicines, she knew Peleus had little chance of recovery.

'Tell me about your family,' Danae said to distract him as she dabbed a wine-sodden cloth against his infected flesh. Peleus winced.

'My wife, Thetis. You'll not meet a cleverer woman. Nor a more tricksome one.' He chuckled then gasped in pain.

'You have a son, don't you?'

'Yes.' Peleus' pride was evident, even through clenched teeth. 'My Achilles.'

'Telamon says he's a good fighter.'

'He's not good, he's extraordinary. He was training with the palace guard at ten years old. I don't know where he gets it from. I was useless at his age.'

She smiled. 'I doubt that's true. I've seen you and your brother in action. I bet you were a pair of troublemakers.'

She finished wiping Peleus' wounds and began to wind a fresh piece of cloth around his torso. His skin was clammy beneath her fingers.

'I worry about him.'

'Achilles?' She realized Peleus was looking past her at the rowing benches. She glanced behind at Telamon. 'Oh, that one can look after himself.'

'It wasn't his fault.'

'What wasn't?'

'He didn't mean to do it.' Peleus sounded distressed.

She paused her wrapping and placed a hand on his forehead. He was burning up. Her heart sank. A fever meant the infection had spread.

'I'm sure he didn't,' she said softly and continued bandaging.

'Father was so angry. But Telamon didn't deserve to be cast out. He didn't know Phocus was standing there.'

She had no idea what Peleus was talking about. He might well be delusional from the fever. She knew so little of Telamon's origins, except that he used to be a prince.

'What happened?'

Peleus made a sound somewhere between a whimper and a moan. 'It was an accident. Telamon threw the discus, then poor Phocus appeared from nowhere. The sound was awful . . . his little skull cracked like an egg.' Peleus' face crumpled in pain. At the memory or his wounds, she couldn't tell.

She glanced back at Telamon. She remembered what Hylas had said, about Heracles giving second chances to those others had shunned. The hero and Telamon had more in common than she'd realized.

'He still blames himself, I know he does. If anything happens . . . will you look after him? You're a kind girl.'

Danae bit the inside of her lip until she drew blood. She'd been doing it a lot lately, and as a result her mouth was raw with ulcers. The pain helped distract from her guilt. He wouldn't call her kind if he knew the choices she'd made.

The following day was relentless. The wind lulled to barely a whisper, and by the afternoon they'd run out of water. Danae offered the last skin around the benches, so the rowers could wet their lips, but it would be impossible to keep going without replenishing the barrels before nightfall. So, it came as a great relief to all when Tiphys spotted a break in the cliff face.

'Captain!' the navigator called. 'There's a beach ahead. Do we land?'

'Yes!' Jason barely let him finish. 'Thank the gods. Steer her in.'

The *Argo* ground to a halt in the shallows, and the crew hauled in the oars.

'Argonauts,' Jason called from the prow deck. 'You know the routine. We go in pairs and –'

'There's someone on the beach!' shouted Pollux.

Danae turned. A figure was riding down the dunes towards the ship. Sunlight blazed behind them, the sand kicked up by the horse's hooves a sparkling cloud of golden dust. The powerful flanks of the chestnut stallion gleamed, and the bronze fur flying behind its rider seemed to capture the sun itself.

She gasped. It couldn't be.

Heracles.

'I fucking knew it!' Atalanta leapt onto her bench and punched the air.

'You beautiful bastard!' Telamon shouted, then lifted Atalanta off her feet and kissed her.

The warrior shoved him off and wiped her cheek, but she didn't stop grinning.

Danae couldn't believe it. A moment later another horse appeared. It was Dolos, charging after Heracles. She couldn't breathe, couldn't speak, couldn't even blink as she waited for Hylas to appear.

But he didn't come.

Jason looked like he might vomit. None of the other Argonauts were celebrating. They floundered, eyes flicking between the approaching hero and their captain.

Danae didn't move either. She stared resolutely at the horizon, waiting. Perhaps Hylas was lagging behind, his horse might not be as fast as the other two. Heracles wouldn't have left the Doliones' shore without him, she knew he wouldn't.

The moments felt like years as they dragged by, each one chipping away at her hope until the awful truth swallowed the last glimmer.

Hylas was dead.

She felt like it was happening all over again. He was being taken from her afresh, and she was just standing there while the Earthborn dragged him away.

She was brought back to the present by the sound of Heracles shouting. But he was too far away for her to make it out.

'What's he saying?' asked Telamon.

Heracles was waving now, his words still distorted by the wind. Danae strained to listen, running to the prow as the hero hurtled towards them.

'Get off the ship!' yelled Heracles. 'Run!'

Shaken from his stupor, Jason shouted back, 'Why?'

There was a choking sound from the stern deck. Danae spun around as Tiphys collapsed, what appeared to be a bronze knife sticking out of his neck.

'Take cover!' shouted Jason.

The crew dived below the benches, and Telamon threw himself on top of Peleus as a slew of metal thudded into the wood. One sliced through the fabric of Danae's dress, grazing her thigh. Up close she could see it wasn't a knife at all, but a feather, cast in bronze and razor sharp.

The weight of dread heavy in her chest, she eased her head out from under the bench and looked up.

A flock of birds was circling the ship. They were large as vultures with feathers of bronze that dazzled in the sunlight. Danae hurriedly squeezed herself back under the bench as the birds flicked their wings and another round of deadly feathers rained down.

'Shit!' Jason was cowering under the adjacent bench. 'Why in Tartarus is this happening?'

'It's the Stymphalian birds,' called Telamon as he dragged Peleus to cover.

'The *what*?'

'We faced them on one of Heracles' labours for Eurystheus – argh!' Telamon cried out as a feather sliced his arm.

'How did you defeat them?' Jason shouted.

'We didn't,' called back Atalanta. 'We ran away.'

'They answer to Ares,' said Telamon as he tried to pull his brother further under the bench. 'Gods know why they're here.'

'That brute led them to us!' shouted Pollux. 'He's going to be the death of us all.'

Danae's mind was racing. As she desperately tried to formulate a plan, her father's words rang through her thoughts, 'All seas are the same beast.' She had always been a child of the ocean. She'd grown up swimming in its tides and diving its swells. The Black Sea was no different.

Now it will answer to you, said the voice.

She summoned the energy of her life-threads and stepped out from under the bench. Someone tried to grab her leg. Jason was shouting at her to take cover. But she ignored him and thrust out her arms. A glowing tangle of life-threads shot out from each palm into the sea on either side of the ship. She tilted her head back and set her gaze on the swarm of bronze birds circling above. Then she gathered the threads in her fists like a pair of ropes and whipped them into the sky.

Two torrents of water arced over her head and smashed in a crescendo of foam and feathers above the *Argo*. The ship dipped violently, and for a moment there was stillness, the birds suspended in a clear archway of ocean. Then the water crashed back into the sea and broken metallic bodies clanged down onto the deck.

Danae staggered but did not fall. She licked the salt from her lips and smiled.

'What the fuck was that?' Atalanta stared at Danae, face taut with shock.

Everyone was staring at her.

The Argonauts emerged from their benches and backed

away. Some reached for their weapons. Most looked at her with a fusion of fear and anger.

Jason alone did not move. He was gazing at her in amazement. 'What are you?'

'She's a kakodaimon!' said Castor. The crew tensed.

It was happening again. She could see her mother's terror-stricken eyes in their sea-worn faces. She had saved them, but at what cost? This time, she could not hide behind the gods.

'She's no evil spirit.'

Heracles heaved himself over the side of the ship. He stepped over the broken birds and came to stand beside her.

She was met with a beaming smile. 'Which god is it?'

Danae was utterly confused.

He put a hand on her shoulder. 'You don't have to pretend any more. I suspected since the mountain village, but I could tell you wanted to hide it.' His blue eyes sparkled. 'I had no idea you were this powerful.'

'I say we kill her!' growled Castor.

'Say that again and I will end you.' Heracles turned to Jason. 'Daeira is no daimon. She is a demi-god.'

Collectively, the Argonauts gaped. Jason looked like he was trying to form words but couldn't get them over his tongue.

'For the love of the gods, put down your weapons,' said Telamon. 'She just saved our lives.'

They did as he said.

Danae's heart was thundering. Heracles had jumped to the wrong conclusion, but he might have just given her a gift.

'He's right.' She returned the hero's smile. 'My father is Poseidon, Lord of the Sea and Shaker of the Earth.'

There were so many questions, but the lies came easily. By now, Danae was well practised.

'My village shunned my mother after Poseidon impregnated her. My family lived in poverty and we kept to ourselves. But when the villagers discovered I had a gift for prophecy and these unearthly powers, they were afraid, and I was driven away. So, I left my home and became a seer.'

She hoped it would be enough to satisfy them. Jason looked torn. She didn't blame him.

'Why didn't you reveal yourself sooner? We are warriors not superstitious peasants.' Jason glanced pointedly at Castor, who looked at his feet. 'Why didn't you intervene with the storm, on *that* island, with the Earthborn? Lives could have been saved.'

Now was hardly the moment to confess she'd started the fire on Lemnos. She bowed her head. 'You're right. My fear of persecution is to blame. I carry the guilt for all those we've lost.' That was no lie.

Jason continued to stare at her like she was a cub who had suddenly grown into a lion right in front of him. She could see the pressure building behind his eyes. She wondered if he was going to banish her from the *Argo*, but then he turned away.

'Heracles.' Jason couldn't quite meet his eyes. 'How in the name of the gods did you survive the Earthborn?'

Heracles grinned at the Argonauts. 'I wish I could say it was all down to me. I killed a good few more of those six-armed bastards and managed to scare the rest back to their mountain. The Doliones came round when they saw how many I'd butchered.' He paused, frowning slightly at the lack of enthusiasm his story was rousing. 'We stayed with them for a couple of days until, as luck would have it, a merchant ship was passing and –'

'What happened to Hylas?'

Danae couldn't wait any longer. It was the question she'd

been burning and dreading to ask since the hero had appeared over the dunes. She already knew the answer, but she needed to hear it from him.

Heracles' huge shoulders sank. 'The Earthborn took him back to their nest. I couldn't save him.'

'You left him unburied?'

How dare Heracles stand there, bragging about killing Earthborn, when he'd left Hylas' ghost to wander the banks of the Styx. He would never find peace, forever separated from the souls of everyone who ever cared for him. He was the last person in the world who deserved that fate.

'How could you?' Tears blurted down her cheeks. 'You abandoned him! If you killed so many Earthborn, why couldn't you –'

'I can't save everyone.'

'You didn't try hard enough!'

'Neither did you!'

She flinched. The Argonauts cringed away from the hero. Heracles stared at them, his blue eyes muddled with surprise and confusion.

Furiously, she wiped her face. In that moment she couldn't bear the sight of him, but she needed to tell him what Jason had revealed somewhere private, where he couldn't react in front of the crew, or Tiphys' might not be the only body that needed burying.

'Jason, before the attack we were going ashore to fetch water,' she prompted.

'Yes,' the captain said distractedly. He was still staring at Heracles.

'And Tiphys will need burying.'

Jason's gaze snapped back to her, then behind him to the stern, as though he'd forgotten they'd lost their navigator.

'Yes,' he said again, then cleared his throat. 'Argonauts,

clear the deck of these birds. We'll camp here tonight and replenish our supplies. At dawn we'll send Tiphys on his way to the Underworld. Then, we sail for Colchis.'

Dolos was waiting with the horses on the shore. As soon as they cleared the shallows, Telamon sprinted over to the healer.

'Thank the gods, you need to come to the ship. Peleus is hurt.'

As the pair hurried back to the *Argo*, Danae took Heracles' arm and steered him towards the dunes.

'Daeira, wait,' Jason called as he waded onto the beach. 'Where are you going?'

'Heracles and I need to speak in private.'

Revealing her abilities had shifted the power dynamic, and they both knew it. He was still the captain and she his seer, but she could end his life as easily as blowing out a candle.

Jason pressed his mouth into a line. 'All right. But don't go too far.'

She nodded, then turned back to Heracles. Together, they paced up the sandy dunes away from the shore.

'I'm sorry,' he said gruffly. 'I didn't mean . . .'

'No, you were right.' It had never really been Heracles she was angry with.

If she'd known that staying on the *Argo* would result in Hylas being slaughtered and left unburied, she might have gone back. But what upset her more than learning his fate was the part of her that knew, even if she'd had the foresight, she would still have left him.

Danae and Heracles sat side by side on the hero's lion hide, hidden behind the dunes as they gazed out over the ocean.

He hadn't looked at her since she'd told him what Jason had revealed about his family.

'You must think me a monster.'

Her eyes traced the outline of his face against the darkening sky. He'd never looked more human.

'I know you were drugged. Telamon told me the truth, that Hera was to blame. But the rest of the crew . . .' She hesitated. 'They think you killed them in cold blood.'

Heracles said nothing. She loathed twisting the knife in further, but he had to know.

'They believe all the misfortune that's befallen us on this voyage is because you broke your agreement with Eurystheus. They think Hera's been punishing you.'

Heracles barked out a laugh. 'Hera's methods are far more underhand than storms and monsters. Besides, Jason is her golden boy.' His voice tightened with spite. 'She wouldn't jeopardize him. If the gods are meddling with us, it's nothing to do with me.'

He was right, but she couldn't tell him. Not yet.

The hero leaned forward and buried his head in his hands. She hated seeing him like this.

'I know nothing I say will ease your guilt. But please believe me when I say you are not alone. I know what it feels like to see those you care for hurt because of who you are.'

She wanted to touch him, but she didn't dare. He was so powerful and so powerless at the same time. They both were.

Heracles rubbed his face and let out a bone-weary sigh. 'I would have been happy if I was born an ordinary man. Could have grown old with grandchildren pulling at my tunic.' His voice cracked. 'I see their faces, every time I can't save someone . . .'

His grief reached into her chest and wrapped its fingers around her heart. She saw Arius in Alea's arms, his tiny fists tangled in her sister's hair.

'All I have is my reputation. Heracles, the living legend.

That's what Zeus wanted me to be, what he made me become. You know, I've never even met him. My own father. He's controlled my entire life, and I've never seen his face.'

She was stunned. 'Never? Not even when you were younger?'

Heracles shook his head. 'I don't remember much of my childhood. Just empty marble rooms. Then Dolos came to look after me.'

Heracles' mother had been a queen, Danae knew that much. Little was told of her beyond being the womb that bore the greatest hero who had ever lived.

'When Zeus came to your mother . . . how did he . . .?'

'He abducted and raped her,' Heracles said flatly.

Her throat thickened. There had been moments on the voyage, in the quiet, dark hours when sleep would not come, that she wondered. Could Alea have been right about Zeus being Arius' father? But if that were true, surely the King of Heaven would not have let his son join the Missing?

'When you were a baby . . . were you ever taken by a shade?'

He frowned. 'No, I'm sure that's something my mother would have told me. Why?'

'It doesn't matter.' She felt foolish for asking. For allowing herself a spark of hope that Arius might still be out there somewhere.

'Can I tell you a secret?' Heracles turned his face from the waves and looked at her.

'Yes.'

'I've always hated my father. All of the gods, in fact.'

Excitement thrummed through her limbs as possibility solidified into certainty.

This was why she'd been drawn to him. He too saw the gods as the tyrants they really were. They would find Prometheus together and, with Heracles at her side, taking on the Twelve wouldn't be such an insurmountable task. She desperately wanted to tell him everything, all at once, but she had to be delicate.

'So have I.'

Heracles' gaze grew so intense, she felt as though she'd been stripped bare. 'I didn't think there was anyone else like me in the world.'

They were so close, she could feel the heat rising from his bare torso. Her body tingled, her gut a tangle of emotions.

His lips met hers and he kissed her, softly at first, then her mouth opened and she let him drink her in, her entire body pulsing with every heartbeat.

He drew back. 'I don't want to hurt you.'

'You won't,' she breathed, barely able to form the words. 'I'm like you, remember.'

He took her face in his hands. 'Are you sure you want this?'

In that moment, it was all she wanted.

'Yes.'

Her skin shivered as he slipped his hands under her dress. She gasped, shocks of pleasure vibrating through her as they edged up her thighs. Then he lifted her and lay her down on his lion hide. She let him pull up her dress and shuddered as he kissed her bare stomach. As his lips moved slowly downwards, the ache of longing was so great, she thought she was going to explode.

She didn't care if someone found them, she didn't care about Prometheus or the prophecy. All she wanted was to disappear into the ecstasy.

38. Sand and Stars

Moonlight pooled over Danae and Heracles' tangled bodies. They lay on their backs, sandy and sweaty despite the chill air.

She couldn't stop smiling. She'd lain with Heracles. *The* Heracles. She couldn't wait to see the look on Alea's face.

The giddiness left her in an instant. For a heartbeat, she'd forgotten.

Heracles drew her close. 'Was that your first time?'

Holy Tartarus, was it that obvious?

'No.' She blinked the salt from her eyes, then said quickly, 'How did you get this?' She traced a silver scar that sliced the hero's abdomen like a crescent moon.

Heracles peered down at his stomach. 'Tusk of the Erymanthian boar.'

'Let me guess, this one was the many-headed hydra?'

Heracles laughed. 'No, just a regular battle wound, I'm afraid.'

'What about this?' She trailed her finger down the scar that sliced the skin from his eyebrow to his jaw.

'That,' he took her fingers and kissed them, 'was a feather from one of those birds you . . . drowned?'

She sat up, suddenly remembering something that had occurred to her earlier on the ship. 'How did you come to arrive at the beach at the same time as the *Argo*?'

'Lucky coincidence. Dolos and I spotted the Stymphalian birds a few weeks ago. We were tracking them.' He pointed to his face. 'I had some unfinished business.'

He drew her back to the sand, and they lay for a while, staring at the night sky.

Heracles brushed his fingers along the curve of her waist. 'Dolos told me, if I do what my father wants, I'll be transformed into a star when I die.'

Danae looked at the lights twinkling above them. 'Is that what you want?'

Heracles shrugged. 'It is the highest honour the gods can bestow. But it always seems lonely to me. Burning alone in the firmament, forever staring down at earth. Always so far away.'

She wondered if he was thinking of his family. She knew if he could, he would be with his wife and children. When her time came, she would always choose to be with Alea.

'My mother loves the stars. She knows the stories of every soul the gods have placed up there to shine for all eternity. Most of them anyway – some she definitely made up.'

'Tell me about them.'

She pointed to the sky, tracing the lights with her finger. 'That cluster is the queen Cassiopeia; she's upside down as punishment for being vain.' Heracles snorted. 'Those three there are the belt of the giant Orion, and those are Andromeda, the princess rescued by Perseus from the jaws of a sea monster.'

Her mind went blank. She dropped her hand, suddenly feeling foolish. A crack appeared in the cocoon of their intimacy. A prickle of guilt that she was wasting time.

'Heracles,' she propped herself onto her elbow and looked at him. 'Would you ever challenge your father?'

The hero frowned. 'That's a big thing to ask.'

'Heracles!' The cry echoed across the dunes.

'Shit.' Danae scrabbled to find her dress, only just tugging it on before Dolos appeared. Heracles made no attempt to cover himself.

The healer stopped still when he saw them. His eyes hardened like frosted earth.

'Jason is asking for you both.'

'How's Peleus?' Danae hurriedly got to her feet.

'I've done all I can. How he recovers over the next day will be crucial. That stitching was terrible, no wonder it got infected.' Dolos cleared his throat. 'But without it, he would have certainly bled to death. You saved his life. For now, anyway.'

She smiled. 'Thank you, Dolos, I'm so glad you're back.'

The healer nodded curtly then turned to Heracles. 'Are you coming?'

The hero grinned, stretched like a cat, then slowly got to his feet. Dolos tapped his foot as Heracles fastened his kilt about his waist and flicked the sand from his lion hide.

'I'll catch you up,' Danae said as the two men headed back towards the beach.

As she watched them walk away, worry crept into her heart.

In his arms, she'd felt so strongly that her own and Heracles' destinies were entwined. He'd been returned to her. Surely that meant they were fated to walk the same path. The odds of him finding the *Argo* at the exact moment he did were too slim to be chance.

But Phineus' words echoed through her mind. *Trust no one*.

She slipped her hand into the pocket of her dress and pulled out the omphalos shard. Ever since she'd learnt of its origins, she'd kept it on her at all times. She unwrapped it and let it roll, naked, into her palm. Immediately, her life-threads rushed into her hand, clustering against her skin like fish seeking crumbs on the surface of a pool. She breathed out slowly as they were sucked into the stone. Then she was plunged into darkness, suspended outside her body in the void.

She let her mind empty, then formulated her question.
Will Heracles join my quest?

A single thread danced across the blackness. She focused on it and felt the now familiar tug as her mind travelled down its length, weaving into the tapestry of life. Then the strands unravelled and threaded together to create a new image.

She saw a figure, wearing Heracles' impenetrable lion hide, climbing what appeared to be a storm-swathed mountain. It must be the Caucasus Mountains, where Prometheus was tethered.

She dropped the stone and returned with a sickening jolt to the dunes. She had her proof, the stone did not lie. She didn't have to do it alone.

Heracles would come with her to find Prometheus.

By the time Danae arrived back on the beach, a camp had been erected. A cluster of tents lined the shore, and the *Argo* had been dragged onto the sand, a tarpaulin stretched over the deck to shelter Peleus and any others who wished to sleep aboard. She spotted Heracles sitting with Telamon and Atalanta beside a large stone-ringed fire.

'Daeira!' Telamon set down the metallic bird he was stripping and beckoned her over with a large hand, encased in several pairs of hide gloves. Atalanta was fixing the discarded feathers to the ends of her arrows.

The warrior took in the sand on Heracles' lion hide and the grains in Danae's ruffled hair. She twisted the feather in her hand so violently it flicked off the end of the arrow and landed between Danae's feet.

Their eyes met, and Atalanta looked at her with all the disdain of their first encounter, as though the months they'd travelled together had been swept away. Danae didn't know why she cared so much, but it hurt, like a fist to her gut.

Heracles placed a hand on the warrior's shoulder. 'Daeira is one of us. I trust her, and that is enough.' His tone was friendly, but the look in his eyes was final.

Telamon's gaze slid from the hero to Danae. 'Now I know why Dolos went to sulk with the horses,' he said with a smirk.

'Daeira!'

Danae looked across the camp to see Jason, sat on a large piece of driftwood, beckoning to her.

She sighed, 'Back in a moment,' and strode across the beach.

'Sit.' Jason gestured beside him as she approached. 'Why has he returned?'

She was taken aback by the abruptness of his question.

'You must have got something out of him on the dunes?'

Her mouth twitched. She lowered herself onto the log. 'He and Dolos were tracking the Stymphalian birds, which led them to us.'

Jason's scowl deepened.

'He can't rejoin the crew.'

A whisper of panic fluttered through her. 'Why not?'

'The men aren't happy about it.'

She knew exactly which men he meant and shot a barbed glance at Castor and Pollux on the other side of the camp.

Attempting to smooth the worry from her face, she said, 'But think of the strength you would command with two demi-gods in your crew.'

Jason laughed. 'That man is a law unto himself. He's dangerous and volatile. The others won't have it. Not now they know his true nature.'

Jason was a coward who didn't want to be overshadowed. That's what this was about.

'They will do what you tell them to, Captain.' Before he could respond she added, 'Let me speak to my father before we sail tomorrow. It would be wise to arrive at Colchis knowing what the fates have in store for us.'

Jason regarded her for a moment. Then nodded.

She was about to leave when he said, 'You should have told me.'

'I explained –'

'I'm your captain, you swore loyalty to me. Don't make me regret what I offered you.'

'Yes, Captain.' She inclined her head and rose to her feet. As she walked away, a smile spread across her lips. Phineus said most seers were liars or fools. She was about to prove him right.

She would make sure the omens were in Heracles' favour.

They gave Tiphys a sea burial. It was what he would have wanted. Danae spoke the funeral rights as the navigator's body bobbed away across the waves, two obols tucked into his wrappings for the ferryman.

Then Jason instructed the Argonauts to build an altar.

In the early hours before dawn, they combed the beach for driftwood and piled it high on the shore. They'd saved the Stymphalian birds' thighs to roast on the pyre as an offering to Poseidon. It was a strange but welcome discovery that underneath their knife-like feathers, the birds were flesh and bone like any other. For the first time in a long while, everyone had gone to bed with a full stomach.

Danae made sure she looked the part. She brought out her midnight cloak for the occasion and finished the effect by smudging charcoal from the ashes of the fire around her eyes.

'Just like the first time I saw you,' Heracles whispered as she walked past.

A thrill rippled through her.

Castor and Pollux stood at either side of the altar. At her nod, they threw burning torches on the pyre and stepped back to join the others.

Danae fell to her knees and lifted her arms into the air.

'Father Poseidon, hear my prayer. Bless the *Argo* and all who sail in her. Keep us safe on your waters, protect the crew from harm. As your daughter, I ask this of you.'

She sang an old tune of Naxos that told of Poseidon's love for a mortal girl he'd seen dancing barefoot on the island's shore. Orpheus wove a lilting harmony with her melody, but as they serenaded the dawn, sadness sank into her bones. She would have given anything to be singing with her father.

As the song ended, Jason stepped forward and placed the body of a Stymphalian bird in front of her, then handed her a knife. She plunged the blade down and with a mixture of repulsion and fascination, pulled the entrails through her fingers, making a display of examining the folds of blood and gristle.

Silently she said her own prayer. She didn't know if anyone could hear her. But something had given her these powers. Perhaps they were listening, whoever they were.

Please keep my family safe. Help me get back to them one day.

She straightened up, blood dripping from her hands, and turned to face the crew. 'The omens are clear. The gods are satisfied with the penance Heracles has paid for his crimes. If our mission is to succeed, he must rejoin the Argonauts.'

Silence rolled over the beach. The Argonauts glanced at one another. Jason looked furious.

'I'm not sharing a ship with a child murderer,' growled Castor.

There was a collective intake of breath. Castor was either

very brave or incredibly foolish. Heracles could crush him as easily as breathing.

The crew muttered amongst themselves. She'd hoped their faith would be enough to convince them, but clearly these warriors needed to be spoken to in the only language they really understood: power.

The sand trembled. Then the sea nearest the altar began to churn, foam flecking the boiling waves.

'You dare question the omens?' Danae threw the full force of divine anger behind her words.

Castor paled and shook his head.

You are like a god to them, said the voice.

I know, she thought.

She let the sea go calm. 'Captain.'

Jason glanced around at the now quivering Argonauts, then back at her. Angry as he was, he couldn't contradict her without denying the gods. She'd trapped him.

Through gritted teeth, he said, 'We will obey the omens. Heracles and Dolos will rejoin the Argonauts.'

It was a subdued crew that packed up the *Argo* and headed back out onto the Black Sea. Without their navigator, Jason took charge of the steering oar.

'I've consulted Tiphys' maps, and if we keep the coast to our right, we should reach Colchis in a month. From there we need to watch out for a river that flows inland, that should take us close to the city. The end is in sight, Argonauts!'

The crew mustered a cheer.

And beyond the city lay the Caucasus Mountains. Danae's chest fluttered with excitement. Finding Prometheus was the beacon that had guided her through the darkest moments of the voyage. Now it felt tangible, like she could almost grasp hold of it.

And she didn't have to do it alone.

As the crew moved to take their places on the rowing benches, Heracles brushed past her, and their fingers touched.

She felt the prickle of eyes on her and glanced around to see Dolos turning away. Since rejoining the *Argo*, he'd behaved like Heracles was a child in his care, rather than a seasoned hero who'd seen more danger than the rest of Greece put together. Perhaps there was some truth in what Telamon had said on the beach. Maybe Dolos held more than friendship in his heart for Heracles.

In the weeks that followed, the cold became an onslaught. Danae had never known a chill like it. She shivered constantly, despite the full body furs the crew now wore. Gone were the days of sweat glistening on bare backs. The rowers pulled the oars with numb hands, red noses and cracked lips. At least having Heracles back on the benches relieved a great deal of strain from the rest of the Argonauts, his strength nearly doubling their speed. The men were still wary of the hero, but he was an undeniable asset.

Since the Stymphalian birds attack, there hadn't been any interference from the gods. Danae wasn't comforted by this. If anything, it made her more uneasy. It felt like they were playing a game, keeping her at arm's length and testing her powers. Studying her.

But despite the peril of her situation, her mind was elsewhere.

She knew she must tell Heracles about Prometheus and the prophecy before they reached Colchis, but despite her best efforts she hadn't been able to engineer time alone with him.

The Argonauts took their breaks from the benches in shifts. Being so few, only two men at a time were given respite from rowing to quickly eat and wick their thirst, before returning to the oars.

Danae sat huddled on the stern platform, her furs wound so tightly around her she could barely draw a full breath. Her gaze began its usual haunt across the mountainous regions of Heracles' shoulders, when Jason called, 'Castor, Pollux, back to the benches and relieve Heracles.'

Danae's heart clenched like a fist as the hero set down his oar and turned, his face seeking hers. Their eyes met, and his ocean-deep gaze struck through her like one of his father's thunderbolts. Without hesitating to think, she eased herself down onto the mid-deck and slipped into the store cabin. Once inside, her eyes darted around at the cramped interior, unable to settle while her heartbeat thumped in her stomach.

A moment passed, then another. And another.

The vibration in her body slowed, and a deep flush prickled her cheeks. She was being foolish: of course he wasn't going to follow her in. She cast around for something she could claim brought her to the store cabin. She settled on a waterskin, then moved towards the door. Her hand was almost at the latch when it opened.

Heracles squeezed himself into the room. Danae dropped the waterskin as the hero closed the door behind him. He was so tall he had to bow his head, his shoulders resting against the cabin ceiling.

They looked at each other for a breath, then Heracles sank to his knees, still almost as tall as she was, and pulled her into him. Their fingers tangled in each other's furs as they fought through the layers of hide to the skin beneath. The heat of him under her hands set a fire roaring up her arms and down to the furnace of her stomach. She gasped as his mouth moved up her neck, his teeth grazing her flesh. She pushed the lion hide from his head and buried her face in his hair as his hands gripped her back. She drank in the smell of him, that intoxicating musk that was only his. She had been tentative before, a stranger to the intricacies of his body, but emboldened by the pleasure she now knew how to give, she reached for him.

The door opened. Like a whip had been cracked between them, they leapt apart.

Dolos stood in the doorway, a statue of displeasure. 'The wind has died. Jason wants you back on the bench.'

'Jason can fuck off,' growled Heracles.

The volcano that had been brewing inside Danae erupted. 'Get out,' she spat at the healer, and beneath her feet the floorboards cracked.

For a moment, she didn't realize what she'd done, then she saw fear flicker across Dolos' face and followed his gaze downwards.

The healer backed out of the cabin and she heard Jason calling, 'Did we hit something?'

'No,' Dolos replied. 'A barrel fell in the store.'

She could feel the reproach in Heracles' movements as he fastened his lion hide.

'You need to be more careful.'

'You're one to talk.' Her words came out with far more venom than she intended.

Heracles looked like he was going to say something else, then he turned towards the door.

'You're not going?'

'This was foolish,' he said curtly. 'We were lucky it was Dolos.' He paused. 'We shouldn't do this again until we reach Colchis.'

Even now, all she wanted to do was touch him. They'd stolen a fleeting moment together, and she had wasted it on appeasing her desire. The narrow planks between them felt the size of a continent, but there was still time. She couldn't let the opportunity slip away.

'Heracles, there's something I need to tell you.'

He reached out and stroked the back of his fingers along her jaw, tracing his thumb across the contours of her mouth. 'Not here.'

Then he kissed her, one last time.

True to his word, Heracles did not seek out Danae again. She was left to comfort herself with the vision the omphalos shard had shown her. She and Heracles were going to find Prometheus together, it was written by the fates. She would just have to be patient and wait until they landed at Colchis to reveal their shared destiny.

Two weeks later, she was back in the store, taking an inventory of their remaining rations, when Peleus threw open the door. She smiled at him. He was still not well enough to row, but every day the man grew stronger. With Dolos busy at the oars, Danae carefully followed the healer's instructions and kept a watchful eye over Peleus. The morning he'd woken and asked for wine, she knew his battle with the fever was won.

'Daeira, come look at this.'

She followed him out onto the deck and nearly dropped the pack of biscuits she was carrying. She had only seen snow once before, one particularly cold winter on Naxos. She'd thought the stars were falling from the heavens.

She tilted her face to the sky, laughing as the flakes dissolved on her skin. They were so delicate, like the cold spectres of spring blossom.

'Look, there!' Pollux was pointing to something in the distance.

Danae squinted through the snow. On the horizon she could just make out jagged mounds of grey rearing up into the clouds.

'It's Colchis!' shouted Jason.

The Caucasus Mountains, Prometheus. They were almost there.

39. The Farthest Shore

As they travelled inland, Danae gazed at the Caucasus Mountains towering in the distance, her stomach tingling in anticipation. Rising above the spines of the dark-green trees that clustered the bank, the snowy crags dominated the sky. They were the largest mountains she'd ever seen. Forests of dense pine trees carpeted their slopes, giving way to ice-coated rock at their peaks. She could just make out the great stone walls of Colchis city, which harboured Jason's golden fleece, nestled between the forest and the mountains.

She thought of the Titanomachy, how the Titans had supposedly ripped the earth apart until the Olympians ended their destructive rampage. She'd been told that mountains and ravines were the scars left behind.

Her eyes trailed along the Caucasus range to the highest crest, barely visible through the clouds. That's where Prometheus would be. The highest peak of the largest mountain. That was where she and Heracles must go.

Eventually, the river became too narrow for the *Argo*, and they were forced to stop.

'Pull in the oars and tether the ship.' Jason jumped down from the stern and clambered across the benches to the prow deck. 'First three rows, gather anything you can to camouflage the *Argo*. Next three, set up camp. At first light we stake out the city and get a look at what we're up against.'

The crew disembarked, and Danae leapt down, her feet encased in fur boots, crunching on the snowy ground. It creaked underfoot as she walked. There was an oppressive silence to the blanketing whiteness. When the crew's voices lulled and no birds sang, the quiet was deafening. But it was beautiful too. Spiders' webs hung like fine necklaces from the branches of ice-crisped trees, and their leaves looked like they were laced with tiny flecks of glass.

She walked over to where Heracles was stripping branches from a pine tree, her gut a nest of writhing snakes.

'I need to tell you something.'

He straightened up.

'We should go somewhere private,' she whispered.

'Heracles!' Jason shouted from the *Argo*. 'Bring the whole tree.'

The hero sighed. 'Come to me tonight. I'll leave my lion hide outside my tent . . .' His blue eyes twinkled. 'So you don't go into the wrong one.'

Her lips quirked. 'Oh, I won't.' She held his gaze, desire unfurling in the pit of her stomach.

'Heracles!' shouted Jason. 'What are you waiting for?'

Danae stepped back as he grasped the trunk and pulled it from the earth in a shower of needles. Watching him carry the tree over to the *Argo*, she simmered with frustration.

She would just have to wait a few more hours.

Nightfall took an age to come. Despite the cold, Jason had forbidden them to make a fire in case it alerted the city guards to their presence.

Danae sat in her makeshift tent waiting for dark. Legs drawn into her chest, she rocked back and forth, trying to work out what she was going to say to Heracles.

You know how you hate your father? Well, the good news is I'm prophesied to destroy him. Want to join me?

She groaned. Why was this so difficult? She knew what the outcome would be. All she had to do was tell him the truth.

Finally, the shard of light faded from the gap in the

tarpaulin. Leaving her bag inside, she slid her knife into her belt and crept out through the opening. With no fire to cluster round, the Argonauts had all retired to their beds. Across the encampment she saw Heracles' lion hide outside his tent, propped up on a branch he'd stuck into the ground. She smiled. Just as he'd promised.

It had stopped snowing, but trails of white still lined the branches of the trees. Danae's breath clouded in front of her as she walked. This was it, the moment her destiny became theirs.

Nearby, a twig crunched underfoot.

She shrank back into the shadow of a tent and was still. A figure darted into the trees. It was hard to be sure in the dark, but it moved just like Dolos.

She looked back at the entrance of Heracles' tent. She could not let herself be distracted. This was too important.

Follow the healer, said the voice.

She hesitated, caught between her plan and the spark of intuition ignited by the voice. Then she turned away from the camp and followed Dolos into the trees.

Eventually the pines thinned, and Danae glimpsed a clearing ahead. She hung back under the cover of the branches.

Dolos was standing in the centre, his face daubed in moonlight. The healer glanced around like he was waiting for someone. Danae stayed very still, her hand clamped over her mouth so her frozen breath wouldn't give her away.

Then she stopped breathing altogether.

Lurking in the trees on the other side of the clearing was a pair of crimson eyes. The pines oscillated as the shade moved towards Dolos. The healer hadn't seen it yet.

Without waiting to summon her life-threads, she drew her knife and sprinted across the clearing. She knocked the shade bodily to the ground, half surprised it had a solid form.

Dolos was shouting, but she couldn't hear him over the thumping of her pulse as she plunged her knife into the rippling space beneath those terrible red eyes.

Blood splattered her furs as she stabbed over and over again, thrusting until the shade stopped moving. Then Dolos yanked her away. She staggered back, staring at the shade's body in amazement. She could see it. In death its skin was no longer invisible, but a dull grey, cracked and rough like a lizard's. It looked chillingly human, from the shape of its head and face to the composition of its limbs.

'What have you done?' whispered Dolos.

She turned to him, breathing heavily. 'I just saved your life.'

Dolos fell to his knees, scrabbling around the icy ground. She watched him with mounting confusion. Then he pulled a bag towards him from the shadow of the trees. Fumbling with its clasp, he rushed to open it, pulling out bottle after bottle of the blue health tonic she'd seen him use to revive Heracles on Lemnos.

'Thank the gods,' he muttered. 'They're not broken.'

Lastly, he drew out a small amulet. She recognized the design. It took her a moment to remember where from. It was identical to the one she'd seen in Polyxo's hut save for the crest, which on this was a thunderbolt.

A terrible realization unfurled in Danae's mind.

'Dolos, were you waiting for that thing?'

The healer stared at the amulet, his face stricken. She wasn't sure he'd even heard her.

'Why was that shade carrying a bag of Heracles' medicine?'

Dolos remained silent as he carefully placed the vials and amulet back into the bag. Then he rose to his feet, the pack clasped to his chest.

'There are things at play here you would never understand.'

'Try me.'

'I can't,' he hissed.

'If you won't tell me, you can explain it to Heracles.'

Dolos' face tightened. 'He can't know.'

She took a step towards him. 'Why, Dolos?'

The healer looked like a cornered rodent, eyes darting from her to the dead shade. Then his body sagged.

'Heracles' power isn't his own.'

Danae's brow creased in confusion.

Dolos' hand trembled as he held up the bag. 'This elixir is what makes him strong. He doesn't know . . . he thinks it's just a tonic to help heal his wounds. Can you imagine what the truth would do to him?'

She couldn't grasp what he was saying. 'He's a demi-god . . . that's why he's strong.'

'There are no demi-gods.' Dolos' eyes shone bright with fear. 'The mortal children of gods have no powers.'

A cold ripple ran down her spine.

'Of course we do.'

'There's no point lying. I know the truth.'

Her heart beat at a nauseating pace. 'What about the heroes of old? Perseus, Bellerophon –'

'All lies,' Dolos whispered. 'Gods-woven illusions to extend the reach of the Twelve's divinity.' Anger, deep and long repressed, twisted the healer's face. 'But that was not enough for Zeus. He is fixated on passing on his divine powers to a mortal son. He believed Heracles might finally be the one, but it was not to be. Still, Zeus wanted him to be the greatest hero that ever lived. He did terrible things to Heracles, things no one, especially not a child, should ever have to endure. He's been taking the elixir for so long he'd die within a year without it.'

'But . . . all the deeds he's done . . . he *is* a hero,' Danae said weakly.

Sadness shone in Dolos' eyes. 'Zeus arranged everything. He planted creatures for Heracles to defeat – the hydra, the Nemean lion, the Erymanthian boar. All so his son's heroic deeds would be a part of his legacy.' He barked a mirthless laugh. 'Do you really think a merchant ship just happened to be passing at the exact moment he and I needed rescuing from the Doliones' shore? I sent a message to Olympus. I got us out of there and back on course as I have always done.'

The legend of Heracles, just another deception by the gods.

'All this time, you've been working for his father.'

Dolos twitched, rage pulsing through his jaw. 'I hid the truth from him so he could have some sort of enjoyment from the life Zeus has forced him to lead, and because of me when he finally leaves the mortal world, he will be raised up to the heavens. He will be made into a star and shine forever, and all of this, all the pain, will have been worth it.'

Silence, glaring as the snow, settled between them.

Danae's mind was a cacophony of confusion, but one thought rang clear above the rest. The healer had known all this time that she was no demi-god.

'Dolos, I can explain . . .' She took a step towards him.

'You lied to him too. You lied to all of us.'

Fear curled around her like smoke. But she did not need to be afraid. She knew that, whatever happened, Heracles would come with her. The omphalos shard did not lie. It was fate.

'You're right. We should both tell him the truth. Together.'

Dolos expelled a sharp breath. 'You don't know Heracles like I do. He'd kill us both.'

Danae took another step towards him. 'I won't let that happen.'

His eyes grew hard. 'Whatever you are,' he whispered. 'You are no match for Zeus. No one is.'

She was so focused on the healer's face, she didn't notice the knife Dolos slid from his belt. Didn't have time to stop him as he plunged the blade into her gut.

Blood seeped into the snow, dark as ink against the dazzling whiteness.

Gasping, Danae staggered back and slumped against a tree, her lungs constricted in agony.

'I'm sorry,' Dolos whispered, his knife glistening. 'You should never have followed me here.'

Pain blurred her vision. With each breath her stomach felt like it was being ripped apart.

Dolos stepped back, his knife still raised between them. 'I will tell Heracles the truth. That you deceived him, that your powers are far from divine, that you would have been his destruction had I not stopped you.'

Moaning in agony, she tried to press down on her wound and hold her life-threads inside her, but they were slipping away like the blood spilling through her fingers. She was diminishing, her energy weaving back into the world, into the earth, the grass, the trees.

The *trees*.

She'd seen it in every vision, the tapestry of life that circulated through all living things. Not just mortals and animals, everything that lived.

Fighting each excruciating heave of her chest, she placed a bloody hand on the trunk behind her and felt for the tree's life-threads. They did not come willingly as the panther's and the harpy's had done. They resisted as she reached out her will to grasp them. The tree was healthy, it was not the time for these strands to pass back into the tapestry of life. But she had to consume them, or she would die.

Danae ground her teeth against the pain as she strained, pouring every ounce of her strength, mental and physical, into sucking the tree's life-threads into her palm. Finally, they answered her call, rising through the bark to pierce her skin. Once the connection was made, they flowed freely, like water bursting through a dam, and with as deep a breath as she could muster, she drew them into her.

'What are you doing?' Dolos' face tightened with fear.

In her periphery she could see pine needles dropping as the branches withered. It was different, absorbing the life of a tree. A slow and steady glow of warmth rather than a heady rush. But just as before, her wounds knitted together and the pain in her gut faded away.

She leapt to her feet, a storm of rage erupting inside her as she imagined the twisted words spewing from Dolos' mouth, the horror and hatred spreading across Heracles' face.

Dolos stared, his jaw slack with terror, then he turned to run.

But he was not fast enough.

He must be silenced, the voice commanded.

She threw out her arms, whipping up a gust of wind so strong the healer was thrown across the clearing into the trees beyond. There was a sickening crack. She faltered, and the wind died.

'Dolos?'

There was no sound, save for the rustling of pine needles.

She ran towards him. The healer lay crumpled, face down at the base of a tree. Trembling, she rolled him over.

His skull was split down to his nose, blood trickling between his sightless eyes. She placed her hand on his chest and felt for his life-threads. They were already gone.

Her ears rang. What had she done?

She staggered back and almost tripped over the dead body

of the shade. As she stared down at its mottled grey skin, realization sank into her bones.

Dolos had been working for Zeus, and the shade presumably had brought him Heracles' medicine on the god's command.

The shades were servants of the Twelve.

And that meant the Olympians were responsible for the Missing. Rage speared her heart as she thought of Arius, of her family ripped apart by the gods.

Run, said the voice. *Run while you still can.*

She picked up the healer's bloody knife and the bag of strength elixir and sprinted back towards the camp.

By the time she reached the tents she knew what she must do.

She ducked into her tent, stowing Dolos' knife with her own and securing her bag across her chest. Then she crept through the camp and boarded the *Argo*, picking her way between the camouflaging tree branches to the store cabin. She took only what she needed: a pack of biscuits, a couple of slices of salted meat, a heel of bread and a waterskin.

Lastly, she walked towards Heracles' tent.

The closer she came, the more her limbs shook. She stood outside his tent flap, the blood of his closest friend staining her hands. She wanted to go inside and explain. Dolos had tried to kill her, he was in league with Zeus, it hadn't been her fault. But then she would have to tell him everything else. Dolos was right. It would break him. Heracles said it himself: all he had was his legendary reputation. It would kill him to know he was just an ordinary man.

Silently, she laid the bag of strength elixir by the tent flap. She didn't want him to be without it, now she knew how much he needed it.

She'd been full of hope when she believed destiny had

twined Heracles' path with hers. But now she saw it was just a fantasy. An illusion, like Heracles himself.

She looked at the impenetrable lion hide propped up on the branch outside his tent, like a real beast standing guard at his door. Her vision had allowed her to believe that she didn't have to do it alone. But now she saw with searing clarity what the omphalos shard had really shown her. There had only been one person climbing the mountain.

It is you, said the voice. *It has always been you. You are the last daughter. You alone are the reckoning.*

40. A Mountain at the End of the World

Danae shielded her eyes against the rioting snow and peered up at the peak of the mountain. The path had ended long ago, but she'd pressed on, clambering over boulders of frozen rock until she could go no further. Above her was a sheer sheet of ice. Torrents of flakes whipped by so fast, the mountain appeared to be moving. The longer she stared at it, the smaller she became.

There was no other way up.

She swallowed. She'd scaled cliffs this steep back home. But on Naxos they were sun-drenched, and she'd been unencumbered by thick furs wound around her limbs. In this place of ice and snow, even when the sun was at its brightest it had no warmth.

She made sure Heracles' lion hide was tied securely around her chest, tightened the strap of her bag and pulled the knives from her belt. She drove the first into the ice and gave it a wiggle. It held. She plunged in the second, then began to climb.

The higher she went, the harder it became to keep her balance in the buffeting gale. Each time the blades pierced the ice she held her breath, waiting for it to crumble. Soon she became so used to the ache in her limbs she no longer registered the pain.

After a while, time lost all meaning. She tried to track her progress by counting each heave of her body towards the peak. But when she got to somewhere in the hundreds, her thoughts wandered. She saw home in her mind's eye, imagined running up the dirt track from the beach, the smell of her mother's honey cakes wafting through the yard.

Then her foot slipped.

She flailed, panic exploding through her as she fell. The world fragmented in a blur of white, protruding rocks bashing her as she tumbled down the ice.

Then her fingers caught a jutting ledge. She clung on, sucking in stabbing lungfuls of frozen air, fighting to claw her mind back together. She still had her bag and one of the knives, the other was lost to the storm.

Squinting through watery eyes, she looked up. A slash of black cracked the snow coverage above the ledge. Beyond it, the mountain seemed to stretch endlessly into the raging sky.

Defeat wound its fingers around her chest. Hours of climbing wasted.

She ground the hopelessness between her teeth. She couldn't give up now. Not when she'd come this far. With a grunt of pain, she swung her left arm up. Her one remaining blade clattered onto the rock as her fingers scraped over the lip. She could feel herself slipping, her legs sliding uselessly down the ice as she pushed against it. Willing the last of her strength into her arms, she heaved, sinews screaming with the effort, and slumped onto the ledge.

It was the entrance to a cave.

She dragged her body forwards, pulling her legs up onto the rock. Pain twitched through her limbs, snatching her breath. There was no room to stand, and even if there had been it was beyond her now. As she lay there, calm settled over her. She knew she had to get up, had to keep climbing, but she couldn't move.

She stared into the dark belly of the cave, her breath dancing like little ghosts in the gloom.

*

Tawny feathers drifted through the air, still restless after her struggle with the griffin the night before. The blood around the creature's carcass had dried overnight, staining the cave floor the colour of rust. Danae looked at the gruesome remains dispassionately. It was just a dead thing. It couldn't hurt her now.

After killing it, she'd pillaged the griffin's hoard and built a fire with every scrap of wood she could find. She'd melted the frozen waterskin, then stripped the beast's feathers, sliced chunks from its breast and roasted them over the flames. The meat was rich and surprisingly tender. It was the first hot meal she'd eaten since the Stymphalian birds.

Even after several hours of sleep, her body still tingled with the griffin's life-threads. Manto's pipe was in her lap. She must have fallen asleep smoking it. She was grateful she'd had something to take the edge off spending the night in an icy cave with only a dead griffin for company. She picked it up and traced the outline of the tree painted on the barrel.

'I'm almost there,' she whispered. She wished her friend could see how far she'd come.

She packed the pipe away in her bag, then carved up what meat she could carry and wrapped the portions in the remnants of her dress. Once harvested, she heaved the remains of the griffin to the mouth of the cave and pushed its body over the ledge. It gave her a glimmer of satisfaction to watch it bash unceremoniously against the ice. Fitting, for a creature half formed from the sacred bird of Zeus.

She breathed in a lungful of freezing air. There was a calmness to the mountain now. The storm had dissipated, and rods of sunlight pierced the clouds that yesterday seemed impenetrable.

After one last sweep of the cave, she secured the lion hide

around her neck and slung her bag across her chest. Knife in her fist, she edged out onto the lip of rock and continued to climb. It was hard going with only one blade. She was at the mercy of finding natural rivets and the shards of protruding rock that yesterday had bruised her as she fell. But the lashing snow was gone and, thanks to the griffin's life-threads, so was her weariness.

As she hauled herself up the ice, she wondered if the legend was true, that every day an eagle ripped open Prometheus' abdomen and feasted on his liver, then every night the organ grew back to be devoured anew.

She would find out soon enough.

She paused for a moment to catch her breath, pressing her body against the ice as she twisted to look at her surroundings.

She was at the top of the world. It was eerily quiet without the screaming wind.

The city of Colchis looked like a child's toy beneath her, the pine forests like swathes of emerald moss. When the sun broke free of the clouds it illuminated the mountain in gleaming light, so bright it was almost blinding, like she was climbing the surface of a diamond.

The Argonauts would have reached the city by now. She hoped Jason found the fleece he so desperately craved, and they all made it back to the ship unharmed.

Dolos' face loomed into her thoughts, his lifeless eyes staring into nothing as blood trickled down his forehead. She wobbled and pressed herself against the ice to stop herself falling. She'd killed him. She'd murdered the only man who knew the truth about Heracles. What would happen to the hero without him?

She bit down on her lip and tasted metal. It jolted her back to the mountain. She could no longer feel her hands and feet, but she had to keep going. It would all be worth it once she reached Prometheus. It had to be.

She set her eyes on the next rivet and continued to climb.

Near the crest, she reached a narrow ridge that slanted upwards. She hauled herself onto it, clinging to the knife as she pulled herself up to standing and shuffled her feet sideways. It was perilously narrow. She tugged the knife free and flattened herself against the icy rock, edging slowly along its length.

She couldn't tell if it was the hours of climbing, or being so high up, but she felt increasingly dizzy. Wisps of cloud trailed past, crisping her hair and swallowing her in hazes of grey, only to be chased away again by the blinding sun. She was reminded of the mist Athena had conjured on the Doliones' shore. She must stay vigilant. It had been three days since she'd abandoned the Argonauts. Surely it would not be long before the gods worked out where she was going.

As she neared the top of the peak, the sun was eclipsed behind the mountain. The summit was close now.

A screech pierced the air.

She froze, heart hammering as she scoured the sky. A pair of golden wings soared above her. An eagle. She flattened herself to the mountain, expecting the bird to dive at her, but it sailed on overhead. It must be going to Prometheus.

Shuffling as fast as the ice would allow, she continued up the ridge.

The dark side of the pinnacle came into view. A sheer section of rock stretched down, as though a giant blade had sliced a chunk out of the mountain. The vertical drop was swathed in shadow and ended in a bed of snow, heaped on the crag below. She slowed as she caught sight of a figure chained to the rock.

Whatever she'd expected, it wasn't this.

Prometheus hung from the rock by rusted chains cuffed to his wrists. The Titan was the height of a mortal and skeletally thin. He looked more rotten than some of the corpses on Lemnos. A circle of iron that would have once fitted his neck balanced loosely on his collar bones, and his spindly arms looked like they'd long ago been dislocated from holding the weight of his body. He was wrapped in furs like she was, but his extremities were bare and blackened with frostbite. He was missing several fingers, and the tip of his nose and his ears were gone.

The eagle swooped down and landed on the iron ring around Prometheus' neck. The Titan didn't flinch as the bird clawed its way up his face and prised his scarred lips apart with its talons.

Danae stared in horror as the bird proceeded to regurgitate into Prometheus' mouth. It wasn't torturing him. It was feeding him.

Its task complete, the eagle launched itself into the air, leaving Prometheus with fresh scratches on his face and neck. His head lolled to one side, eyes closed.

She waited until the bird was out of sight, then edged along the last stretch of ridge and climbed up onto the snowy crag beneath the Titan.

'Prometheus?'

He didn't move.

She raised her voice against the whistling wind. 'I'm the one from your prophecy.'

It was somehow even colder than it had been on the ridge. They were completely exposed to the elements.

Prometheus' left eye cracked open.

Her heart clattered against her ribs. 'I am the last daughter.'

Both eyes opened. There was a heavy pause as they stared at each other. She waited. Maybe he hadn't heard her.

'I'm the last daughter!'

Prometheus blinked.

'When the prophet falls, and gold that grows bears no fruit, the last daughter will come. She will end the reign of thunder and become the light that frees mankind.'

He continued to stare at her.

'I destroyed the oracle at Delphi.' Her throat ached as she strained against the wind. 'And I've had visions of a golden apple tree. How am I meant to end the reign of thunder and become the light that frees mankind?'

The Titan tilted his head, his bones crunching. Waiting for him to speak was agonizing.

'I've come such a long way to find you. I've worked some things out on my own, but there's so much I don't understand . . . Even with my powers, how can I ever hope to defeat the King of the Gods?'

'There are no gods.' Brittle with disuse, his voice scraped like nails over stone.

She must have misheard. He couldn't have said what she thought he had.

She shuffled closer. 'Sorry, what did you say?'

'There are no gods.'

She gaped. 'I don't . . .'

Prometheus' gaze shifted to focus on something behind her. Danae turned around.

Flying towards them through the clouds was a chariot pulled by two winged horses, one russet, one white as the mountain snow. Its rider was clad in golden armour overlaid with a filigree of peacock feathers that matched the trim on her billowing purple cloak.

As the figure drew closer, Danae could make out the face beneath the indigo-plumed helm. To call it beautiful would have been reductive. None of the likenesses carved on statues or painted on murals did her justice. Even Alea's radiant features would have looked clumsy next to these. Her skin was flawless ebony, her eyes dazzling umber. Her face was that of a lioness and the most delicate flower all at once. A face so perfectly formed it didn't look real. It was the most devastating face Danae had ever seen.

Hera, Queen of the Gods, had come.

41. The Last Titan

Hera tugged on the reins of her chariot. Her flying horses beat their magnificent wings as they trod the air, sending gusts of freezing wind lashing across Danae's face. Like Athena's, Hera's armour covered every inch of her body from neck to toe.

The Queen of Heaven raised a golden, gauntleted hand.

The shock wore off just in time for Danae to dive out of the way. A jet of wind, so powerful it drilled a hole through the snow into the rock beneath, hit the place where she'd just been standing.

Hera aimed again. Danae tried to move, but her bag caught on a shard of rock. Her numb fingers were clumsy in her gloves, and she only just freed herself in time to narrowly avoid the next blast. Ice hailed down as she scrambled to the far corner of the ridge.

The cold stabbed her lungs with each panting breath. Frantically, she felt for her life-threads and sent them hurtling into the snow. Like she'd done with the water of the Black Sea, she grasped the glowing strands and flung them upwards. Whipped by her life-threads, a wave of white reared up and before Hera could move, her chariot was engulfed. Danae dropped her arms and for a joyful moment she thought she'd done it.

Then the chariot broke free, the horses tossing their heads to clear their eyes of snow.

Hera stared down at Danae, her luminous eyes round with disbelief.

'It is true.' The goddess's voice was sharp and rich like poisoned wine.

Hera let go of the reins and with both hands sent out her life-threads to rip chunks of ice from the rock. She held the frozen slabs suspended in the air, then whipped them forwards. Mid-air, they split into knife-sharp splinters, long as branches, and smashed into the mountain.

Danae threw herself out of the way, tumbling from the crag to land with a sickening crack against the jutting rock below. Pain spiked through her back, but she didn't have time to dwell on it, or the fact that Hera's power seemed to be a stronger version of her own. She gathered more life-threads and cast them into the snow.

Hera was quicker.

The goddess snapped her metallic fingers, and flames burst from her palm. Danae gaped. Hera manipulated the fire into a burning orb, until it was the size of her head, then hurled it at Danae. She raised a sheet of snow in front of her just in time to absorb the worst of the fire, but it still charred her furs and burnt the hairs from her face.

Hera was unbelievably strong. The goddess didn't look like she was weakening at all, whereas Danae could feel herself depleting each time she cast her life-threads out of her body. She didn't have the energy to keep defending herself.

Clenching her jaw, she sent two torrents of threads into the air as Hera sparked another fireball into being. Danae whirled the strands over her head, faster and faster, until a tiny maelstrom formed beneath Hera's chariot. The goddess was about to discharge her fire when she stumbled, then screamed as the miniature typhoon swallowed her.

Danae could feel her energy waning; she was dangerously close to losing too many life-threads. With one last push, she yanked her threads downwards and let go.

The chariot tumbled from the sky, falling out of sight. She heard it collide with the mountain below. A few moments later the white winged horse reappeared, braying and flapping away from the swirling cloud of snow.

Danae slumped against the rock, her limbs heavy as iron.

Through the falling flakes, she spotted a glint of golden armour. Hera was on the back of the russet horse, flying away into the clouds.

Danae groaned and pulled herself back onto the ridge, wincing at the spasms shooting across her back. The rock face looked as though it had been hacked by an axe.

And Prometheus was gone.

She stared around frantically, then spotted the Titan crumpled in the snow where the sheer rock met the crag below. Hera's attack must have broken his chains.

She scrambled forward. Even before she reached him, she could feel the life-threads leaving his body. When she drew closer, she saw shards of razor-sharp ice protruding from his chest. His furs were matted with blood.

'You're dying?' He couldn't be. He was a Titan. He was immortal.

Prometheus' skull-like face was placid. 'At last.'

Up close, his eyes were so pale they almost looked white.

'No.' Danae placed her hands on his chest. 'If I can heal myself, so can you.'

'What is your name, daughter?'

'Danae.'

Prometheus curled what was left of his bony fingers around her hand. 'You must cast aside your fear, Danae, or you will not be able to do what needs to be done.'

'I'm not afraid,' she lied.

Prometheus stretched back his scarred lips into what once might have been a smile.

'What did you mean about the gods?'

Prometheus drew a rattling breath. 'The world you know is an illusion. Those you call gods have spent centuries weaving lies.' He spluttered as wheezing coughs racked his body.

She waited. Every moment that slipped by fed her desperation to understand.

'The religion you slave under is false. There have only ever been mortals and those mortals who were chosen to become Titans.'

Her head felt like it was going to explode. 'But . . . the gods are real. They created mortals. *You* made the first man's body out of clay.'

'Lies,' Prometheus rasped. 'Man is not made from clay. Demeter does not command the seasons, just as Apollo does not drive the sun across the sky. Hades rules the Underworld, but there is no afterlife there.'

She felt as though he'd pushed her off the mountain and she was falling endlessly into darkness. She jerked her hands away from his. 'What do you mean?'

'You are more powerful than you know . . . Just like me and those who call themselves gods . . . you are a Titan.'

She stared at him, unable to ground herself as Prometheus' revelations smashed through the structure of her reality.

'That's impossible.'

'Seek out Metis on the island of Delos . . . She will help you.'

Prometheus' breath was so shallow she could barely see it in front of his mangled lips. The skin on her palms began to itch, and a longing ache spread up her arms. It was there, it was so close, the ecstasy, she could have it again.

Do it, said the voice. *Take his life-threads. He's dying anyway.*

She shoved her hands into the snow. The shock of the cold brought her back to her senses.

'Where is my sister?'

Prometheus' eyelids began to flutter.

'No!' She launched forward and grabbed his furs. 'My sister is dead. If she's not in the Underworld, where is her soul?'

'I . . . don't . . .'

'Prometheus!' She shook him so hard his jaws clattered together. But when she let go, she could no longer feel his life-threads. He was gone.

She dropped the lifeless body of the Titan and screamed into the sky.

Danae sat on the highest peak of the tallest mountain at the end of the world, staring at the rock where Prometheus had been chained. She didn't know how long she'd been there. She didn't care.

You must leave, said the voice. *They will return.*

She did not move.

Seek out Metis, like Prometheus said.

She laughed. Her throat burnt but she couldn't stop. The mountain echoed the sound back as though it were mocking her. Everything she'd done, everything she'd sacrificed, had been for nothing. The gods would never stop hunting her. She could never go home.

Every time she tried to entertain the possibility that Prometheus' claims could be true, she felt like she was falling again. Her sister had to be in the Underworld. All the dead went there. If there was no afterlife, then what happened to every mortal soul after death?

Anger shook her body. She'd battled to the ends of the earth. She'd lied, manipulated, and abandoned her friends, all to be told things that could not possibly be true.

But you have powers just like the gods.

She raked her hands over her face. She wished she could block out the voice, but it invaded every crevice in her mind.

Yes, the Twelve had lied and exaggerated the scope of their powers to keep mortals in line, but how could she and they be the same? They had existed since the dawn of time. They were immortal and . . .

Her gaze slid to Prometheus' body.

Immortal but not invulnerable.

So the gods could be killed, just like mortals.

Something snorted behind her. She turned and saw the winged horse that had escaped the fallen chariot sniffing her bag. It gave the strap an exploratory nibble, then picked it up in its mouth and tossed it towards her. It hit her in the legs.

She stared at it for a moment, then leant forward and undid the fastening. She slipped her hand inside, drew out the crumbled remains of the last biscuit and held them out on her palm. The horse lowered its muzzle and munched. The sensation of its teeth nipping through her glove was strangely comforting.

She raised her other hand and stroked its neck.

'What do I do now?'

The horse whinnied and flexed its wings.

With great effort, she pushed herself to her feet, slung her bag across her chest and rested her head against the creature's neck. It was good to touch something warm, something alive.

She didn't know what was real any more and she'd lost too many life-threads to ask questions of the omphalos shard. The only thing she could count on was what she could see in front of her.

She raised a hand and grasped hold of the horse's mane. It didn't back away as she'd expected but lowered its front legs so she could climb on. She was grateful; she didn't know if she'd have the strength to heave herself onto its back.

Burrowing her gloved fingers into its milky hair, she supposed she should give it a name.

'I don't know where we're going, Hylas. But I'm going to find out.'

Seek out Metis, fulfil your destiny.

She knew she should listen to the voice, that her fate was tied to the destruction of the gods. But after Prometheus' claim, the idea that Alea's soul was not in the Underworld threatened to tear her apart.

She had to know.

There was only one way to find out for sure if Alea's ghost was in the Asphodel Meadows. She would have to go to the Underworld. She had no idea if it was even possible for the living to visit the realm of the dead. But she had to try.

Then, once she found Alea and knew her sister's soul was at peace, she would go to Delos.

She took a deep breath of frozen air, then gave Hylas a kick and clung on as the horse beat its snowy wings, carrying her up through beams of sunlight, beyond the clouds.

Destiny could wait. She was going to find her sister.

Epilogue
Olympus

The winged horse landed on the balcony, its hooves scraping across the polished marble as it skidded to a halt. The rider slid from its back and clattered to the ground.

A cloud of nymphs, the Twelve's mortal servants, ran forwards, twittering with concern. Their gossamer dresses billowed as they reached out and hauled Hera to her feet.

'You're hurt!'

'My Queen, who has done this?'

'Come inside, we will tend to you.'

A gauntleted hand shot out and grabbed one of the nymphs by the neck. The girl's eyes bulged as her twitching feet left the floor. Hera drew a deep breath, then sighed as the girl's life-threads rushed into her body. She cracked her neck and dropped the dead nymph, the pain in her bruised limbs melting away as she stalked inside.

She unfastened her snow-soaked cloak and let it slide to the patterned topaz floor. A nymph darted forward and picked it up, before scuttling out of reach.

Hera removed her helm and appraised her reflection in an ornate mirror that spanned the entire wall. The remnants of a cut were still fading above one perfectly sculpted eyebrow. She smoothed her black curls. One of the golden strands that wove through her hair stuck up at an unpleasing angle. Despite her efforts, she couldn't bend it to her will.

She pressed her full lips together. Normally, she would

never leave her chambers in such a state, but the events of this day were unprecedented.

'Where is my husband?'

The nymphs exchanged furtive glances behind her back. Pathetic creatures.

'The King of Heaven is in the throne room . . .'

She could sense a 'but'. He was with that boy again.

'Say it.'

Two girls pushed a third forward. The nymph quaked.

'He said he's not to be disturbed.'

She flinched as Hera shoved the helm into her trembling hands. Then the Queen of Heaven strode out through the open doors.

Hera paced down the corridor, the clink of her armour echoing off the marble columns. The wall mosaics changed as she passed, her presence triggering them to swirl into a different pattern. You could tell which deity had last walked by depending on the scene depicted by the tiny pieces of precious stone. They always clustered to show a triumphant frieze from the present god's life. Her son, Hephaestus, had designed it to honour their family, he'd said. She thought it was so he could keep track of them.

The current mosaic showed Hera lifting an infant Ares into the air, the sun shining behind them like his birth had brought forth the dawn. Hera didn't bother to look at it. After hundreds of years of walking down this hall, she knew the placement of every gem.

In the flickering light from the chandeliers, the mother-of-pearl clouds inlaid on the megaron doors looked like they were threatening to storm. Gold thunderbolts spiked down from their swollen bellies. She breathed a short sigh. She'd had enough of the elements for one day.

Two guards stood on either side. Their handsome faces

tightened with unease as she approached. Hera's eyes flicked over them in disdain. They were always pretty. Calling them guards was an exaggeration. The only thing they guarded was her husband's infidelity.

Not today.

She raised her chin. She could see them weighing up their dilemma. Enrage her now or enrage Zeus later? Either way their futures didn't look bright. She flexed the fingers of her right gauntleted hand.

The guard on the left cracked first and heaved one door open with a decoratively muscled arm. Hera strode past without looking at him. She paced across the cavernous circular hall, over the twelve diamonds set into the floor that fanned around a golden sun, each encasing a likeness of the gods' favoured animals.

The King of the Gods was sat on his throne. It was the central and largest of the twelve. Vast marble statues of each god sat impassively around the circle, the real deities' seats carved into their giant feet.

Zeus wore an ivory robe draped over his muscular limbs. His skin was as pale as his marble sculpture, his raven hair slicked back to the nape of his neck, and his cerulean eyes, colder than a winter sky, were fixed on Hera.

Perched on the armrest of her husband's throne was Ganymede. The boy's beautiful face fell slack with fear as she strode towards them. He stumbled to his feet and backed away from Zeus.

'Get out.'

The youth didn't move.

Zeus' eyes swept over his wife's armour, then he nodded to Ganymede. The young man half walked, half ran out of the room, his lithe body twisting away from Hera as he passed her.

She knelt before her husband.

'My lord, I went after the girl.'

Zeus' face betrayed nothing.

'Ares came to me after she escaped his attempt . . .'

The King of the Gods took her apart with his gaze. 'She is still alive.'

Her hands began to tremble. She tried to calm them, but her temper got the better of her. 'The girl from *his* prophecy appears, and you didn't tell me. How could you send the children after her not knowing what she truly is? She could have destroyed them!'

Zeus rose from his throne and walked slowly down the marble steps. Hera backed away.

'Where is she now?'

'The Caucasus Mountains.'

Zeus' brow darkened. Hera could see the life-threads pulsing in his eyes.

'You let her speak to Prometheus.'

'I . . .'

Zeus snapped his fingers. The click of the golden gauntlet he always wore on his right hand echoed around the chamber. A bolt of lightning sizzled between his fingers.

He advanced on her. 'I gave you the world. I raised our family to the heavens, I banished death from our halls, and what do I receive in return? A cold disappointment of a wife and spoiled children, consumed by petty games. You have all grown soft and careless. No more.'

He was standing so close the heat of his thunderbolt burned her cheeks. She knew better than to run.

'You were right about one thing, my Queen.'

The thunderbolt expanded in Zeus' hand until it was almost blinding. Hera could smell her hair burning. She wondered if this time he was going to kill her.

Zeus rammed the bolt down into the mosaic of the sun. The floor exploded around them, shards of glazed stone smashing into the marble legs of the gods. Through the lights bursting in front of Hera's eyes, she saw deep cracks splinter through the statues of her family.

Standing in the centre of his destruction, Zeus' eyes bore into her like two burning stars.

'I will never underestimate her again.'

Acknowledgements

This book was born of love, grief, and a pandemic. I began writing *Daughter of Chaos* in the lockdown of 2020 after the death of my mother, because it was the story I needed to read. At the time, I had no idea it would be published. I have many, many people to thank for making that happen.

Firstly, my agent, Sebastian Godwin – thank you for being the best possible champion of my work, for all the coffees and lunches spent listening to the latest book idea, and the compassion with which you have supported me through the roller coaster that is debut year. Thanks also to the inimitable David Godwin and the rest of the brilliant team at DGA; Heather Godwin, Philippa Sitters, Aparna Kumar, and Rachel Taylor. You are the best agents in the biz!

To my editor at Penguin Michael Joseph, Rebecca Hilsdon; thank you for passion, vision, and dedication to making this story shine. You made my dreams come true. And thank you to the rest of the wonderful team at PMJ; Clare Bowron, Emily Van Blanken, Jorgie Bain, Riana Dixon, David Watson, Hayley Shepherd, Serena Nazareth, Sriya Varadharajan, Kallie Townsend, Jessie Beswick, Courtney Barclay, Stephanie Biddle, Stella Newing, Colin Brush, Lee Motley, Becci Livingstone, Christina Ellicott, Emily Harvey, Kelly Mason, Richard Rowlands, and Akua Akowuah. Thanks also to Sarah Scarlett, Lucy Beresford-Knox, Lucie Deacon-Thomas, Beth Wood, Sophie Brownlow and the rest of the Penguin Random House rights team for all your efforts in bringing this book to readers in other languages and across the globe.

To my US editor, Dina Davis; from our first meeting I was blown away by how much you loved Danae's story. Thank you for everything you've done in helping shape this book and to the rest of the brilliant Mira, HarperCollins team; Margaret Marbury, Nicole Brebner, Evan Yeong, Tamara Shifman, Gina Macdonald, Tracy Wilson, Ana Luxton, Ashley MacDonald, Puja Lad, Randy Chan, Pamela Osti, Maahi Patel, Lindsey Reeder, Brianna Wodabek, Riffat Ali, Ciara Loader, Erin Craig, Denise Thomson, Reka Rubin, Christine Tsai, Nora Rawn, Fiona Smallman, Heather Connor, Loriana Sacilotto, Amy Jones, Katie-Lynn Golakovich, Stephanie Choo, Jennifer O'Keefe, Sara Watson, Carly Katz, and to everyone in sales and anyone I've missed working behind the scenes.

Thank you to the incredibly talented Tom Roberts for illustrating not one, but two gorgeous covers, and to the amazing designers; Lauren Wakefield for the UK and Elita Sidiropoulou for the US.

To my authenticity reader, Hamza Jahanzeb, and my early readers, Poppy Rowley and Sophie Quaile; your honest feedback has been invaluable.

To my fellow City Lit writers and my tutors, Rowan Hisayo Buchanan and Jonathan Barnes; thank you for your critique on those early scenes. Special thanks to Jonathan for being the first person outside of my family and close friends to praise my work and encourage me to finish the book – you gave me hope.

Thank you to all the writers who've scooped me up with kindness and friendship on this mad debut journey, especially: Saara El Arifi, Frances White, A.Y. Chao, Venetia Constantine, Kat Dunn, Marvellous Michael Anson, and Kate Dylan.

To the Southwark Playhouse and the wonderful humans

who work there; thank you for supporting me through the rough times and cheering me on while I pursued publication. An extra thanks to Emma Bentley for the home-made penguin cake.

To my wonderful cousin, Beatie Edney; thank you for all your love and support, for taking me to Naxos, and always encouraging me to write.

Thank you to the friends who've been there though it all; Constance Bamford, Hannah Griffith, Lucy Haworth, Lulu Branth, Natalie Otusanya, Tessa Rowse and Katharine Horgan. And to Vanessa Declercq, who's guidance and wisdom changed my life.

To the family who are no longer here – you all live in my heart. Special thanks to; Grandad Billy, who loved the sea and with a gleam in his eye always told me to read 'just a chapter' before bed, knowing it would never be just one. My glorious dad, we had so little time, but your talent lives on and never fails to inspire me. My mum, my hero, the Lorelai to my Rory, who raised me on stories of magic, adventure and wonder, and taught me that anything is possible. I know you'd be so proud. My love for you is in these pages. I wish you were here to read them.

To Brian, the silliest, loveliest dog; I know you can't read but I'm thanking you anyway for the unconditional love, muddy walks, and big, golden cuddles. You are the BEST BOY.

To Sam, who reads every word – this book would never have been finished without you. In Plato's *Symposium,* Aristophanes speaks of the first humans being conjoined, only to be split apart by Zeus, their souls divided, for fear of their strength threatening the gods. I did not believe in soulmates until I met you. Thank you for your tireless love, partnership, and kindness. You are the best human I know, and I will be forever grateful that you make me believe my stories are worth telling.

And finally, thank you to the readers who've given this book a chance, for coming on this journey with me (and lingering long enough to read the acknowledgments). This story belongs to you now.

CONTINUE THE JOURNEY AND READ THE FIRST CHAPTER OF *DAUGHTER OF FATE*, THE NEXT BOOK IN THIS EPIC SERIES...

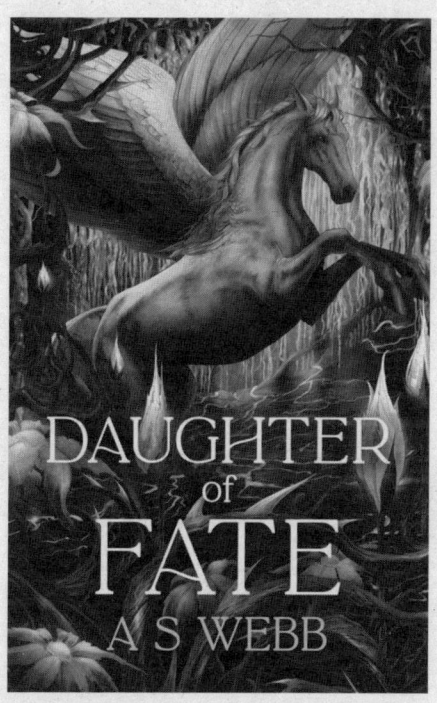

'A S Webb weaves familiar myths within an intricate plot to great accomplishment succeeding in a story that is both fresh and dynamic'

Saara El-Arifi, bestselling author of *Faebound*

NURTURING WRITERS SINCE 1935

One Thousand Years Prior

Kronos lifted his torch, staring through sweat-stung eyes at the looming peaks of Mount Olympus. Banks of beech trees towered either side of him like verdant sentries, their leaves whispering in the wind. He drew a deep breath. Bushes of wild oregano clustered between the silver trunks, the herb's minty, earthen scent carrying on the chill breeze. Beyond the sloping swathes of forest, bare ridges of rock stood free of ice and cloud, silhouetted against a coal-dark sky scattered with stars. Watching, waiting.

'Father!'

Kronos looked back. His eldest son, Zeus, was climbing the trail behind him, his own flaming torch spilling streaks of light and shadow across his face.

Kronos sighed. 'You should not have followed me.'

Zeus stood firm: weary yet defiant.

Suddenly, Kronos saw not a man, but a boy. All gangly limbs and wide, sea-blue eyes, the same expression etched across his face as at the injustice of his younger brother, Poseidon, stealing the wooden cow he had lovingly crafted. Kronos wondered how Zeus had grown so fast. Sun-crinkled skin spread from the corners of his eyes, and his jaw was lean and bearded. He was almost thirty. When Kronos was younger people had remarked that they looked more like twins than father and son. He could not recall at what age his body had revealed the truth.

It felt strange now to contemplate the passing of time, when he was about to become ageless.

'Father, please...'

Kronos turned back to the path with an aching heart.

'You could save her.'

He froze, his chest constricting as he thought of the last time he'd seen his youngest daughter, Hestia, still only a babe, wrapped in blankets by the hearth, her wan little face looking up at his. He thrust the memory away. He could not allow himself to be drawn down that road. Once he tasted the sacred fruit, he would no longer be a father and a husband. He had been called, and all that he once was must be set aside. It was the greatest sacrifice and the greatest honour a person could ever hope for: to become a Titan.

'We have spoken on this. Go home, Zeus.'

'Do you not care?'

Kronos took a couple of steps.

'Father! Do not walk away from me.'

His son's words were arrows in his heart as he continued on, fighting the urge to glance back. Eventually, Zeus grew quiet, but Kronos could hear his son's ragged breath as he followed like a spectre behind him.

Kronos' progress was slow in the dark with the burden of his pack and torch, and the small stones that slipped under foot. For a while the trees grew so tall, he could no longer see the mountain's peak above him, only a sliver of star-flecked sky. The way grew tangled, thick roots lying like steps across his path, the vivid green leaves of beeches giving way to the jade spines of towering pines. Owls and other creatures of the night called to one another from the shadows. Then a rustling sounded up ahead. Kronos' eyes darted between the trees, lingering on a churned patch of earth between two pines.

Wild boar.

He paused, his free hand leaping to the handle of the knife sheathed in his belt. A tusk to the gut could be deadly.

After a while, the noise faded, and Kronos once more resumed his ascent.

He had not gone far when there was a cry behind him.

Despite himself, he spun around. Zeus, still following, had tripped on a root, his torch sputtering on the ground.

Kronos cursed under his breath. Damn the boy's stubbornness.

Fighting every instinct, he turned away from his son and pressed on.

He clambered over great channels of rock and long-dead trees that had been shaken free by storms to pour like rivers from the peaks. He did not slow as the way steepened and the pines thinned, the tufted earth replaced by loose grey stones. The wind grew fierce, whipping Kronos' thick woollen cloak and threatening to extinguish his fire. He was forced to scramble up the scree, using his free hand to steady himself on the lichen-stained boulders littering his way. The urge to glance back at his son gnawed at him like the cold air lancing across his skin. All the while the sky paled, the stars fading into the cold blue light that creeps before the dawn.

In the shadow of the highest peak, he came across a flat bank of rocks perched on the edge of a sharp ridge, falling in a sheer drop to the forested valley below. Beyond the trees and the grassy plain and sandy beach stretching away from the foot of the mountain lay the Aegean Sea: a dark foil to the brightening sky.

Kronos set his torch in the centre of a clutch of stones and heaped a few twigs and bracken onto the little fire. For a brief moment he thought Zeus had finally abandoned his pursuit. Then his son emerged from scrambling up the scree to stand at the edge of the light, his clothes smeared with dust, his eyes blazing brighter than the flames.

Kronos could not help the spark of pride that warmed his chest.

'Sit with me.'

Zeus added his torch to Kronos' fire and lowered himself onto a rock beside his father. Kronos delved into his pack and handed his son a couple of strips of dried goat meat, then took a swig from his waterskin. Zeus devoured the goat, groaning as he chewed.

A smile twitched Kronos' lips. He held out his hand. In the centre of his palm lay an almond.

Zeus swallowed his mouthful.

Kronos curled his fingers around the nut and blew on his knuckles. Then he opened his hand to reveal the almond vanished.

Zeus' brow darkened. 'I'm not a child.'

Kronos sighed, retrieving the almond from his tunic pocket.

'I care,' he said softly. 'You, Poseidon, Hades, Demeter, Hestia, Hera . . . You will always have my heart.'

Zeus leant forward, his voice nothing but a hoarse whisper, as though he feared the mountain might be listening. 'Once you have become a Titan you could come home in secret, use your power to heal Hestia, then return.'

Kronos shook his head. 'You know I cannot. You must be strong now. Take up the responsibility as head of your family.'

Zeus recoiled, the fire in his eyes cooling to ice. '*Our* family. You always said we came above all else. Was that a lie?'

Kronos' ribs tightened. 'I have never lied to you, son.'

'Then why will you not save your own child?'

Kronos gazed up at the mountain's highest peak, his heart aching. 'I have been chosen for a higher purpose. As one of the Twelve, maintaining the balance of the tapestry of life will be my responsibility. I cannot place my own loves above every living being on the earth.'

The look in Zeus' eyes was too painful to hold. So many words lay piled between them, and yet still he could not make his son understand.

After a long pause he added, 'I saw the face of creation. This is how it must be.'

Zeus' expression grew thunderous. 'My mother gave her life so Hestia could join this world. Do you care so little for her sacrifice?'

At the mention of his wife, Rhea, Kronos flinched.

'Your anger shames your tongue.'

'It is you, Father, who should be ashamed.'

Kronos clenched his jaw, swallowing the torrent of words he longed to hurl at his son. Silence raged between them. Drawing deep, calming breaths, Kronos let Zeus' anger wash over him until the tidal waves faded to ripples and the fight in his son's eyes ebbed away.

Zeus hung his head. The knot in Kronos' chest eased. Finally, acceptance.

Brightness crept along the edge of his vision. He looked to the east, where the sun crested the sea, spilling its rosy glow across the world. Then he turned to gaze at the ridge of stone behind him. Tears flowed freely down his cheeks as that honeyed light burnished the mountain, transforming its grey crags into golden rock and, below their stony ridge, its dark forests into swathes of gleaming emerald.

Then he heard it.

A melody sang to him that before, he had only heard in his dreams. Harmonies of bright birdsong, rasping leaves, whistling wind and the pulse of rumbling stone. The heartbeat of the world. The song of life itself.

The tangle of emotions roiling in his gut melted away.

'It is time. This is where I must leave you.'

They both rose to their feet, and the air between them grew tight as a drum skin. Then Zeus threw his arms around Kronos, clinging to him as though he were driftwood in a tumultuous sea.

'I'm sorry, Father.'

Something in his tone struck unease through Kronos. He tried to pull away, but as he moved pain seared through his back. He gasped, unable to fill his lungs as Zeus let go of him. Kronos fell to his knees, palms hitting the hard rock as he coughed blood onto the ground.

Zeus stood over him, Kronos' knife clenched in his trembling hand.

'W-why?'

'For *our* family.' Zeus' face twisted into a mask of grief. Then his shoulders broadened as he said, '*I* am Kronos, chosen to become one of the Twelve.'

Kronos' mouth stretched wide, tears muddling with the blood seeping between his lips.

'You cannot . . . the Mother will . . .'

'She will do nothing. Just like she did nothing when Rhea died, when plague took half the village, when our crops failed and whole families starved. The Mother does not care for us. Neither do you.'

Kronos no longer saw the boy he'd raised, but a wild thing that had stolen his son's skin.

Zeus' face glowed in the swelling light. 'I will use the apple's gifts to help those in need. I will be a saviour. I will be the coming of a new dawn.'

Then Zeus dragged Kronos across the stony ridge. Kronos struggled in vain, his hands slick with his own blood as Zeus hauled him to the edge, then pushed him down the mountainside.